FRIVOLOUS

Frivolous

Edited by: Alex M.

Beta read by: Oana D.

DEDICATION

For anyone struggling with invisible illnesses.

You're not alone.

PREFACE

Dear reader,

Frivolous is a standalone in the Morally Questionable world and it takes place ten years before the events in the Morally Questionable Series.

This isn't as dark as my other books, but it still tackles a number of sensitive issues.

There are mentions and depictions of sexual assault/abuse as well as situations that would fall under the umbrella of non-con/dub-con (perpetuated by the hero). There are also depictions of substance abuse, self-harm and suicide that might be triggering to some.

Please proceed with care!

P.S. The hero is an asshole and you might hate him.

TRIGGER WARNINGS: anxiety, death, derogatory terms, child abuse, drugs, guns, graphic violence, graphic sexual situations, depictions of torture, grooming, mental illness, murder, molestation, rape, non-con/dubcon, self-harm, sexual assault, substance abuse, suicide.

MAIN DEVILLE FAMILY BRANCH

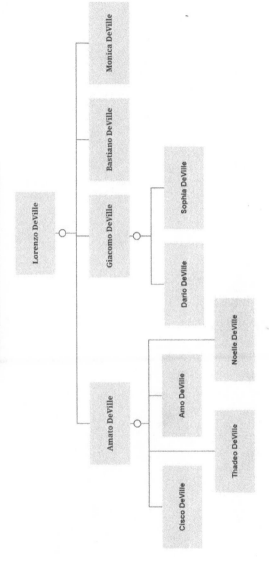

MAIN GUERRA FAMILY BRANCH

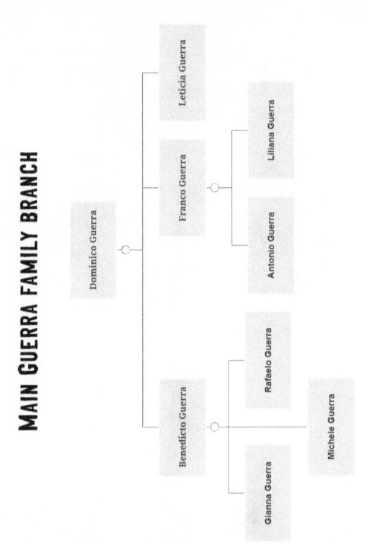

Chapter One

BASS

Wiping the blood off my knuckles, I give one last kick to the man currently writhing in pain on the floor. I already had an inkling that my welcome party would include fists. Good thing I'd had plenty of exercise over the years, my entire body primed for fighting.

The perks of spending half a decade in a state prison.

Known for their lax regulations, every day had basically been a battlefield. And when *everyone* hates you, there's an unlimited supply of challengers.

Ah, but I'd never lost.

Funny how my fists had landed me in jail and my fists had kept me alive there. It seems fitting, though, since my entire measure has always been the amount of destruction I could wreck on an enemy.

But that's just who I am.

I live, breathe, and kill for the famiglia.

Leaving the injured men behind, I head down to the basement where my welcome committee is. Reaching the landing, I nod to the guard and open the door.

My nephews are all sitting by a round table, thick smoke permeating the air as they bicker over poker chips.

I can see the shape of a woman under the table, on her knees as she's servicing two men at once. Rolling my eyes, I head straight to the empty seat, unholstering my gun and placing it on the table with a resounding thud.

Their voices stop, and I wait for their reactions as they scrutinize my face, unspoken questions on their lips.

"Bass," Cisco is the first to speak, rising to his feet. "Good to see you old man," he exclaims, drawing me into a hug. He's also the only one looking at me with a straight face.

And the only one keeping it in his pants.

I grunt, shaking his hand and resuming my seat.

Dario's eyes are bulging in his head, and he blinks rapidly as he stares into my face—or what's left of it.

Yet no one dares to say anything.

The woman, who I can only assume is a hooker, places one hand on my knee, the other already on my zipper.

"Don't," I swat her hand aside, my voice grave.

Her eyes peek at me from under the table, the horror on her face unmistakable, as well as her relief as she scoots back, resuming her previous activities.

"Bass, old man, don't tell me your time in jail has turned you away from women," Dario jokes amid sloppy blowjob sounds.

"I don't want your fucking STDs," I growl, already growing tired of their antics.

I should have known five years would be too little for them to grow the fuck up.

"What STDs?" Dario asks, eyes wide. "There's no such thing here," he smirks, his hand in the woman's hair as he makes her gag on his cock.

Children…

I shake my head at him, his ignorance not my business. If he wants to believe that mouths don't carry STDs then he's my guest. I simply can't wait to hear when he gets the itches, and then we'll see who's laughing.

"You'd think that after five years you'd be eager to resume your life, uncle." Cisco notes with the rise of an eyebrow.

I just shrug.

"I can't help it if I have standards. Unlike some of us…" I trail off, tilting my head in Dario and Amo's directions.

8

Amo's kept quiet until now, but I see the trace of a sheepish smile on his face. After all, as the youngest, he's always seen Dario as his role model and had always taken after him. Too bad he's chosen the worst he could follow.

"I have standards too," Dario chimes in, "she needs a cunt and two spare holes," he winks smugly at Amo, as if he just said the greatest piece of western philosophy.

I don't know if I'd call that standards or desperation.

Everyone knows that Dario hasn't been the best at getting female attention until way after he'd reached puberty. And since then, he's decided to plow his way through the entire population of willing females.

But if that's his minimum requirement, then so be it.

I've always preferred quality over quantity, proof being that I haven't gotten laid in over eight years. Or is it more? Fuck, I can't even remember, and that's saying something. But even before my short layover in jail I'd been very discerning about potential partners. And the minimum requirement has always been a clean bill of health.

You'd think that would be easy, but the evidence points to the contrary. I should know since I've been visiting my father's bordellos for years to collect fees. And when you're privy to the inner workings of whorehouses, you tend to become a little pickier. The number of times johns refuse to wrap it up is insane, and I can only imagine the shit that they spread in and out of the brothels. That's not to say the cases in my own family…

Just like Dario, who even now snorts arrogantly as if having his cock in a whore's mouth is such an achievement. Although… I doubt anyone would fuck him for free, so there's that.

"Dario." Cisco raises an eyebrow, after which Dario promptly shuts up. Not without a pout though, before he concentrates his attention on the whore at his feet.

If anyone's able to rein these two under control, it's Cisco. Only a few years older than them, he's decades ahead in maturity and life experience.

And it shows.

His father's heir, he is the one who calls the shots in the absence of the capo. And since my brother's health had gotten progressively worse, now unable to move around except in a wheelchair, Cisco's in charge of everything. Though he is four years younger than me, I can only comply, since I simply follow the chain of command. It's not a hardship, though. Not when I respect the man and agree with his decisions.

My brother is lucky his first born wasn't an idiot like Dario, or we'd have a revolution on our hands.

"Can't say I missed this." I mutter under my breath, suddenly my cold cell sounding more appealing than the squabbling of children. "Why don't we get to the point of this meeting," I nod at them.

"Guerra," Amo blurts out, though he immediately censors himself when Cisco gives him a grim look.

"I know it's been just…" Cisco looks at his watch, "twenty-one hours since you got out of prison, uncle. But this job requires your expertise."

"Out with it." I lean back in my chair, curious what they'd have to say.

It might be less than a day since I've been released from jail, but it's not as if I have any pending matters. After all, I've given my entire life to the famiglia. They were the reason I did time, but they were the reason I got out before my time too.

The corner of my mouth pulls up as I remember just how the cops had caught me. In the middle of nowhere, without a care for who might hear or see, I'd just snapped. My fists had been red soaked in blood as I was pummeling away at an already dead man. I'd only stopped from my rage when headlights had shined down on me.

Faced with irrefutable proof, there hadn't been much anyone could do to get me off the hook. And so they had charged me with manslaughter and slapped me with a life sentence. Of course, a few bribes here, a few threats there, and I'd managed to get out early.

That doesn't mean the time I did behind bars didn't leave its mark on me. Hell, I'm yet to find out just how much four walls and exquisite company can change a man in five years.

And I'll have the eternal memento staring me in the face every time I look in the mirror, the jagged lines crossing my face a perpetual reminder of what can happen when you're the most hated man inside.

Jail isn't that pleasant when you're part of the most insular crime family on the East Coast. I might not have gone to war, but I've become used to sleeping with an eye open to avoid a knife wound in a critical spot. Other areas? Cool. It happens. But while a scratch here, one there is nothing to worry about, a mortal wound is. I do still value my life, even though it might not seem so.

"What's with Guerra?" I grind my teeth as I say the name.

The reason we're the most insular crime family.

The conflict with Guerra originates on the continent, before our families came to America to start a new life. There are different versions, depending on who you ask. From land disputes, to betrayal to simply a squabble over women—since, when is it not?

From what I'd gathered, though, the squabble had been over *one* particular woman, who'd been playing with two men at the same time—a Guerra and a DeVille.

This had been around the turn of the century, and both men had been too proud to admit that they'd been played. Instead, they'd decided to solve matters in a very public duel which had resulted in both their deaths. The families had been incensed and had vowed retribution against the other. And so a game of cat and mouse had begun, each family trying to one up and ruin the other.

The reason for the conflict might have been paltry, but the enmity had gotten progressively worse with *every* generation. And in our generation the conflict had only been exacerbated by personal differences between my brother, Giacomo, and Benedicto's brother, Franco, who had once more quarreled over a woman. So our family had decided to go all out on Guerra.

After all, it's not as if they aren't constantly trying to do the same to us. But this is a game of who can outsmart the other first.

"Benedicto's daughter is of age," Cisco says, his eyes on me.

Tilting my head back, I raise an eyebrow, waiting to hear the entire story.

"He's been trying to marry her off to Agosti."

"I should hope that's not the case anymore," I reply slowly.

A connection with Agosti, one of the most powerful families in New York, would certainly give Benedicto the advantage to take us head on.

For years now we've managed to keep them leashed into a financial submission of sorts, by never allowing them to make good alliances or investments. It's given us an edge in dealing with them, but it has also been satisfying to watch them struggle. While their own businesses are doing well enough, our interference has ensured they've never been able to grow and expand.

A wolfish smile appears on Cisco's face as he pours himself more alcohol.

"Indeed. And we didn't even have to kill the groom," he chuckles, "though we tried."

"He still lives?" I inquire, both in shock and surprise. The former because I know Cisco never plays around, and the latter because he'd been daring enough to go after the son of a capo.

"His death became... unnecessary." His eyes glint dangerously. "He's officially a married man and unlikely to disrupt our plans."

"Then why did you call me if you have everything figured out?"

"Because," he pauses, a lopsided smile appearing on his face, "war never stops. War is eternal," his face suddenly morphs in a perverse grin.

"Right," I add drily. "And how can I be of help in this eternal war?"

"Benedicto's looking for another groom," Amo rolls his eyes. "And we think he has several businessmen lined up."

"Business interests," Cisco nods. "We can't exactly ensure he won't turn to anyone else unless we do something about his daughter."

"What did you have in mind?" I ask, curious.

Cisco might be many things, but I've never heard of him being cruel to women. In fact, it might be said that he's *only* human to them.

"Don't worry, uncle," he's quick to say when he sees my apprehensive expression. "She's not that innocent."

"I'm surprised Dario hasn't fucked her yet," Amo interjects, amused. "Since she fucks *everyone*," he drawls towards his cousin.

I frown.

Regardless of our animosity towards the Guerra, I know for a fact that Benedicto is a very traditional man. I doubt he would allow his daughter to go off the rails as they are implying.

"Explain." I prompt Cisco, ignoring the way Amo and Dario tease each other with their former conquests.

"She's very popular in high society circles, and rumors fly," he shrugs.

"And you believe these rumors?"

"I do. I have no reason not to. There have been numerous accounts of the debauchery she partakes in. Why, the parties those *nouveau riche* throw," he whistles. "You've never seen so much coke in your life."

"He's right," Dario interrupts. "I've been to a few, and man, those rich girls?" he shakes his head, an amused smile on his face, "they suck cock better than a seasoned whore. No offense, dear," he pats the woman still gagging on his dick.

"I've never seen one so willing for a quickie. You just have to listen to them complain about rich girl problems and up their skirts go," he laughs.

"And Benedicto knows about this?" I ask, my eyebrows furrowing.

I just can't believe that someone as traditional as Benedicto would stand by and let his daughter engage in that type of behavior. It's not only her reputation, but the honor of the family too.

Cisco shrugs.

"I don't think he has the ears to hear. Gianna is the apple of her father's eye. By all accounts, he'd sanctioned the match with Agosti because Gianna had wanted it. You know the drama with his first wife," he rolls his eyes.

Benedicto might be traditional, but he isn't any less facetious than other made men. His first marriage had been one of convenience, and everyone had been aware that there had been no lost love between him and his wife. He'd had two children by her, Gianna and her brother Michele. But not long before Michele's birth he'd met and fallen in love with Cosima, a poor first generation Italian girl from the Bronx. She'd quickly become his mistress, and his entire attention had been focused solely on her.

Suspiciously, his wife had dropped dead soon after she'd given birth to Michele. By this point, Cosima had also fallen pregnant, and

Benedicto had wasted no time in marrying her to legitimize their child—Rafaelo.

"Gianna doesn't get along with Cosima," Cisco continues. "So like any man full of regret, Benedicto's overcompensating by spoiling her rotten. He's simply blinded by his *dutiful* daughter. Do you think someone like that would believe she's anything less than perfect?"

"I don't get it." I mutter. "Wouldn't Gianna's behavior reflect on her entire family? I've never heard of a made man allowing *any* woman in his family those liberties."

"I can assure you, uncle, that he doesn't know the extent of it. Gianna is allowed to go to her private academy and to soirees with other people from her rich girl circle. To the outside world, everything is fancy and sophisticated. Think caviar and wine tasting events. You need to be present at one of those parties to know what really goes on."

I grunt, remembering my own run-ins with trust fund kids back in the day. Cisco is right that from the outside everything looks absolutely *perfect.* It certainly does an amazing job to hide the fact that they're rotting from the inside.

All these Wall Street people and their rich entourage pretend their money is clean, when in fact they all have secret accounts in the Cayman Islands.

At least we're honest about *not* being honest.

"What he doesn't know can't hurt him. His businesses are floundering, uncle. He'll soon become desperate about finding a match to pull him out of the financial mess he's in. The last thing he'll have time to worry about is what his daughter does on a Friday night. Or who," he smirks. "And my last report tells me he already has a list of back-up grooms lined up."

"What do you want me to do?" a muscle twitches in my jaw.

"I want you to turn the rumors into reality." He turns to me, his expression serious.

"Excuse me?" I laugh.

"Rumors are rumors. It's up to people to believe them or… not. But we can't risk that," he smiles insidiously. "We can't have *any* potential groom go forward with a match. And that's where you go in."

"Jesus, Cisco. You want me to rape the girl?"

"Rape?" He frowns. "Of course not. Seduction? Yes," his lips tug up in a wide smile, his white teeth gleaming. "Or *forced* seduction," he shrugs. "Your choice."

I look at him for a moment before I burst out in laughter.

"Seduce her?" I ask. "With this face?" I point at my scars, but he doesn't seem to share my amusement.

"Indeed. I don't know if you've heard of Gianna, but she's stunning."

"She is." Both Amo and Dario agree.

"I wish I could tap that," Dario continues with a sigh.

"Then why don't *you* do it?" I fire back.

"Because," Cisco intervenes before Dario can answer, shifting our focus back to him. "They know us. They know how we look, and no Guerra is going to allow a DeVille anywhere near them. You, on the other hand," he pauses, his eyes perusing my face. "Not only have you been absent for the last five years, but no one would recognize you with your new look."

"Tell me you're not serious about this," I groan. "Why not just kill her?"

"We don't kill women," he replies dismissively. "And besides, death is too honorable. I need her fall from grace to be public, loud, and simply degrading."

"Fuck, Cisco, but you really planned this, didn't you?" I shake my head, the entire idea crazy to my ears.

First of all because who the fuck would fall prey to my *irresistible* charm? And second, because Cisco knows fully well that I don't mix with whores—of the paid or unpaid variety.

"Of course," he smirks. "*Defile, debase, destroy*. That is your mission. I want you to turn those rumors into reality so that *no one* will doubt the type of woman Gianna Guerra is."

"I'm sure she'll fall right into my arms. If she doesn't run when she sees my face," I grumble.

"How old is she?" I quickly sober up, remembering she can't be older than twenty or so.

"She just turned eighteen." Cisco replies, watching me closely.

"Eighteen?" I narrow my eyes at him. "She's barely legal, Cisco. She's a child." I shake my head in disgust.

"So?" He shrugs. "She's a Guerra. That means she's the enemy, uncle. And *that* means she's fair game."

"Cisco," I groan in frustration.

Of all the things I thought he'd ask me to do, I never realized he'd go this far to ruin Guerra. Do I hate them? As much as the next DeVille. But she's barely legal for fuck's sake. God, I may not be old enough to be her father, but I sure am old enough to be *something*.

She's what… twelve years younger than me?

"Not doing it." I reply firmly, my hand on my gun as I holster it and get up to leave.

"Uncle," Cisco's voice changes as he calls out. "May I remind you *who* you swore your allegiance to?"

"Yes. Your father," I reply, turning my head slightly. "And I don't think he'd approve of using a fucking child to get his revenge on Guerra."

"And I make the decisions with *his* blessing. Let's not forget for a moment where we both stand," he raises an eyebrow. "You swore to do *everything* for the family's well-being. And I'm telling you that this mission requires *your* expertise. And when the boss tells you something, what do you do?"

Those steely eyes of his regard me expectantly, and I know he has me cornered. And I can't refuse the mission when it was the famiglia that got me out of jail, too.

"I do it," I mumble, resuming my seat.

I've always been loyal to a fault, and I've *never* questioned my capo's decisions. But in this case? I have a bad feeling about this.

There's only one way this can end—in disaster.

Taking a folder from the table, he throws it towards me.

"I outlined a plan."

Opening the folder, I look to see my new identity, complete with detailed work history and a background in the military.

"You're going to become her bodyguard."

And suddenly it's clear why I was out of jail earlier. Why I was specifically chosen for this job.

Because I'm the perfect obedient soldier.

Because there's no one else who would blindly agree to anything the boss says.

A week later and I'm armed with knowledge of *everything* that is Gianna. Cisco hadn't been kidding when he'd said she was the furthest thing from innocent.

Parties with alcohol, drugs and sex. Orgies in fifth avenue penthouses. Trading partners like trading clothes.

She sounds like a female Dario.

And that makes me even disgusted about my mission.

Not only will I have to share a space with her and pretend to *protect* her, but I'll also have to touch her eventually.

I scowl at that, the thought of touching *that* filling me with revulsion. I don't know what went through Cisco's mind to give *me* this mission, when he knows I have my own hang-ups with loose women, my own mother being a prime example of one.

But it's not enough that she spreads her legs for *anyone,* she's also the resident mean girl.

God, but I'd perused so many reports of her outrageous behavior that I'd been wholly shocked that such a vile woman can exist.

From humiliating and betraying her friends, to throwing fits in public and playing with people's feelings, I don't think there's anything that Gianna is not guilty of.

Why, there are detailed accounts of her going off on restaurant staff, going as far as to throw a bowl of soup on a waiter who'd merely inquired if she liked her food. The man had been drenched in food, and Gianna had continued to belittle him until he'd almost burst into tears.

Safe to say, I can already imagine the barrage of insults she'll send *my* way when she sees my face.

Pulling my cap lower, I try to blend with the crowd as I let my eyes roam around the area.

And there she is.

For a second, I have to remind myself to breathe. The boys hadn't been joking.

She *is* stunning.

And pictures don't do her justice.

Honey blonde hair that reaches her knees, she has it styled in a braid that's held together with a pink bow. Her *entire* outfit is pink.

She's wearing a matching skirt and blazer set, both short and cropped to fit the summer weather. Underneath her blazer, I note a sheer white top, her skin peeking through, her white bra fully on display.

Her clothes don't do much to disguise what lies beneath her clothes, and fuck me if she doesn't look like any man's fantasy brought to life.

And she doesn't look like a child. No, she's all woman.

Long legs, slim waist, and perfectly sized breasts, she has a body made for fucking. And not the gentle type of fucking, the wall banging, legs wrapped around the waist, tits bouncing in the air type of fucking.

Suddenly, I can see why *no one* would turn down an invitation between her thighs. She probably only needs to nod at men and they drop to their knees for her.

"Goddamn," I mutter just as she turns around, her small eyebrows pinched together in a frown.

If her body is the epitome of fuckable, then her face is the type poets write sonnets about.

Not me. *Definitely* not me.

But fuck if she doesn't have the most exquisite face I've ever seen. A dainty, heart-shaped face, full lips and big luminous eyes, she looks like a doll come to life.

And I'm certainly not the only one to think so.

Gianna is walking around with her nose up in the air, as if she's assessing everyone and finding them lacking. Behind her, a throng of men are following her around, all sporting the same lost puppy look, as if one acknowledgement from her would be celestial manna.

She moves and they follow.

And I follow too.

Keeping my distance, I silently observe her interactions.

She's looking at some shoes, taking a pair from the shelf and grabbing a seat nearby to try them on.

I watch in fascination as she takes off her sandals, her feet just as small and dainty as the rest of her.

Damn it all to hell!

It takes me repeated mental exercises and reciting everything I know about her so that I *don't* react. But even the smallest movement of her fingers as they skim over her calves is fucking sensual and my cock refuses to heed my mental warnings.

And I'm not the only one.

There are at least a couple of men that are sporting visible erections as they simply watch her in awe, their eyes following her every move.

One rather impatient bloke hurries to help her by handing her the second shoe to put on, his fingers grazing her hand.

Fuck.

I don't think I've seen such a sudden transformation in my entire life.

One moment she looks serene, her beauty almost ethereal, the next her entire face becomes a mottled mass of anger.

Snatching the shoe from his hand, she stands up, her eyes shooting daggers at him as she's saying something.

I move closer until the sound of her voice reaches my ears.

"Did *anyone* give you permission to touch me? With your filthy hands?"

The man doesn't reply, taking all her insults in stride.

She yells at him, calling him names no young lady of her age should know.

But if it's not enough, she takes it one step too far as she drops the shoes, her arm stretching out, her palm connecting with his cheek in a resounding slap that gets *everyone's* attention.

She shakes her head, a scowl on her face as she quickly puts her sandals back on. Then, grabbing her bag, she bursts out of the shopping center and into a waiting car.

Not entirely surprised by her outburst, I watch the departing sedan and I realize two things.

Touching her shouldn't be such a hardship if I manage to shut down my disgust at her past. She is, after all, delectable enough for a quick fuck.

But most of all, she needs a lesson.

FRIVOLOUS

She needs a nudge to fall off her high horse and realize that her beauty doesn't give her carte blanche to behave like a brat.

Ah, but suddenly this mission doesn't seem so hard.

CHAPTER TWO

GIANNA

"Can you believe they gave *her* the bag? I've been building a relationship with the sales assistant for a *year*," Lindsay chatters away, complaining that her favorite exclusive brand had given her desired bag to someone else.

I just nod, turning my attention to my plate and willing my hand to move and grab the sandwich.

"I'm so glad I have you, girls. Who else would come with me on a Wednesday and binge on finger sandwiches," she sighs, taking her cucumber sandwich and gulping it in one go.

My eyes are still on my untouched food and I know I'll need to eat something before they start asking questions. It wouldn't be the first time.

Is this how you maintain your figure?

Are you on a diet?

Are you starving yourself?

A sandwich won't make you fat.

Come on, don't be such a party pooper. Eat something.

Even as the accusations ring in my ears, I have a hard time moving my hand. Like a weight holding it down, I can barely budge it. My heart is beating loudly in my chest, my mind fogging as I try to get my breathing under control—it's the only way I can get through this meal without issue.

But as I stare at the food, my mouth waters, both in hunger and at the acid reflux coming back up. My feet can't stop shaking, and so I tap my soles against the floor to hide my reactions.

A smile plastered on my face, it's like nothing is wrong. *Nothing at all.*

"Aren't you eating?" Anna asks the dreaded question. "That's your favorite," she mentions, taking a bite of a small cake.

"I was just lost in thought," I wave my hand, my cheeks stretching in a painful smile.

My hand is on the table, closer to the food. Now if I could just…

Two deep breaths, and my fingers are on the fluffy bread that contains my favorite food. I open my mouth, taking a small bite of the sandwich and forcing myself to swallow.

The girls, seeing me eat, return to their previous conversation, their curiosity assuaged.

It's not like they care if I eat or not. But they do care if I'm starving myself, or if I'm on a strict diet, because that's one more piece of information to use against me.

You see, they aren't and have *never* been my friends. Not my real friends. They are who society dictates be my friends. They have the status, the wealth, the rearing. They go to the same private academy, live in the same residential area on the Upper East Side, and dine at the most exclusive restaurants.

They are the people my *father* wants me to befriend. And like the dutiful daughter that I am, I have.

"There's a party at Tommy's house this Friday," Anna suddenly says and my eyes snap to hers.

Dropping the sandwich on the plate, I gather my hands in my lap, my fists clenched as I know what's coming.

"We should meet at my place beforehand," Lindsay says. "We can dress up and I can show you my new Louis Vuitton dress. I got it custom made in Paris last week…"

I tune out her words, my eyes suddenly on my wrist watch as I count down the minutes until I can excuse myself from the table.

"You're coming, right?" Anna addresses me, and I blink twice, grounding myself.

"Of course," I reply with a fake smile. "I wouldn't dream of missing it. Everyone will be there, right?"

"Exactly. It's the last party before everyone goes on summer break," she says with a huff. "Where are you spending yours this year? Milan?"

"Cannes. At my uncle's *palazzo*." I reply absentmindedly.

It's where the entire family meets and plots their various illegal businesses. But I'm not supposed to know that.

"Must be nice being European," Anna mutters under her breath.

I just shrug, not deigning a reply.

The meal is soon over and I'm finally free from my social obligations for the day. As I leave the hotel, my car is outside waiting for me. My bodyguard, Manuello, nods at me and opens my door.

"Home?" he asks when I'm inside.

I shake my head slightly. "I need to grab some school books from the Strand. I need some old editions for an assignment," I lie.

Manuello purses his lips, regarding me skeptically.

"It's for a final assignment," I amend, since he knows very well school finishes in a few weeks.

Reluctantly, he nods, instructing the driver to drive towards the Strand. My attention on my watch, I keep track of the seconds that pass as we make our way through the infernal downtown traffic. I try not to think of the fact that we're on the second lane, far from the sidewalk where Manuello could swiftly pull over so I could get out and take a clean breath. Or how there are cars everywhere, in a cacophony of sounds as they drown out everything, even my voice.

Suddenly, I have a short flashback, seeing myself panicking and getting out of the car mid-ride, surrounded by other speeding cars and at the mercy of fate.

But just as quickly as I see the direction of my thoughts, I will myself to think of something else, pinching my arm and mentally counting to ten.

It seems to help. A little.

And as the journey continues, I try to think of the books I'll be able to peruse at the Strand, since I know it might be the last time I get to do this until we leave for Europe.

When I'll already be married.

I shut that thought down too.

I have my freedom for a bit longer, and that's the only thing that matters. I've known about my fate from when I was old enough to understand what marriage meant, and the fact that I got to choose my future husband means less horrors await me.

Because the alternative…

A shudder envelops me as my mind strays into that territory and I already feel that small bite of food coming back up.

Nails digging in the insides of my palms, my entire body tenses as I clench my fists, my breath coming in short, painful spurts.

Already, I feel my heart racing, a wave of dizziness taking over me.

I chose him. I chose Enzo.

I continue to tell myself that, since it's the only thing that gives me a sense of control over my own life.

And until the contract is signed and the ink dried on the marriage certificate, I'm still free. I'm still… me.

Once the car stops, Manuello turns to me, his expression grim.

"You have half an hour."

Biting my lip, I nod.

I would love nothing more than to argue and tell him half an hour isn't nearly enough, but I'm aware that being in a bookstore is enough of an extravagance.

For all my freedom to move in high society circles, mingling with the rich and the uber rich, my movements are rather restricted.

A party? I need to attend. A social gathering? I must be present.

Because in our world connections are everything. Education? Not so much. At least not in my case.

My father is what I like to call a *hypocritically* traditional Italian man. For him, a woman is only as good as her child bearing abilities, his current wife—the love of his life—included. The only education required is the ability to read, write and hold a grammatically correct conversation in a few languages. Enough to play the perfect hostess, but not enough to get strange, enlightened ideas.

Of course, that doesn't stop him from using me to achieve his goals.

For years now our family has suffered financial losses because of an ongoing conflict with another Italian family. That has prompted my father to look for connections and potential business partners outside our normal sphere of influence. So he's crafted a plan to insinuate himself into the high society circles of Manhattan. And what better way to do it than use *me*?

And so my enrollment at the academy was all for status, since my father knew that other rich kids would attend, so he wanted me to make friends in high places. When it comes to the actual education I'm getting at the academy? I'm only enrolled in the basic courses that give me enough credits to graduate, but not to do much else.

In a world where college admissions are cutthroat, where students break their backs taking courses on top of courses just to get a tiny advantage over the others, I'm simply a failure. With my credentials, my only hope would be a community college. And while I'd take that in a heartbeat, it's completely out of the question.

I'm free, yet trapped. The worst paradox possible, because I can feel the taste of freedom, but I'm doomed to never truly get it.

For girls in my family, even completing high school is a luxury. The only available stage after that is marriage.

Being a wife. A mother. *No one.*

"I still have a few months," I whisper to myself as I enter the bookstore.

Since my father looks down on women getting an education, he'd have an apoplexy if he knew I was here, looking at books that are decidedly *not* for an assignment. It's also the reason why Manuello was reluctant to take me to the bookstore in the first place, since he has to report it back to my father.

Knowing that time is precious, I simply lose myself among the many rows of books, finding some interesting ones and quickly perusing them. Since I know I can't buy anything that might raise suspicions, I simply take pictures of the pages with my phone, leaving everything for later when I'm alone in my room.

Thirty minutes pass quickly, and I find myself again in the car, this time going back home. Knowing I don't have to interact with more people puts me more at ease, and I finally let myself relax.

But everything is short-lived because the moment I enter the house, Cosima's screeching voice resounds in my ears.

"Gianna!" she yells, coming towards me at full force. I blink twice and before I know it her palm makes contact with my cheek, the force of it making me reel back. "What did Mrs. Dumont tell me? You refused her invitation to the Hamptons? When you know how much your father and I need their support," she continues with a barrage of insults, all aimed at me and my useless self.

I ball my hands into fists, feeling my temper rise too.

"Why don't you get your own invitation then?" I ask, tilting my head to the side and regarding her with disgust. "Oh, wait, you can't," I scoff. "Because they don't mix with trash, do they?"

"Wh-what?' she sputters, her eyes going wide.

"You know exactly what I'm talking about," I smirk at her. "They would never mingle with a second-rate actress who was a mistress before a wife. You think they don't know?" Satisfaction blooms in my chest when I see her react to my words.

"They whisper about you, you know?" I continue, my voice low and calm. "They call you a home-wrecker. Not that it's not true." I shrug, leaning back and watching the successful delivery of my jibe.

I make to move past her, but she wraps her fingers around my wrist, pulling me back, her arm stretched in the air and ready to slap me again. This time I see it coming, so I stop her hand mid-air, pushing it backwards.

She stumbles a few steps, her eyes shooting daggers at me.

"You? You dare insult me when you're nothing else than a little slut," she starts just as I'm about to leave again. "Just like your mother," she adds, her voice dripping with malice.

I don't know what comes over me, but as I turn on my heel, my fingers clenched together, I simply let my fist fly to her face.

She gasps, her gaze full of hatred before it suddenly morphs into one of distress, tears making their way down her cheeks.

I frown at the sudden change, but it doesn't take long for me to figure out why.

"Gianna!" My father's voice booms from behind.

I watch stupefied as Cosima runs to my father, jumping in his arms and crying her eyes out.

"I just..." she says, sobbing, her words barely coherent, "wanted her to reconsider the Hamptons trip." Lies drip from her tongue as she paints herself the victim and me the assailant.

"Gianna, how could you hit your mother?"

"Mother?" I spit in disbelief. "She's not my mother. Now or ever." I shake my head at him, unable to believe he'd side with her.

But then he always does, doesn't he? It's in the tiny gestures, the way he always values her words more, her well-being more important than mine.

"Gianna! Apologize to her immediately!" He raises his voice, and the hairs on my arm stand up.

"No," I shake my head. "I won't."

"You will." His eyes narrow at me while Cosima smiles conspiratorially in his chest.

"No," I say with more conviction.

"Then you'll be grounded," he decrees, and I hide a smile.

Little does he know that being grounded isn't all that bad.

"But Tommy is holding a party on Friday," I reply in a fake voice, waiting for him to prohibit me from going.

He pauses for a minute as he thinks about it.

"You'll go to Tommy's, but aside from that you go to school and back home."

My eyes widen in shock. For a moment I'd been happy thinking I'd have an excuse not to go to that stupid party. But of course my father wouldn't miss an opportunity to pimp me out and profit off my social connections.

I don't even reply as I turn and dash to my room, my entire body trembling with unreleased tension. And the frustration only increases as I start thinking of the bleak days ahead.

"You should put on some lipstick. Your lips are too pale." I advise Lindsay as she's putting the finishing touches on her makeup.

"I don't think so. I like how it looks like this" she pouts, puckering her lips and sucking in her cheeks as she checks her face from every angle. She's added so much powder that her face has a sickly hue to it.

I shrug. "Not my business if you look like a corpse in those neon lights."

"Don't mind her," Anna says as I move back, assessing my own makeup. "You know she always finds something wrong." She casually throws the jibe.

I don't reply. Instead, I take out a red lipstick from my bag, carefully applying it to my lips.

"Besides, red is her signature," she continues, her tone changing slightly. "She likes her dick to look bloody by the time she's done with it," she chuckles.

I merely glance over at her, arching an eyebrow. I knew she was going to go for that. Just like I know she can never help the way her envy seeps through her *nice* façade.

"You would know," I shrug. "Since you always help yourself to my sloppy seconds." I smile sweetly at her, batting my lashes. Satisfaction brims inside of me as I watch her expression change from smugness to outrage.

"Wh-what…" she sputters.

"Oh, come on, Anna," Lindsay closes her eyeshadow palette, placing it on the desk and turning to face us. "Everyone knows you two are like Eskimo sisters," she giggles.

"It's not my fault that they come to me once they see how frigid Miss Perfect is." Anna gives me a challenging look, the corner of her lip trembling as she tries hard not to smirk at her own statement.

"How is it my fault if they don't know how to get me hot?" I ask in a feigned pleasant tone.

It's not the first time we've had arguments on the topic. Of course, they're *never* actual arguments. They are all *friendly* discussions where we covertly insult each other.

After all, it's well known that Anna goes after whatever guy shows an interest in me. I've never cared about what she does or who she fucks, just as I have never cared if she took on the whole male population for a gang bang. Good riddance then, since they would stop bothering me.

Standing up, I head to the mirror to arrange my outfit.

The dress is uncomfortably short, barely covering my ass and molding to my body in a tight fit—uncomfortably tight.

But I can only act how it's expected of me. I am, after all, Miss Perfect. I almost roll my eyes at that thought, and with a last tug at the dress, I tell the girls I'm ready to go.

In this circle, you're only someone if you show up to events. Everything hinges on being seen out and about, socializing and *networking*. It is, after all, the reason I'm always present to these parties.

My father has made it clear that he expects me to pave the way for him to reach his business contacts, and more often than not, his financial successes have occurred because I'd smiled and flirted with potential investors, or befriended someone whose parents owned entire chains of luxury stores.

He was pimping me alright, but he just didn't want to call it that way.

Networking. It's all networking.

Ready for the evening and with the girls dressed in equally short or even shorter dresses than me, we get into a limo and head to Tommy's place.

The son of an internationally acclaimed fashion designer and a supermodel, Tommy lives in an apartment right off Fifth Avenue. While not exactly a penthouse, the apartment stretches over two levels and six bedrooms. Perfect for parties, drugs, and underage drinking.

My fingers tighten over my small purse, mentally going over all the items inside to make sure I haven't forgotten anything.

Because even if one thing is missing… I'm screwed.

Convinced that everything is in place, I do my best to listen to Lindsay and Anna's inane chatter.

The car soon pulls into the underground party, and we are ushered directly into the private elevator taking us to the apartment.

It's not much later that the doors open, loud music and stringent lights filtering in. We step inside, and there are already people dancing right and left.

"I need a drink." Lindsay mutters as she leaves us in the middle of the room to head to the kitchen where someone is already serving hefty doses of jungle juice.

"We should say hi to Tommy." I add, already heading towards the living room, knowing I'm likely to find him there.

My connection to Tommy is feeble at best. We go to the same academy and maybe we've interacted a few times in the past. Given his parents' occupation in the art field, my father has never pushed me for a deeper relationship.

Tommy is not a bad person, if one overlooked the fact that nine times out of ten he's high out of his mind. Even now, as I enter the room, throngs of people coming and going, I immediately spot him on a couch, bent over the desk as he's snorting cocaine.

He barely notices me when I offer some pleasantries, his eyes completely glazed.

Job done, I move around the apartment, trying to find a less crowded space to spend the next couple of hours until I can go home.

The balcony is the only place that's a little quieter, and so I prop myself against the railing, taking out my phone and connecting to the Wi-Fi.

Another perk of having a controlling father is the fact that I can't access most websites at home. After all, they would only give me strange ideas not befitting of the daughter of an Italian don. But my father is a hypocrite like that. He doesn't bat an eye at pimping me out to get his prized connections, but is instantly incensed should I know more than I'm allowed to.

Biddable.

Because if I knew more, then he wouldn't be able to control me anymore.

Aware that my time is limited, I try to download as many free books as I can, since if I paid for something *educational* he would be able to tell from my card statement—which he closely monitors.

After all, for all our show of money, we're not swimming in it. Far from it, which is why he's desperately been looking to get me a husband.

I'm focused on my phone when I feel someone poking me from the side.

Scrunching my nose, I look up into the face of one of the most disgusting human beings I've ever had the displeasure of knowing— Max Connor.

I want to gag just finding myself in such proximity to him, and especially as the smell of alcohol coming from his breath drifts towards me, I can't help but take a step back.

"There you are, GG," he slurs, coming even closer to me.

"Go find someone else to bother," I say flippantly. "Loser," I mutter under my breath.

He doesn't seem to get the message as he crowds me in the corner of the balcony, his gaze a mix of malice and lust that makes my skin crawl with disgust.

"Oh, come on, G. I know all about you." His breath is suddenly on my face, that awful smell invading my nostrils.

"Get lost," I push against him, moving to go back to the house.

Max Connor has never been one to take no for an answer, evidence being the *many* times I've had to reject his advances.

But just as I bump into him when I try to maneuver my way out, his hand shoots out, his fingers wrapping around my wrist and pushing me back.

My back connects with the glass railing.

"What the fuck is wrong with you?"

"Come on, G. I know you want this," he trails his nose down the side of my face, inhaling.

Suddenly my annoyance turns to fear as my heart starts beating loudly in my chest. His touch is enough to detonate the self-destruct mode—the only mode my body knows. And my bravery slowly fades away, replaced with revulsion, dread, and panic.

"Take your fucking hands off me," I push against him in another attempt to move away.

"You're suck a cock tease. You think I don't know you've fucked half the people here? What's one more, huh? You know I've wanted between those sweet thighs of yours for a long time." I don't let him finish as I bring my hand up, slapping him across the face.

"Fuck off."

"Feisty. I like it," he smirks. "Fuck but I bet that pussy's just as fiery as the rest of you. That's how you drive everyone crazy. That's how you drive me crazy," he rasps, and a sickening feeling forms in the pit of my stomach.

His grip tightens over my wrist as he brings my hand over his crotch, thrusting into my palm and letting me feel his erection.

What was the start of a small attack mounts into a full-blown panic as he continues to whisper all the things he'd like to do to me.

No... Not again.

Momentarily stuck, it only takes me one flashback of what could *actually* happen for me to go into fight or flight mode.

Raising my knee, I don't even think as I aim it straight at his dick, hitting as hard as I can while wrenching my hand free from him. He stumbles back, hunched over in pain.

But I can't stop.

I bring my foot up, my heel directed at him as I simply push it to his crotch. There's this sick need inside of me that wants me to make sure he won't be able to recover and come after me. That he won't be able to hurt me.

And so even while he's down, I keep on stomping on him, his cries of pain and the sound of my tears drowned by the loud music.

It's only when a little bit of clarity makes its way into my mind that I realize I need to leave. I need to get away from the crowd. I need...

My breathing is harsh as I feel my pulse pick up, my mind fogging with what I know is an incoming attack.

I barely make it to the bathroom in time, locking myself inside and spilling the contents of my stomach in the toilet.

I heave and heave until nothing comes out anymore, but still, my pulse won't quiet.

The voices in my head won't quiet.

Leaning back against the cold tile, I bring my hands over my arms, my nails digging in my skin as I search to cleanse his touch from me.

He touched me.

He touched me.

He fucking touched me.

It's like I'm in a trance as my unblinking eyes focus on a small spot on the wall, my breathing out of control as I keep on replaying the events of the evening.

He fucking touched me.

There's a reason why I avoid interacting with people like the plague. There's a reason I can't be in a crowded place. And there's a reason why I can't even eat with people present.

"I need to calm down," I mutter to myself, my arms going around my body in a shield, trying to separate myself from the events of tonight.

But seeing that my attempts are in vain, that my mind still feels foggy, the tension in my temples throbbing and culminating in a lump in my throat, I carelessly grab at my bag, spilling the contents on the floor and picking up the small pouch with pills.

On shaky legs, I raise myself to the sink to chase the pill with water.

Then I just wait for it to take effect.

Bracing myself on the sink, I stare into the mirror at my tear-streaked face, and my smeared red lipstick and I'm suddenly reminded of *that* night again.

Only then it had been worse. Way worse.

CHAPTER THREE

BASS

Splashing some water on my face, I take a deep breath as I open my eyes to see my destroyed features staring back at me in the mirror. Not for the first time, I want to look away, pretend that the last five years never happened. That *I* didn't change.

But I can't. Not when the evidence is right in front of me.

I still remember the night I'd woken up with strangers in my cell, hulking men holding me down on my bunk while someone wielded a knife in front of my face. I guess I should be lucky he'd only given me a new look instead of taking an eye–or two. The fact that I still have my sight should make me grateful that I escaped that hell. That I survived.

As my eyes flicker over the harsh ridges of my scar, the slash starting from my hairline and going down my chin in a diagonal line, I can only see the change–both on the outside and on the inside. It's the latter that concerns me the most because there's a violence inside of me that wants to be let out. A need to wreck everything around me in a maddening show of destruction. Because the truth is, I don't know how to be normal anymore.

I don't know how to act with other people and I don't know how to stop myself from seeing *everyone* as a potential danger.

Even now, a week later, I still can't truly sleep, one eye always open to make sure there's no incoming attack.

I'm primed for danger like a caged animal suddenly set free, the lure of the wilderness seemingly treacherous as only memories of captivity suffuse my mind.

And people have noticed. *Everyone* has noticed.

I've paid my respects to my brother at his home, and even him, bedridden and barely in command of all his faculties, could see I wasn't the same.

But while most seem to be wary of my new attitude, Cisco's seen it as a thing to exploit.

He is his father's son.

He knows that there's something simmering just beneath the surface. Something angry and deadly that he wants to use to destroy Guerra.

And I'm itching so much for a fight that I'm going to let him.

After all, my life begins and ends with the famiglia. I've been its fists and shield for so long, I don't know how to be anything but an instrument of punishment. Even more so now that my entire existence for the past five years has revolved around using my fists.

Going back to the kitchen I set about preparing something to eat. The space is small, and I'd chosen this apartment specifically for its compactness.

After I'd gotten out, I had been unable to sleep at my old place. Too much open space led to paranoia, and I could never get comfortable enough to rest. I'd immediately relocated, finding a small studio with everything contained in one room.

There's a degree of familiarity in not having the freedom to move, even when I know I am now *free.*

A whooshing sound gets my attention. Slowly leaving the utensils on the counter, I step away from the kitchen, following the foreign sound. My ears prickle with awareness, and while a side of me thinks it's my sick paranoia, I'm not about to take any risks.

On the pads of my feet, I move stealthily towards the source of the sound, my muscles straining, my fists clenched for action. And in that moment, I *wish* someone tried to barge in. Just so I can have an excuse to exercise this violence out of me.

As expected, the door rattles for a few seconds before the knob slowly turns.

I fit myself to the wall as I wait for whoever is on the other side to come in. It's enough for me to see the outline of a silhouette and I act.

Extending my arm to the side, I bring it into his neck, hitting him in his Adam's apple and making him fall to the ground with a groan.

Adrenaline coursing through my veins, I'm ready to dispatch the motherfucker, consequences be damned. At that moment, all I can see are my fists smeared with blood, my knuckles hitting until I reach the bone.

But a hint of blonde hair manages to get me out of my rage, my eyebrows pinched together as I realize just who my intruder is.

"Dario," I mutter under my breath, disappointment settling deep in my gut.

Damn, I'm not getting a kill today.

All this time I'd behaved. I'd told myself that as long as I don't kill or attack anyone unprovoked, then I'm fine. That doesn't mean that I don't always wait for the moment when someone *will* attack me. The only excuse I need to let loose. To finally feel some familiarity as I watch life leave a body.

And as I look at the pitiful form of my nephew, I can only shake my head at him, turning back and heading to the kitchen to continue preparing my food.

"You could have..." he wheezes, trying to get himself off the floor, "killed me."

"I *would* have," I reply, my attention already back to the stove.

"Damn uncle, is that my welcome?" He tries to make light of it as he teeters towards me.

I look him up from the corner of my eyes, refraining from snorting at his less than stellar physical condition.

Dario looks exactly as you would expect of a pampered child, never used to the hardships of life. Tall and lanky, there's no muscle mass, nothing to help him hold his own against *anyone.* But then again, he doesn't have to. He has his many bodyguards for that.

His fluffy existence doesn't revolve around death, or blood, or violence. No, he's only concerned about his next fuck, or his next fix. It's not as if I haven't noticed the way he sniffles his nose, always touching his nostrils with his fingers. I've spent enough time with addicts to recognize one. Dario lives up to his spoiled kid persona to the T.

"You know better than to provoke me, boy. In any way." I arch a brow.

He knows that even before my stint in prison I was a hardened man. It happens when you're taught to use your fists instead of your words from a young age.

He rolls his eyes at me, taking a seat at the small table in the middle of the room.

"Wonderful accommodation," he snides, looking around in disgust. "Very... spacious."

"Careful, Dario. Less space for me to catch you and..."

One look and he shuts up, pursing his lips in annoyance.

"Why are you here?" I get straight to the point, not wanting the *pleasure* of his company for more than necessary.

He might be my blood, and that makes it my duty to protect him, but that doesn't mean I have to like the little shit.

"My cousin sends his love," he snorts, pushing an envelope on the table.

"What's that?" I frown.

"Gianna's new schedule. You need to make your move this week." He shrugs. "Cisco said to use his men to do whatever you want, but you need to get that job by the end of the week."

"If not?" I raise an eyebrow.

I admit that I've been biding my time because her age makes me uncomfortable—no matter how hot she is. I may be the family's instrument of vengeance, but even I have my scruples—few as they may be.

"Not my business." He gets up. "You know better than me what happens to people who don't follow the boss' orders. Your sister's still in Sicily, isn't she?" He has the gall to smirk.

I barely hold myself in check as I level him with my gaze.

"My sister happens to be Cisco's aunt too."

"You're a little late to the party, uncle. Cisco isn't the same boy you used to know," he comes closer to me, and for the first time he has a serious expression on his face. "He doesn't make idle threats." He says and an emotion passes over his face.

Before he can turn to leave, I grasp his shoulder, holding him in place.

"What did he do?"

He blinks, slowly raising his gaze. And for a moment, the immature Dario seems to disappear.

"What didn't he do?" He gives a dry laugh. "Heed the warning. When Cisco wants something, he gets it. He doesn't care who gets hurt in the process," he says and suddenly he's back to his nonchalant self, giving me a derisive smirk as he heads for the door.

I keep in the background as I watch Gianna step out of her car, her bodyguard hot on her trail. Right before entering the store, she meets with another girl that seems to be her age. They both giggle as they hug each other, waiting for the concierge to open the door for them.

For the first time in years, I'm dressed in a suit, trying my hand at showing some respectability since no doubt I'll be assessed from head to toe the moment I enter the fancy store.

Pushing my glasses up my nose to hide at least half of the monstrosity that lies beneath, I follow.

The man in charge of the door gives me an odd look, but opens the door wide for me. The entire showroom is filled with see-through glass cases that house incredibly expensive jewelry.

The only type Gianna would ever wear.

I keep my distance, pretending to study some designs while ignoring the annoying sales assistant following me like a shadow.

Just like the last time I'd seen her, Gianna looks absolutely stunning in a yellow sundress, her creamy shoulders naked and drawing everyone's attention to the pearly white skin peeking through. And as she turns her gleaming smile to the sales assistant, I can see how anyone would become a blubbering fool in her presence.

Fuck but she's beautiful.

If I didn't know how nasty she was, I may have enjoyed my assignment more. As it stands, I can only regret that such a perfect face is wasted on a shit human being.

Like a lecherous old man, I let my eyes rove over her generous curves, over the deep cleavage of her dress that emphasizes the swell of her breasts with every breath she takes.

She's eighteen now.

I have to chant that piece of information to myself, though it does nothing to lessen the disgust I feel at myself for feeling so attracted to her.

And just as I make no secret of my perusal of her, she turns slightly, raising her head, her eyes meeting mine. There's no mistaking the disdain that replaces the former cordiality, not in the way her upper lip curls up in a snarl, a scowl taking hold of her features, her beauty eclipsed by derisive condescension.

She doesn't glance at me more than once before she turns with a huff, her attention once more on the sales assistant.

She's also a bitch.

The reminder is like a cold shower, and as I look down at my watch, I note that only a few minutes remain until showdown.

Deep in conversation, Gianna turns so that her back greets my view. Intentional or not, I feel a need to rile her up. And as I move closer, I note the stiffening of the shoulders. The way she's probably aware I'm just a few steps behind her.

Her hands are balled into fists and as her friend asks her a question, she takes a moment to reply.

I disgust her.

Even with the glasses on my face, my scar is still visible, the white line stretching all across my cheek. The sight of me probably offends her tender sensibilities, the ones used to luxury and pretty, useless boys that probably fuck like they do everything else–with the enthusiasm of a sloth.

"What was it?" Gianna asks her friend to repeat her question.

"Why didn't you tell me you fucked Max Connors. I had to find out from Emily," her friend rolls her eyes.

My entire body tenses, my lip twitching in displeasure. And as my mind conjures images of this luscious creature, limbs tangled with some fumbling boy, his dick sliding in and out... My nostrils flare as I realize just how distasteful the thought is. Even while knowing all about her reputation, hearing about it firsthand seems to do something to me.

"I don't kiss and tell," she giggles, waving her hand dismissively and turning her attention to the jewelry.

"Come on. You know I'm curious," the girl continues in an enthusiastic voice. "How big is his dick?" She asks in a shushed voice.

"Really Marie? That's what you want to know?" Gianna shakes her head, still refusing to engage her friend. Instead, she just addresses the sales assistant, asking for a few pieces to try on.

I'm hovering a few steps behind, but as I pretend to look at the jewelry case before me, I see Gianna quietly signal her bodyguard.

Two steps and his hand is on my shoulder.

"If you could come with me," his voice greets my ear just as my lips pull in a smile.

If before I thought I offended her, now I'm sure.

Ah, but this is going to make my victory much sweeter, knowing I truly disgust her. Let's see how she's going to feel about herself when she's slumming it with the beast.

I don't have to act though. Not immediately.

Because just as I turn to answer her bodyguard, the door to the store opens. Five men fully masked with black balaclavas enter, wildly waving their guns around.

The concierge is the first to fall as he tries to struggle with one of the masked men.

I'm immediately forgotten as the bodyguard hurries towards Gianna, telling her to get down.

I stretch my foot out, tripping him just as he dashes to her side, falling to the floor instead.

One nod at the men, and I'm down on my belly, behaving like the other hostages.

The men shoot a few rounds in the ceiling as a threat, quickly giving the store manager a list of demands.

I have to give the bodyguard his due. Even with the men aiming guns at everyone in the store and telling them to stay still, he tries to crawl towards his charge.

An errant thought enters my mind, and I have to wonder about the nature of their relationship. Especially as Gianna keeps calling out his name in a low voice.

Manuello.

Lover or not, he's not making it out alive. That was for sure before. But now...

There are a few glass cases separating Manuello and I from Gianna and her friend. And because the lower part is made from wood, we can't see them and they can't see us.

A smile pulls at my lips as I wrap my hand around Manuello's foot, easily pulling him to my side. His eyes widen as he sees my expression, his brows drawing together in a frown.

But any surprise is short lived as I have him in my hold.

Not only does he need to die today for this plan to be successful, but I also find that I don't quite like his face—or the fact that he may have taken his guarding too seriously. Ironic, considering I plan to do the same.

And as he opens his mouth to protest, trying to push me off him, I just use my other hand to reach for his neck, my fingers snug against his throat as I squeeze swiftly. With the force I'm applying, only a few, barely audible sounds escape his lips. And as I press on his Adam's apple just a little more, I feel his entire larynx collapse under my fingertips. One more ragged breath and he's out–forever.

There's a side of me that regrets the circumstances of the kill, a need to give him a more violent death just as I imagine him guarding Gianna—guarding her very well indeed.

The noise from the masked men covers any sounds Manuello might have made, and as soon as I release his body, I focus on the next part of the plan.

One of the men meets my eyes, a small signal with his fingers letting me know it will happen any moment.

The staff hurry around the store as they remove more jewelry from the back for the robbers, directly handing them all their prized possessions.

"No," one says, throwing a box to the ground, a diamond necklace rolling on the soft carpet. "I know you have more in the back," he barks. "In the safe. I want everything. Now."

"We don't... I swear, this is all we have."

"If you don't... then how about I give you some incentive," one man laughs, striding between the rows of cases and stopping where Gianna and Marie are.

The sound of struggles reaches my ears just as he plucks Marie off the floor, gun to her temple as he drags her back to the center.

"You either bring me the good shit, or she drops dead," he announces.

I frown.

He was supposed to grab Gianna, not her friend.

"Let her go!" my head snaps back as I hear Gianna's voice ring out in the store. I raise myself just in time to see her try to rush towards the armed man.

What the...

I don't even think as I react, jumping to my feet and reaching her side just in time. From the corner of my eyes, I see a man raise his gun, aiming straight for Gianna.

Grabbing on to her arm, I whirl her around just as I put myself in front of her.

The shot is quick, the pain sharp as the bullet makes contact with my shoulder.

Her eyes go wide as she sees me, but she doesn't protest as I pull her to the ground.

"That..." she trails off, her eyes on my shoulder that's no doubt leaking blood.

"Fuck," I mutter under my breath, confused about the change of plans.

None of this should have happened. Certainly they shouldn't have tried to shoot *anyone.*

As if nothing happened, they continue to order the staff around, assessing the variety of jewelry brought for their inspection.

I'm still trying to understand what's happening when a jab in my ribs takes me by surprise. I turn around to see Gianna kicking me aside, the scowl from before back on her face.

"Don't touch me," she hisses, her eyes shooting daggers at me. That's when I realize that I'm still holding on to her, her front molded to my chest, her lush tits digging into me.

"Let me go!" She continues to squirm against me, doing nothing but further inflame me despite the pain in my shoulder.

I blink twice, taken aback by the viciousness of her tone. I just saved her a bullet hole and this is how she repays me?

Pushing her away, I lift my hands up, a smile on my lips.

"Go ahead, sunshine. If you don't mind an extra hole," I shrug, delighted to see the way her expression morphs into one of fury.

"Fucking asshole," she grits, her small fist making contact with my wounded shoulder.

Damn but that shit hurts!

She quickly sobers up as she sees the amusement leave my gaze, especially when I catch her hand in mine, my fingers tightening around her dainty wrist. One tug, and her face is inches away from mine. My other hand is quick to wrap around her throat as I bring her even closer.

There's still defiance in her eyes as she looks at me, but there's no mistaking the way her lower lip trembles, her body tense.

"Careful, little one. I might still feed you to the wolves," I whisper, my breath on her cheek as I inhale her sweet, most definitely expensive scent. It's just like her. Classy, yet wrapped in perversion, the underlying aroma promising long nights of reckless abandon and unsubdued passion.

Just like the fire cat in my arms.

"Let me go," she whispers on a small voice, and that soft plea does wonders to my cock.

Suddenly, all I can see is her on her knees as she begs me to let her go, to leave her alone. But even as she utters the sounds, her mouth is parted, her luscious lips open as they wait for my cock.

Fuck.

Just as soon as that thought enters my mind, I thrust her away from me, disgusted with myself.

She's an ungrateful little bitch.

I keep repeating that in my mind, trying to convince myself that's all she is, and urging my body to react accordingly.

Fuck, but I don't think I've ever had a stronger reaction to a woman in my life. And I've no doubt it's the allure of the forbidden. Because while my mind loathes everything that she is and stands for, my body can't help but be taken by her physical beauty. The duality of my desire for her only enhances its potency, and I know that while I'll *definitely* enjoy fucking her, I'll hate doing it nonetheless. And that combination forecasts itself to be explosive.

I've always prided myself on conducting my affairs in a quiet, almost clinical fashion. After all, I never wanted to descend into the same madness that took my parents.

But as I look at the woman by my side, her expression feral as she tries to put distance between the two of us, that's all I can see.

Recklessness.

Pure abandon, because there's no way I could detach myself while I'm balls deep inside of her, those long legs wrapped around my waist, her sweet cries ringing out as I thrust…

Goddamn it.

I need to keep myself in check if I'm to approach this logically. *She's a Guerra!*

Yes. Not only does she embody *everything* I loathe in a woman, since my own mother's shameless example is still fresh in my mind, but she's also a Guerra.

From birth, every DeVille is indoctrinated to see Guerra as the epitome of evil—that who should be vanquished. And I'm no different. I've killed Guerras and Guerras have tried to kill me. There's simply no middle way between our families. That thought helps me recenter myself, her physical appeal suddenly paling in the face of decades-old grudges.

But just as I manage to put a damper on my growing arousal, Marie starts screaming and kicking at the man holding her, tears pooling down her cheeks as she tries to get free. She pushes her heel onto the man's foot with enough force that he's momentarily distracted. Running towards Gianna, the sound of the gunshot echoes through the store.

Eyes wide, mouth open in pain, Marie drops to the floor, the carpet quickly soaked in the blood pouring from her wound.

Fuck.

They nabbed her in the neck, too. And as I raise my gaze towards the shooter, I note the chuckles that permeate the air.

What men did Cisco send me? They're fucking ruining *everything*.

Gianna shakes her head as she tries to crawl towards her fallen friend, a sob escaping her lips. Before I can pull her back, the man who'd shot Marie is on her, dragging her to her feet.

"Seems like we need a new one," he tells the others.

Everyone is frozen on the spot as the masked men start loading the goods into their bags.

I move slowly, catching Gianna's eyes.

She tries to look fearless, but there's no mistaking the way her legs are trembling, her muscles strained as she tries to keep herself from moving.

She meets my gaze and I give her a slow nod.

She blinks, panicked, but she returns my signal with one of her own as she bobs her chin down ever so slightly.

On my elbows, I move quickly as I spot the nearest man. Since this is a race against the clock, I don't give him any opportunity to spot me before I tackle him, his neck in the crook of my arm as I hold him tightly from behind.

The others turn their attention to me, but I move faster, using the gun in the man's hand to shoot round after round, managing to nick all the men save for the one holding Gianna. And in their attempts to get back at me, they did me a favor by killing the man in front of me, now his entire body riddled with bullets.

Eyes wide, the last man standing keeps jamming the end of his gun against Gianna's temple, his eyes wide with terror as he sees me approach.

"No, stop!" he cries out. "No, this wasn't how it was supposed to go," he mutters. "No one was supposed to die," he continues to prattle, wildly looking around the corpses on the floor.

"You pulled the first shot." I tsk at him before I aim the gun I'd taken from the dead man straight for his face.

Since he's at least a head taller than Gianna, I'm not afraid I'm going to hit her.

My finger squeezes the trigger and sure enough, the shot is clean. His arms go slack around Gianna and he drops to the floor.

By this point all the staff is on the floor, crawling as far away from the site of the gunshots as possible.

"He's dead," Gianna whispers, her shoulders quaking. She blinks rapidly as she stares at the dead man at her feet, blood leaking from the round circle on his forehead. "You killed him…" she continues, finally raising her gaze to meet mine.

She shakes her head, taking a step back as if terrified of me. And as she tries to put distance between us, she trips on the man's legs, falling to her ass in the pool of blood, the back of her dress quickly changing color.

As she realizes the situation she finds herself in, she turns those big, gorgeous eyes of hers towards me, looking so achingly vulnerable that for a second I feel my chest contract in an unfamiliar sensation.

She parts her lips as she's about to say something, but no sound comes out. One more flutter of her lashes and her eyes roll to the back of her head.

She's out.

I purse my lips at her, somehow missing the fire she's shown earlier. For fuck's sake, what did I expect? She's a spoiled little girl. Of course, she'd faint at the sight of blood.

Gathering her in my arms, I try to ignore the way my wound pains me as I move her out of the pool of blood. I take a moment to quietly peruse her features, once again noting how exquisite her face is.

Like a fucking painting.

And they sent *me*, a shredded canvas, to take care of her.

Oh, but take care I will. I'll make sure I fulfill my mission and I'll enjoy seeing the look of disgust she's given me earlier morph into one of desire. Because Cisco was right. What punishment would be worse for the belle of the ball than to be seen consorting with the beast?

Her strong reaction to me only makes me want to prove her wrong even more. Knock her down from that mighty tower of hers and show her how we mortals get down and dirty.

And fuck, by the time I'm done with her she *will* be dirty.

The alarm rings, and it's not long after that the police and the ambulance arrive. Not surprisingly, I'm hailed as a hero, and with my new identity devoid of any arrest record, they don't even bat an eye when I tell them what happened. Especially as every eye witness testifies in my favor. Manuello's death is written off as part of the robbery too, with most people too frightened to even remember what happened to him.

And after my arm is patched up, I get the visit that I was most looking forward to.

"I must thank you for saving my daughter's life." A man in his forties says as he shakes my hand.

"Thank you..."

"Benedicto Guerra," he quickly introduces himself, looking at me expectantly.

"Sebastian Bailey. At your service." A wolfish smile spreads on my face.

And so it begins.

Chapter Four

GIANNA

"Fuck this," I mutter to myself as I lift up the mattress, searching for my hidden stash. Immediately, the shiny glint of glass beckons me as I pick up a bottle hidden within the bed frame.

My hands are shaky, my entire body on the verge of a meltdown. And there's only one thing I want to do.

Mute it. Mute everything.

I don't even look for a glass, quickly unscrewing the cap of the vodka bottle and chugging the nasty substance. The liquid burns as it goes down my throat, and tears coat my lashes as I force myself to bear it.

I need this.

I drink as much as I can before I start coughing and sputtering. Taking a deep breath, I allow myself to give over to the warmth that seems to envelop me, making my limbs become numb.

Hand on the neck of the bottle, I raise myself up, heading for the wall length mirror in my closet.

My eyes survey my form, taking in my legs and my slender frame. I move closer, bracing my hands on the mirror as I look at my face.

The face that everyone seems to love.

But it wasn't enough for him.

Bitter laughter bubbles in my throat, and I can't help myself when it reaches the surface, loud sounds combined with tears of frustration reverberating in the tiny room.

"Why am I so unlucky?" I shake my head at my own reflection.

It hadn't been enough that I'd almost died in an armed robbery. That I'd witness a beast murder five men in cold blood without even working a sweat. That I'd had said beast touch me.

Even now, a shiver of revulsion goes down my spine as I remember his icy fingers on my skin, his heavy palm resting against my ribcage. A sob catches in my throat at the memory.

If there's such a thing as the epitome of a personal nightmare, then he's *it*. With his big frame, and hulking muscles, he's everything I fear when I close my eyes at night. When I feel helpless outside of my safe haven where all my vulnerabilities are laid out in the open. He's what I fear the most because that strength has the power to break me—completely.

I'd noticed him from the beginning. One tends to do so when every man in one's vicinity seeks only one thing—to possess. I think I've developed this habit from when I was old enough to realize what my appearance did to people, and how it made *men* react. Since then, I've always been able to see them lurk around, looking me up and down in that lecherous way that always makes the hairs on my body stand up.

So I'd known. From the moment he'd entered the store, I'd felt his gaze on my back, his eyes slowly raking over my form. And when I'd turned to him, trying to give him my best set down, he'd smirked.

He'd fucking smirked.

"Fucking asshole," I mutter, taking another swig of the vodka.

It hadn't been enough that I'd still felt his dirty touch imprinted on my skin when I'd woken up from that ordeal, I'd also received the news that threatened to destroy *everything*.

The moment I woke up at home, my father had to inform me that my engagement was over, since Enzo had married someone else.

My hand tightens over the bottle, and I bring it to my mouth, taking another big gulp.

If Enzo is no longer a viable option then…

The future is bleak indeed, since I have no doubt that my father is already hard at work to find himself another wealthy groom. After all, I know the dire state of our finances. He's gotten himself into quite some trouble by going to the Russians for money. I shouldn't know this. I shouldn't know *anything*. But the situation has become so bad that my father's been arguing with his advisors day and night about our lack of funds.

He'd banked everything on this engagement and on merging his businesses with the Agosti family. Now? Unless he acts fast, we're going to lose everything.

Another husband.

The liquor threatens to come back up at the thought.

The only reason I'd been fine with Enzo had been the fact that he seemed to be disinterested in me.

When my father had announced that I had to marry—and marry well for that matter, I'd begged him for a chance to choose my own husband. After all, he'd been allowed the same privilege, and to my detriment too, when he'd chosen Cosima. I'd played the victim card and for a while I'd managed to soften him enough that he'd allowed me to meet with different prospective husbands.

All of them had been either lecherous old men or perverted fiends, one even going as far as cornering me in the hallway to tell me all the depraved things he'd do to me once he got his hands on me.

Enzo had been the only one who hadn't seemed interested. Hell, he'd barely even glanced at me.

And just to be sure, I'd tried to be a little more suggestive, to try to bring his true nature to the surface. After all, the men of our world are all the same, and they all want one thing—to possess the body and break the spirit.

When I'd been a little too forward, instead of looking excited, he'd looked disgusted with me. Even when I'd tried to place my hand on his shoulder, he'd drawn back as if burned. His reaction had been wholly unexpected and exactly what I needed.

I'd immediately told my father that Enzo was my choice, and he'd been ecstatic, since the Agosti fortune would finally pull us back to the surface.

Now?

"What the fuck am I going to do?"

My knees buckle and I fall to the ground, uncontrollable sobs racking my body as it dawns on me what future awaits me.

I'd met the other men whom my father had considered good matches, one worse than the other. And there was him...

A shiver goes down my back as I realize he might very well give me to *him*.

"No, no, no..." I shake my head, my fists clenched.

I can't let that happen. Anything is better than *him*.

But what can I do? No doubt, even now, father is courting different powerful men trying to pave the way for another match. I probably have a few months left at best.

I bring the bottle to my lips, taking another sip. The alcohol is finally starting to kick in, and I feel a little light-headed.

Taking a deep breath, I let everything fall away, reveling in the moment.

Opening the small window of the closet, I do a quick scan of the outside. When I don't see anyone, I take out the pack of cigarettes I always carry with me, my fingers shaky as I try to light one up.

The first drag is heavenly. The second only complements the alcohol as it makes me even more light-headed. The third is already helping me relax.

"Miss?" A far away voice registers amid dulled senses.

Startled, I whip my head towards the noise, my eyes going wide as I realize I need to hide the bottle and get rid of the cigarette in my hand. Putting it out on the windowsill, I throw it out the window before I quickly open a drawer, shoving the bottle inside. With slight difficulty, I manage to get to my feet just in time to see our housekeeper come in.

"Miss Gianna," she frowns when she sees my tear streaked face.

Shit, I must be all red.

I bring my hands up, quickly dabbing at my eyes.

"What is it, Mia?" I strain a smile.

"Your father is asking for you downstairs. He has a guest with him," she says, pursing her lips as she takes me in. "You should make yourself presentable," she nods at me before turning on her heel and leaving the room.

What could he want now?

A little tipsy—ok, maybe a bit more than tipsy—I take a seat to my vanity and I quickly apply some foundation to mask the red splotches on my face. I put on some make up as well before dousing myself in perfume so I don't smell like cheap alcohol.

Making sure my clothes will meet his approval, I finally head down.

"You wanted to see me *papa*?" I ask when I enter the living room, my voice dying when I see who the guest is.

Rooted to the spot, I can only stare at him wide eyed.

Him…

I feel a flush envelop my entire body, from the alcohol or his presence, I don't know.

He's just as big as I remember. Bigger still, with wide shoulders and bulky arms that could tear me apart.

He's dressed casually. More so than last time when he'd worn an expensive suit. Even then, I could tell that wasn't his go to. He's much more in his element in a black t-shirt and a pair of dark jeans. And the open neck shirt does nothing to hide just how big he is— everywhere.

Instinctively, I take a step back, my body recognizing danger before my mind can register it.

It's in the way his body is slightly angled towards me, his chest rising and falling in a calculated rhythm.

My gaze moves over his form, from his solid, muscular thighs to his defined pecs to the protruding veins on his neck to…

I blink rapidly as I see his face clearly for the first time. Wide, angular jaw peppered with morning growth, he doesn't seem like the preppy type who'd shave every day. No, he seems like the type of man parents use to scare their children into obedience with. The boogeyman that feeds off fear and chaos. And as I survey the rest of his face, I can't help the sliver of fear that courses through me too.

A jagged line starts from his right cheek and slashes diagonally across his face, ending in his hairline. It looks like someone deliberately cut through him.

Like a nightmare brought back to life, he embodies everything I fear when I step out into the unknown. The monsters who feed on my despair, the ones who delight in causing it.

And as I note the slight curl of his lip, the one that emphasizes the monstrosity of his scar even more, I'm reminded of what had happened at the store.

Now, just like then, his gaze follows the contours of my body in a predatory way that makes me want to run to my room and hide. Lock the door and throw the key away. There's nothing covert about the way he peruses my body, his eyes lingering a little too long over the swell of my breasts.

Unnerved by this blatant inspection, I have the urge to cross my arms over my chest and cover myself.

And as I meet his eyes with mine, I feel a strong jolt that almost makes me stagger back.

Gray. His eyes are gray.

I hadn't realized that before. Mostly because I'd been more worried about getting as far away from him and escaping the hostage situation with my life intact.

Then, his big frame, and hulking hands had only inspired fear as they'd settled on my body. Now...

I frown, tilting my head to the side.

His steely gaze follows, and he doesn't even blink as he holds my stare, a wolfish grin appearing on his face.

Monster. He's a monster. A monster that makes me...

"Gianna!" My father's voice startles me and I turn my head to look at him, a little disoriented.

"What's wrong with you, girl?" He makes a tsk sound as he commands me to take a seat.

I refrain from retorting, but I still huff out loud as I sit down, putting as much distance between me and the hulking beast currently occupying my living room.

"What is he doing here, father?" I ask, masking my voice and putting on my haughty persona.

I don't know why this man is here, in my own house, but I *know* he is dangerous. There's something deep within me that tells me to keep my distance from him.

"Didn't you say *mutts* have no place in our home?" I raise an eyebrow. "Why, you threw poor Johnny out before I could even feed him," I smile sweetly.

"Gianna!" my father exclaims, scandalized.

The *mutt*, however, only regards me amused, as if he'd expected my insult.

"He's our guest. Behave," he gives me a grave look.

I shrug.

"Make it quick. I have matters to attend to," I flutter my lashes as I cross my legs.

It doesn't escape me the way *his* eyes follow my movements, his pupils seemingly growing in size. He's still sporting that smug smile on his face, and I'd like nothing better than to wipe it off.

My upper lip twitches in annoyance, my fists clenching as I mentally imagine putting him in his place—anywhere away from me.

"You'll have to excuse my daughter. She's not always this... difficult." My father grimaces as he looks at me, and I recognize the quiet signal.

Behave.

It takes everything in me to not just up and leave, causing a scene before I do as well, since there's this growing desire inside of me to put the *mutt* in his place. Especially after I'd seen the way he'd taken one too many liberties with me the other time. And that he's here... I don't trust him. Not in the least.

"This is Sebastian Bailey, and he's your new bodyguard," my father says before continuing to add something else. But I don't hear that. No, I just hone in on the fact that he just said *this* is my new bodyguard.

"No!" I put my hand up. "No way," I turn to my father, hoping it's all a bad joke. But he's not laughing. He's not even smiling.

"Gianna..."

"*Papa!*" I exclaim, outraged. "He's a creep!" I say the first thing that pops into my head.

And it *is* true. I'd seen him follow me around, trailing behind me as if he didn't think I'd notice. I'd also seen the way his eyes never once left me in the store, even before the robbers showed up.

"Gianna," my father breathes out, annoyed.

"Papa, he was following me. I'm sure of it. How can someone like *that* be my bodyguard."

"I'm sorry about her. She's a little too spoiled and used to getting her way," he apologizes to Sebastian before turning to me. "Gianna, stop."

That one word has me still. I recognize the signs and I know that he's not going to listen to what I have to say.

"But he killed someone, *papa*. He killed those people…" I trail off.

Why can't he see that there's something not quite right with this man? I can't accept him as my bodyguard. I simply can't. Manuello had been with me since I was a child and I'd known him better than my own family. Another man taking his place?

I shake my head. No, impossible. Especially not *him.*

"Yes, Gianna," my father mutters drily. "He killed someone to save your life, which makes him perfect for the job."

I stare between the two of them and I realize that it doesn't matter if I agree to this or not, they've already planned everything.

"But *papa…*"

"No, Gianna. The matter is already decided. He will be your bodyguard for the next few months until I find a way to get us out of the mess Agosti left us in. And considering DeVille had the audacity to go after Enzo, I trust you realize how critical this is. For all I know, you could be their next target."

My hands are balled into fists, but I don't argue further. There's no point.

I just sit in silence as my father proceeds to list all of Sebastian's achievements, how he's been awarded countless medals for his bravery in the army, and how he's an expert in all matters of security.

I only listen with half an ear as I try to stop myself from shaking. Tapping my feet on the floor, I keep glancing at my watch, wishing the time would pass faster so I can go back to my room—back to safety.

I don't know what it is about this man—this beast really, because there's no way any decent man would look like that—that makes me so frightened.

Just thinking about the fact that as my bodyguard he'll be by my side at all times… The hairs on my arm stand up, my entire being recognizing the danger he poses.

"He'll be taking the room next to yours," my father suddenly says and I whip my head around, thinking I'd misheard.

"What?"

"This is a twenty-four seven position, Gianna. I don't think you realize the gravity of the situation. DeVille is out for our heads. They already ruined your engagement. I'll be damned if I let them do more damage."

"But…" I whisper, my father's expression stopping me from continuing.

I know he is right in that DeVille *is* an ongoing danger, and I'd be crazy to go out without a well-trained bodyguard. But *him?*

I refrain from saying more, just nodding my head like an obedient daughter. It's not like he cares about my opinions anyway.

"I'm glad we've managed to reach an understanding," my father nods, appeased. As if he didn't just reach that *understanding* all by himself. "Now, why don't you show Mr. Bailey to his room?"

"Mia can do it," I'm quick to say as I get up, ready to forget the unfortunate conversation we just had, and maybe even finish the bottle of vodka. God knows, all I want is to forget about *everything.*

"Gianna," my father levels me with his stare. "Do what you're told and we'll have a few words later about your behavior."

He doesn't wait around for me to reply, leaving the room.

The *mutt* rises slowly from the couch, lifting a small duffle bag and swinging it over his shoulder.

He grunts at me, a sign to get moving.

He freaking grunts!

If I weren't already sure he was some sort of crossbreed, now I'm convinced.

"Follow me." I throw my hair over my shoulder in a dramatic gesture, hoping he'll get the message to keep his distance.

As we go up the stairs and towards the third floor where my room is located, I can't help but feel a burning sensation in my back, as if his gaze is drilling a hole through me.

FRIVOLOUS

In fact, my entire body feels the weight of his presence as I put one foot in front of the other, goosebumps covering my skin, a small shiver traversing my limbs.

We reach the landing and I quickly motion for the door next to mine, ready to be done with this and retreat to my safe space.

I don't get to take one step though, and I find myself backed against the wall, my back hitting the cold surface as I raise my head to see those silver grayish eyes watching me. His irises are unnaturally light, the pupils like slits as he regards me. He has that mocking smile on his face, and every small movement seems to make his features seem harsher in the dim light of the hallway.

There's a small bubble inside my chest that seems to grow in size with every labored breath I take. My pulse is through the roof as I can only stare at him, my mind blank of anything but the position I find myself in.

His body—that massive body that must have been forged for destruction—is flush against mine, his hand on my neck as he holds me captive.

"What," the word tumbles out of my mouth on a whisper.

There's something euphoric about his nearness, and I don't think I can pinpoint the sensation. It makes me dizzy, but not in the faint way I usually get, though I recognize the danger I find myself in.

Instead, I find myself tingling…

Is this another type of fear?

"I'm a creep?" he asks, amused. His voice is low, so low a shiver envelops my entire body, my lips parting on a harsh breath. I shake my head slightly, not in response to his question, but trying to alleviate this feeling of discomfort that seems to have lodged itself inside my head, in my ears and lower, down my neck and…

"Tell me, sunshine, how am I a creep?" he repeats the question, his mouth closer to my face, his hot breath fanning over my skin.

I turn my head, trying to avoid the direct contact.

That nickname again—sunshine. Who does he think he is to call me by anything other than my name? Even *that* he isn't fit to utter.

But that's quickly forgotten as I hear the pounding echo of my own pulse. My heart is beating wildly in my chest and I don't think

I've ever experienced greater terror than in this moment. Yet, it's of a foreign nature.

There's danger and there's…

His thumb comes to rest under my chin, slowly turning my head so I can face him.

"I'm waiting," he chuckles, a deep sound that makes me even more uncomfortable.

Yet, as I see that smugness in his gaze, the same one I now recognize as his default setting, I realize I can't let myself be intimidated by him.

"You are," I state with as much conviction I can muster. "I saw how you were watching me." I push my chin up so he can see he doesn't scare me.

"And how is that?" There it is, again. The same amused tone, as if everything is a joke.

Instead of answering him, I push against his arms, seeking to get out of his hold.

"I think you're overstepping your boundaries, Mr. Bailey," I add.

"Tell me," he pushes back, a slight show of force that has me pinned to the wall—with no other way out. "Tell me and I'll let you go."

My eyelids flutter closed, my breathing erratic.

Damn, but did the alcohol have to choose *this* moment to get to my head?

Because I'm starting to feel a little faint, a little…

My eyes snap open to meet his as they continue their slow perusal of my face. The corners of his mouth turn up, his head dipping lower.

"Tell me," he whispers, the sound painful to my ears in a way I'd never experienced before.

"You…" I take a deep breath, wetting my lips. "You were undressing me with your eyes," I manage to say the words out loud, heat traveling up my cheeks and staining them with a deep red.

It's the alcohol. It's clearly the alcohol.

"Is that so?" He brings his hand up, his thumb on my mouth as he brushes it against my lips.

I frown, already feeling out of my depth. Even my brain seems to be lagging behind as I look into those wolfish eyes of his.

"Like I'm doing now?" he drawls, bringing his thumb lower down my neck.

"Let me go," I push against him, not liking the direction this is going.

"Why? I'm a mutt, aren't I?" he scoffs derisively at me and his entire countenance shifts. Where before there was a playful quality to his tone, now all traces of amusement are gone, leaving instead a pure disdain that seems to be aimed directly at me. "Not fit to touch you, much less look at you, right?"

"You're hurting me," I croak, his fingers wrapped around my wrist as he holds me against the wall.

"You paint a pretty picture, *sunshine*," he drawls, his mouth quirking up in sick satisfaction as he brings his face close to mine, his nostrils flaring as he nuzzles my cheek, inhaling deeply. "But the inside is rotten."

"Let go!" I snarl, pushing against him.

"You may bathe in perfume, but it won't erase the stench," he grits, his jaw clenched, his entire body rigid with tension.

Danger rolls off him and it seeps into my pores, spurring my body into reacting to the deadly nearness. Tremors rack my entire being as I try to hold myself still, not show him any weakness.

He scares me.

There's something wicked lying behind his façade. Something that wants to get out and harm me. Something that thirsts for blood.

My blood.

His breath on my lips, it takes everything inside of me not to give in to hysterics, mental fog already settling in and drowning my senses.

"You can't fool me, Gianna Guerra. You think you're so high and mighty but you reek of cheap vodka and cigarettes."

My eyes widen.

"Pro tip," he whispers, his tongue peeking out to lick the lobe of my ear. "Next time use mouthwash."

And just as soon as those words register in my brain, he's gone, the door to the room opening and closing with a whoosh.

My knees feel made of jelly as I barely catch myself from falling to the ground. There's a deafening sound in my ears as I can hear the echo of my own heart, violently beating against my ribcage.

It takes Herculean strength for me to get back to my room, locking the door behind me and allowing myself to slide to the ground.

My mouth parts as I try to breathe, a dry sound coming from my throat as I feel myself choking. I bring my fist to my chest, banging it against my lungs to alleviate the discomfort, but there's little improvement.

That *mutt.*

He actually dared…

He dared talk to me, touch me… taunt me.

I fight against the wave of panic that seems to overtake me because I can't let him win. Oh, I know his type. I know the kind of man he is.

The type that thinks women are useless for anything other than a roll in the hay. The type that sees us as nothing but objects.

My fists clench as I replay his words in my head, the way he'd been so arrogant in his delivery, so sure of himself as he'd pressed himself against me.

Humiliation burns in my cheeks at his insults, and a desire to show him *his* place grows within me.

"I'm no man's toy," I mutter to myself, suddenly faced with a new purpose.

I agree with my father that I *do* need a bodyguard in times like these. But Mr. *mutt* is the last man I'll let near me. Just the sight of him causes a deep, visceral reaction inside of me, not unlike the one I get every time I'm on the verge of a panic attack. My entire body seems to be averse to his presence, a low hum activating deep within me and making me wildly agitated, as if I can't run from him fast enough.

I've had enough experience with his type—the arrogant, never take no for an answer type—and I know that he'll keep on pushing my boundaries until he pushes too far.

I vowed I'd never make myself that vulnerable again, and I'll do anything to see that promise through.

If my father won't listen to me, then I'll just have to take matters into my own hands.

A smile spreads on my lips as I realize just how.

Maybe it's time I lived up to the way everyone sees me—a fucking mean bitch.

"Lindsay?" I dial my friend, the words pouring out of me. "Yes. It needs to be perfect," I smile insidiously.

I may not have control over much in my life, but I'll take anything I can.

CHAPTER FIVE

BASS

"I told you I'd get it done, Cisco. Stop bothering me and let me do this my way," I grit into the phone before hanging up.

There are some things that don't entirely add up. Like Cisco's urgency to see Guerra destroyed. If before I would have found it odd, after the robbery incident I've become convinced there is something amiss.

Cisco must have a personal vendetta against Guerra.

And he's being incredibly tight lipped about it, which doesn't help with my overall mood. Especially as I have to wait hand and foot on little miss spoiled. Just thinking about our latest interactions has me clench my fists in frustration, a need to put her in her place festering inside of me.

I'd been her bodyguard now for a few days, and since the job entails being with her twenty-four seven, I'd gotten a front row seat at the spectacle that is Gianna Guerra's life. And of course, I had to be lucky enough to be welcomed on the stage too.

She had spared no minute in insulting me, her favorite nickname *mutt* already a daily constant. But when she'd seen that I'm not particularly bothered by any names she may call me, she started ordering me around like a servant.

Take that, carry that, oh I forgot that, go get it. While the physical exertion is negligible at best, the mental exercises are strenuous as I have to force myself not to strangle her pretty neck and make her shut up once and for all.

Fuck, but in all my years on this earth I don't think I've been as adversely affected by a female before.

I don't hurt women. I never have. But one glance at Gianna and I swear I'm about to forget all my principles, take her over my knee and show her how *mutts* behave when taunted.

"What are you looking at? Eyes down, *peasant*," she huffs at me as she exits the store, her chin up high as she walks like a model on a runway.

I take a deep breath, repeating to myself that murder in daylight is never a good idea—been there, done that.

Certainly, I won't be able to complete her humiliation from the grave, no matter how appealing the thought might be.

So I just grit my teeth and follow, getting in the car just as she plops herself on the back seat, her nose in the air as she refuses to look at me. She's made it perfectly clear that my appearance offends her, and today is no exception.

"Maybe I should wear a bag on my face," I add drily. "Would that help with your tender sensibilities?" I ask sarcastically.

"Why, that's a marvelous idea." She smiles insidiously. "I might become prematurely blind if I keep seeing," she waves her hand in front of me, her face tilted to the side as she tries very hard to avoid my gaze, "that monstrosity." She fakes a shudder.

I purse my lips, willing my rage to remain contained.

I've never been prone to vanity, but the scar on my face is recent enough to still make me self-conscious of the way people look at me. Add to the fact that even *I* think it looks like a monstrosity, and her jibe definitely hits the mark.

Still, I'm not about to show her that any of her mean girl comments affect me.

I grunt at her, taking out a bag and getting my lunch out.

In the meantime, she's barking some orders at the driver, asking him to take her to her equestrian lessons.

A smile pulls at my lips as I slowly open the bag, letting the smell waft through the air. Gianna's nose scrunches up as a small frown appears on that lovely face.

She looks around, dazed, until her eyes settle on the bag in my lap. Her eyes widen.

"Throw that out," she hisses.

"It's," I bring my watch closer to my face, "twelve. I'm allowed a lunch break, you know," I shrug, opening the can of food.

Delight fills me when I see the way her expression changes in a second. Indeed, even I have a hard time keeping a straight face as the smell hits my own nose.

One thing I'd noticed in the few days I've followed little miss spoiled around is that she has an issue with food—specifically food that has strong odors. Why, she rarely even eats in public, picking at her food and finding excuses *not* to eat.

It had certainly given me an idea, and seeing her reaction just now, I know I've also hit the mark. And because I'm just as petty as she is, I'd gone for the smelliest fish in the world—a Swedish type that hadn't been the easiest to procure.

Ah, but payback's a bitch.

"Stop the car!" She shouts at the driver, her hand to her mouth as she looks mightily ill.

"He can't hear you anymore, *Miss* Guerra," I smile widely at her, motioning towards the privacy divider. I'd shut down the microphone and put the divider in place, so the driver can do nothing but take us to our destination. And seeing how the horse farm is upstate, the ride will be long indeed.

"You…" she seethes, barely able to take her hand from her mouth to shout some expletive at me.

"You must be famished too. You barely touched your lunch. Why don't you try some?" I thrust the can towards her, unable to keep the grin off my face as she all but jumps out of her seat, backing away as much as possible to avoid any contact with the smelly fish.

"You're dead," she glares defiantly at me. "My father won't forgive this slight!"

"What? Having lunch?" I snort at her. "Good luck explaining *that* to him," I smirk.

"You…" she trails off, and I wonder if she's out of insults.

But that thought is quickly forgotten as she rummages through her back for something, her expression turning defiant again as she removes a small container.

Before I realize what she means to do, she jumps on me spraying something in my face. I have a hard time balancing the smelly fish in one hand and her in another as I try to drag her off me.

But she doesn't seem easily dissuaded as she clings to me against all odds, limbs flailing, nails out to scratch me.

It's a cacophony of sounds as she tries to land a hit on me, her little spray aimed for my eyes, her other hand reaching for the fish.

She's such a tiny thing, yet she doesn't seem to realize that all her efforts are in vain. Not when I hold her steady with only one arm. And as she continues to spray me with what I can only assume is some kind of pepper spray, my nostrils already feeling some of the sting, I realize there's only one way to end this.

One moment she's screaming at me, the next she's quiet as her eyes widen, the fish sauce coating her hair as I dump the contents of the can on her head.

She blinks. And blinks.

With one shaky hand she reaches in her hair to remove a slice of fish. No sound comes out of her mouth as she stares in horror at it.

"You," she whispers, still unmoving.

She lifts her eyes at me, those big, gorgeous eyes that beg to be painted by renowned artists and displayed for the public to admire them. For a second I forget all about her abysmal behavior and her shitty personality, the sight of moisture accumulating at the corner of her eyes making me feel a little guilty.

Just a little. She's still a bitch.

There's no warning as her mouth opens and she starts retching in my lap, her meager lunch spilled all over my suit.

"Fuck!" I curse out loud, shaking my head and bringing my hand up to massage my temples.

But one second I'm distracted by the sick girl in my lap and it's all it takes for her to complete her attack, raising her arm and spraying that noxious substance in my eyes.

Double fuck…

To say that our interactions worsen with time would be an understatement. In just one week, we've gone from insults to full on body assaults, most of the time it's her lithe little body that jumps on me, intent on scratching my eyes out.

That I've refrained from taking her over my knee...

"You need to change," she tells me as she comes down in one of her glamorous gowns. She's wearing a full face gilded mask for tonight's ball that makes her look mysterious and one thousand percent more fuckable. If only she could mask her personality too...

"I'm not going to be a laughingstock because I have a..." she continues as she scrunches her nose at me in distaste, "hobo as bodyguard. Put on a decent suit and meet me in the living room," she orders before disappearing towards the room.

Again, visions of exactly what I'd do to the little brat swim before my eyes, but just as I start plotting her next punishment, I realize that I'm never going to get her to lower her guard enough to complete my mission.

"Damn it," I mutter as I go and change my clothes.

Damn Cisco and damn the entire family for giving *me* this assignment. I don't think there's greater humiliation than having to withstand miss little spoiled's tantrums on a daily basis. And now I also have to accompany her to her rich girl party, where no doubt, more spoiled kids are going to be present.

I may not have been here long, but I've noticed the way Benedicto treats his daughter. He really isn't that interested in her except to ensure she attends society events and has regular outings with people from the upper circles.

Daily I have to accompany her to different activities—horse riding, archery, golf, polo and other snobbish things—sitting in the background and watching how these people covertly insult each other behind a sweet smile.

Maybe I've spent too much time in the gutter, but I simply can't comprehend how she derives any pleasure from hanging out with such an entourage.

While our family has money, we've never mingled with the *elite* of New York. Instead, we've been involved in the underground world, where things are rarely glamorous. There, the rich are rich because they've gotten their hands dirty, not because daddy left them a trust fund to last them a lifetime.

Sometimes it feels like I'm in a completely different world as I watch these kids that will likely become someone, but never *be* someone.

It's one of the things that makes this job even more annoying. Having to witness good for nothings do worthless things while criticizing the rest of the world for actually *working.*

The more I think about it, the worse my mood gets. And that's *not* a good thing considering I'm going to be surrounded with all those vapid people tonight.

A party at a mansion upstate, the party is supposed to be an end-of-year masquerade for everyone graduating. Of course, Gianna could not miss such an event, not with her being in the center of every single gathering.

Just thinking of the times I'd seen people fawn over her, no shame at literally kissing her feet.

"If I don't kill someone tonight..." I mutter to myself, feeling an insane urge to do harm. It's going to be a lucky day indeed if I don't kill some lanky ass kid for getting too close to her.

Getting too close to her?

Where did that come from?

A scowl appears on my face as I realize the direction of my thoughts. It's not like I care about who gets close to her, but I still need to finish my mission, and that means I have to make sure she has no outstanding attachments.

Yes, that's it.

With a last aggressive tug at my tie, I mumble some curses as I go out, intent on being Gianna's shadow for the night without getting *too* mad—at anything.

For once the car ride is peaceful as she barely even glances at me, her entire attention on her phone as she keeps on texting someone. Interestingly enough though, there are no more insults either.

It takes us almost an hour to reach the mansion, and although a masquerade, I realize that everyone is wearing the same gilded mask as Gianna.

Built in a Georgian style, the mansion houses a huge ball room where everyone is already dancing, drinking and carousing.

Just like Dario had mentioned, drugs seem to be *everywhere*. People are snorting coke off every surface available, a guy bending over so that his friend could sniff the powder off his back.

As soon as we step inside, though, all the eyes are on Gianna. Two girls hurry towards her and she does a quick twirl to show off her dress.

But as people stare at her, their eyes also find me, the only unmasked person at the party.

"I'll be by the door," I mumble, not liking being the object of their attention.

"No, silly!" Gianna turns around, grabbing my hand and all but dragging me towards the dance floor. "You have to dance with me," she giggles.

I lean in to smell her, noting the presence of alcohol on her breath.

Of course.

"Find some other boy toy," I grumble, trying to extricate myself from her.

"Come on, you're no fun," she accuses in a breathy tone that goes straight to my cock.

Damn, but no matter how bratty, or how much of a bitch she is, my cock doesn't seem to get the memo that she's just a means to an end.

Her hands are on my arms, as she feels for my biceps, her fingers testing the strength of the muscle. This is the first time she's touched me with anything other than aggression, and I find myself stunned on the spot.

"My, but you're strong, aren't you?" she purrs, leaning closer to me—too close.

If there's anything I've learned about Gianna during this time, is that she *hates* getting close to people. She doesn't let anyone in her personal space, and is often biting in her replies when people dare to touch her uninvited.

That she's doing this... I'm immediately suspicious.

My hands against her shoulders, I push her back.

"What are you doing?" I ask, trying to control my tone.

"Dancing with you," she fires back, but she's not completely focused on me. No, one eye is on her wrist watch.

I immediately catch her hand, bringing it towards me.

"What are you planning, Gianna?" my voice comes rougher than intended. But I know her by now, and she's always up to something nefarious, almost always resulting in some unsuspecting fool getting hurt.

And I seem to be the unsuspecting fool.

The hands of her watch move in alignment just as a loud noise permeates the air. Everyone removes their masks, all at once, throwing them in the air.

I frown, not comprehending what's happening at first. But as I zone in on one person after person—their faces specifically—I realize what her game was.

Gianna's mask, too, falls to the ground, and she's sporting the same prosthetic on her face as everyone else. Blended seamlessly with her skin, a long scar starts from her chin to her nose before appearing again from her brow and ending in her hairline. The wound is red and raw, resulting in a monstrosity fit for Halloween, not for *this*.

But it was all calculated. It was all a game.

She flutters her lashes at me, a satisfied smile on her face as she comes closer.

"See, Mr. Bailey? I'm nothing if not thoughtful," she drawls as she smiles, her white teeth gleaming in the light. "Now you're not the ugliest person at the party," she says sweetly, barely able to contain her laughter.

And as I turn my head around, I realize that everyone is staring at me with a hidden smile on their faces, probably secretly laughing at me.

My fists clench, and I don't think as I grab her by the arm, dragging her with me towards an area with less people.

"Let go!" she kicks at my hand, *now* trying to get free.

A sick grin pulls at my lips as I effortlessly tug her along, all her attempts to free herself in vain.

As soon as I see an empty corner, I push her in front of me, her back hitting the wall. Her smile is gone as she looks at me wide-eyed.

"So this is all for my benefit?" I drawl, enjoying the way the amusement leaves her features, giving way to fear.

And she should fear me. Because fuck if I don't want to teach her a lesson right this moment.

Backing her even further into the wall, I cage her with my arms. She looks so small next to me, even in her high heels. And as I cover her with my body, a whimper escapes her lips.

"Not so brave now, are you, sunshine?"

"You're a beast!" she hisses at me in that wild cat voice of hers that only manages to make me harder, my cock straining against my zipper. I continue to smile at her, enjoying the way she doesn't seem as powerful now that she's alone, without her friends or anyone to save her from me.

"Take your filthy hands off me," she commands me in a last show of strength, her small hands on my wrist as she tries to push me aside.

"You should have realized that before, Gianna," I tsk at her, lowering my head to nuzzle her hair as I inhale her lovely scent. "Before poking the beast," I whisper when my mouth reaches her ear. Fuck, but why is all this perfection wasted on her?

I note the sudden stiffening of her body against mine. The way her skin is suddenly covered in goosebumps, a slight quiver going down her spine. She's not indifferent. Oh, she's definitely not indifferent, no matter how much she might protest to the contrary.

And just to prove my point, I let my mouth trail over her jaw, blowing softly over her skin, but not touching it.

A gasp escapes her, her hands slack on my arm.

To test something, I pull back, just looking at her.

Her eyes are wide, her lips slightly parted as she looks at me. Shock—or something similar to shock—is painted on her features. There's also a look of wonder as she seems rooted to the spot, barely even realizing I'm giving her an out.

But as soon as she shows that hint of vulnerability, it's gone. She shakes herself, quickly making to dash past me.

"No, no, no," I say, amused, grabbing her wrist and pushing her back.

I remove a switchblade from the back of my pants, the knife gleaming even in the dark corner.

"You seem rather fond of your new look," I start, noting the quickening of her pulse under my hand. "Why don't I make it permanent?" Just as the words are out of my mouth, the tip of the blade touches her fake skin, right where the prosthetic scar covers her cheek.

Cutting in the middle, I slowly drag the knife up.

She's almost shaking with fear—almost. Yet she still looks at me with that defiant gaze of hers.

"Go ahead," she pushes her chin up, thrusting her face further into my blade.

The corner of my mouth curls up, but I don't let her see how impressed I am with her resilience, or the fact that she's not attacking me as it's become the norm. I simply continue to cut through the fake skin until it's all but detached from her face.

Flinging the flap of silicone to the floor, I resume the position of the blade, but this time over her real skin.

"What would people say if this perfect skin was no longer… perfect?" I murmur against her cheek, my hot breath mingling with the cold of the steel and making her tremble. Her tongue peeks out to wet her lips as she regards me unblinking.

"Do it!" she challenges, bringing her hand up, her fingers wrapping around mine as she forces me to push the blade into her face. "Make me as ugly as you," she whispers, and I note the hint of determination in her gaze.

She's… serious—a sobering realization.

Suddenly, I find myself unable to go through with my threat. I don't know if it's the way she's glaring at me, a mix of misplaced courage and resolve, or the way she's slightly trembling in my arms, her body betraying her and belying her expression.

Instead of digging the blade into her cheek, I bring it lower, down her neck and towards the swell of her tits.

She's wearing a low-cut gown, perfectly molded to her body as it pushes those bountiful tits up, making them look too fucking perfect.

But that's what she is. *Too fucking perfect.* On the outside, at least.

I'd seen the way everyone was eating her up, no doubt already visions of her enticing curves dancing through their minds. All those puny boys are probably already thinking how to woo her better, how to reserve a spot between the sweet thighs that hide under her gown.

I grind my teeth in frustration as I realize how much the thought of her offering herself up to *anyone* bothers me. She's too perfect for mere mortals to touch. Too perfect for someone like *me* to touch. Yet touch I am as I let the blade rest between the valley of her breasts.

"You need someone to teach you a lesson, Gianna. You need a firm hand to show you how to behave like a human being. For once." I give her a lopsided smile.

Her chest expands with every inhale, the knife brushing against her skin and making her shiver. Her eyes are still on me, wild, her expression almost feral as she shoots that disdainful gaze at me.

I can't help the way my mind conjures up images of her on my lap, my palm resting against the curve of her ass as I spank the brat out of her. But those thoughts are dangerous, because my hand on her ass means my fingers would be close to her pussy, and damn if I have no doubt I'd find her dripping wet and ready to soak my digits. Not with this fire that seems to be hidden within her, this arrogance that makes me want to orgasm her into submission.

Fuck!

This is dangerous. Too dangerous. I know her track record and I know her personality, and yet I can't help my own fucking reaction to her. I've never been this turned on by a woman before, especially a nasty one like Gianna. But God if I don't want to fuck the arrogance out of her and make her scream my name so that all those posh boys can hear who she belongs to.

"And you think you're the man to do it?" She asks snidely. "You're not fit to lick the dirt off my shoes, Mr. Bailey." Her hand on my knife, she keeps it to her breasts as she leans in, her mouth close to my ear. "You disgust me," she whispers, and I feel the satisfaction dripping from her voice. "I know you want me. I see the way your eyes follow me around. Even now, you're hard just being in my presence, aren't you?" she states with certainty, her eyes dropping to my crotch.

"Ah, sunshine, you're a touch too confident, aren't you?" I drawl, my other hand on her back as I bring my fingers down her spine in a soft caress. "My cock may think you'd do for a quick fuck, but I wouldn't touch you if my life depended on it," I reply, pushing the knife down her bodice and feeling the material give way with a snap, her tits bouncing ever so slightly at being freed from their confines.

She tenses, but she doesn't move.

"Good, because there will be a cold day in hell before you'll *ever* lay a finger on me," she does her best to keep her voice steady, even as I feel her body tremble under my fingertips.

"Not as cold as your touch, *sunshine*. There's only ice in this body of yours, and I'd rather not have my cock freeze off," I smirk down at her, keeping her against me.

If there's such a thing as a truthful lie, then this is mine. Because I *don't* want to touch her, yet I do.

Fuck but I do.

She raises her head slightly, her eyes meeting mine, a small battle of wills ensuing as we stare at each other.

"And yet," I continue, a smirk on my face, "I like you at my mercy." I tell her and her features pale.

"You're sick," she spits out, pushing against me so suddenly the knife grazes the creamy skin of her tits, drawing blood. A quick intake of breath and her eyes widen when she sees the gash that seems to grow larger.

Before I can help myself, I dip my head low, my tongue sneaking out to lick the liquid, tasting the metallic tinge of the blood as well as the sweetness of her skin.

A gasp escapes her lips as I close my mouth over her flesh, sucking on her wound. She holds herself still, her heart thumping fast in her chest.

"Let go," she whispers, but her voice lacks strength.

I don't.

I continue to flick my tongue over the small expanse of flesh, teasing the small cut and eliciting more gasps from her.

Her hands are balled into fists, her entire body taut with tension.

"Let go," she repeats, this time a little louder.

It's not until I start trailing my lips up her neck that she finally reacts, her hands pushing at my shoulders, her fiery eyes shooting daggers at me.

"You…" she seethes, her lips drawn in a thin line as her nostrils flare at me. "You'll pay for this," she threatens, giving me a slight shove before running away.

I watch her retreating figure, chuckling at her promise of retribution.

She's cold. Yes, she's very cold. But she has the potential to be hot too.

CHAPTER SIX

GIANNA

"Gigi, where were you?" Lindsay calls out when I make it back to the ballroom. My heart is beating loudly against my chest, my cheeks flushed and my…

God, why does he make me react like this? Why does he make me so angry I forget myself? He'd held me against the wall, that big body of his flush against mine as he'd threatened to do *things* to me, and there had been no hint of my usual panic. Yes, I'd felt feverish, and a little out of breath, and maybe a bit dizzy… But it hadn't been the regular faintness I get when I see someone encroach my space. There had been none of the mental fog that usually accompanies those episodes.

There had only been heat. Dangerous, disgusting heat that seemed to emanate from every pore in his body and transfer into mine.

My entire being had nearly quaked when he'd put his mouth on me, a tingling starting in my lower belly and moving lower.

"Fuck," I curse out, a little terrified by what happened.

I've never felt something like this before, and to have it happen for the first time for *him?* My lip curls in disgust as my mind conjures up that scarred face of his, a monstrosity not fit to grace my field of view.

"We need to move to Plan B," I say suddenly.

I can't allow myself any weakness. He makes me feel *weak*, and I can't have that.

"Are you sure? Isn't that a little extreme, even for us?" she asks, concerned.

"No. I need him to resign. Tonight. As soon as possible," the words tumble out of my mouth.

I just need him to be out of my life. Somewhere far away where he can't make me feel strange things, where my body can't react like it's not my own anymore.

"Gigi…"

"We're doing it Lindsay! Tell the boys to bring it into positions. I'll lure him to the spot," I say resolutely.

A cruel smile pulls at my lips as I imagine how he's going to react to what I have prepared for him.

I thought that maybe going after his appearance would hurt him enough to resign. But I should have realized that someone like him would never care about that. Why, it's probably a badge of honor.

While everyone is doing their bit, I hover around the entrance to see if the *mutt* is anywhere in sight.

When I'd planned this, I hadn't thought I'd actually have to do it. Mostly because it's over the top—even for me. But with how things are progressing between the two of us, I find myself unable to continue like this.

Since he started working I haven't been able to have one moment of peace, his presence unnerving me, his nearness often making me tremble with unreleased tension.

Angry. He makes me so damn angry.

He frustrates me like no one's been able to before, and I know that I won't be able to last a few months with him by my side. Already a week and all I want is to jump on him and do him bodily harm.

A snort escapes me. As if I could. He's such a hulking giant that he can lift me in the air with one hand. He's already done that the many time I'd tried to attack him.

I catch Lindsay's eye at the top of the stairs as she signals me that everything is in place.

Just as I turn towards the entrance, I note Sebastian there, a smirk on his face as he takes up his position. His hawkish eyes are fixed on me, his eyebrows moving up and down in a quiet dare.

After the incident in the hallway, it might prove a little difficult to get him to follow me. But I'm nothing if not persuasive, especially when it's something I want.

And oh, I so want to see him thoroughly humiliated in the worst of fashion.

My resolve strong, I straighten my back as I go towards him, painting a smile on my face.

Everyone is aware of my plan, as I'd instructed them what to do at any point, so no one is particularly concerned with me as I glide towards my unsuspecting victim.

"I've been thinking," I say as I reach his side.

I need to be smart about this, especially after the first prank he's not likely to believe me and my *good* intentions.

"Oh, you think?" He mocks, that stupid smile of his wide and inviting. It shows a hint of white straight teeth, and his mouth that...

"You're an asshole. But what's new," I give him a smile of my own as I join his side.

"Why don't we call a truce?" I propose, curious to see his reaction.

"A truce?" He raises an eyebrow.

"Is that your way of making sure I won't embarrass you in front of your friends?"

The corner of my mouth pulls up. It's not *me* who's going to be embarrassed. That's for sure.

"You're going to be my bodyguard for at least another couple of months. It's already been a week and we've all but killed each other," I pause, tilting my head to look at him.

"Go on," he narrows his eyes in skepticism.

"It's going to be hell if we continue like this. For both of us. I was thinking we could act more," I purse my lips as if I'm deep in thought, "cordially."

"It's not in your nature, Gianna," he chuckles.

"It can be," I counter. And it is technically true. I don't have to be a bitch. But it works—it keeps people away.

"Can you tell me what brought this on?" he asks, his tone serious for the first time.

"I'm tired," I sigh. "At home I fight with my father and stepmother. Outside, I fight with you. At these parties," I wave towards the ballroom, "I fight with even more people. I want a moment of peace," I admit.

Again, technically true, but not in the context I'm implying.

He studies me for a moment, his eyes moving over my face and lower, towards the torn bodice that I'd barely managed to fix. Heat travels up my body at his perusal, but I can't break character. I certainly can't yell at him to avert his fucking eyes.

It takes everything in me to just smile sweetly at him.

"So, what do you say? Truce?" I hold my hand out to him.

He doesn't answer for a second and I fear that doesn't believe me. But then he surprises me when his big hand engulfs mine, my skin tingling from the contact.

Why the hell is it tingling?

I barely mask a scowl at that thought, trying my damned hardest to keep myself in check as I slowly shake his hand.

"You're an odd person, Gianna Guerra," he states, his eyes still glued to my face. The r in my name rolls effortlessly on his tongue, and for the first time I note a tinge of accent. It doesn't help that it sounds like a low purr, sending shivers to my back and making me feel even more feverish.

The plan. Yes, I must stick to the plan.

"I'm glad we can put everything besides us. If you'll excuse me, I need to get something to drink."

"Wait here. I'll bring it to you. It's not a good idea to drink from foreign places," he immediately interjects, almost frowning at his words.

I nod thoughtfully.

"You're right. Thank you," I smile shyly, his eyes dipping to my lips.

"Right," he says, blinking twice.

The drinks station is at the other end of the ballroom, and to make it there, he has to walk by the balustrade that divides the top floor from the lower one.

I'm a little giddy as I watch him stride across the dance floor, a determined look on his face. It also serves as a mighty contrast, his body big and imposing—so very different from those scrawny boys pretending to be men. He's at least a head taller than everyone at the party, his figure easily discernible in the crowd.

And as he reaches the designated spot, I pull my phone from my bag, hitting record.

It all happens in slow motion. One second he's fine, the next he's covered in a white, almost translucent sticky substance. It pours down his head and face, staining the top of his black suit.

"What," his startled voice echoes through the ballroom as the music stops, everyone staring at him and laughing to their heart's content.

I take a step forward, walking until I reach his side, my phone still capturing his reaction.

He turns sharply towards me, his eyes blazing.

"Gianna," he grits my name, his jaw clenched, his nostrils flared.

"I'm sorry Mr. Bailey," I start in a dramatic voice, "but ours isn't meant to be," I raise a hand to my forehead, closing my eyes and releasing a tragic sigh. "Not when you're covered from head to toe in horse cum." I have to purse my lips so I don't break into a satisfied smile.

Last time we'd gone for my riding lessons, I'd put a—rather large—order of horse semen, already plotting my revenge for the fish incident. Still, I don't think I could have ever imagined how gratifying this could be.

And now the entire internet will know too, because I'm not the only one with my phone out. Everyone is recording him, videos from all angles hitting the online space all at once.

No longer able to hold on to my laughter, I burst out loud, my hand on my stomach as I let everything out. I don't think I've ever been more satisfied by a prank than now. Seeing him covered in horse spunk has to be the best humiliation.

"You should even thank me," I add, barely able to get the words out. "That spunk is probably worth more than your entire pathetic self," I giggle.

And it had been expensive. But when you know enough rich people that derive just as much pleasure from humiliating others, you don't have to pay a penny.

He takes a step towards me, and as I see his grave expression, aggression rolling off him, I stop laughing, worry bubbling to the surface.

But he can't do anything to me here, right? There are so many people, all filming the events, that he can't possibly think to harm me in plain sight.

He comes right to my side, giving me a look of disgust before shaking his head at me and striding away from the ballroom.

I release a relieved sigh, and immediately I'm met with a barrage of comments from people around me, everyone praising my idea and telling me that he should go viral by tomorrow. Considering that some of the people in this room have millions of followers, I have no doubt that Mr. Scarface will be Mr. Spunkface tomorrow.

When he doesn't return even after half an hour, I'm *almost* convinced my mission has reached its goal.

I continue to chat with everyone who comes up to me, until at some point it becomes too tiring.

Making my way to the back terrace, I finally take a moment to myself.

"Who knew revenge would be this tiring?" A smile spreads on my lips.

Father might have tossed me to the sharks when he'd decided to pimp me out to the New York elites, but I learned very quickly to survive. You don't get at the top of the chain unless you're tough. And in these circles, you need to be more than tough—you need to be cruel.

"Gianna," a voice calls from behind me.

I turn, frowning when I see Garett, one of Lindsay's friends, come forward.

"Yes?" I raise an eyebrow. I'm not in the mood for company, especially of the male variety.

"Damn," he whistles, "what you did back there?" He shakes his head, an amused expression on his face. "I knew you were smart, but I didn't realize you'd be devious too."

"Excuse me?" I narrow my eyes at him.

Being Lindsay's friend meant that we'd seen each other regularly at events. But I'd never had a conversation with him alone. Hell, I don't *ever* have conversations with men alone.

"When I heard from Lindsay what you had planned, I doubted you'd actually go through with it. But you did," the corner of his mouth curls up as he steps closer to me.

"Yeah, well, thanks," I say dismissively, making to bypass him.

"Where are you going?" He stops me, his hand on my elbow.

Already I feel an incoming wave of anger and panic, but I know better than to outwardly show it.

"Back inside. The party's still going, right?" I attempt a smile of my own to put him more at ease.

I've already seen—many times—what rejection does to these boys' egos, and they only become nastier if I say no to them.

I'm already on my way when he grabs my arm again, this time more forcefully, pulling me backwards and into his embrace.

His entire body is flush against mine, and my eyes go wide for a second, unable to react.

"I've wanted to tell you how I feel for a long time, Gianna," he starts, whispering in my hair. "I've been in love with you for years now, but I've never had the courage to tell you how I felt. Not when I knew the men you were with," he sighs, continuing his confession.

I can only stand still, my body stiff as a wooden plank as my mind tries to catch up with what's happening. Even the words to tell him to let me go fail to come out of my mouth. There's only a sense of loss, so profound my entire being starts shaking, my body remembering what it's like to be held against my will, to be...

"I'm sorry if I laid this out on you too suddenly," he says eventually, moving away. His eyes are studying me for a reaction, but I simply can't give him anything. I can barely move as it is.

"You don't have to reply immediately. Please, just think about it?" He asks in a hopeful tone.

I barely find the strength to nod slowly, my eyes unblinking as I will some clarity to return to my mind.

He beams at me before quickly retreating, leaving me alone once more.

It's only then that it finally dawns on me that this could have been worse. So much worse than a sweet boy declaring his crush. And I would have been powerless to do anything. Not with how my body froze up, my mind a minefield of panic.

A sob catches in my throat as my entire body starts vibrating with the intensity of my emotions.

"Fuck, fuck, fuck," I whisper to myself, agitation and terror overtaking me.

I don't have a bag with me, but I do have a small pouch in my dress reserved for emergency situations.

My fingers fumble with the opening of the dress, taking out the small container to reveal my prized pills. But my panic is still too intense, my fingers shaking as I try to open it and take the pills out.

And I'm so focused on getting to them that I don't hear the figure sneaking behind me. I only realize there's someone else in the garden with me when I feel a hand on my arm.

I jump, startled by the sudden touch, my pills all tumbling to the ground, spilling from their container.

"No, no," I shake my head, muttering under my breath.

"Now, what do we have here?" *His* voice resounds as he holds tightly on to my arm, not letting me stoop to gather my pills.

"Let me go," I whisper, knowing he's here to wreck his revenge. And I'll take it. I'll take everything as long as I get my pills.

I just need one…

"You didn't think I'd let you off the hook for what you did, did you *sunshine?*"

I gather the courage to look up, my limbs still trembling with residual adrenaline from my close encounter with a panic attack.

He cleaned himself up. He's no longer wearing his suit. Instead, he put on a black t-shirt that's molded to his muscular frame, only serving to emphasize further the disparity in our sizes.

And what he could do to me.

"Just let me get that, and then we can talk."

I try to wrench my arm from his hold, but it's in vain as he tightens his fingers over my skin. His hands are so big, he's easily circling the entirety of my arm, making sure I can't possibly escape.

"Please," the words tumble out of my mouth, a shameful admission, but necessary when my brain is craving—no, demanding—the pills.

"Hmm," he smirks, bending over to pick up the container.

"Xanax," he reads the label, an eyebrow raised as he turns to study my face. "So little miss perfect is taking Xanax," he drawls.

"Give it back," I burst out, my eyes fixed on the pill he's holding, the only thing that can help me escape the hell that is my mind. "Please, give it back," I whisper, resenting saying the words out loud, hating that he caught me at my weakest, but nonetheless unable to ignore the way my body is fighting me, my mind sending sharp reminders of the nightmare that will begin if I don't get them. They are the only thing standing between me and a total breakdown, and for that… I'd do anything.

I don't know if it's this show of vulnerability that gets through to him, but he ends up extending his palm, the pill in the middle.

I don't even think as I snatch it, popping it into my mouth and swallowing. I close my eyes, a sigh of relief escaping me as I simply wait for the calm to settle over me.

I don't know how long I stand like that, eyes closed, mouth parted as I simply breathe in and out. The effect is slow to come, but come it does, rewarding me with a heavenly inner peace as I finally ground myself enough to open my eyes and face my bitter enemy.

"What do you want?" I spit at him, a little more in control of myself. Now that I got my fix, I know there's nothing he can do to me that's worse than the throes of an attack.

He's sporting an amused expression on his face, slowly chuckling as he looks me up and down.

"Does anyone else know what a little addict you are?"

"I'm not an addict."

"Really? Could have fooled me," he arches a brow. "I wonder what your father would say about this pastime of yours," he drawls, folding his arms over his chest.

My eyes widen at his threat and I shake my head at him.

Fuck, but that's the worst thing that could *ever* happen. If my father knew about my pills, he'd not only prohibit me from taking them, but he'd ensure I never find somewhere to get them from.

And a life without pills. No, a day without pills… Hell, even an hour without them would save me living through mental and physical hell.

"Don't tell him," I say, "please," I add, since that word seems to work wonders with him.

I'm willing to beg him if that's what he wants. I'm willing to even apologize for my prank as long as he doesn't tell my father about the pills.

But even in my frightened mind I can realize he now has something over my head, and he will no doubt continue to use it to get me to behave.

What's the alternative, though? Because without those pills… No, that's out of the question. I *can't* live without them. I'd sooner kill myself than withstand even *one* day without them, knowing the agony that awaits me, my mind my worst tormenter.

"Maybe," he shrugs, still maintaining that smug expression on his face. "But why would I help you after what you just did?"

I purse my lips, realizing he has me cornered. Especially after what I did to him I have no doubt that he's going to go ratting to my father and…

I squeeze my eyes shut at the imminent nightmare, and I do the one thing I'd never done before. I lower myself to my knees in front of him.

"Please," I bow my head down so he sees I'm serious, but my hands are still clenched as my entire being rebels at this gesture of submission. "Please don't tell him."

"My, but you look quite at home on your knees, sunshine," he laughs at me.

Coming closer, he grasps my jaw in his hands, forcing me to look up at him.

"Tell me, why should I help you?"

It's that lopsided smile that drives me crazy, the way his entire face appears monstrous, the ridges of his scar prominent and looking like my own personified nightmare.

"I'm begging you," I grit the words out, physical pain assaulting me at this humiliation.

"You're begging me?" he asks, his fingers tightening over my jaw. "How nice of you," he drawls, his thumb suddenly on my lips. Without any tenderness, he pushes against my lips, parting them.

"What's in it for me?" his eyes seem to darken as he looks down on me, his size even more frightening from my position.

"What… what do you want?" I try to hold my voice steady, even though there's only fake confidence at this point.

He's threatening me with the one thing that allows me to live like a normal person. And for that I'm afraid to admit to myself that I would do *anything*.

And he sees it too, as his mouth slowly curls up, an insidious smile that would make *anyone* weep at the horrific sight.

"What do I want indeed," he pauses, smirking. He's keeping me on my toes by delaying the inevitable. And he's doing a perfect job with it, because even in my semi-high state, I can feel a sliver of anxiety spike through.

My hands are balled into fists as I stare into his arrogant face.

"Show me how good you are on your knees, and I *might* not tell your father." He raises his eyebrows at me expectantly, and I can only gape at him, flabbergasted.

"What do you mean?" I ask softly, although my heart is beating like crazy in my chest.

Didn't I already know he was going to ask for that?

"You wound me, sunshine!" He spreads his palm over his chest, feigning pain. "You know exactly what I mean. I want you to take my cock out and show me how good you are on your knees," he smirks.

My tongue peeks out to wet my lips, my palms sweaty, my entire being on the verge of an attack.

I can't do it. I can't… But do I have a choice? If he tells my father, then he'll make sure I'm never going to be able to get my pills. Even worse, my father will no doubt inform my future husband too, and that… I can't have that.

I already know my life is going to be a living hell from the moment I say *I do*, but at least the pills will help me bear the brunt of it. Without them…

"No? Fine," he shrugs, pulling out his phone to dial my father.

"I'll do it," the words are bitter in my mouth as I say them.

And just like that, I'm once more put in a position where all choices are taken away from me—not that I've ever had many to begin with.

God, am I doing the right thing? Is this humiliation worth it? Because I know that for him it's nothing more than payback for what I did to him.

Yet just as the thought surfaces, I know that it's worth it. The pills are worth it.

They are worth everything.

"What are you waiting for then?" His voice startles me from my thoughts.

"Aren't you going to…" I trail off, pointing towards his pants, a blush creeping up on my face.

"And do all the work for you?" he shakes his head, his arms once more crossed over his chest as he watches me closely, waiting for my next move.

I steel myself, somewhat thankful I'd managed to take a pill before this. It will make me more likely to withstand it.

With shaky fingers, I reach out for his belt, unbuckling it. He's still wearing the dress pants from before, and the material makes it easy to recognize he's already hard, the outline of his cock a little daunting.

I fumble with the zipper, my mind in a million places as I reach inside to cup his dick.

"That's it, sunshine. Now take it out and put it in your mouth," he says as my palm brushes over his warm flesh.

And it is warm. I guess I'd never stopped to think about that, everything else about him so cold and mean.

I try to circle my fingers around his girth, but I can't. And when I take it out of his pants, I can see why.

Instinctively, I bite my lip at the sight.

It's huge. Thick and veiny, it looks so angry as it seems to twitch in my direction.

"Are you going to just stare at it?" I look up to see him watching me with narrowed eyes, as if he's convinced I'm going to bail at any minute. The phone is still in his hand, peeking through the crook of his arm, a perpetual reminder of what's at stake.

"No," I mumble, swallowing hard and taking a deep breath.

I can do this.

Tucking my hair behind my ears, I place both hands on his cock as I angle my face towards it. Without giving it more thought than necessary, I open my mouth, closing my lips over the head.

It doesn't taste as bad as I thought it would. There's just a tinge of saltiness as my tongue makes contact with his flesh.

"Fuck," he mutters, and I quickly look up, afraid I've done something wrong.

His eyes are droopy, his lips slightly parted and I take it to mean I'm doing something right. The faster I get this over with, the sooner I'll be able to forget it.

Forget him.

My hands are awkwardly gripping the shaft as I push him further into my mouth, my teeth slightly grazing his skin.

"No teeth," he hisses, his hand suddenly in my hair as he pulls my head back. "Don't even think about biting my dick off." He dangles the phone in front of me, the threat clear.

I frown a little. I hadn't meant to do that. Of course, I would love nothing more than to geld him, but that would only make him more eager to tell my father about my pills.

I nod slowly, and he grunts, his hand leaving my hair and urging me to return to what I was doing.

I'm a little unsure how to proceed, but I try my best to mask my teeth with my lips as I guide the head back into my mouth. I open wide, attempting to fit as much of him into my mouth as I can. When the head of his cock reaches the back of my throat, I stop.

"What are you doing?" His raised voice takes me by surprise, and I lift my eyes to his.

"Fuck, you're useless, aren't you?" He grits the words, his fingers back in my hair, pulling so hard, my scalp burns with pain. I blink twice, looking at him and trying to understand what he wants from me.

He's holding my head back, his dick sliding out of my mouth and leaving a trail of saliva in its wake.

"For all your beauty you give a man a limp cock with those stiff lips of yours," he jibes, a sick smile on his face. He leans down, his face close to mine as he whispers, "you just let the man do all the work, don't you, sunshine? You just lie back and let them rut between your thighs, don't you?" he drawls in my ear, the sound almost painful.

There are so many things I wish I could say, so many insults I wish I could hurl at him. But I can't. Not when he owns my secret.

Instead, I just shake my head slightly, trying to get out of his painful hold.

"Show me how you suck, sunshine. Properly," he speaks low in his throat, the bass of his voice making me shiver. "Show me how that pretty mouth of yours works dick, because it ain't good for much else," he chuckles.

Humiliation burns at my cheeks but I can't show him that. Damn, but I can't do anything.

I'm truly caught.

Leaning back, he nods at me to continue.

For all my show of bravado earlier, I'm a little afraid now. Because I don't know what I'm doing and if I don't do it right, he *will* call my father.

I think back to all the things Anna and Lindsay had said over the years, coming up slightly empty because I'd never paid attention.

I look up to see him waiting, his brow slightly raised, the ridge of his scar even more prominent in the harsh lighting of the night.

Swallowing hard, I turn my attention to his dick, tightening my hands around it and leading it back to my mouth. I let my tongue play with the head, all the while watching him and his reactions to know if I'm doing something right.

His breath hitches when I lick a spot under the head, and I see the sudden clench of his fists. Convinced this might work, I continue to lick and tickle the area before sucking his head deep into my mouth, being mindful of my teeth.

"Fuck," he curses out, his hand in my hair as he pushes me forward, his cock going in deeper. "That's it, sunshine, suck that real nice," he grunts, thrusting his hips towards my face.

The head makes contact with the back of my throat and I gag, my hands immediately on his hips as I push him from me. I find it hard to breathe as he all but chokes me with his dick.

Tears gather at the corners of my eyes as he keeps me still. His palm spread across the back of my head, he doesn't allow me to pull back. He pushes his dick in and out of my mouth, his breathing harsh as he increases his speed, fucking my mouth even harder.

The urge to bite is overwhelming, but I know I can't do that without suffering dire consequences, so I just take it. I force myself to stay there as he keeps on thrusting in and out of me.

When at last he slows his movements, he looks down at me, his hand coming to rest on my face as he swirls his thumb on my cheek, closer and closer to my mouth until he slips it between my lips, forcing them to open wider.

"You can't even work a cock, but you want to work a man," he tsks at me, amused.

Spit is dribbling down my jaw, and he swipes it up, lathering it over his cock as he takes it in his own hand, fisting the length up and down.

"Eyes on me, sunshine," he commands, and I do. I look up to find him staring at me with a mix of rage and desire. His silver eyes look black in the darkness of the night, his irises indistinguishable from his pupils.

He continues to work his cock up and down, his movements increasing in speed as he holds eye contact.

Out of nowhere, spurts of warm liquid land on my face. Startled, I make to pull back. But one look at him, and I know he wouldn't like that. So I keep myself still as more and more drops of his cum spray on my face.

"Good girl," he rumbles, his thumb still on my cheek as he splays the cum around before pushing it into my mouth.

I keep on staring into his eyes, even as he keeps on feeding me his cum, the taste slightly bitter, but not as unpleasant as I would have thought.

For a second, everything falls away as I lose myself in his gaze. Even his scar fails to register, the intensity of his eyes almost addictive.

His lips pull up in a sinister smile as he leans down, his mouth close to my ear. I can feel his breath on my skin, the effect immediate as goosebumps appear all over my body. I feel shivery, and I don't know if it's a good thing or not.

"Check mate," he rasps, his voice like molten lava to my senses. "Who's covered in cum now?"

Just as soon as he utters the words, he's gone from my side. He tucks himself back in his pants, his back a retreating figure.

It takes me a moment to find my words, and as I realize why he'd done this—the ultimate humiliation for me—I can't help but yell after him.

"Fuck you, asshole!"

He doesn't hear me. Or if he does, he doesn't care.

My knees hurt, the small pebbles on the ground imprinted in my flesh. There are still streaks of cum on my face and in my hair. My lips are swollen and puffy, my face red and tear-streaked.

But that's nothing compared to how I feel inside. Compared with how *he* made me feel.

Shame burns even deeper in my gut as I stand up, a gust of air brushing under my dress and making the wetness between my legs feel even more humiliating.

I hate that he caught me at my worst. I hate that he knows my secret and can now control me. But more than anything, I hate that a part of me wasn't indifferent to it. A part of me… liked it.

And that's the worst offence of all.

Chapter Seven

BASS

"Where are we going? My dance lessons are in the opposite direction!" She demands, scandalized. Her hands are splayed on the window of the car as she looks outside, frowning as she sees us go in the wrong direction.

Fortuitously, or not, her driver had gotten sick the day before, and now it's up to me to drive her around while he's on leave.

Fuck! This is exactly what I did *not* need. Unfettered access to little miss spoiled is only going to get me in more trouble.

I clench my hands on the steering wheel, the memory of the disaster of last night still fresh in my mind.

I never thought I had it in me to react like that, yet I couldn't help myself. Not when I saw her hugging that scrawny little kid, looking so fucking content in his embrace.

If before I would have overlooked her little pranks and the way she'd wanted to embarrass me to get me to resign, when I saw that boy touch her—and even worse, her accepting the touch—I'd gone nuclear.

An angry fog had descended upon my mind and I'd wanted nothing better than to take her. Take her and erase all traces of that kid's hands from her body.

When I'd recognized the pills she'd dropped on the floor, I'd known that I had an opening.

And I'd taken full advantage of it.

Fuck, but I don't know what had come over me, but in that moment I would have done anything to mark her—in any way.

I wanted her to hate me. Oh, I wanted her to despise me, but I also wanted something else.

Something that seemed hidden in those beautiful eyes of hers, behind all the glitz and glamor, behind the façade that she shows to the world.

I wanted to see *her*.

Vulnerable. Exposed.

At my mercy.

Fuck me and my impulsive behavior.

I don't think I've ever reacted so viscerally to something in my life.

I've never been a jealous man.

Hell, I've never even been in an actual relationship. When you do what I do, it's hard to find someone to put up with it. It's especially hard to find someone who wouldn't call the cops on you if they saw you covered in blood at four A.M., rummaging through the fridge for a goddamn beer.

I'm reacting to her in ways that are completely foreign to me.

But most importantly, I've *never* gone without a condom, even for a blowjob. The mere fact that it had slipped my mind when I knew her reputation is astounding.

I've *never* been careless before. Never.

And it had taken me just a second of seeing her in the arms of another man to throw caution to the wind.

Fuck. Fuck. Fuck.

There's also the other elephant in the room. The fact that I'd basically blackmailed her into blowing me. But, God, if her mouth on my bare cock hadn't been the most intense thing I've ever felt...

I don't think there are words to describe the high I'd felt when I'd looked down to see those pretty lips of hers wrapped around my cock. Fuck, I've been fantasizing about that since the first time I saw her. To actually have that turn into reality…

"Where are you taking me?" She repeats, turning those fiery eyes towards me, and damn if I'm not hard again.

In a way, I'd thought that one taste of her and I'd get her out of my system. But now, she's wormed her way into my head even more.

I look at her and all I can think is her spread out on the backseat, my cock in her pussy and my name on her lips as she moans her pleasure.

I want to tame her. Fuck the mean girl out of her and…

"Damn," I grumble, realizing I'm having a fucking hard time putting a damper on my attraction to her.

But this isn't even attraction. It's something else. Something bordering on obsession, since there's not a minute when I don't think of her luscious lips and…

I groan out loud.

It must be the fact that she hates me just as much as I hate her, and her dislike of me only serves to make me harder like I'm some sick bastard.

"You'll see," is all I say when she gets restless, and I try my damned hardest to not look at her. At how her long legs are barely covered by the skirt she's wearing, or how every time she shifts in her seat I can get a little peek at her panties and…

I'm painfully hard, my dick straining against my zipper and I know I can find no relief. Not unless I hold her secret addiction over her head again, and I don't want to do that. Not again.

No, the next time she comes to me it will be of her own volition, and she's going to beg me to fuck her.

I just need to get myself under control so I don't screw up again like last night. For all my dislike of her, she's making me act out of character.

Maybe it's the fact that I haven't gotten laid in too long. Or maybe it's just her otherworldly beauty, because there's no one in the world who would not concede that she's a perfectly shaped feminine specimen. Hell, I doubt there's anyone who would dare say she's anything other than spectacular.

Yes, that must be it. Her beauty must be addling my brains, since there's no way in hell I'd ever like a harpy like her.

She's spoiled, mean and downright nasty.

The horse semen prank and the many videos of me drenched in it circulating online should tell me as much.

Even with ninety percent negative qualities, there's still something about her that makes me want to go crazy at thinking anyone would dare come close to her. Why, I'd been ready to fucking murder that kid for hugging her.

This isn't normal.

I pull in the parking lot of a clinic, adjusting my pants as I get out of the car so that my erection isn't as visible.

Then, I all but drag her to the lab.

"What are we doing here?" She frowns when she sees that it's a health clinic.

"You're getting tested," I tell her, none too nicely.

"Tested? What do you mean?"

"You'll see," I grunt.

Opening the door, I quickly grab two forms, watching closely as she fills hers in.

"STDs?" She frowns when she reads the small print. "Why?" She looks up at me and fuck… If angels were ever to come down on earth, they'd look like her. But they sure as hell wouldn't be as mean.

"I need to know you didn't give me any weird shit," I tell her as I take the form from her, checking the boxes to test for all diseases.

"Maybe *you* gave me something," she snickers, turning her nose up at me.

"As if," I snort. "Your pretty mouth's the only place I've been in a long time." I grab her jaw as I turn her face towards me. "The same can't be said for you, though," I grit my teeth as I say the words out loud, the thought of another touching her, or worse, her welcoming that touch, sending me over the edge.

"You're an asshole," she hisses at me, finally showing her claws.

"Good on you to notice, *sunshine*," I say as I lean in, teasing her with the ghost of a touch, my lips hovering on hers, my breath on her lips.

But I don't go further. No, I *can't* go further. Because I know if I got one taste of those lips, she'd be on her back, legs spread, without a care for who's watching.

Fuck! I need to get myself under control.

Taking the form to the front desk, I wait until we're called to have our blood drawn. When it's Gianna's turn, though, I don't leave her side as I watch every step of the way, ensuring she does go through with it.

She's silent as we go back to the car, and I realize she's quietly seething at me, so I just wait until it's time for her outburst—knowing one is imminent.

"I hate you," she spits at me as she holds on to the arm where she'd gotten her blood drawn from.

"The feeling's mutual," I smirk at her.

"Really? It sure didn't seem like that from where I was standing," she arches a brow at me. "You know, on my knees, with your cock in my mouth," she makes a sick expression, trying to show me how much I disgust her.

"But that's just the thing. You're good for a fuck. For anything else…" I trail off, enjoying the quick outrage that crosses her features.

"Wow, said the guy who has to blackmail someone to suck his dick," the corner of her mouth curls up. "That's why it's been a long time, isn't it?" A cruel smile appears on her face. "With that face you have to force someone to blow you."

"Careful, *sunshine*," I warn her.

"But that's just it, isn't it?" she continues goading me, and I see how much she's enjoying it. She leans towards me in her seat, her face close to mine as she moves slowly, almost sensually. "Even whores scoff at your money, don't they? How could *anyone* want to look at this?" Her finger comes up to trace the scarred ridge above my brow.

I stiffen, her touch on me the last drop.

Before I know it, my hand is on her neck as I push her back against the seat and settle on top of her.

"What is it, *mutt?*" she flutters her lashes at me. "Don't tell me you'll fuck me now? Is that the next step so you won't tell my father my secret?"

Even with my hands around her throat, she leans closer into me, her lips close to my ear.

"Do it. Fuck me. Who knows, I might even enjoy it," she taunts, pausing as her tongue peeks out to lick the lobe of my ear. "Or maybe I'll just give you more STDs. Why don't you find out?" She asks in a seductive voice and fuck if it doesn't send the perfect signal to my cock.

It takes everything in me to fling her away, resuming my own seat as I buckle my seatbelt and trying to ignore the way she's spread out on her seat, her dress hiked up a little too high, her panties…

I'm in trouble.

"I'm on it. I already told you that," I grind my teeth as I try to get Cisco to back the fuck off.

"Bass," he calls me by my name, something he almost never does. "Benedicto has had several meetings this week alone. He'll soon find someone, and we can't afford for that to happen, can we?"

"Why are you so set against Guerra? Because this doesn't seem like a game anymore, Cisco. It seems personal."

"My business is my business," he says, his tone clipped. "It's not for you to know. You only need to follow your orders and do the goddamn job. What's so hard about fucking a slut, uncle? Lift up her skirt, fuck her, destroy her and it's done."

I don't know why him calling Gianna a slut rubs me the wrong way, but it does. Especially as he proceeds to detail how I need to broadcast her fall from grace for the entire world to see.

I'd been apprehensive about the mission from the beginning, but now…?

"And I told you I'd do it, but at my pace. Don't worry. You'll have a very public spectacle," I say as I hang up, throwing my phone on the bed.

Fuck, but Cisco's been on my back nonstop to get me to finish the mission. And like I told him, I *will* do it. Eventually. But it's going to be on my terms.

Still, even if fucking little miss spoiled might be the culmination of all my fantasies come to life, I'm a little reluctant to do it in such a public manner. I know what a nasty piece of work she is. And I know all about our enmity with Guerra. Even so, I'm starting to have doubts about this whole thing.

Fuck!

She has me wrapped around her little finger, that's for sure. Maybe if I *do* get to fuck her I'll be able to look at matters a little more objectively.

It's lust. Pure, unadulterated lust that's made even more potent by the fact that I hate myself for desiring her so much.

Opening the door to the balcony, I lean on the railing, inhaling the fresh air of the night and wishing I had a cigarette. It would certainly alleviate this emptiness I feel inside. But I'd sworn them off in prison, when someone had sold me a counterfeit that put me in the hospital for a week. Who knows what noxious substance they'd put inside, but it hadn't been the first attempt nor the last.

The only good thing about this mission is that it's taken my mind off my newly found freedom. It's certainly not given me *any* time to think how much the world's changed in only five years. Still, that doesn't take away from the uneasiness that completing this mission causes me.

I've never once questioned an order given by my boss. I've never had to.

But now? Even knowing what I do about Gianna, and seeing firsthand how she treats other people, there's a part of me that's not keen on broadcasting her humiliation for the entire world to see.

Yet for all my doubts, my allegiance is first and foremost to the famiglia. Everything else comes secondary.

My attraction to her comes secondary.

There's a small noise coming from below, and I lean over to see little miss spoiled step into the night, tiptoeing her way around the garden as she looks left and right.

What is she up to?

The moment that thought crosses my mind, I still. What if she's meeting someone?

"Damn it!" I mutter as I all but dash out of the room, hot on her trail.

The thought of her having clandestine meetings with some boy in the middle of the night has me almost going mad. And so I increase the speed of my steps, all the while making sure I'm as stealthy as she is.

Crossing the garden, I spot her again at the other end of the property. She's stooping low against the fence, picking something off the ground.

A love letter? More drugs?

Fuck, my imagination is ripe with all kinds of scenarios, none of them helpful to my mood in any way. Not when all I want is to stalk over to her side, grab her to me, and demand her to tell me *who* she's meeting.

And then killing him.

Damnation! I'd seen where killing a civilian got me, and yet I'm contemplating doing it again. Repeatedly. As many times it's necessary to remove any temptation from her side.

I move closer to where she's standing, still trying to keep myself to the shadows.

She's wearing a pink robe on top of a sheer nightgown. But even with all that material covering her skin, I can see the outline of her breasts, the way her nipples peek through the almost see-through gown.

And just like that, I'm taken back to the night of the party, when I'd had my mouth on those generous globes. When I sucked on her skin, its warmth and taste imprinted on my tongue.

Just as I get more impatient to see what she's doing, she strengthens her back, taking a few steps back but still looking down at the ground. It's only when she moves slightly to the right, dropping to her knees on the grass that I finally see what she's doing.

"I'll be damned," the words are out of my mouth before I can help myself.

Crouched on the ground, she's sporting an expression I've never seen on her face until now. She looks… content. Her lips are drawn up in an effortless smile, her eyes crinkling at the corners. Even in the darkness of the night I can bet they are sparkling with joy. There's a lightness on her features that has me simply enthralled. It goes beyond just physical beauty—and she has that in spades.

No, there's something about her now, in her element, that has my heart racing.

Surrounded by the green of the grass and bathed in moonlight, she looks like a forest nymph descended from the heavens to take pity on mere mortals and let them gaze upon her beauty.

Because as I continue to watch her smile, that fucking blinding smile that has my pulse throbbing with need, I realize that it's impossible for someone to look like that.

The malice gone from her face, it's like I'm staring at another Gianna.

And it's all because of... fucking kittens.

The urge to rub at my eyes is overwhelming, unsure if what I'm seeing is real in *any* way.

Three small kittens are huddled together as they eat from the bowl Gianna had placed in front of them.

So focused they are on their food, that they even allow her to pet them.

She's softly caressing the fur of a white kitten, her features so serene it's like she's an entirely different person. Gone is the malice and the perpetual scowls that mar her features. Instead, she looks relaxed, happiness reflected on her face as she gazes lovingly at the kittens.

She sits with them for minutes on end, until they finish their food. And as I see her return to the house, I hide deeper in the shadows of the night, watching her take the bowl back to the kitchen.

A slow smile appears on my face as I keep my eyes on her retreating figure. Queen B might have a heart after all. But it's definitely buried under layers and layers of bitchiness.

It seems I should start peeling away.

The next morning, as I drive her to her archery practice, I can't help but gaze at her every now and then, trying to superimpose the expression she'd had on last night to the one she's currently sporting.

There's this burning need inside of me to see her that carefree and happy again—but in my presence. An absurd want blooms in my chest as I realize I want her to smile like that *because* of me. Which is entirely hypocritical since all I seem to do is make her glower at me in anger, most times actually threatening bodily harm.

"You should stand in the back. I don't want people to see me with you," she huffs at me as I lock the car and we step towards the archery center.

"Should I remind you that you're not in a position to make demands, sunshine?" I raise an eyebrow at her.

She's dressed in a pair of brown pants and a black top, both molded to her body and showing her curves in such a delicious way I have no doubt she's about to give a few heart attacks as she steps inside the venues.

Yes, they should die before I kill them.

Fuck!

My fists clench as I once more realize the direction of my thoughts. I don't even like her, and yet I seem to have a perpetual problem thinking about her with *anyone* else. It's like a sickness eating at me, more often than not the picture of her in an intimate setting with another man making me want to lose my temper.

That's not even the worst thing, since I've realized that the mere thought of her in bed with some other man has the power to make me physically ill.

"Or what?" She turns towards me, hands on her hips as she tries to give me a stare down.

I've already learned her cues, and I can tell exactly what's going to come out of that pretty mouth of hers.

Folding my arms over my chest, I just wait.

"Let me guess," she rolls her eyes, "you want me to get on my knees again? Right here?" She asks sarcastically as she comes towards me, ready to drop to her knees.

I catch her before her knees hit the pavement, my fingers on her arm as I all but pull her towards me, her firm breasts making contact with my chest.

"You just know how to get under someone's skin, don't you, Gianna?" I lower my mouth to her ear as I whisper, feeling the way her body trembles slightly at my touch.

"What, want to fuck me now?" she retorts like a misbehaving brat.

"Oh, no," I chuckle, my voice low. "On the contrary, you provoke such a visceral reaction in me that all I can think about is strangling this pretty neck of yours," I say as I trail my fingers up the column of her neck, leaving a trail of goosebumps behind.

No matter how much she'd like to argue to the contrary, she's not unaffected. She can insult my appearance as much as she'd like, but it seems that the *mutt* turns her on.

And it's even more evident as I lean back, my gaze on the same level as hers as I look at the change in her.

Her pupils are dilated, her skin flushed, her lips slightly parted as her breath comes in short spurts. There's a delay in reaction as she raises those big orbs towards me, looking at me as if she's never seen me before.

And that's when I see *her.*

The Gianna behind the mask. The vulnerable side of hers that she keeps tucked away, preferring to come across as cold and unfeeling.

She's anything but, though. Not with the way she's looking at me, her eyes begging to be seen, her lips yearning to be kissed. Her body is slightly leaning towards me, the desire to be fucked clear in the way arousal drips from her every pore.

But just as soon as I see it, it's gone.

She shuts down.

Pushing at my shoulders, she proceeds to insult me with every word she might think of before dashing off towards the field.

My lips pull in a satisfied smirk as I watch her retreating figure.

It seems Gianna and I are more alike than I'd thought. And both of us resent the fact that we're attracted to each other.

Well, too bad for her that my mission is to take advantage of that attraction until she'll beg me to take her to bed.

Because while I may have acted entirely out of character when I'd blackmailed her, I won't be using that tactic to get her in my bed. No, she's going to come there willingly. Maybe she'll even beg.

And I'll enjoy every minute.

There are only a few people present on the field, and Gianna quickly takes her spot on a lane more secluded than the others.

She's strapped with everything she needs, and she tries very hard to ignore me when I take my position by the sidelines.

But as I watch her take her stance, her fingers masterfully gliding over her bow to aim the arrow, I have to begrudgingly admit that she is very skilled. I'd noticed this from the first time I'd come here with her, and she'd let it slip that she's been practicing since she was a child.

The years of work are visible as her posture is flawless, the arrow flying from her hands and towards the target. I don't even have to look to know that she's hit bull's eye.

She continues to fire arrow after arrow, her speed equally as impressive.

Her features are drawn up in concentration, her lips pursed as she's watching for her targets. Increasingly, her shots seem more aggressive, until she finally snaps, yelling at me.

"Mutt!" Of course she can't help herself from using her favorite insult. I still wonder why she'd chosen that particular one. I have no doubt it's somehow in connection with my scar, but I'd like a small trip inside her mind to see just what had made her think of *that* word.

"What?" I ask drily as I casually stroll up to her side.

She raises her hand, placing it to her forehead to keep the sun from her eyes as she's squinting towards the targets.

"Go check the targets and get my arrows back," she barks the order. Still, I don't move, a smile playing at my lips.

It takes her a couple of seconds to notice I'm still by her side.

"Now!" she turns sharply, her eyes blazing at me.

"Gianna, Gianna," I whistle, "I guess you forgot who owns who," I raise an eyebrow as I lean closer to her, wrapping my finger around a stray strand of hair.

As expected, it's soft. Maybe deceivingly soft for someone like her.

Her nostrils flare as she stares at me.

"I might," I start, watching the play of emotions on her face and loving the way I seem to have a knack for making her lose her cool. "If you say *please*," I whisper against her earlobe.

She stiffens, but she doesn't move away.

Her eyes are still defiantly glaring at me, her entire body quaking with anger… or something else.

My lips twitch as it finally dawns on me that all this anger is to mask her growing arousal. The fact that she can't stand herself that she lusts after a *mutt*.

"Please," she grits her teeth as she says the word, and my eyes widen in surprise. I can't say I expected her to actually say it. Hell, I doubt she's said it too many times in her life.

"There you go sunshine. Wasn't so hard, was it?" I drawl, visions of her saying please to something entirely different assaulting me.

Fuck, but I feel myself growing hard just from that.

"Well?" She taps her foot. "What are you waiting for?"

I shake my head at her, starting towards the target to get her arrows. I guess I can't expect her to change too fast. I'm still the most hated person in her life.

I reach the target, and I start removing her arrows, truly impressed to see she'd hit center every time. But just as I'm about to turn around, I feel an arrowhead penetrate my shoulder from the front, tearing through muscle.

"Fuck," I curse out, momentarily blinded by the pain. "That brat…" I grit my teeth, taking a deep breath to ground myself.

Turning back, I see her bow at her feet, her arms crossed over her chest as she gloats at my pain.

I don't think anymore as I stalk towards her, intent on showing her just how wrong she is to mess with me like this.

When I'm only a few feet away from her, I raise my hand, gripping the shaft of the arrow and breaking it close to my skin.

She gasps when she sees me fling the wooden piece to the ground, her eyes snapping to mine. Horror crosses her features as she realizes that she's in much deeper waters than she thought.

Taking a step back, her eyes are still on mine as she tries to keep her bravado intact, the slow tremble of her hands giving her away though.

"You're really brave from a distance, aren't you?" I ask as I continue to walk towards her, all the while she keeps on moving back.

"It was a mistake," she mumbles when she sees me gain ground on her.

"A mistake?" I repeat, almost amused at the flimsy excuse.

"Yes. I didn't mean to. I…" As she nears the wall of a building, she looks left and right for a place to run and hide, but that ship's sailed.

She makes a dash to the right, but I'm faster as I cage her in, stretching my arms and placing my palms on the wall, on either side of her head.

"What was your plan, Gianna? Kill me?" I drawl, loving the way her mask is quickly slipping from her.

Until now she's been great at keeping the pretense that I don't scare her, but as she looks into my eyes and sees the violence simmering inside, she's smart enough to realize she *should* be afraid.

"But that's not right, is it?" I continue, bringing my hand to my wound as it's already leaking blood. Swiping some of the red liquid with my fingers, I bring it in front of my face, staring at it. "Someone with your skill wouldn't miss it if they wanted me dead. No…" I tsk at her. "You wanted me out of commission, didn't you?"

She blinks rapidly, still looking around for a way out.

"Gianna, Gianna," I lean into her, bringing my fingers to her face and smearing some of my blood on her pristine skin. "You should have said so if you wanted war. It's something I'm…" I trail off as I see her teeth peek through as they bite on her lower lip, "an expert on."

"It was a mistake," she continues, shaking her head.

"You made me mad, Gianna. Very mad," I tell her in a serious tone, enjoying seeing her squirm. God, but it's only making me harder, in spite of the pain in my shoulder.

Funny, I took a shot in my left shoulder saving her at the jewelry store, and now I took an arrow to my right shoulder because of her spoiled girl tantrums.

Because I see exactly why she did it. She wants me replaced as soon as possible. And I know why too.

"I'm… sorry," she whispers, and I can't help the way my brows shoot up in surprise at those words.

Damn, but she must be terrified if she's resorting to the magic words.

"I'm not a very nice man when I'm mad. But you already know that, don't you, sunshine?"

"I…" she raises her eyes to meet mine, her mouth open on a word that won't come out.

Slowly, I bring my bloodied fingers down her cheek and to her neck, smearing myself on her perfect skin. When I reach her pulse, I wrap my hand around her pretty neck, giving it a quick squeeze.

Her eyes widen, and she looks at me questioningly.

"You're scared," I state, and she blinks, her eyes pressed together as she inhales like she's truly caught. "But you're not scared of what I'll do to you," I chuckle, my voice low, my breath brushing against her skin. "You're scared of liking it."

Her eyes snap open, those gorgeous golden irises raging at me.

"Yes, that's just it. You keep on lying to yourself." I trail the back of my knuckles down her front, slowly caressing her breasts. The shudder that goes through her body is unmistakable, the way her skin flushes, her tongue sneaking out to wet her lips. "You think you hate me," I continue, my ears attuned to the small shifts in her breathing, "but you don't. Not really. You just hate yourself for wanting me." I say confidently.

Her eyes widen in shock, and she shakes her head slowly at me.

"You know it's true. You *want* me to fuck you. You may not like me, but I bet your pussy's already wet from having my hands on you. Ain't that right?" I smirk, my hand going lower and hovering on top of her mound.

Her breath hitches, her back arching slightly, her head angled in my direction as she stares at me with confusion in her eyes.

"You like having my rough, *peasant* hands on your body, don't you sunshine? Just like you loved having my cock in your mouth, fucking your throat and coming all over your face. Having my *mutt* cum in your pretty mouth as you swallow every bit."

She's not even hiding her reactions anymore, her pupils already engulfing her irises and turning her eyes into black, bottomless pits. Her slight cleavage allows me to see a flush creeping up from her chest and towards her neck, slowly marring her cheeks with a red tinge that makes her look even more fuckable.

"And I bet you touched yourself, imagining your soft, dainty fingers are coarse, calloused ones that scratch and give both pleasure and pain," I continue to rile her, enjoying the way her body reacts to my words. "And I would. I'd slide my thick fingers between your wet lips, searching for that sweet little hole you have hidden between your legs. And I'd slowly dip them in," she gasps, her head thrown back as she closes her eyes, biting her lip. "I'd stretch and fill you, sunshine. I'd bring you to the brink but I wouldn't give you any satisfaction. Not until you beg me."

Fuck, but my cock is already leaking in my pants, my words conjuring images of her spread out and at my mercy.

"Stop," she whispers, her voice barely above a whisper.

"What was that?" A smile pulls at my lips at her capitulation.

"Please… stop," she repeats, squeezing her eyes shut and trying to regulate her breaths.

I bring my hand back to her neck, tipping her chin up with my thumb so she's looking directly at me. Lowering my head, I tease her with my mouth, not touching, but *almost* touching.

I blow hot air on her lips, the urge to kiss her almost unbearable. But I can't. Not yet. Not until *she* comes to me.

"I could fuck you right now, sunshine. I could fuck you and you wouldn't say no. Why," I pause, my tone amused, "you'd probably beg me to."

The moment the words are out of my mouth, though, the spell is broken as she jams her hand into my arm, right where the arrow head is lodged into my skin.

It takes everything in me not to wince in pain, but I don't want her to give her any satisfaction. Because she has to realize that none of her pranks will work.

I'm here to stay. And eventually, she *will* be mine.

"You're an asshole," she spits at me when I release her.

"Good on you to notice," I roll my eyes at her. She's going on the defensive because she knows I hit a sore spot with my words.

And I'm *sure* I could have fucked her and she would have never protested a thing. She would have welcomed me into her body, might have even ripped at her clothes to get her pussy ready and open for me to plunge into.

But it would have been a mistake. Though my cock weeps at the missed opportunity, I need to approach this with my other head.

I need to plan this thoroughly.

"I should have aimed for your heart," Gianna mutters under her breath as I'm admitted to the emergency room.

"You would have, wouldn't you?" I raise an eyebrow at her as I take a seat on a bed.

She looks away, but not before I see a steely determination in her eyes.

She would have. If she thought I was an *actual* danger to her, she would have killed me. And I don't know why the notion that she would so readily take a human life shifts something in me.

Gianna is unlike any of the women I've ever associated with. The ones in my family are demure, well-behaved and sweet. They don't swear, smoke, or drink alcohol; much less engage in the outrageous behavior I've come to expect from her. But all scandalous things aside, there's something else too. There's a strength besides her bitchy façade, but there's also a weakness—a vulnerability that only makes me more intrigued by her.

Certainly, at first glance she's just a spoiled high society girl enjoying the luxury of life all the while snubbing those who are lower than her.

But the more time I spend in her presence, the more I realize that her mean front might just be a defense mechanism. The question remains, though. Defense against what?

A doctor and a nurse follow suit, and they cut the shirt from my body, quickly assessing the wound and applying some anesthetic before carefully removing the arrow.

Arms crossed over her chest, Gianna tries her best to seem disinterested. A smile pulls at my lips as I see her gaze stray to me every now and then, curiosity written all over her features. But more than anything, I see the way her eyes widen when my shirt is thrown to the side. This time she can't hide the interest as she peruses my chest.

Even riddled with a multitude of scars, both from my time in prison and before, I know she likes what she sees. I've kept fit my entire life, but for the past five years I've really dedicated myself to building up muscles so I could take out every inmate that was out for my head.

And as I note the slight blush that stains her pale skin, I know she's anything but indifferent.

"It doesn't hurt, does it?" A voice asks, and I turn my head, noting that the nurse is trying to engage me in conversation.

"No," I grunt before returning my attention to Gianna.

To my surprise, I see a flash of anger cross her features as she stares at the nurse and her proximity to me.

I'll be damned.

My lip twitches, and I decide to play a little with her.

And as the doctor leaves, instructing the nurse to dress my wound, I have the perfect opportunity to do so.

"The doctor said I shouldn't strain myself. For how long?" I ask the nurse, still watching Gianna from the corner of my eye.

"At least a week. You should avoid lifting heavy things, or..." she purses her lips, momentarily scanning Gianna's form, "do other things," she eventually says.

Ah, but she is flirting with me. And Gianna notes that as well, immediately stiffening at her words.

"Thank you," I nod to her as she adds the finishing touches to my wound, realizing it's best if I don't give her any false hope—for all my desire to rile up Gianna.

"You'll need to complete your discharge papers before you go," the nurse adds, standing up straight. Addressing Gianna, she continues, "can you go grab the forms? He shouldn't move too much."

I frown, since I don't see how walking could interfere with a shoulder wound. But before I can say anything, Gianna shakes her head at both of us, stalking off almost in anger.

Damn, but one might say she is *actually* jealous.

"Isn't she a little too young for you?" The nurse asks on a husky voice, leaning towards me as she all but thrusts her tits in my face.

"Isn't it none of your business?" I retort, gritting my teeth in annoyance.

But it is sobering enough to remind me of our age difference. With our back and forth, and Gianna's ability to hold her own, it's easy to forget that I'm so much older than her.

She just finished high school and I... Well, I've certainly finished high school, but I haven't done much after that except killing, more killing, going to jail and then more killing.

"Unbelievable," she mutters, drawing my attention to her.

Until now, I hadn't even looked at her properly. She looks to be in her thirties, a scowl on her face as she stares me down.

"Isn't it unethical to flirt with patients?"

"You..." she frowns, almost scandalized that I'd be so direct.

She continues to say something, but I tune her out when I see a new message on my phone. When she sees I'm simply ignoring her, she finally takes the hint and leaves.

Opening the text, I realize my test results have arrived, and all are negative.

I nod appreciatively at that, relieved it had been a scare and nothing else. Another beep sounds from the table in front of me, and as I spy a glint of metal, I realize Gianna must have forgotten her phone.

"Damn," I whistle as I pick up her phone from the table, unable to believe my luck.

Even more fortuitous is the fact that it's not password protected, so I'm easily able to open her messages and access her own test results.

Negative.

FRIVOLOUS

I finally release a relieved breath as I read through the entire report, pleased to see that she'd tested negative for all of them. Well, that certainly gives me *some* peace of mind. Especially as she won't have the chance to change them since *no one* but me will touch her from now on.

Unable to resist temptation, I start going through her phone, checking all her texts first. I'm a little surprised to see there isn't a single one from guys. There are only a couple of people that text her, all female friends I'd met before from her posh circles.

Even more intrigued, I go through her gallery, once again taken aback to see it's mostly empty. There aren't thousands of selfies as you would expect of a girl her age, especially one of her beauty and social standing. If anything, the only pictures she has saved are of animals, and some pretty sights.

"This can't be it," I mumble as I proceed to go through her documents.

It makes no sense that someone who thrives off attention and has a massive social media presence would have no pictures of themselves. So far, everything I've found has been entirely impersonal. If a random person picked up this phone, they wouldn't be able to guess who the owner was.

It takes me some serious digging before I finally find a folder filled with something. And it's what I least expect—books. Hundreds—if not more—books on every subject, some academic, some fiction. From philosophy, to history and religion, there's no topic that's not covered here.

And as I continue to browse through the list of titles, I'm having the hardest time believing what I'm seeing.

"What the hell are you doing?" Gianna's voice rings out before she snatches her phone from my hands, her eyes wild as she looks like a deer caught in a headlight.

"Relax, I didn't delete anything."

"You'd better," she replies, almost absentmindedly as she makes sure everything is in place. "You're an asshole," she grits, closing her phone and tucking it safely in her pocket before hurling the discharge papers at me.

Her shoulders are stiff as she places herself in a corner, putting some distance between us. And as I fill in the forms, I can't help but notice her repeatedly going back to her phone, almost as if she's anxious I might have done something to it.

"What are you so prickly about?" I stand up, coming to her side. "Are you afraid I saw your nudes collection?" I drawl, wanting to play a little with her. But more than anything, I want to know *who* she is. Because it's becoming increasingly clear that the Gianna she shows to the world is *not* the real Gianna.

"I don't have any nudes, *mutt.* Get your head out of the gutter," she huffs at me, her eyes looking anywhere but *at* me.

"Then what are you so worried about? That I know you read Descartes? Or that I saw all those books from Project Gutenberg on your phone?"

Her eyes widen, her lips trembling slightly.

"I don't know what you're talking about," she lies.

"You're not a very good liar, sunshine." I lean into her, inhaling the sweet scent of her perfume as I all but nuzzle my nose in her hair.

"Why don't you go flirt with your nurse and leave me alone," she pushes past me, but I'm faster as I wrap one arm around her waist, bringing her into me.

The anesthetic the doctor had given me is still going strong, so I don't feel any pain when she squirms, trying to get out of my embrace.

"Jealous?" I bury my face in her hair, enjoying the feel of those silken locks as they brush over my skin. "Tell me, are you jealous, sunshine?" I ask, nibbling at her earlobe.

"Let me go," she lets out on a strangled tone. "I don't care who you fuck," she continues, trying to regain the strength in her voice. "As long as it's not me," she adds cheekily.

"But that's just the issue, Gianna. *You* are the only one I'll be fucking. I don't care about other women. I don't even *see* other women," I tell her honestly. The truth is that she's bewitched me, awakening sensations in me I'd never experienced before.

"You're lying," she shakes her head, still trying to get out of my hold.

"I'm not," I state, bringing my fingers to her jaw and tipping it up so she can look into my eyes.

"Because make no mistake, sunshine. I *will* fuck you. But only when you beg me. I'm not going to hold anything over your head. I want *you*, but only of your own volition," I stroke my thumb across her satin skin as I gaze into her eyes. "I will only fuck you when you ask for it."

There's no fun in it otherwise. I want to tease and torment her until she surrenders to me of her own free will. I want her to suffer from sexual frustration, knowing I'm the only one who can provide relief. And only then will I act.

I want her to be vulnerable. Open.

I want the real her.

And I know I'm not getting that if I blackmail her into fucking me. Certainly it would get Cisco off my back and help me fulfill the mission faster. But I don't want that. Why should I take the easy way out when I could enjoy watching this unravel softly? Because for all my dislike of her, I have to admit that no woman's ever caused such visceral reactions within me. And I want to explore this to the end.

No matter the consequences.

"You..." she trails off, swallowing hard. "You won't tell my father about the books?" she asks in a small voice.

There it is. Vulnerability. And it's all because of some free books?

"No. I won't. I won't tell him about the pills either."

I don't know if I'm making a mistake by not taking advantage of it further, but I've never been one to prefer easy conquests. And Gianna at my beck and call because I have something on her? No. I'd rather she came to me because she craves my touch. Because I'm the only one who can provide her with what she needs the most.

Her eyes widen. "Why?"

"Because I want *you*, Gianna."

And because I *will* have you.

CHAPTER EIGHT

GIANNA

"Is there something you're not telling us?" Lindsay asks, her tone suggestive as she pokes my side.

"I don't know what you're talking about," I reply, a bored expression on my face.

"Come on! He hasn't taken his eyes off you the entire night!"

"He's my bodyguard. It's his job." I roll my eyes at her.

"But he's not watching you like *that*." She makes a funny face. "He's watching you like…" she pauses to think.

"Like?"

"Like he's ready to whisk you away any moment and have his wicked way with you," she giggles, the alcohol clearly having gone to her head.

"He's my bodyguard." I repeat. "Besides," I lift my hand to tuck my hair behind my ear, "have you seen him? I would die before I associated with… *that*," I add in a disgusted tone.

Both Anna and Lindsay burst into laughter, and the matter is promptly forgotten.

Lindsay is not wrong, however. Sebastian does look at me like that, and sometimes the intensity of his gaze scares me. But not in the way most things usually scare me. No, it's in a much more debilitating way, because it's stripping every protective layer I have on, ready to lay me bare for him to devour me.

Even now, as I sneak a peek at him, he's watching me closely, that smug smile still on his face. He's dressed entirely in black, and the suit does nothing but emphasize his impressive physique.

My cheeks burn as I remember the way he'd looked at the hospital, when the doctor had cut the shirt off his body. His chest had been pure muscle. Strong and manly, it had looked like a work of art, the hard planes of his stomach drawing my attention lower, to the v of his hips, all leading down to...

Damn!

Not for the first time, I feel a flush envelop my body as I imagine him in the nude. And I have. God, but I have. I've even had dreams where he...

I close my eyes to calm myself, my breathing already harsh, my body covered in goosebumps.

I don't know what it is about him that makes me react so. I've been numb for so long that it's even more surprising that all it takes is for me to think about his body—his strong, threatening body—and I'm wet.

The gathering continues well after midnight, and I pretend I'm enjoying myself as I chat a little with everyone. Of course, *he* needs to think I'm enjoying myself.

After he'd snooped through my phone, I'd been terrified that he'd try to use that over my head too. More than anything, I'd felt completely naked as he'd looked into my eyes, inquiring about my collection of books.

Damn it!

I thought I'd hidden the folder well, but if *he* can find it, then so can my father at the next inspection.

All night I'd tried to think of ways to better hide the books, knowing that if my father got wind of them, I'd be in a lot of trouble. That Sebastian hadn't used that opportunity to make me do more things for him...

My cheeks are already red as my mind conjures some scenarios he could have blackmailed me into.

But he hadn't. He hadn't even tried to hold my pills over my head again.

My gaze skitters to him, my teeth nibbling at my bottom lip. I admit that I can't help but be curious about him. Just when I think he's going to do something, he surprises me by doing something completely different.

Saying goodbye to everyone, I nod to Sebastian as I pass by him, heading to the car.

It's becoming harder and harder to ignore the way his proximity affects me. It's enough to feel his body heat next to mine that I break out in shivers, my skin covered in goosebumps, my breath labored.

It's taken me a while to make peace with the fact that I am, indeed, attracted to him—much to my dismay. And if I allow for extra sincerity, I have felt like this since the first meeting, the reason why I'd reacted so vehemently to his appointment as my bodyguard. Because having him near me at all times has only exacerbated those feelings.

And at night... it's even worse.

Knowing he sleeps in the room next to mine fills me with thoughts that should have never made their home in my mind. And lately, even my dreams have become filled with him.

With the way his mouth had felt on my breast, or his hot breath on my skin, teasing the surface and increasing my frustration. But most of all, I can't escape his voice. That deep, rumbly voice that whispered dirty words in my ear, detailing all the things he'd do to me.

I clench my thighs, moisture pooling between them as my thoughts become increasingly graphic.

Damn my body for betraying me like this.

I sneak a peek at his profile.

He's focused on driving, the road dark, almost no other cars on the driveway at this hour.

I can make out the scar on his left side, the one that crosses his forehead and disappears into his hairline. It's a harsh, jagged line, and for the first time I stop to wonder how he got it. Because it doesn't look accidental. No, it looks like someone dragged a knife across his face in some type of monstrous revenge.

FRIVOLOUS

A shiver goes down my back as I remember a similar experience. A long blade pressed to my face, a vile voice commanding me to be quiet or suffer the consequences, strong, unyielding hands holding me down.

My breath hitches, my fingers tightening on my armrest as I try to control myself.

It's not often that I find myself thinking back to that event. Years of mental exercises have helped me push the memory back, but little things like sights, smells... touches, can trigger it. And when it hits, it's usually full force.

Like now.

Closing my eyes, I take a deep breath, trying to think of something else. But the pain hits me again, my chest constricting, my throat clogging up.

I swallow hard, trying to banish *his* image from my mind.

I can't let him win. Not again.

But no matter how much I tell myself that, my reaction is as severe as always.

My limbs start trembling uncontrollably, my mouth dry as I continue to swallow non-existent saliva.

"S..." my teeth are clattering, the words hard to make out. "Stop t-the c-car," I manage to grit out, my hand suddenly on his arm.

He turns to me, frowning slightly.

I tighten my fingers on his arm, digging my nails in his flesh. "Stop," I repeat.

He must note the urgency in my tone, because he does stop by the side of the road. I fumble with my seatbelt before pushing the door open, gasping for air as I jump out of the car and head towards an open field.

Still, nothing helps.

The night air blowing in my face, I pant like I've just run a marathon. And no matter how much I try to catch my breath, I can't.

My pulse is through the roof, my heart beating so hard it feels like it's going to jump out of my chest. My knees feel weak as I all but fall to the ground, the soft grass breaking my fall. I bring my fist to my chest, thumping it against my ribcage in an attempt to alleviate the pressure inside.

"Gianna?" I think I hear a voice, the mental fog clouding my perception. "Gianna?"

A hand touches my back, and it's all it takes to make me lose myself even more, the mere touch making me hyperventilate.

"Shit! Look at me," he whispers, slowly turning me to face him. I try to blink some clarity in my eyes, but everything's so blurry, I can barely make out the outline of his body.

"Shh, here," he says, one hand slowly stroking my hair while the other extends in front of me, offering me something.

I frown, unable to understand what he wants me to do. But as he presses his hand to my mouth, prying my lips open and pushing a pill inside, I realize what he's trying to do.

I nearly choke on the pill, my throat too dry to swallow it without water. But after a couple of tries, I manage to get it down.

"Shh, it's ok," he speaks in a soft voice, his knuckles moving slowly down my back in a sweet caress.

My gasps for air soon turn into hiccups as I start to regain control of my body. The pill is starting to calm me down, already my heartbeats slowing down, my breathing more regulated.

"Thank you," I whisper when I can finally utter the words.

Tilting my head towards him, I note he's on his knees in front of me, a worried expression on his face.

"What happened?" he asks, no trace of his previous smugness. Instead, he actually sounds… concerned.

"Nothing," I immediately reply, forcing myself to get up.

It's enough that he saw me in the throes of an attack. I don't want him to know more things he could use as leverage in the future.

Dusting my knees and removing some of the grass from my dress, I turn to head back to the car.

"What was that, Gianna? Don't lie to me." His fingers circle my wrist as he stops me, his voice gave.

"I told you," I roll my eyes at him, easily slipping my usual mask in place. "Nothing. Now let me go. I want to get home and sleep." I swipe his hand aside, continuing towards the car.

"Is this why you need the Xanax? You're not going anywhere until you answer me," he declares, plopping himself in front of me.

"I don't owe you any answers," I push at his shoulder, purposefully aiming for his injured side. It's only been a few days since he's gotten it, so it must still hurt like a bitch.

His cheek twitches as my hand makes contact with the area, but he doesn't give away that it's paining him. Instead, he traps my hand in place, squeezing my wrist and bringing me closer to his body.

"You don't. But you *will* tell me," he states, back to his usual self-assuredness.

"Really?" A sardonic smile pulls at my lips. "Make me," I whisper, leaning towards him.

But just as he's about to reply to my dare, a loud noise comes from the direction of the car. The wind is knocked out of me as I end up on the ground, my back hitting the ground.

I groan in pain, especially as I open my eyes to see the *mutt* on top of me, his entire body covering my own.

"Get off me," I grit, shoving him aside.

He rolls to the grass, covering his forehead with the back of his hand.

"Damn," he curses.

Getting myself together, I raise myself into a sitting position, my eyes going wide when I see what had been the source of the noise.

"The car…" I whisper, watching the flames enveloping what's left of the car.

"You could have said thank you," he mutters dryly, joining me, "since I did shield you with my body," he wiggles his eyebrows suggestively.

"That was a bomb, wasn't it?" I ask, ignoring him. My gaze is still fixed on the wreckage.

Shit! That could have been us.

He nods grimly.

"But… who would want to kill me?" There's a slight tremor in my voice as I turn to look at him. His lips are set in a thin line, his features rigid.

"Not you," he replies and I frown. "Your father," he corrects, telling me that he'd had to switch cars last minute because the engine had died on our regular car.

"But who..." I shake my head, unable to come to grips with the fact that I'd barely escaped death.

"Best ask that of your father." He gets to his feet, extending a hand to help me up.

"How are we going to get home, then? Please tell me you have your phone with you," I plead, since I'd left my own in the car.

"No," he states grimly. "I left it on my seat."

"Damn!" I curse out loud.

How is this happening to me? How am I this freaking unlucky?

"I think it will take us a couple of hours to reach home," he states pensively. "Maybe more since it's night," he looks at his watch.

"You mean to walk home?" I ask, scandalized.

It's an hour drive away. I can't imagine *walking* that distance.

"Come on, sunshine. Nothing better than fresh air and some midnight exercise," he winks at me, already walking ahead of me.

"You have to be kidding me. Sebastian!" I yell after him, trying to catch up. "I'm not walking home. Go by the street and hitchhike me a car or whatever."

He stops, turning and studying me with an amused smile.

"You want me to hitchhike for you?" He repeats, as if it's the most outrageous thing.

"Of course. I'm not walking," I cross my arms over my chest. "And that's final," I push my chin up so he can see I'm serious about this.

"Fine," he shrugs, and I'm surprised at his easy acquiesce. "I'll see you home," he says before turning and walking once more.

"Sebastian!" I shout after him when I see he is *serious* about leaving me here. By myself.

"You're my bodyguard. You're hired to protect *me*. Not to leave me in the middle of nowhere, with a burning car, no cell phone, and no shoes fit for walking," I yell.

And to prove my point, I take off one of my heels and throw it at his back.

Just as it hits him, he stops, slowly turning towards me.

"Can't you stop your tantrums for once?"

"Tantrums? Should I remind you that you're the employee and I'm your boss?"

"Oh, so you're playing the boss card now?" He arches an eyebrow.

"You can't just leave me here!"

"I don't know if you realized, *sunshine,* but there are *no* cars driving around here," he points to the empty street. "But suit yourself and wait for one. Who knows, they might take pity on you if you play your cards right."

"What…" I frown, "what do you mean?" I grit my teeth at him.

"There's only one reason a woman would be alone around here at night, Gianna. And dressed like that," he nods to my dress, "they're going to expect a performance."

"You…" I seethe, baring my teeth at him in anger. "You're implying…"

"I'm not implying anything. I'm telling you the reality. No one is going to believe you're anything but a hooker," his eyes move over my body. "Maybe a high class hooker, but one nonetheless."

"I'm not a prostitute," I all but yell at him.

"Right," he smirks. "You don't charge for it."

My mouth drops open in shock, outrage written all over my features.

Before I even know what I'm doing, I'm on him, tackling him with my body.

"You're a fucking asshole," I push at his shoulders, itching to scratch him and feel his blood under my nails.

"Always so ready to hit me," he drawls, his arm easily immobilizing me. "Why so violent, sunshine? If you like it rough, you just have to say it. I'm ready to accommodate you."

There's something oddly annoying about his arrogant smile. The way he looks down at me and mocks me right to my face. But more than anything, I hate the way he gets to me, making me angrier than I've ever been.

"I'm going to kill you," I spit the words out, frustration mounting when he subdues me with just a few moves.

Not one to give up though, I do something that surprises him.

Jumping on him, I wrap my legs around his waist and wound my arms around his neck, ready to use my head to hit him. I'm so heated from the argument, that all I can think of is causing him bodily harm—no matter how.

His big hands come to rest at the junction between my hips and my waist, holding me close to him.

Before I lose my courage, I tilt my head back, bringing it into him at full force.

Instead of hitting him, though, I hit empty air, his chuckle reaching my ears as he moves his head to the side.

"You're a bloodthirsty little thing, aren't you?" He murmurs, his voice sending shivers down my back.

I blink, my gaze meeting his.

His irises are an even deeper gray than before, the color so cold it makes the hairs on my body stand up. His mouth is curled up in half a smirk, but as he sees me looking at him, it slowly dies down.

There's an intensity to the way he looks at me. His eyes are like two whirlpools, sucking the life out of me even when I'm not ready to surrender.

I don't know how it happens. I don't know who reaches first for the other.

All I know is that one moment I'm staring at him and thinking six other ways to draw blood, and the next my lips are on his, my teeth clashing against his in what I can only describe as a violent mashing of the mouths.

It's not a kiss. It can't be a kiss when all I want is to rip the flesh off his mouth. And as I bite down on his lower lip, I can only enjoy the hiss of pleasure mixed with pain that escapes him.

I suck it into my mouth, clamping my teeth down on it until blood breaks free, coating my tongue. But I don't let go. No, I *can't* let go.

His hand goes higher up my back as he brings my chest flush against his. He's so strong, he can easily hold my entire body mass in the air as his mouth simply devours me.

He doesn't hold anything back. And neither do I.

His tongue probes into my mouth, meeting mine and stroking it in a tantalizing dance that heats up my entire body, my own blood boiling in my veins and seeking to be let free.

I feel mindless as I claw at him, using my nails not as I intended, but damned near the same thing.

Everywhere he touches he leaves a trail of fire behind, and as he devours my mouth in a searing claiming, I feel myself melt against him. Every bone in my body turns to jelly, the desire to do harm slowly morphing into one of being consumed.

My core aches in a way it's never done before, and I feel the wetness that drips out of me, drenching my panties.

He drags my body lower and I can feel the tip of his erection settle right between my folds. His hands on my ass, he starts kneading the cheeks, moving me slowly over that hard part of him and stimulating that spot between my legs.

I gasp into his mouth, my eyes wide with wonder as I feel him hit a spot. He swallows my cry. He swallows everything that I am as he leaves me no room to breathe, or simply be.

I lose all notion of space or time, of anything but him and his body as it touches mine. It's only when we break apart, breathing hard, that we look into each other's eyes again and realize what just happened.

The enormity of what just happened.

As if burned, I jump off him, in the process losing my balance and ending up on my ass in the grass. Still it's better than the alternative. Than…

Contrary to what he seems to think of me, I don't go around kissing strangers. I don't go around kissing anyone. And that kiss…

I bring my fingers up to my lips to find them puffy and swollen.

"Already regretting it?" He asks, taking a seat next to me.

I don't dare look at him. Not when he could see everything written in my features. I'd lost control over myself and… I shake my head. I can't dwell on that.

"Of course. You know how it is. Spiked adrenaline levels got the best of me. It could have been anyone," I shrug, not wanting him to think he is in any way special.

"Is that so?" he drawls, that dangerous sound that seems to emanate from deep in his throat.

I shiver.

"Yes." I push my chin up. "Do you really think I'd go for you?" I tilt my head towards him to show him a disgusted expression.

Before I can blink, his hand is on my jaw, his fingers digging in my flesh as he brings my face closer to his.

"Tell yourself what you want, sunshine," he whispers, his breath on my lips as I clench my thighs at the memory of his body under mine. "But I know you want me. Me, not anyone else." He holds me captive in his grasp and I can only stare into his eyes.

"You can tell yourself that too," I retort sweetly, "if it helps you sleep better at night."

"Oh, don't worry. I have enough to help me sleep well at night," his lips curl up, "like these pretty lips," his thumb brushes across my lower lip, "wrapped around my cock. You have no idea how many times I've jerked off picturing you on your knees."

My breath catches in my throat, the image vivid in my mind.

"Well, continue to imagine it," I smile, "because it's never going to happen again."

He chuckles, the sound almost as arousing as his touch. God, what's wrong with me?

"Oh it will. Many, many times."

"Keep dreaming," I huff, wrenching myself from his hold and turning my head away.

"Why do you fight it?" He asks, his tone serious. "I know you feel it too, this attraction. This maddening attraction between us."

When he sees I'm not answering he continues. "Fuck, you're such a vexing woman," he groans. "I don't understand why you're so against me when I see the way your body reacts when I barely touch you. You're driving me insane, Gianna."

"I don't like it." I answer quietly, bringing my knees to my chest and wrapping my arms around them. "It makes me feel out of control. *You* make me feel out of control," I admit, the most I'm willing to share with him.

Leaning my head on the top of my knees, I turn my gaze towards him.

"You think you're the only one?" He asks, his brows pinched in the middle. "Hell, woman, you have no idea how out of control *you* make me feel. I've never met someone like you. Someone who defies me at every turn yet melts at my touch. Someone who makes me feel..." he trails off.

"Makes you feel what?"

"Not like myself." His confession manages to elicit a smile from me.

"You make me feel not like myself too," I admit, and for a moment there seems to be an understanding in our gazes.

"Why do you need the Xanax?" he eventually asks, like I knew he would.

I sigh. It's not an easy question to answer without opening a can of warms I'm not ready for. So I reply with a deal.

"Quid pro quo," I suggest, and he raises a brow. "You tell me something and I tell you something."

"Good for me," he readily agrees. "What do you want to know?"

I pause for a moment, *really* studying him.

There are so many things I'd like to ask. How did you get your scar? Where did you get all those marks on your body? Why are you so strong and...

Good Lord, but my mind is going in the wrong direction.

Again.

Instead of going for a more complicated one, since he'd expect a similar answer from me too, I decide to ask something more basic that could give me some insight into his past.

"Why are you so obsessed with STDs?"

His eyes widen slightly and initially he seems taken aback by my question.

Not only had he taken me to a clinic to have my blood tested for all possible STDs, but in the days following that, he'd kept making snide remarks as if he expected me to be riddled with syphilis and other similar ailments. More than anything, his reaction to seeing the negative results had been extremely telling, and he'd brought that up repeatedly afterwards.

"Why do you think I'm obsessed?" He counters.

"Come on, we both know you're a little OCD about them. God, I bet you test yourself weekly with how concerned you are about that."

He smiles.

"I don't. I don't need to test myself weekly because I'm not fucking anyone," he says, his eyes glinting as if he knows I was fishing for information.

Which I totally was, but I'm not about to show him that.

"And I've never *not* used a condom. You were the first one."

I frown at his words.

"What do you mean?" I'm a little confused because people talk, and I've never heard anyone use a condom for a blowjob.

"Exactly that." He smirks in that arrogant way I've come to expect of him. "Your mouth's the only thing I've ever been bare in."

The urge to gloat at the fact is overwhelming. But I keep my mask on as I nod thoughtfully.

"That doesn't explain why you were so adamant about the test," I continue, mentally cringing at my words. I hope he's not about to throw my reputation in my face.

I've gotten used to the way people talk about me, but somehow him believing it and scorning me for it would hurt more than anything.

He sighs deeply, leaning back on his elbows as he raises his face towards the sky.

"My mother used to cheat on my father a lot," he starts, and I can tell it's not something he likes to talk about. "With anyone, really," his lips form a sad smile. "She ended up giving my father HIV. This was some time ago, and there was a lot of stigma against HIV. My father was a proud man and he never wanted to admit to the disease, thinking people would brand him a gay man."

I nod. It's true that in the past the disease was mostly associated with homosexuals, and it breaks my heart that someone would prefer dying than facing the stigma.

"He ignored it for as long as he could, until it turned into AIDS. His immunity was so compromised, he died of a common cold," he gives a dry laugh.

"I'm sorry." I say softly, not knowing how to comfort him.

"Don't. It was his choice. But it was sobering enough for me to *never* want to put myself in that position in the first place," he continues, and somehow I feel that he's not telling me the whole story.

But he's opening up to me and... It feels good. I can't believe I'm even thinking this, but there's a warmth that seems to unfurl in my chest.

"Your turn now," he turns towards me, his eyes a quiet challenge.

"I have chronic anxiety and panic attacks, or at least that's what I think I have." I admit, a little embarrassed. Since I don't have access to a doctor, I'd self-diagnosed myself on the internet.

"You think?"

"My father doesn't believe in mental illness. He thinks it's bogus and an invention of the modern era. He also doesn't believe in depression, or," I snort, "homosexuality. He doesn't really believe in science either." Or education. Or women being independent. But I don't say that too.

"But what's happening to you isn't normal," he frowns. "When I saw you..." he shakes his head. "Hell, you were trembling uncontrollably from head to toe. You couldn't even form words."

"I know," I purse my lips in a forced smile. "I've been living with this for years. And after a bit of research I found out about Xanax. I know it's not ok that I'm taking it without prescription," I sigh, "but it's the only thing that calms me down. The only thing that makes me feel normal."

"That's why you were willing to do anything for them." He adds quietly.

"Yes. I can't imagine what life would be like *without* them. The attacks," I take a deep breath, unable to believe I'm confessing my biggest weakness to my enemy. "Sometimes they are so bad I can't function properly. Whatever I have, it's debilitating."

"You should still get a proper diagnosis."

"I wish. You have no idea how much I wish I could do that. But my father won't have it. Especially now that he needs to find me a husband, he can't afford to sell a defective product."

"Gianna..."

"Don't. Don't pity me. Please." I turn to him. "It's the way our world is, and I've long been resigned to my fate. The pills..." I give him a sad smile. "They are the only thing that make me able to withstand it."

"You're eighteen. You're an adult. Surely you can..."

"And do what? I don't know if you've noticed, Sebastian, but my father's kept me on a *very* tight leash. I depend on him for everything. As for me?" I shake my head. "I barely have any education. No credentials. Nothing to make it by myself in the real world. Nothing except..." I trail off, the truth bitter on my tongue.

"Except what?"

"Except my body." I whisper, my eyes suddenly moist. "And I would never resort to that."

Somehow we make it back home before dawn. My father is scandalized when he finds out about the attack and the bomb in the car, immediately starting to plan the offensive against whoever dared to threaten his life.

When he realizes that both Sebastian and I are unharmed, he just nods, appeased. And if anyone doubted how much he cared about me, he squashed those doubts when he sighed in relief at still having a bride to sell.

Sebastian noticed too, and he shot me a worried glance.

I don't know why, but since our little chat in the grass, the air seems to have shifted between us. Even as we walked home, we talked amiably without resorting to fighting anymore. It had been a nice change.

But also bad because it had served to emphasize my attraction to him even more. If before it was easier to ignore it because I thought he was an ogre, now that I know there's an actual person behind his tough guy persona I find myself confused and a little too intrigued by him.

After we leave my father to deal with whatever he needs to deal with, we head upstairs to our rooms.

I don't know why, but when we reach the landing of the stairs, I'm a little reluctant to go inside, a part of me craving his company.

He sees me teetering in front of my door, and a strange look crosses his features.

"Sunshine?" he calls out, and my ears perk up immediately.

"Yes?" I ask, my voice a little too breathless.

In two steps, he's in front of me. His big hands cup the sides of my face as he leans down, his lips a soft caress on mine.

I'm too stunned to react, the action taking me wholly by surprise. I can only soak in the contact, wishing he would do more, but knowing how unwise that would be.

"From now on, call me Bass," he whispers against my lips.

"Bass," I test the name, wetting my lips as I look in his eyes.

He has a satisfied smile on his face as he gazes down at me.

"Dream of me, sunshine. I sure will," he winks at me and before I know it, he's gone.

I barely find the strength to enter my own room, my feet sore, my entire body tired from tonight's exertion.

Yet I can't help the silly smile that's spread all over my face.

"Bass," I repeat, a little too giddy.

Even his nickname sounds hard—like him.

A blush envelops my features at the thought, and as I drift off to sleep I do end up dreaming about him.

CHAPTER NINE

BASS

A pretty blush stains her features as she promptly looks away from me.

"You're not very subtle, sunshine," I remark, fairly amused.

"I don't know what you're talking about," she feigns a shrug, even though the corner of her mouth is slightly raised.

Since our conversation in the middle of nowhere, Gianna has started to relax more around me. Certainly, she's stopped using her favorite nickname *mutt*. To hear my actual name on her lips might just be the highlight of my day.

"And you're staring," she replies, still not meeting my eyes.

"I find it hard *not* to stare, all things considered," I tell her, my eyes roving over her body. She's dressed casually, but even casual looks stunning on Gianna.

A pair of high waisted dark jeans and a pink cropped top, the outfit emphasizes her tiny waist and her long legs.

And I'm not the only one who's noticed. I caught at least a dozen men turning their heads around to get a better look at her, and it had taken everything in me not to remove their eyeballs from their sockets.

But then again, she does have that effect on people.

"Just because I'm not actively trying to kill you anymore doesn't mean you have permission to stare," she raises an eyebrow at me.

"So you *were* trying to kill me," I reply, referring to the archery incident.

"Maybe," she shrugs. "You do have a way of getting on people's nerves, you know."

"I think I have a way of getting on *your* nerves. Although I don't think it's your nerves you should be worried about," I drawl suggestively as I let my eyes move over her chest. Even *she* can't hide her reaction to me, and her pebbled nipples are proof enough of how much I affect her.

"Eyes here, big guy," she motions towards her eyes before crossing her arms over her chest to hide the evidence of her desire for me.

"Don't worry, sunshine," I lean in, brushing my mouth over her hair as I breathe hot air on her ear. I feel her shuddering at the close contact, but she still keeps herself upright, trying to show me I don't affect her. "I'm not about to ravish you in the middle of the street. No matter how much you may want it," I whisper, letting one finger trail down her front, barely touching her.

"I still hate you," she retorts, her voice breathless, her eyes already glazed with desire.

"Good," I smirk. "Keep on to that hate," I say and her eyebrows draw up together in a small frown. "I hear hate sex is better than regular one."

Her mouth parts, at first on a whimper, before she regains control over herself, schooling her features to reflect feigned outrage.

"You're an asshole," she grumbles, promptly turning her back to me and continuing to walk.

"Damn, sunshine. And here I thought you liked my assholishness," I call after her.

She turns her head back, a sheepish smile on her face as she shrugs, continuing on.

We walk in silence for a while, enjoying the sunny weather. She'd insisted on parking the car a small distance from the location of her lecture, saying a walk would help her clear her mind.

"You promise not to tell my father?" She asks as we get to the car. Only her profile is visible, but even so, I note her lower lip trembling as she nibbles at it—the only sign of weakness.

One thing I've noticed about this *other* Gianna is that she has a hard time trusting people. It's not the first time she's asked me something similar, trying to ascertain whether I will betray her or not.

"No. I told you I wouldn't."

She nods thoughtfully, but doesn't seem entirely convinced.

Since Gianna's schedule is always packed with a myriad of activities, I've never really paid attention to whether it's dance, or golf, or pottery or whatever. I know that these classes are part of her networking routine and the way she keeps in touch with a lot of her so-called friends.

By chance, though, I'd stumbled upon the fact that her dance practice was not a dance practice at all. Hosted in the same building, instead of going to her dance lessons, she's been attending some psychology lectures.

At first I'd simply been baffled about the discovery, and I hadn't brought it up with her simply because I wanted to observe her more.

Soon, though, more and more inconsistencies started appearing, more cracks showing in the perfectly crafted façade Gianna shows to the world. And I slowly started to realize that I'd been wrong about her.

But even as I find more things about her, I don't think I'm anywhere near to solving the puzzle that is Gianna Guerra.

"Why risk it, though?" I ask. I'd been wondering about this for quite some time, and I've never been able to figure out why she'd go through so much trouble just to attend a lecture. She's already running a risk with the books on her phone, since, by all accounts, Benedicto detests the idea of education for women.

She sighs, suddenly looking distant.

"Because it's the only thing that's mine," she raises her finger to her forehead. "This," she taps her temple, "is the only thing that *no one* can take away from me."

I frown.

"What do you mean?"

"Sometimes I forget you're not used to our world," she shakes her head ruefully before proceeding to explain. "I've known since young that one day I was going to marry a man of my father's choosing. And over the years it's become increasingly clear that my father was going to sell me to the highest bidder, since, let's face it, he's not doing well financially. My first engagement fell through, and now he's scrambling to find a replacement. He's desperate, which doesn't bode well for me." She takes a deep breath, her small fingers balled into fists.

"I'll just switch hands from my father, who may not be the worst tyrant, but he's certainly no walk in the park, to God knows whom," she shakes her head, her lips curled in disgust. "I'll become that man's property and I'll have *nothing*."

Hearing her call herself another man's property doesn't sit well with me. Mostly because I can't imagine her with anyone else. Anyone but me that is.

"I don't know what I'm going to walk into for that marriage, or how strict my future husband will be. Who knows, he might not even allow me a phone," she gives a sad smile. "As long as everything is in my head, then no one can take it away from me."

"Have you never thought about running away?" I throw the idea out there, even though I know it to be impossible. No one gets out of this life. Not alive, anyway.

She chuckles at my question.

"Running away..." she snorts, amused. "Probably every day?" She angles her shoulders up in a lazy shrug. "It's certainly my fantasy. But I'm smart enough to know I have no way of getting too far. I'd need another identity, first of all, and the ability to move around unrecognizable. I've thought about it... so many times," she releases a sigh. "But I'd never be able to do it on my own. And if I did run away and my father caught me... let's just say some things are better left unsaid."

"You're very brave," I offer a sincere praise.

Over the years, I've seen many women succumb to the same fate as her. But there had been one major difference. They'd never fought it. My father had arranged a match for my sister the moment she turned eighteen. She'd been married off to a nobleman from Sicily.

While he hadn't needed the money the match had brought to the table, he'd benefited from the connection with the aristocracy, which had ultimately given us more legitimacy in some regions.

Anna had been apprehensive about her marriage, since her husband-to-be had been at least a decade older than her. But she'd never once thought about defying our father. She didn't have Gianna's rebellious spirit, or her broad knowledge of the world.

She'd simply... settled. But was it really settling if it was all she'd ever known?

The same can't be said about Gianna, since Benedicto has been parading her in front of the New York high society since she reached her puberty, all in hopes of finding someone with enough resources to save his drowning businesses.

She's seen what the world has to offer, and she's learned how to think for herself. To take everything away from her and make her fit into an anachronistic mold is simply cruel.

And for a moment I feel grateful for my mission. Because once she's truly ruined she won't have any other choice than live her own life—for herself.

Her eyes widen at my praise, her brows shooting up as she looks at me with an incredulous expression on her face.

"What happened to spoiled, terrible, and whatever other names you used to call me?"

"It was the truth. For what you wanted me to see. Because that's what you want, don't you? For people to discount you as a spoiled bratty heiress."

"Easy, big guy," she laughs softly. "Let's not turn me into some kind of saint. I know my faults," she waves her hand dismissively.

"Why do you have to pretend, though? Why the mean persona?" I ask, trying to understand her better.

"Why indeed," she purses her lips. "Sometimes, the only way to survive amongst wolves is to learn to behave like one," she says quietly.

"You're quite the philosopher, aren't you, sunshine?"

Somehow, she keeps surprising me.

She turns to me, a silly grin on her face.

"Not really. Often, philosophy is just the idea of wisdom without the experience to back it up. In my case, I've experienced everything on my own skin."

Her smile dies, her upper lips twitching as her forehead creases in a frown.

"Never mind that," she takes my hand, pointing at my watch. "We need to get home fast. I've been thinking about that cake all day."

Her brother, Michele, turns thirteen today, and Benedicto had organized a mini bash for him and his schoolmates. And if we hurry, we might even get there before the party starts.

"Hmm, I know what type of cake I'd like, and I don't think our visions match," I wink at her.

"When are you *not* thinking about that," she giggles before leaning towards me to whisper. "If you behave, I might give you a kiss."

"It's a deal," I immediately exclaim, aiming to hold her to that.

As we'd slowly moved away from our arguments and the mutual dislike that seemed to lead our previous interactions, we realized we *could* get along. For days now, we've slowly slipped into a comfortable routine and we'd stopped antagonizing one another. In fact, we'd also had a discussion about our attraction and we'd agreed to take it slow and see what comes out of it. Certainly, that's going to make my mission much easier, and more enjoyable.

I don't think there's anything more satisfying than having a woman like Gianna come to me of her own accord, giving in to her desire because she wants to.

Because she wants me.

And for as long as this lasts, I aim to take advantage of it to the maximum. Fuck knows, I've already gotten used to being in her presence at all times, the thought of being without her inconceivable.

We quickly arrive at the house, the preparations for the party still ongoing, with staff hurrying from one corner of the house to the other to add last minute touches to the decorations.

"Damn, but Benedicto went wild with this one," I note the lavish ensemble—balloons, props, costumes and all types of role-play stations for the kids to play at.

"Not my father," Gianna purses her lips. "I spoke with my uncle to help organize everything. My father isn't very present in Michele's life, and the few times I tried to bring it up he ignored me," she explains, but is interrupted by a loud voice.

"Gigi!" A lanky boy runs down the stairs as he flings himself in her arms. He's almost as tall as Gianna, and from what I'd gathered, his growth spurt hasn't kicked in still. He might be the tallest in the family yet, given that Benedicto himself is a rather short man.

Black hair and eerily light amber eyes, Michele is a very pretty boy. He's definitely going to have a hard time fending off the girls when he grows up.

"There you are," she replies affectionately, threading her fingers through his thick locks. "This is your costume?" she asks, looking down at his clothes.

"Yes! Do you like it?" he takes a step back to show the entire costume. "It's from that popular superhero show," he continues to prattle, telling Gianna all about his favorite characters. She listens attentively, her hand still on his as her smile never wavers.

For a thirteen year old, Michele's past times might seem a little too childish, but he's not exactly a normal boy.

As a little boy he was diagnosed with leukemia and he's been in and out of hospitals for treatments. It wasn't until they found a miraculous donor that matched that he managed to beat cancer. But his immunity was compromised, and he's never been completely healthy, even something as little as a cold taking its toll on his body.

Safe to say, he's never had a normal childhood. And that's only from what I've heard.

What I'd witnessed, however, has only made me feel even sorrier for the lad.

Benedicto completely ignores him while Cosima, his step-mother, always finds ways to mistreat him to benefit her own son.

The only person in the family who seems to give a damn about him is Gianna, and sometimes I have the vague impression that she's taken it upon herself to be both a mother and a sister for him.

FRIVOLOUS

"I can't wait to meet your classmates," Gianna comments at some point, and Michele's smile falls.

"You think they'll come?" he asks in a small voice.

"Why wouldn't they? I'm sure they will all be here. I sent the invites myself," she winks at him, and he gives her a tremulous smile.

A while later, the party doesn't seem very promising. I sit in my corner, watching and observing everyone. Gianna is constantly on the move as she tries to ensure everything goes smoothly.

Michele's friends for school arrived as planned, but instead of hanging out with him, they abandoned him in favor of his brother. Not before laughing about his superhero suit, though, a conversation that I'd eavesdropped on and heard exactly how cruel his classmates had been.

Gianna hadn't been around to notice, mostly moving between the kitchen and the living room to make sure the food is served on time. And so while she'd been busy with the logistics of the party, I'd had to watch Michele get his heart broken by his *friends* as they all but laughed at him at his own birthday.

Even now, he's sitting in a corner, watching the others talk about some new video games, but not daring to join the conversation.

Taking pity on the lad, I move from my corner, going to his side.

"They're not your friends, are they?" I ask, nodding to the small crowd occupying the living room, all surrounding his brother Rafaelo as he shows them how to pass a more difficult level.

"How did you notice?" He asks drily, but I note the disappointment in his tone, no matter how much he tries to hide it.

"They barely said two words to you. One didn't even know your name," I raise an eyebrow.

Closing his eyes, he sighs.

"They're not my friends. They are Raf's friends," he confesses.

"Why invite them then?"

He doesn't reply for a second, his shoulders squared.

"Gigi was so excited about planning the party that I didn't want to tell her," he starts, before continuing in a low voice, "that I don't have any friends."

"I don't buy that. Why would you not have any friends?"

He shrugs.

"They don't like me. They prefer Raf. Clearly," he adds sarcastically, looking at the small gathering with longing in his eyes.

"Have you tried to talk to them? You won't solve anything if you sulk in a corner."

"I'm not sulking."

"Yes, you are," I point out, and he frowns at me as if he doesn't understand what I mean.

"It's your party, Michele. You need to put yourself out there if you want to interact with people. What does Raf have that you don't?"

"I don't know," he sighs. "People always like him better. *Everyone* likes him better."

"I don't. Your sister doesn't."

He blinks slowly. "You don't?"

"I think you're pretty cool. You just need to be more confident and open and people will flock to you too," I give him a smile.

"I wish I could. But I don't know…" he continues to shake his head, as if he doesn't know what to do to change his circumstances.

"Go to them," I motion towards the others. "Go and make an effort. Who knows, you might be surprised too."

He seems to weigh my words for a moment, before nodding enthusiastically.

"You're right. Thank you," he gives me a quick smile before dashing towards the living room.

"I didn't know you had such a way with kids," a voice calls from behind me. Gianna comes to my side, carrying two plates of food. She hands me one before starting to eat from her own.

"Michele is already a young man. He should act like one," I grunt, a little peeved she'd overheard our conversation.

"He is, and he isn't," she says quietly, her eyes on the boys.

Michele is saying something to the crowd and we both wait, almost holding our breath, for the result. There is a tense moment where the boys seem to debate whether to accept him in their midst, but Raf pats his back affectionately, inviting him to play with them.

"He's not like the others," Gianna confesses with a sad smile. "I've tried to help him as much as I could, but the absence of a mother figure really affected him. After everything he went through," she shakes her head. "When kids his age were actually dressing up as superheroes, he was in the hospital, his head shaved, his arm hooked to IVs. He never got to go through the normal stages a kid would. And I fear it's marked him… irrevocably."

"You're good to him," I praise gently. "You heard what he said. He lied about his friends so he wouldn't upset you."

"He's a darling. That doesn't stop me from worrying about him. Especially since both my father and Cosima seem to forget he even exists."

We eat in silence as we watch them continue to play, Michele slowly becoming more integrated in their group.

"Thank you for what you said to him. He needed to hear that," she gives my hand a quick squeeze before heading back to the kitchen with the dishes.

It's not much later that Cosima makes an appearance. The timing, however, is completely off, as the boys are playing some kind of wrestling match.

Raf and Michele are enjoying themselves, simulating a fight but not actually hitting each other when Cosima bursts in the room. She takes one look at the scene in front of her before yelling at the top of her lungs for them to stop.

Without waiting, though, she dashes to Raf's side, wrenching him away from Michele.

Michele looks confused as he turns his gaze to his step-mother, trying to explain it wasn't serious.

"Haven't I told you? You don't *touch* him!" She yells at Michele before she slaps him—hard enough to throw him to the ground.

"What…" Gianna's voice rings out as she hurries to the scene.

"And you," Cosima turns to Gianna. "Who gave you permission for this? Was everyone just watching while this *monster,*" she spits at Michele, "was hitting my son?"

"He wasn't hitting him. They were playing," Gianna tries to explain at the same time as Raf and Michele interject that they were, indeed, playing.

"You might think it was a game," she berates her son, "but he didn't. He wants to hurt you, but I won't let him," she continues, pure malice dripping from her words.

Stopping the party, she orders Raf to go to his room before turning once more towards Michele.

Realizing she won't stop at just one slap, and that Gianna might not be able to deal with her alone, I intervene.

"Ma'am, you need to stand down," I say as I put myself between her, Gianna and Michele.

"You? Who do you think you are to tell me what to do? He was harming my son!" she yells at me.

"They were playing," I explained in an even tone.

"No! He's a monster and he isn't fit to touch a hair on my son's body. You hear me?" she points towards Michele, her eyes bulging in her head. "You stay the hell away from Rafaelo, or I will make sure you never see the light of the day again."

"Really, Cosima?" Gianna rolls her eyes at her. "You think you can order everyone around just because you spread your legs for my father every night?" She raises an eyebrow, and the insult hits its mark as Cosima becomes a red mottled mess of anger.

"Oh, this is just marvelous. Who's calling who a whore, Gianna? At least I spread my legs *only* for your father. Who knows how many have taken turns with you already," she retorts.

"Go to your room, Michele," I turn to the boy, urging him to leave so that he doesn't listen to the shitshow that's about to start. It never ends well when Cosima and Gianna start arguing, and Michele shouldn't hear what Cosima has to say about his sister.

"But..." his eyes drift to Gianna, and I see his quiet desire to defend her, even as he himself is a target for her malice.

"I got her. Go," I nod at him.

He looks me in the eye, man to man, and he nods, placing his trust in me.

"Take care of her," he whispers before running.

"Where the hell do you think you're going to?" Cosima screams when she sees him dash up the stairs.

The staff are all on the periphery, likely listening to everything that's happening, ready to gossip about it later.

But as Cosima makes to go after Michele, Gianna wraps her hand around her arm, stopping her.

"You have no right to touch my brother, witch. And if I hear you try anything with him, you're going to wish you were never born," she threatens.

"You? Your father will never believe you. But you know that already, don't you? That he doesn't care about you or that brat of your brother. He only cares about my Raf, which is why he's making him his heir."

"You're lying."

"I'm not," she replies smugly. "Ask him. Raf's the next capo, and he will make the most marvelous boss."

"Oh so you think that your son will protect you?" Gianna chuckles. "Make no mistake that if I hear you did anything to Michele, I'm coming for you."

"You and what army? Let's face it, dear. You're useless."

"But I'm not," I take a step forward, grabbing Gianna and pushing her behind me. "Gianna is my charge and as such it's my duty to protect her from those who mean her harm. I believe her father mentioned eliminating all targets." I state, my expression serious.

"Is she a danger?" I turn to Gianna, asking.

"Hmm, she might be," she replies, feigning fear.

"OK," I reply, and already my hand is wrapped around Cosima's throat as I lift her in the air, putting enough pressure on her neck to make her gasp for breath.

"Gahh," she squeaks, eliciting a smile from Gianna.

"Not so tough are you now, Cosima?"

"Call… call off your pit bull," she spits, her eyes shooting daggers at me.

"I don't know. I feel that you're still a danger to me." Gianna replies and I tighten my hold over her neck.

She starts having trouble breathing, and flailing her arms to the side, she tries to get me off her.

"Apologize to Gianna and I'll let you go," I tell her, my expression leaving no room for compromise.

Her eyes widen and she shakes her head. Of course, I only continue to tighten my fingers until she screams out.

"I'm sorry!"

"What was that?" Gianna asks again, looking bored. "I don't think I can hear her from that height. Maybe if she was lower…" she drifts off and I immediately catch her meaning.

None too gently, I push Cosima to her knees in front of Gianna, my hand still on her throat as I keep her in place.

"Apologize," I prompt her.

She's trembling with a mix of fear and anger as she looks up at Gianna, but eventually she does say as directed.

"I'm sorry," she apologizes and Gianna smirks.

"Good," she nods at me to release her. "Now bear this in mind Cosima. The next time you mess with me, or with Michele, I won't ask him to let go." She leans closer to Cosima to whisper, "I'll ask him to squeeze tighter."

Eyes wide as two saucers, Cosima barely scrambles to her feet before dashing upstairs.

Gianna lingers a little longer as she instructs the staff to clean up the house and to pack the food.

Eventually, we both head upstairs.

Luckily, Gianna's room is a floor above Cosima's and the boys so the risk of running into her again is minimal. However, I am extremely surprised when we reach her door and instead of saying goodbye she tugs me inside her room.

She doesn't even let me say anything as she pushes me on her bed before coming to my side, her hands on my shoulders, her body between my spread thighs. One moment she's looking at me with those fuck me eyes of hers, the next she's kissing me, a sweet, gentle kiss that belies her sexy appearance but nonetheless tugs at my heartstrings with its intensity.

Her lips are soft on top of mine as they brush ever so slowly. It's nothing like the first kiss where we'd been one moment from ripping the clothes off our back. No, this is totally opposite, yet just as potent.

Maybe even more.

"Thank you," she whispers against my mouth, her arms wound around my neck as she nuzzles her cheek to mine. "I've never heard Cosima apologize to me before, much less on her knees."

"She was being unreasonable."

"Mhm," she purrs, fitting her cheek to mine, "she's always been a witch. She hates my brother because he's the first born. But if what she's saying is true… I just don't see how my father would make Raf his heir."

"She seems to have a great deal of control over him."

"Yes," she sighs. "He's smitten with her. He's always been. And I have no doubt she's going to spin the story to her advantage this time too."

"I'll back you up."

"Why, Bass, if someone saw us now versus a week ago they'd think we've had a personality transplant."

"I don't know," I smile. "Have we?"

"Maybe. Maybe not." Her lips brush more against mine. "You got your promised kiss," she whispers, "now go back to your room."

And just like that she's off me and showing me to the door.

CHAPTER TEN

GIANNA

My eyes snap open the minute I hear the rumble of thunder in the sky. I blink repeatedly, trying to make sense of the darkness enveloping the room, my entire skin covered in goosebumps as fear starts to settle in.

The play of shadows on the wall opposite my bed only adds to my terror, my limbs trembling, my eyes squeezed shut as I will the memories to leave me alone.

It's just like that night.

The storm had caught everyone unaware and we'd had to relocate inside. It had all been going perfectly fine until I'd had to go to the bathroom and…

I bring my hands to my ears as I try to block the sound, the tree branches moving and enhancing the howl of the wind.

There had been a window open then too, and all I could hear were the sounds of my clamoring heart and the raging storm outside.

For minutes on end I try to shut those thoughts down, knowing that if I truly go down that rabbit hole I won't be able to come out of it unharmed.

My breathing becomes erratic, my entire body shuddering with unreleased pressure as I struggle to keep that night from intruding in my mind.

But I can't.

Not like this. Not now, when every sound, every *single* flash of lightning threatens to bring me back right to that moment.

Without even thinking, I get out of bed, draping a robe over my nightgown and exiting the room. A little unnerved, but convinced only *he* can help me, I make the courage to knock on his door.

The seconds trickle by, and I cross my arms over my body. It's not cold, yet my teeth are clattering from an unknown chill.

The door opens slowly. His eyes are the first thing I see. Those steely eyes that have become my strange comfort.

"Can I..." I start, wanting to ask him to let me in. But I can't even bring myself to complete the sentence. Not when my mouth doesn't seem to be working properly.

Still, he senses my desperation, opening the door for me to come inside.

My arms still wrapped around my midriff, I take a seat on his bed, my eyes facing forward.

The room is completely bare save for a couple of clothes stored in a corner. I don't know what I expected to find, but it's certainly not this... not this emptiness.

"Gianna?" His voice startles me from my thoughts, and I dare look up at him.

He's not dressed. At least not fully.

His chest is bare, his lower half covered only by a pair of gray sweatpants.

My eyes hone in on every detail of his chest as my gaze sweeps him in. There's only muscle. Pure, hard muscle that flexes and extends right under my eyes.

He's... magnificent.

It should scare me. It should terrify me. The way his body is so big and hard, double, no... almost triple my own size. He could easily subdue me.

He could do anything to me.

But as I meet his eyes, I only see concern in them. And somehow, I know I'm safe.

"Can I... sit with you for a bit?" I ask, steadying my voice.

"Of course," he immediately replies, coming to sit by my side. "Are you ok? Are you feeling ill?" His voice is full of worry, his question eliciting a small frown for me.

When was the last time someone's asked me if I was ok?

Has anyone ever?

I tilt my head to gaze up at him.

The light peering through the window serves to emphasize his scar even more. Yet the more I look at him, the more it seems to fade away. It's there... yet it's not.

Before I know what I'm doing, my arm shoots out, my hand on his cheek as I trace those hard planes.

There's shock written all over his features as I slowly bring my fingers over the jagged scar crossing his face. I feel the rough skin under my fingertips, the small bumps on his scar telling me the healing journey was anything but smooth.

"What are you doing, Gianna?" He asks, catching my hand and holding it captive. He's looking at me intently, as if he's trying to figure me out.

"I don't know," I confess. "I don't know anything anymore."

I wet my lips with my tongue, and his eyes dip to my mouth, his pupils growing in size as he takes in every small movement I make.

"You shouldn't have come here," he rasps, his voice thick and husky. "You shouldn't have come anywhere near me at night. Not when all I can think of..." he trails off, his thumb on my lower lip as he touches it reverently.

"What? What are you thinking of?" I ask breathlessly.

"You." He states squarely. "Naked, and in my bed. Your legs spread, your pussy bared to me," he continues and I gasp. His crude words should scare me away, the taste of danger imminent. Instead, they only inflame me more, turning my fear into something else. Something stronger, more potent. Something that has the power to truly make me forget.

"And what would you do to me?" I don't recognize myself as I ask the question. I can't even recognize my own voice, so suave, almost like the seductress everyone brands me to be.

"What wouldn't I do, sunshine? I'd worship your body with my mouth," he says, and my eyes close, my lips parted on a soft whimper. He leans into me, his breath on my skin as he continues to whisper the wicked things he'd do to me, making my core tingle, my pussy gush with wetness as my walls contract on a shiver.

"I'd lick every inch of your delectable body. I'd suck on those tight nipples that even now strain against your dress. Then, I'd mark every bit of exposed flesh with my teeth, sucking, nibbling, biting. I'd make it so that everyone can see who you belong to."

"And who do I belong to?" I ask saucily, a heat unlike any other traveling down my body.

"Me," he states in a gruff voice. "You've been mine since the first moment I saw you."

The intensity of his eyes as he looks me up and down in such a primal way has my toes curling, the urge to clench my thighs to relieve the pressure building there almost unbearable.

"What if I don't want that?" I shoot back, trying to seem defiant but failing as my voice comes out breathy and excited.

"Too bad, sunshine," he smiles arrogantly. "You never had a choice to begin with."

Damn but that cockiness of his makes me even hotter, and there's a part of me that would like nothing more than to just jump on him and melt against his skin.

"Why? Why me?" I don't know what I'm asking exactly, but I want to hear how I affect him. I want to know it's not just me suffering from this strange affliction, from this longing that seems to have seared itself into my bones.

"Because you drive me crazy, Gianna. I've never met someone like you before. Someone I'd like to both kiss and strangle at the same time," he smirks, "someone who defies me at every turn but makes me so fucking hard I can barely think straight. You make my blood boil."

My breath hitches. I feel drunk on his words, lightheaded from his presence alone.

"You make me lose my fucking head, Gianna. And I've *never* been this distracted before," he groans.

"Touch me," I blurt out, the sincerity in his voice my undoing. Because I know what it's like to want something but not be able to act on it—I've been wanting him from the first, but I'd been too scared to admit it to myself.

His eyes widen and he doesn't move for a moment. Then, out of the sudden, his big hands reach for me, easily lifting me up and moving me to his lap.

My palms come to rest on his chest, the warmth of his skin seeping into mine. He's massive. All muscle and brawn, coiling under my fingertips, flexing right under my gaze.

And as I drink him up, I realize just how easy it would be for him to push me on my back, spread my legs and...

I blink, raising my eyes to his and noting he's not moving to go further. Instead, he's waiting for me to make the first move. His hands are on my waist, and I feel his fingers burning through my light dress. My skin tingles everywhere he touches me.

He's like a tornado to my senses, and I think I realized that from the beginning. I'd just been so terrified of his size and my own desire for him that I'd tried to shut everything down.

I continue to move my hands over his chest, enjoying the slight twitch of his muscles under my palms. My knees are on each side of his thighs, yet I'm not close enough to feel his hardness. And I know he's hard. I saw it from the moment he started talking to me.

Briefly, my mind takes me to that night, when he'd pushed me to my knees and blackmailed me into giving him a blowjob. To the frightening yet arousing way his dick thrust in my face had made me feel.

I've been lying to myself from the beginning, telling myself I hated him when all I wanted was to be held by him.

Closing my eyes, I revel in this touch, the way he makes me feel both safe and breathless at the same time. It's the first time I've allowed myself to touch a man freely, without being disgusted by the proximity, or fearful of what he might try.

I don't know what it is about him that makes me feel like this. That simply erases all my history and gives me back a portion of my lost identity.

His steely gray eyes glint in the moonlight, emphasizing their wolfish quality and the way they simply eat me up.

I bring my fingers to his face, cupping his jaw right where his scar is thickest. He tenses immediately, his jaw locked tight as he barely contains himself.

"What are you doing to me?" I whisper, the question more to myself.

Two years I'd led a hellish existence, afraid of my own shadow but unable to show any weakness. And yet his presence seems to cancel that out. It makes my fear... fall away.

"What's that, sunshine?" He smirks at me, prying my fingers from his face and bringing them to his mouth. Slowly parting his lips, his tongue peeks out to lick each finger, all the while his eyes never leave mine.

I zero in on those lips, licking my own in response.

There's this desire inside of me that threatens to overtake me. It both scares and delights me. Because I've never experienced this before. I don't know how to react to it and I don't know how to deal with... him.

Men like him probably expect more... more than a kiss, more than this simple nearness that fills me with giddiness and a profound sense of fulfillment. He'd expect... sex.

Of course he'd expect sex. I barely stop myself from snorting out loud. He's heard the whispers. He knows what people say about me. That I'm easy. That I'd sleep with anyone.

I wish he realized just how special this is for me. The mere fact that I'm laying myself bare for him—defenseless—should show him how in earnest I am and how much I want him.

"You make me forget myself," I admit vaguely.

It's not the most blatant invitation, but it's not an untruth either. Because he does make me forget myself, and everything I've built for myself these past years.

He makes me... feel.

"You make me forget myself too," he leans forward and I feel his breath on my face.

In the past, I would have recoiled. Now... I lean in too, meeting him almost halfway.

"You tempt me, sunshine." He rasps. "You tempt me to forget my job, and you tempt me to forget I'm a gentleman. You tempt me to do wicked, wicked things to you," he pauses, and I gulp down, almost lost in his words.

"You tempt me too," I whisper, wounding my arms around his neck.

It's all the incentive he needs to finally smash his lips to mine. Because this isn't a gentle kiss.

Far from it.

The contact is bruising as his teeth take hold of my lower lip, nibbling. His tongue licks the seam of my semi parted lips, searching for a way in.

I don't even think as I open wide, molding myself to him as I press closer, deeper.

I reach out with my tongue, meeting his in a light stroke that seems to inflame him further as he all but drags me in his lap, my chest flush to his.

A small gasp escapes me, my center suddenly in contact with that very hard part of him and…

I moan.

God, the sound escapes my lips and I'm powerless to stop it, the friction so potent it makes me shiver in pleasure.

His mouth is still on mine, tasting, devouring. There's no gentleness as wet lips meet wet lips, teeth clashing as we give ourselves to chaos. There's nothing organized about the way he makes love to my mouth.

His hands on my back, they move lower until he cups my ass, bringing me even closer to his erection and grounding me on it.

"Fuck, sunshine," he groans against my lips, his breathing harsh.

He pulls back a little, leaving me dazed, lips swollen, eyes glazed.

He stares at me as if he's never seen me before. But just as soon, that look is gone.

Instead of pulling away though, he raises my hips slightly, molding my pelvis over his hard cock.

My mouth parts on a breathless moan as I feel the ridge of him brush against my clit. My hands are suddenly on his shoulders as I hold on tight, my hips continuing to roll over his, seeking a repeat of the previous feeling.

A spear of pleasure goes through me just as I move again, and I find him watching me closely, his nostrils flared as he takes in my flushed cheeks and my hardened nipples peeking through my dress.

He continues to gently move me over his erection, his eyes never leaving me as he catalogues every emotion that crosses my face.

And just as I feel something build inside of me, he increases the tempo, lowering his mouth to my breasts and giving my nipple a quick bite through the material.

The loud moan takes me by surprise and I have a hard time believing it's coming from my own lips. But as my eyes flutter closed, my muscles spasming all around, I find that I'm not in control of anything.

He is.

He is masterfully playing my body like I never thought it capable.

And as I'm coming down from my high, I can only stare at him dazedly and in confusion.

"You're exquisite when you come," his hand goes up to my face, his thumb caressing my cheek.

"I don't think I've ever seen a more luscious sight. You bewitch me Gianna," he tells me, and I note the harshness of his tone, the way he doesn't like how I affect him.

But so gone I am from this newly found pleasure that I don't mind it.

I just sigh deeply and contently, nestling closer to him as I lay my head on his shoulder.

I do realize, though, that he hasn't finished, his cock still hard under me. Yet he doesn't seem in any hurry to do so. He doesn't even mention it as we stay like that for minutes on end.

That's when I gain a new found respect for this hulking beast.

He could have taken his relief from my body. I know he could have. Not only would the position have allowed for him to take out his cock and fuck me right there, but I don't know if I would have done much to stop him.

He says I bewitch him, but I fear I am the one bewitched.

Because he makes me feel safe. He drives the fear away.

And that is the biggest wonder of all.

He trails his fingers down my back as he holds me to his chest, and a sense of peace settles over me.

"Will you tell me what happened?" He asks, his voice low.

"I don't like storms," I reply, not giving more details.

"Hmm," he hums, and I don't think he buys my flimsy excuse. Still, he doesn't force me to answer him.

Instead, he takes me into his arms and settles us both on the bed.

Sitting on my side, my front is flush against his. I can still feel the outline of his hard cock against my stomach, and the fact that he hasn't asked for anything in return for the orgasm makes me a little more daring.

Holding his eye contact, I lower my hand between our bodies, tugging at the band of his sweats and reaching inside to cup him.

His hand immediately covers mine, stopping me.

"No," he whispers, and I frown. "You don't have to do anything. This isn't about me."

"But... don't you want to..." I trail off, a blush enveloping my features.

"That's not why you came here, sunshine," he removes my hand from his pants. "No matter how much I'd like to fuck you and come all over your perfect body, I won't."

"Why?"

"Because I already took what you were reluctant to give once. I don't want you to feel pressured to do anything you don't want to."

I can't help but look at him in confusion, the notion that he wouldn't want me to get him off baffling.

All my life I'd been told that I was only good for one thing—to serve as an outlet for a man's pleasure. And here he was, this man that refused my touch.

"I don't understand," I tell him sincerely.

"And that's exactly the issue, Gianna," his lips curl up. "You came to me for shelter from the storm. Let me give it to you, no strings attached."

He drags me closer to his body, his arms coming to rest around me as he nestles me to his chest. He lays his chin on top of my head, his touch healing and comforting.

"Thank you," I whisper.

"Sleep. I've got you."

And for the first time, I do sleep. In spite of the loud rain hitting the windows, or the howling wind screeching in the distance. I hear the thunder, but I'm no longer afraid.

Because I'm enveloped in a searing heat, with big, strong arms wrapped around me and keeping me away from harm.

I am at peace.

But why does it feel like life as I used to know it is all but gone?

I feel his warmth seep into my skin. And as I slowly come to, I realize this might be the best sleep I've had in… forever. My eyes snap open and he's right there, next to me, his gaze boring into mine with an intensity that leaves me breathless.

The morning sounds envelop the room, birds chirping, people moving around the house and shouting random things.

"You're so fucking beautiful, sunshine," he brushes his thumb across my cheek, his voice thick and full of emotion as he looks at me like he's never seen me before.

I can't help but blush at his words, especially since I know I must not look that great this early in the morning.

"I should go," I whisper, although I'm not making any effort to move.

"You should," he agrees, though his hand comes to rest in my hair, his fingers twirling some strands around.

"I can't if you don't let go," I say softly when I see he has no intention of letting me up.

"I don't know if I want to," the corners of his mouth curl up. "When are you going to be so pliant in my arms again?"

"Maybe if you behave yourself…" I trail off, running my fingers down his naked chest.

There are a myriad of scars there too, and I can only assume they are from his time in the army. I still hadn't had the courage to ask more about that, mostly because we've just started to become more open with each other. I don't want to ask the wrong question and have him push me away.

That smirk of his makes another appearance, his hands dropping to my waist as he pulls me on top of him, his mouth fitted to mine in a heated kiss.

"I have to get ready for the gala tonight," I blurt out, breathless and a little overwhelmed.

"I know," he replies, his lips trailing kisses all over my chin and down my neck, "and I also know there will be other men sniffing around you," he rasps before closing his mouth over the spot right above my clavicle, sucking on the skin.

I gasp, realizing what he's trying to do.

"Bass," I push at his shoulders.

He doesn't let go, sucking until I know all the blood's already rushed to the surface.

"There you go," he gives the mark another long lick, "now any bastard who looks your way will know you're claimed."

"What? You..." I shake my head, scandalized.

Before I know it, though, he wraps his fingers around my jaw, holding me tight and bringing me into him.

His eyes look unyielding as he stares at me.

"I meant what I said, Gianna. You belong to me now. And I don't share," he states in a deadpan voice. "If I see another man so much as lay a finger on you, I'm going to kill them and I'm going to make you watch," his tone is chilling, and the more I study his face for any sign he's joking, I realize he's not—he's serious.

"You're crazy."

"Yes, you got that right. You've seen me kill before." His other hand is trailing down my back, the tips of his fingers slowly brushing along my spine and making me shiver in response. "I do it very easily. And I *will* kill anyone who even dares to look the wrong way at you."

"You can't just..."

"Yes. I can, and I will," he leans in, his teeth catching my lower lip as he gives it a soft bite. "Now run along before I lose all my control," he grits, resting his forehead on mine.

One look at his strained features and I realize he's telling the truth. Especially as I'm sitting on top of the *very* hard evidence of his feeble control.

I scramble to my feet, and with one last look at him, I dash back to my room.

The rest of the day is a flurry of activities as I'm rushed from make-up, to hair, to getting one last fit for my gown.

Unlike the other events I'd attended in the past, for this one I'll be accompanied by my father and Cosima, and I've already had strict instructions to behave myself so that it looks like we are all one happy family.

I have to give it to Cosima. She hadn't gone to rat me out to my father, and I think I have Bass to thank for that.

It's no secret that he terrifies her. Every time she sees him around the house she turns sharply on her heel, pretending she has business somewhere else. And I, of course, can't help but gloat at the fact.

No one's ever defended me before, and the rush I'd felt when Bass had stood up for me had been like no other. It would be so easy to get used to it—to him. To know I have a strong protector ready to have my back at any point could get addictive. And that's a problem. Especially since I know whatever we have going on right now can't last.

I've caught myself a few times when my thoughts had veered in that direction, because I hadn't wanted to mar this small amount of happiness that I have for the first time in my life. Still, I've always been a realist. And while my thing with Bass may bring me joy and make me feel unlike ever before, I know it has an expiration date.

Until my marriage.

And because of that, I aim to make the best out of it. I will try to put my fears aside and focus on what is in front of me—on him.

Certainly, it doesn't seem as hard as I would have thought. His touch doesn't scare me. The potential for more doesn't terrify me as it should.

It just… leaves me breathless.

Sometimes I have a hard time identifying the emotions he awakens in me. So used I've become to terror and anxiety taking over my body, that at first, I'd become scared I may be getting an attack. It had taken me a while to realize that my physical reaction was not one of dread, but of excitement.

Simmering low in my belly, they can feel the same, but they are not.

He makes me feel like my body is my own again.

And that's probably the most precious gift.

I thought I'd lost myself that night two years ago. Since then I've felt like drowning, struggling in a turbulent sea with a few gasps of air here and there. I'd never thought I would make it to the shore. I never thought I would breathe again.

But Bass' arrival in my life has shown me that my body is still capable of desire—much as I fought it in the beginning. It's still capable of feeling.

Adding the last touches to my outfit, I head down.

Bass is already in the background, watching closely. The moment I step in his field of view, though, I feel his eyes on me as they rake over every inch of my body.

I'd be lying if I said I hadn't thought about him when I chose this outfit. I'd wanted to get exactly that reaction out of him.

His eyes slightly widen, his mouth semi-parted as he continues to peruse the way the dress hugs my curves, the tight fit emphasizing my body's shape.

He likes what he sees.

My eyes meet his across the room and a slow, sensuous smile appears on his face as he drinks me in, not at all shy about checking me out in front of my father.

"There you are, Gianna," my father purses his lips, barely looking at me, his eyes on his watch as he goes on and on about being late.

Cosima gives me a scowl, but as I raise an eyebrow at her, calling Bass over to my side, she turns away with a huff, her arm hooked through my father's elbow as they walk ahead.

And as we step outside the house, two limos are waiting for us, and a few other cars with guards to follow behind. Undoubtedly, Cosima hadn't wanted to share a space with me and she'd asked my father for separate rides. Normally, I would have thrown a fit just to make her uncomfortable and to ensure she's not getting away with her plan. But as it stands, spending some extra time with Bass alone will help me settle my nerves.

"Are you ok?" He asks me when we're finally alone in the car and heading towards the Met where the gala is being held.

"Yes," I nod. "I took a pill before I left. It should help me get through the night."

"I'll be your shadow at all times. You have nothing to worry about," he squeezes my hand, before tugging me to his side of the limo.

I stumble, rather awkwardly, falling to his lap.

"What are you doing?" I push at his shoulder, amused. "I can't get my dress wrinkled. Or my makeup ruined," I say with a pout.

"I know," he tips my chin up, his eyes boldly staring into mine. "That doesn't mean I can't do something else," he trails his finger down my neck, lingering over the spot he'd sucked on earlier this morning.

"You covered it up," he rasps, his breath against my skin. "What did I tell you, sunshine?" he nuzzles his face against my throat, the gesture gentle but the threat in his voice is unmistakable.

"What...did you tell me?" I ask breathlessly, lost in the sensation of his warm lips on my skin.

"Those posh bastards need to see you're marked," he continues, opening his mouth and trailing wet kisses down the column on my neck.

"I couldn't... my father would have seen," I try to reason with him.

No matter how much I'd liked having his mark on me, I couldn't risk it. Especially at such a public event where it will only serve to fuel the gossip about me.

"But that's just the thing. The entire world needs to know you're off limits. That you're taken..." he trails off as he reaches my cleavage.

The dress has a square cut cleavage, the tight bodice making my boobs pop.

His hands on my ribcage, he leans forward and wraps his mouth on top of the swell of one breast, licking the skin languidly before sucking in.

"Bass, stop it!" I give him a playful punch.

I was serious that I can't be seen with a hickey on—not today.

"No," he speaks against me, his hot breath blowing on my skin and making me shiver.

There's already a tingling in my lower region, and as much as I try to not react, I can't help the moan that escapes me when he starts making love to my breasts with his mouth.

"Bass," I whimper, my hands going to his hair.

He keeps on sucking and licking, concentrating only on the visible areas.

My nipples are already hard, my entire body convulsing with need. And as his hands travel up and down my dress in a slow caress, I'm one second away from asking him to put me out of my misery.

My body remembers the pleasure he'd given me the other night, and it wants a repeat.

"There you go," he whispers in that thick voice of his as he raises his eyes to meet mine. "Now everyone will know," he continues, lifting one finger and bringing him to my breast, tracing the red mark he'd put on me.

"You're an asshole," I mumble, half-annoyed, half too turned on to mind it.

"I know," he smirks. "And you love it," he winks.

Just as I'm about to reply, the car draws to a stop, having reached the destination.

I quickly try to compose myself before getting out and joining my father. Bass follows quietly behind, promptly putting his serious persona on as he assumes his bodyguard stance.

The Met is teeming with people, all invited for an exclusive charity gala in the form of an auction.

A few rooms on the first floor, in the Greek and Roman galleries, are open to the guests to mingle. The entire atmosphere is intoxicating as I walk around the many statues, the high ceiling and splendid lighting of the room providing an authentic ancient feel.

It's a pity that I have to interact with all the people my father keeps on throwing my way, otherwise I would have enjoyed the gala much more.

Cosima quickly finds her circle of *friends*, or at least people she wished she could be friends with, trying to pepper them with fake praises in hopes she could get an invitation at their next afternoon tea.

My father, on the other hand, seems to have an exclusive agenda for tonight's event—and it's not bidding on priceless artifacts.

He zeroes in on some men, bringing me along as he attempts to sway the conversation to my failed engagement and the fact that I'm back on the marriage mart.

"This is Mr. Collins, Mr. Edwards and Mr. Lovell," my father does some quick introductions before he jumps back to extolling my virtues.

I keep a stiff smile on, even though hearing him talk about me as if it's the nineteenth century is enough to send me in a fit.

I keep my back straight, my posture excellent as I pretend to listen to the conversation, nodding every now and then.

"Your daughter is exquisite. I fail to imagine anyone would say no to her," one of the men comments, his eyes moving suggestively over my body. I keep myself from shuddering in disgust, instead trying to look for Bass from the corner of my eye.

He's right by a Bernini sculpture depicting Bacchus. And just like the God of wine, he's holding a plate of grapes in his hand, slowly bringing the fruit to his mouth in a sensual move.

It's… decadent.

His eyes are fixed on me as he opens his mouth to swallow one grape, that simple act making *me* swallow in return.

"Gianna?" My father's voice startles me.

"Yes, sorry I was woolgathering," I give them a pleasant smile, even though inside I'm all but cursing them and their lecherous gazes.

"If you'll excuse me, I'll go grab some refreshments," I say as I leave the conversation.

One of the men, Mr. Collins, I think, decides to offer his services and accompany me.

I walk stiffly by his side, trying to keep a distance so we're not touching, even though I can see that's all he's trying to do.

"Thank you, but it wasn't necessary to come with me," I tell him, hoping he'd take the hint and leave me alone.

"A pretty girl like you always needs a knight in shining armor," he says in what he wants to come across as a seductive tone, but only makes me want to gag.

"Right," I add drily, "I think there are enough armors in here. I don't need another one."

If he's not going to take the hint then I'm going to be a little more direct. I know my father all but gave them the green signal to me when he jumped into his rehearsed monologue for tonight, but I'm not about to let him parade me around for everyone to cop a feel—like this guy is clearly trying to do.

I increase my pace, hoping to get rid of him by simply losing him in the crowd.

"Be a good girl and don't shout," he says and I frown for a moment before he roughly pushes me to the right, my back quickly hitting a wall. Everyone around is too busy to realize he's basically dragged me to a dark corner.

His hand is on my mouth before I can even attempt to call out for Bass.

"Your father owes me, Gianna. A few millions. It's not enough that I'd…" his eyes trail down my body and he snarls as he focuses on the mark Bass had put on me, "marry you. But who said you're not good for a few minutes of fun. If you're a good girl, I might wipe his slate clean," he drawls, right before his hand goes for the opening of my dress.

My eyes widen in terror as I realize what he's trying to do, and it takes me a moment to get my bearings and try to defend myself.

But as the mental fog lifts from my mind and I start to act rationally again, I realize I don't need to do anything.

Not when Bass is twisting the man's hand until I hear bones cracking. Certainly not as he brings him to his knees, continuing to contort his arm until the man is yelping in pain.

Hand over his mouth, he doesn't allow him even the smallest sound.

"Are you ok?" He looks at me, taking in my terrified expression.

I slowly nod, surprised I'm capable of reacting at all.

"Good," he grunts. "I told you I'd have to kill anyone who touched you, sunshine. And it seems I have my first victim," his mouth twists in a cruel smile.

Before I know it, his hand makes contact with the side of Mr. Collins' face, pushing it all the way to the ground, his cheek hitting the marble floor.

"You touched what's mine," Bass leans in to whisper. "No one touches what's mine," he says right before he lifts his face a little, gaining some momentum to slam it again onto the floor.

Mr. Collins' eyes are wide, both fear and pain in his gaze as he flails his arms around in an attempt to get himself out of Bass' hold.

But he stands no chance. Not when he's not even half his size.

Bass continues to bash his head against the floor until the man passes out from pain. Instead of letting him go, though, he lifts him up by his throat, his body limp in his hands.

A loud snap, and Mr. Collins' head falls, bent at an awkward angle.

"You..." I blink. "You actually killed him," I whisper as I take a step back.

"Of course I did," he smiles at me. "I don't make empty promises, sunshine."

He drops the body to the floor, taking a step towards me.

"Are you afraid?" He raises an eyebrow.

My eyes go from him to the body on the floor and back to him, a sense of terror enveloping me but also one of satisfaction.

Because he saved me.

He's the only one who's ever saved me.

I shake my head vehemently.

"No. He wasn't going to let me go. I'm glad you stopped him. Before..."

In two steps he's in front of me, his big body pushing me into the wall and caging me with his huge arms.

"You're mine, little one," he says in a husky voice, his breath coming in short spurts—from the adrenaline of the kill no doubt.

Because I know he enjoyed it. I saw the way his mouth curled up in satisfaction at the sound of bones snapping. I'd seen it before too. When he'd dispatched the robber.

He likes killing.

"I know these motherfuckers want you. You're too perfect for this world, and every fucking man wants to touch you," he brings the back of his hand to my cheek, "feel how soft your skin is, how sweet your lips taste." His lips hover on top of mine, close, but not touching.

"And that's why you have me, sunshine. Because I'm capable of killing them all," he all but growls in my ear. "I'm the only man for you because only *I* can protect you. And because of that, only *I* get to touch you."

"You're saying this now," I give him a sad smile. "But how long will this last? A few weeks? A few months?" I blink rapidly, trying to stop the tears from forming in my eyes. "You know I'll end up marrying someone at some point. We can have our fun but..."

"No buts." He tips my chin up to look at him. "This isn't some temporary shit for me, Gianna. I'm in it for the long haul. I'm not going to give you up for anyone, much less let some bastard put his slimy hands on you. If I have to kill all your husbands, then so be it. If I have to steal you away, even better. But make no mistake." His nostrils flare, his breathing harsh. I'm so captivated by his steely eyes that I can only nod at everything he says.

"You. Are. Mine," he enunciates each word before his lips are finally on mine, giving me the peace I'd been searching for all along.

Because he has the power to rile me up and send me over the edge. But he's also there to calm me.

"Now here's what we're going to do. I'm going to get rid of this body, make the crime scene look like a robbery, and you're going to say that he remembered he had something to do and he left you alone at the refreshments' table."

"What about the CCTV?" I ask, worried. I don't want Bass to get in trouble for me.

"Don't worry about it, sunshine. Go back and put on your best smile and I'll do the dirty work."

"Ok," I nod, placing my trust in him.

"Just remember. When I'm done," he pauses, licking his lips as he stares at me. "I'm coming for my due."

And just like that, he's gone, body in tow.

I remain in the same spot for a moment, trying to understand what it is that he makes me feel. Because it's not ordinary. No, it's anything but ordinary when he's capable of killing for me.

He already killed for me.

His parting words are both a warning and a promise. And I find that I can't wait... for both.

Chapter Eleven

Bass

"I've taken care of it already," Cisco confirms as I return to the party.

"Good. Thank you," I reply, about to hang up.

"You're taking an awful long time with that mission, uncle. I hope you haven't had a change of heart," he chuckles.

"Don't worry. I'm on it," I answer curtly.

"I'll be waiting." He hangs up first.

I should have asked him if he was behind the bomb on Benedicto's car, but something tells me he wouldn't have been too forthcoming with that answer.

Dario was right that Cisco isn't the same young man I used to know. Maybe it's the new responsibilities getting to him, but I've noticed a coldness to him that wasn't there before.

It's like he's barely holding himself from wrecking destruction on Guerra—and everyone who stands in his way.

Not only is his urgency suspicious but also the way he wants to go about it.

I know it's not my place to question his orders, but I can't help but be skeptical about his reasoning. Somehow, I don't think it's just the old DeVille-Guerra enmity that's driving his hatred towards the family. I'd suspected before that there might be something more, something of a personal nature. And as I've observed him more, I can bet there's something he's not telling me—or anyone.

As a young kid, he'd always been a little different from the rest. Quiet, withdrawn, not very social. I'd always thought it had been because he'd known what awaited him, and the responsibility had felt heavy on his shoulders. After all, he'd spent all his childhood and teenage years studying and preparing to take over his father's position.

Maybe *he* is trying to prove something by going after Guerra so aggressively, but I don't think I like his approach.

And as much as I know my duty to the famiglia and that I'm not supposed to question my orders, every day it's becoming harder and harder to actually go through with the plan.

More than anything because I've gotten to know Gianna better, and a public ruination like Cisco wants would truly hurt her.

As much as she's never addressed her reputation, I can tell the rumors bother her a great deal, even though she tries not to show it. I've also gotten to know enough of her to realize that she doesn't have a healthy relationship with men, and her reputation might end up being a product of them taking advantage of her.

Benedicto clearly hasn't set a very good example by parading her around all his acquaintances in hopes someone might offer for her. Certainly, he hasn't shown her there's anything more to her than her body.

I'd witnessed that first hand with how she'd reacted to me. Whenever we are in a more intimate setting, her first inclination is to see what *she* can do for me, and not the other way around.

It makes me wonder if she hasn't been conditioned to think that all she can offer someone is her body, and that as long as she gets a man off, her job is done.

The thought that people would have used her like that makes me so mad, I want to kill each and every man that's ever laid a finger on her.

And it also brings me to my current dilemma.

I'd been a fucking asshole when I'd blackmailed her to blow me, and as I build a more accurate picture of who Gianna Guerra is, I can't help but regret I'd treated her like everyone else before—I'd used her.

It doesn't matter that in that moment I'd only wanted to get even with her for her stupid pranks, or get her off her high horse by forcing her to her knees. At the end of the day, I'm just another bastard who'd used her.

Fuck!

I'm going to have my work cut out for me to make sure she understands she has more to give than her body—way more. And because of that, I'm not going to pressure her into anything she doesn't want to do. I'll go slow—though it kills me to—and I'll show her that I'm not with her because I want in her pants.

But as I've gotten to know her better, it's not only her motivations that I've come to understand but also question mine.

For a while now I've known that there's no way I'm going to go through with the plan. I don't think I could stand myself if I was the cause of her tears and sadness. And a public humiliation would no doubt end her.

And make her hate me.

And I can't have that. No matter how much Cisco's on my back to complete the mission, I'm not going to be able to do it.

I've been racking my brain to think of alternatives, but I fear the only way for both of us to make it out alive is to simply disappear.

That means I need to use every single connection I have to get us new identities and a way to escape both Cisco and Benedicto's scrutiny.

As I return to the museum, I immediately spot her at the Greco-Roman exhibit. She's by the sidelines, a glass of champagne in her hand as she looks aloof at everyone trying to approach her.

It's easy to see that every man in her vicinity is smitten with her, their eyes unable to veer off her location.

My lip twitches in displeasure knowing she's alone and defenseless, no trace of Benedicto and Cosima in the vicinity.

I stalk across the room, my eyes fixed on her, and I note the immediate moment she spots me too.

She strengthens her back, the corner of her mouth slightly curling up, her eyes big and luminous as she turns that pretty gaze towards me.

"Is it done?" She comes towards me, her body moving sinuously in what I can only describe as an assault to the senses.

There's simply no match to Gianna, anywhere in the world.

"Yes. It shouldn't give you any problems," I nod, offering her my arm as I take her for a quick stroll around the room.

"People are staring at us," she whispers, her gaze darting around.

And they are. They're probably wondering what someone like *me* could be doing with someone like her.

"Let them stare."

For the first time I find that I don't mind my scar anymore. If Gianna can overlook it, then that's all that matters.

"Where are we going?" she frowns when she sees us exiting the exhibit and heading towards the stairs.

"It's a surprise," I whisper in her hair.

In no time we're in the middle of a dance floor, the Blue Danube in full swing as I swoop her in my arms.

She takes her position immediately, the music calling to her. One hand comes to rest on my shoulder, the other nestled within mine as I lead her into the waltz.

"I didn't know you could waltz," she says, almost breathless. Her cheeks are flushed, a raw smile on her face as she looks at me.

"There's a lot you don't know about me, sunshine," I reply, twirling her in the middle of the floor.

We're surrounded by tens of other couples, all giving themselves to the dance and not minding who else is on the dance floor.

"That's right, isn't it. I don't really know you," her teeth nibble at her lower lip, a small frown appearing on her perfect features.

"I'm not a deep person, Gianna. What you see is what you get with me," I grunt, not liking the line of conversation. Though it is technically true that she doesn't know much about me.

"Who taught you how to waltz?" She asks and I stiffen.

I should have realized this would come up eventually.

"My mother," I answer briskly.

"The one who cheated on your father?"

"The same one." My tone is dry as I reply, but I quickly catch myself. It's not Gianna's fault for my issues with my mother. And it's normal for her to be curious about my past. There's already so much I can't *yet* tell her, I might as well give her *some* glimpses into it.

"She was often lonely at home. I was the youngest of three children and my older brothers were already teenagers when I was born. After they left home, I was the only one left to keep her company."

"So she taught you how to dance?"

I grimace at the question, the memories a tad too unpleasant for such an exquisite night. Still, I indulge her.

"She had a flair for the dramatic. She was used to a glamorous lifestyle, but when my father stopped letting her go out, she started entertaining herself. First it was the dances, and tea parties, and all sorts of things she could come up with. Then, it was the men..." I trail off.

"Why did he stop letting her out?" Gianna asks as I move her towards the back of the room.

"I told you she had a penchant for theatrics. They couldn't go anywhere without her causing a scandal. Retrospectively, I don't think my mother was well... mentally. But my father didn't know that, or he didn't want to accept. Rather than have her embarrass our family, he preferred keeping her out of the public eye."

One twirl, and Gianna comes face to face with me, her chest flush against mine. The proximity is killing me, and I swear I can feel her body heat through both our clothes. It's like a drug, enthralling and intoxicating me.

"You were at home when she would bring the men over, weren't you?" Her voice is concerned, her touch comforting as she slowly moves her hand from my shoulder up my neck, cupping my jaw.

I nod.

"I'm sorry. It must have been horrible to see that," she purses her lips, giving me a sad smile.

"It's in the past," I mumble, though that's not the worst I witnessed during that time.

"I don't really remember my mother," she suddenly admits. "I have flashes of her, and I remember her smile. But other than that... I only know what people tell me about her."

My arm tightens around her, and I bring her closer, realizing this isn't easy for her, either.

Everyone knows the rumors about Benedicto's first wife, and that had been the main reason why he'd gotten away with marrying Cosima so soon after.

"That she was a whore and that she slept with the entire city," she gives a dry laugh. "A bit of a déjà vu, isn't it?"

"Stop it. Don't say that."

I don't want to hear her undervalue herself. Not when she's so precious.

"Why? It's the truth," she sighs. "You know that too, Bass. You don't have to pretend you haven't heard what they say about me."

"Is it true?" I ask her directly, almost beating myself for it. I'd rather not know, all things considered. But I can't stop myself from being curious.

"Would you believe me if I said no?" she asks in a small voice, as if ready to be called a liar.

"I'll believe you," I bring her hand to my mouth, kissing her knuckles.

"You're sweet. Even if you probably don't mean it."

"I do. I'll believe what you tell me." I look her in the eyes, letting her see the sincerity behind my words.

I've already crucified her enough based on appearances' sake. But now I know better. I know *her* better. And I want to learn everything about her.

Because she's mine.

I guess there's no escaping it. Deep down I must have realized this pull I have towards her from the very beginning, and I preferred to fight it, thinking she's everything I despised in a woman.

But I've been lying to myself all along.

There's no escaping her.

"Most of the rumors are made up by guys that I reject," she takes a deep breath, biting her lip again as if she's worried I'm not going to believe her. "If I reject their advances, or refuse to go out with them, they're quick to say they've already fucked me," she shrugs, but I can see that it hurts her.

"Haven't you tried to refute the rumors?"

"Who will people believe," she laughs. "A guy who thinks he's the shit and can fuck anything that walks, or a girl that's already branded a sinful Jezebel?" She shakes her head. "I did try in the beginning. But it didn't solve anything. People believe what they want to believe. After that, why bother trying?"

"Thank you for telling me," I tell her, and a slight blush creeps up her cheeks as she turns her face away.

"No one's asked me for my side of the story, you know…" she trails off, looking in the distance. "They automatically assume it's true. They ask for details, and stuff like that. But no one's ever asked me if it was true."

"Because they're jealous of you, sunshine. It's easier for other girls to turn you into the enemy because you're so much better than them. And it's even easier for guys to malign you because you're too unattainable. They want to have you, even if it's just a fantasy."

"I guess so," she nods dispassionately.

Without even thinking of who might be watching, I stop moving, my fingers on her jaw as I force her to look at me.

"Listen to me, Gianna, and listen well. You don't owe anyone anything. Let them talk because *you* know the truth." She blinks repeatedly at my words, almost confused. "And because *I* know the truth."

"I… I don't know what to say…" So many emotions seem to cross over her features at my words, her eyes watery as she just raises herself on her tiptoes to give me a sweet kiss.

In the middle of the ballroom, where everyone can see, she's kissing her bodyguard—her ugly ass bodyguard.

But no one minds us. Not when they are all caught up in their own little bubble. And I take advantage of that to tug her to me, finding an exit and taking her down a dark corridor and towards an exhibit that isn't open to the party.

"Bass?" she asks, that soft voice of hers only going straight to my cock and making me harder than I've been in my entire life.

"I have you, sunshine," I rasp just as I push her towards the wall, my hands on her waist as I lower my head to taste her lips.

The entire area is dark, the only source of light coming from some exhibit cases in the middle of the room.

Still, I easily find my way around her body, my palms molding to the contour of her ass.

"This feels so wicked, Bass," she giggles as I make my way down her neck, kissing and licking at the flesh until she's breathing hard, her own hands moving down my shoulders as she keeps me glued to her side.

"I want to taste you," I speak against her skin. I have to make a conscious effort to slow down, my desire for her too overwhelming.

Fuck, but I've never reacted like this to anyone in the past. Her presence is an instantaneous aphrodisiac, my body always primed for hers.

"Taste me?" she asks on a breathless tone, almost uncertain of what I mean.

I slowly bring my hand up her thigh, caressing her leg as I lift up her dress.

"A taste of your sweet little pussy, that's all I want."

For now. But I don't say that out loud. Because fuck knows I want more. So much more and in such depraved ways that I'd only scare her. But I don't want her to think I'm a horndog and that I'm only in it for the sex.

But I'm already salivating for a taste of her. Hell, I want to bathe in her scent, cover myself from head to toe in her aroma. For the first time, I'm curious what it's like to fully let go with a woman.

"Oh, ok," she immediately agrees, but her voice seems anything but certain.

"I need you to be sure of this, sunshine. Otherwise I'm not going to do something you don't want me to," I tell her, bringing my hand to her hair and brushing it from her face so I can see her expression.

I've already made that mistake once. No way I'm going to repeat it.

She turns those stunning eyes of hers towards me, her tongue peeking out to wet her lower lip.

"I do. It's just..." she stammers, "I've never..." she doesn't finish the sentence, immediately looking away in embarrassment.

Shit! No one's ever gone down on her.

Fucking bastards!

Though I'm incensed that no one's ever cared about her pleasure before, there's also a side of me that preens at being the one to give it to her. And I will. Fuck but I will. I'll make sure she comes on my face until I'm drowning in her juices.

Pretty sure there's no death sweeter than that.

"Ah, sunshine," I close my eyes at the new tidbit of information, satisfaction simmering inside of me. "I promise I'll take care of you," I continue as I swipe my thumb over her cheek.

"I know you will," she replies affectionately, spreading my open palm to her face as she nuzzles her cheek to it. "You always do."

Her trust in me floors me, especially when it's unwarranted, and I feel compelled to share a piece of myself with her too.

"I'll let you in on a secret," I whisper, "I've never gone down on a woman before either."

She gasps, her mouth parted in shock as she just stares at me.

"You're lying," she exclaims.

"Nope," I give her a lopsided smile. "Scouts honor," I wink at her.

And it *is* the truth. That might make me an asshole, but I'd never wanted to before. Now... The more I look into her lovely face the more mesmerized I become by the sight of her.

"I'd like that then," she says softly, fluttering her lashes at me.

It's all the encouragement I need to get to my knees.

She's watching me closely, her eyes glazed with desire as they follow my every movement.

Slowly—tantalizingly so—I lift her dress until it rests over her hips, getting her to hold on to it while I stare at the wonder in front of me.

She's wearing a pair of white silky panties, her arousal evident as I see them already molded to her pussy lips, already drenched.

Now that I have her in front of me, spread open like this, I want to take my time learning her—learning her reactions.

I take one finger and I dip it between her legs, slowly stroking her over her panties.

The effect is immediate as her knees buckle, a tremor going through her entire body.

"Bass," her throaty voice is only urging me on, the thought of making her come on my tongue enough to make *me* come.

"I got you, pretty girl," I murmur, bringing my nose to her pussy and inhaling her musky scent.

Fuck!

This right here is going to drive me mad. Because one taste isn't going to be enough. I'll need to fucking feast on her forever.

I slide her panties to the side, gently probing her folds. She's so fucking wet, her arousal immediately coating my finger.

I don't even think as I bring it to my lips, tasting her essence.

Damn, how am I supposed to last if just the taste of her is enough to make me combust?

I quickly palm my cock through my pants, adjusting my erection.

This is about her. All about her.

Sliding her panties down her legs, I quickly pocket them, my gaze riveted on her small pussy, her lips glistening with need even in the dimly lit room.

Fuck, but I don't think I've ever seen a more perfect sight.

Once I've looked my fill, I prop her against the wall, cupping her ass as I lift her legs and place them over my shoulders.

She's light enough and I'm strong enough that the position isn't uncomfortable. In fact, as my tongue makes contact with her pussy, I'd say it's the most comfortable position I've ever been in.

Her hands find my hair as I give her a long lick, her gasps and whimpers my guides as I try out things she might like. And when I wrap my lips around her clit, sucking it into my mouth before gently biting it, her loud moan tells me everything I need to know.

"Bass, that feels…" she trails off on a moan as I continue to make love to her pussy with my mouth, alternating between sucking and licking, concentrating my attention on her clit until it's swollen and crying for relief.

"I think…" she doesn't get to finish her sentence when she starts coming, her thighs clenching around my head, the opening of her pussy spasming around my tongue.

More juices gush out of her and I continue to lap at her, swallowing it all.

Fuck. Me.

I'm an addict. One taste. That's what it took for me to become wholly and irreparably addicted to her.

"Bass," she cries out when I continue to suck on her clit, wanting to see if I can wring yet another orgasm from her.

My scalp is all but sore as she continues to tug at my hair, all of it telling me that her pussy and my tongue have just become best friends.

I only release her when she's begging me to stop, telling me she can't take it anymore. Reluctant, but already looking forward to my next meal between her legs, I place her feet back on the ground.

She's shaking and she can barely stand upright as I move up her body. I snake my arm around her waist, letting her hold on to me for support.

"Wow," she breathes out, her skin shiny with perspiration. "That was wow," she continues, shaking her head in disbelief.

"I'll eat your pussy anytime you want me to, sunshine. *Any* time," I drawl suggestively. Her face is flushed, some of her make up already ruined.

She looks like someone who's been thoroughly fucked. And pride swells in my chest that *I* did that.

The evening ends uneventfully as we all get back to the house. Benedicto is visibly upset that his attempt at selling his daughter wasn't as successful as he'd wanted it to be.

And as I retire to my room, I can't help but reminisce the way she'd felt against me, the taste of her as she'd come undone all over my face.

"Damn," I shake my head at myself in the mirror, slowly unbuttoning my shirt.

I have it bad.

There's this aching vulnerability to Gianna that sometimes makes me want to take her in my arms and never let go—show her that the world doesn't have to be an awful place.

Because from everything I've seen so far, Gianna isn't living. She's just alive.

Despite her glamorous lifestyle, her fancy clothes and cars, and all those ostentatious social media pictures, she's not enjoying any of it.

She's simply existing.

I take my clothes off and hop into the shower, all the while my thoughts revolving around her and trying to understand her better.

There's just something about her that awakens a part of me I thought did not exist. A gentle part that wants to protect and not destroy. In truth, every time I'm in her presence, my heart clenches in an unfamiliar way, the need to shield her of the evils of the world so overwhelming, it makes me want to act out of character.

Stopping the water, I put on a fresh pair of boxer briefs before going back to the room.

But just as I exit the bathroom, I stop dead in my tracks at the vision in front of me, daintily sitting on my bed.

"Oh," the word flies out of her mouth as she takes me in, her eyes greedily roaming all over my body in an appreciative manner.

It's times like this that I'm thankful I had the foresight to work out and keep in shape, because I love having at *least* something that's pleasing to her eyes.

"What are you doing here?" I ask, my lips quirking up in amusement.

It's the last place I expected to see her, especially since she'd suddenly gotten very shy after what happened at the gala.

"I was wondering..." she pauses to wet her lips, her eyes fixed on my chest as if she's making a conscious effort to not let them go lower. Catching herself staring, she fakes a cough before continuing. "I was wondering if I could sleep here again."

"Why?"

Her eyes widen at my sudden question but I feel compelled to ask.

"It's not that I don't want that, sunshine. Hell, I'll be a lucky bastard if I get to sleep *anywhere* near you. But what prompted this?"

She releases a breath, relieved.

"I think I sleep better with you," she admits, a blush staining her features.

"You think?"

"I do," she amends, "I can't remember the last time I slept that well. You make me feel safe."

"I make you feel safe?" I repeat, pleased with her words. And as I come closer to her, that night gown she's wearing is teasing me to perdition with the way her body peeks through, her nipples hard and puckered against the material.

She nods, looking up at me with those big eyes of hers, and suddenly I'm struck by the innocence and vulnerability I see reflected in them.

"I'm glad," I tell her, moving to drop a kiss on her forehead. "That's the highest praise a man could get from his woman," I tell her, wrapping my arms around her and gently placing her in the middle of the bed before stretching out next to her.

"I'm your woman?" Her lashes flutter as she looks at me in wonder.

"Of course," I reply, almost incensed. "I told you, sunshine. You were mine from the moment we met. You just didn't know it then," I smirk at her.

"Yours… I think I like that," she whispers, borrowing deeper into my chest. "I think I like that very much."

"Sleep," I murmur, holding her close until her breathing starts to regulate before joining her too.

Gianna wasn't wrong, though. Sleeping next to her is, indeed, the best sleep I've ever had. And for the first time since I got out of prison, I feel like a normal man again.

It's the following day that I find out that Gianna's demons might run deeper than I'd thought.

She'd already gone back to her room early in the morning, so I'm surprised to see her knock on my door again, asking me to accompany her downstairs.

"My father says he wants to speak to me, and I'd rather you were there," she tells me, her voice lacking her usual confidence.

"Do you know why?" I ask as we make our way downstairs. She shakes her head.

"I can only hope it's something trivial," she sighs, and she looks like someone heading for the guillotine, her features pale, her lips pursed.

But as we enter the living room, her expression worsens tenfold. She stops in her tracks, looking as if she'd seen a ghost.

"Ah, there you are, Gianna," Benedicto exclaims as he gets to his feet, coming over to our side and gesturing to his guest to do the same.

A man around Benedicto's age, his body is on the leaner side, his features smooth and attractive.

"You remember Clark Goode, don't you? He used to come with us to Newport a few years back." Benedicto starts introducing Goode, a former associate of his.

"Right," is the only word that comes out of Gianna's mouth, and I note distress in her body language.

Goode immediately goes for the kill, taking a step towards her to give her a hug and kiss her cheeks.

One step back, and I can tell Gianna is beyond uncomfortable, so I promptly place myself between the two of them.

"If you could keep your distance," I say, knowing I'm courting Benedicto's anger for my interference.

"And who are you?" he frowns at me.

"Her bodyguard." I reply tersely.

There's something about the man that doesn't sit well with me, from his overly familiar gestures with Gianna to the way he regards me now, as if I weren't fit to lick the dirt off his shoes.

"Mr. Bailey, Clark isn't a danger," Benedicto tries to make light of the situation.

"Miss Gianna is my charge and I need to ensure her protection at all times, Mr. Guerra. It's what you hired me for."

"Bah! Danger in my own house! As if," he exclaims, shaking his head. "Besides, Clark here might very well join the family soon."

"What do you mean?" It's the first time Gianna speaks up, and I note a tremor underlying her tone.

"He's been widowed for some time now, and he's decided it's time to find a new wife." Benedicto continues, and I don't like where this is going.

Worse still is Gianna's reaction and the way I know there's something wrong with her but I can't openly comfort her and ask her what's happening.

"Widowed?" She snickers. "How come? Didn't you rob the cradle? What was she? Eighteen, nineteen? How could she be dead unless you killed her yourself?" She asks, condemnation clear in her voice.

It also tells me all I need to know about the man in front of me and Gianna's stance towards him.

"Gianna!" Benedicto is quick to call her out, telling her to behave herself. "Don't be rude! Clark has offered to merge our businesses. You know what that means for this family," he raises an eyebrow at her.

"So that's it," she shakes her head in disbelief. "You found me a husband."

"Gianna," Goode addresses her, a sinister smile on his face. "I know you're a willful young lady. But I believe we'll suit perfectly." He smirks, before turning to Benedicto and adding. "Why, I know just the way to make her behave, Benedicto," he says with a creepy laugh, as if he's not openly stating his intentions with her.

My fists are balled in my lap, and it takes everything in me not to get up and smash his head against the glass table in the middle of the room.

In fact, that image continues to haunt my mind as I imagine myself holding him down and cutting him to shreds for even daring to imagine that he'd get to Gianna—ever.

Not while I'm here.

But I know I can't act. I can't give away my feelings for Gianna, or our relationship.

I need to bear it.

Fuck! Restraint has never been my strong suit, but if I ruin everything right now, then I won't be able to help Gianna from behind bars, or worse—dead.

Her back straight, she keeps on looking from her father to Clark, her eyes moist as if she's barely holding out her tears.

Benedicto and Clark continue to talk, but my focus is wholly on Gianna and the way she's trying her hardest not to break down in front of them. And the way Goode is looking at her as if he can't wait to get his hands on her does nothing to calm me.

"We can hold the engagement party in a month, and the wedding soon after," Benedicto suggests, and Gianna's sudden intake of breath alerts me to her distress.

Fuck, how I wish I could at least hold her hand so that she knows I'm here for her. Instead, I can only search for her eyes and give her a small nod, wanting her to know I'm here for her.

A few more tense minutes, and Gianna excuses herself, all but dashing towards her room. I don't look back at Benedicto or Goode as I follow after her.

There's a loud thud as she shuts her door with a bang.

"Gianna?" I knock on her door, worried about her vehement reaction.

"I need a moment alone," her voice comes from the other side of the door. "Please," she adds, just as I want to insist.

"Are you ok?" I ask, needing that for my peace of mind.

"Yes. I'll see you in a bit," she mumbles.

With a sigh, I leave her, heading downstairs to where Benedicto is seeing Clark out.

"She'll come around. Besides, she knows you. Better than a stranger," Benedicto tells Clark, trying to appease him.

He doesn't seem very pleased by Gianna's reaction to him, and the more I study him, the more I get this feeling that there's something *wrong* with him.

"Never do that again, Mr. Bailey," Benedicto warns after Goode leaves, telling me that my outburst had been out of place.

"I need to look out for Gianna's welfare, as I've been hired to do," I answer curtly.

"And Clark is not a danger. From now on, consider him an exception—to everything. He can see Gianna whenever he wants, and you have my permission to give them time alone."

My nostrils flare, my lip twitching as I barely contain my anger.

The fact that I still need to keep up my ruse is the only thing that's saving Benedicto from an untimely demise.

Certainly, the more he talks about the upcoming marriage between Gianna and Clark the more I want to rearrange his face and tell him that there isn't going to be *any* marriage.

After he's done with his monologue, he dismisses me, leaving the house.

One look at my watch and I realize Gianna's had enough time to calm herself. Because I need answers, and fast. So that I know when to plan Goode's funeral. Because her reaction had been unusual—too unusual for someone who's usually the first to show her claws. She'd been eerily quiet in his presence and that tells me that he scares her.

What did he do to you, Gianna?

From what I'd gathered, that's the only explanation. And I feel a pain deep in my chest at the thought of anyone harming her.

"Gianna?" I'm back at her door, knocking.

The first knock goes unanswered. The second too. It's only when I start banging against the door that I realize something must be wrong.

"Gianna!" I yell, getting more worried by the second. Without a second thought, I take a step back, placing all my strength in my leg as I kick against the door. It gives way immediately, the lock broken.

"Gianna?" I call out as I enter her room, frowning to find it bare.

"Gianna, where are you?" I continue to ask as I look everywhere.

The sound of running water draws my attention to the bathroom, and as I take a step towards the closed door, I feel my heart plummet in my chest.

She's just taking a shower.

But as I open the door to the bathroom, it's to find a naked Gianna in a half filled tub, her eyes closed, her breathing labored. The water is a murky red as blood flows freely from two cuts in her wrists.

"My God," I mutter, barely finding my voice.

My body mind goes into action mode as I rush to her side, scooping her from the water and taking a few towels to press to her wrists, carefully bandaging them to stop the blood loss.

"What?" I hear a gasp from behind me, the housekeeper mumbling something as I bark at her to call the ambulance.

"Pretty girl, I got you," I whisper to her, brushing my hand over her pale features.

"Don't you dare leave me, sunshine, or I'm going to fucking come after you and I'll make you regret this," I rasp, my voice thick with emotion.

My own eyes feel watery as I feel for her pulse, relieved to see it's there—weak but there.

"I got you," I continue to talk to her, saying a small prayer in my head so that she'll be all right.

She needs to be alright.

"Sunshine, I didn't find you just so you could leave me..." I mumble, my entire being overtaken by the most intense feelings I've ever felt in my life.

I hold on to her frail body, slowly rocking with her and praying I wasn't too late. That the ambulance isn't too late.

You need to live, Gianna. For me. For us, and for everything I never got the chance to tell you.

It feels like an eternity before the ambulance arrives and we're rushed to the hospital.

Neither Benedicto nor Cosima were at home when it happened and I couldn't reach either of them on the way to the hospital.

In a way it's better, since I'm sure Gianna can do away with their fake concerns.

But as they hurry her to the emergency room, I'm not exactly welcomed since I'm not family.

"I'm her fiancé," I lie. "Please just... make sure she's ok."

The waiting is the worst.

Every single scenario crosses my mind, and I have a hard time dealing with everything that's happening.

"Damn," I curse out, resting my head in my hands.

The adrenaline from finding her almost dead in her tub starts wearing off, and a deep pain takes root instead. Because what would I have done if she'd...

Fuck, but I can't even say the word. I can't imagine her being there one minute and gone the next.

I simply can't imagine a world without her.

I've never been prone to sentimental displays, and I don't think I've ever cried in my life. But as I bring my hand up to my eyes, rubbing the weariness away, it's to find them wet.

I stare in wonder at my fingers, the tears fresh, and I realize just how deep my feelings for her run.

How far I've fallen...

Sure, in the beginning it might have been just a maddening physical attraction. But now?

I'm screwed. I'm well and truly screwed.

In my line of work, you protect your heart at all costs, because that is the one weakness that can cost you everything.

And as I stare at the white hallway of the hospital, the smell of bleach permeating my senses, it dawns on me that I've found my weakness—my one debilitating weakness. And she has one foot in the grave.

I failed to protect my heart.

But as I finally realize the extent of my feelings for Gianna, and the fact that she may literally *be* my heart, I vow to myself that if she makes it out alive I'm going to do whatever I can to protect her.

I won't let Clark or anyone else touch a single strand of hair on her head.

And if I have to fight my own family to keep her safe, then so be it.

She's mine.

And it's time I protected what's mine.

CHAPTER TWELVE

GIANNA

It's pure torture to sit still.

From the moment I'd entered the room and seen Clark, my entire body had gone into emergency mode, my mind slowly slipping from me.

The most immediate reaction had been this insane urge to run and hide. But I knew I couldn't do that. Not when he was my father's guest. And so I forced myself to not show the storm brewing inside of me.

It's what I do best after all. It's what's gotten me to this point. After all, isn't there the saying *fake it till you make it*?

I've certainly faked my smile, my posture and my unshaking limbs one too many times. I've been put in enough situations over the years where all I wanted to do was shut down and hide deep inside my mind.

But it's all in vain when my mind is the biggest enemy.

When thoughts become small needles prickling at my skin and making me feel like a stranger in my own body—unwanted, unwelcomed.

Like a crescendo, it starts with small ideas that increase in magnitude until my entire brain is flooded by foreign thoughts—the what ifs. Fear is my best friend, and dread is my only companion.

It's in moments like that I wish I could somehow exit my own body—escape this maddening hell that gives me no respite.

And when the mental fog is at its worst, I can only wish I were anywhere but in the present. Ironic, since the past is even worse, while the future looks bleak.

So I find myself in the paradoxical situation of wishing I both existed and *not*.

Just like that, now I have to exert an extraordinary amount of strength to keep myself from bolting, or doing something worse—like smash the glass table and hold a shard to Clark's jugular, digging it in his skin until he bleeds dry, his blood the only thing that would ever give me a semblance of peace.

Wishful thinking.

I haven't seen him since that night, two years ago. I'd breathed out relieved when I heard he'd gotten married, even though I'd felt sad for the girl he'd chosen to be his wife. Not that much older than me, she fit his mold—beautiful and youthful looking.

And the moment I hear he's been widowed, I know she can't have died of natural causes.

His eyes drift to mine as my father continues talking, that insidious smile of his aimed in my direction as his eyes drift all over my body.

The hairs on my arm stand up, and it takes everything within me not to show how that affects me, and how much revulsion he provokes in me. It's such a visceral feeling, my stomach churning, my heart beating fast as adrenaline courses through my veins.

I'm one second away from being sick on the floor.

I clench my fists, trying to control myself. If anything, I don't want to give him the satisfaction of seeing how much he scares me.

But when my father proclaims that *I* will be his next wife, I can't help myself.

"So that's it," I shake my head in disgust. "You found me a husband."

Of course he'd sell me out to Clark. His business is thriving, and his net worth is nothing to scoff at. And with the way creditors are running after my father...

He continues to chastise me, telling me the decision is final.

But I don't hear it anymore.

I can't hear it.

Not when the only sound is my throbbing pulse, the way I don't know how I'm going to make it out alive.

Bass is sitting next to me, the heat projected by his body the only thing remotely helping me deal with the turmoil forming inside me.

He's like a steady rock, there for me to cling to. And as he looks at me with worry in his eyes, I know he's not indifferent.

But he can't help me.

No one can.

I stare into empty space, avoiding to look at Clark more than I need to and wishing this meeting ended faster.

And when it finally does, I don't care as I run back to my room, barely acknowledging Bass' inquiries whether I am ok.

I'm not. I'm anything but ok.

But I can't deal with anyone right now. I can't deal, period.

Closing the door in his face, I gasp for air, finally allowing myself to show my weakness—but only in the sanctuary of my room.

I'm barely able to stand on two feet as I rummage my room for pills, feeling my lungs closing up, my throat sore as I keep trying to breathe in and out.

Why? Why is this my fate?

Maybe I could have survived a random husband. *Maybe.*

But Clark?

Clark is my nightmare personified. And I know exactly what awaits me with him.

Besides an untimely death.

He's a sadist of the biggest order. And the worst thing is that he *enjoys* hurting women. He gets off on fear. The more you fight him, the harder he gets.

I should know.

"No, no, no," I mumble to myself, barely coherent as images start assaulting me, my skin burning from his invasive touch.

I don't waste any time in taking off my clothes and going to the bathroom, turning the faucet on and climbing inside the empty tub as I wait for it to fill up.

Even so, I need to scrub myself clean. Scrub the memories. Scrub the flesh off my bones.

Anything to erase him from my body.

But the flashes won't stop coming, the images flooding my brain until I'm barely breathing, the pressure in my chest building up until I'm almost screaming.

I bring my fist to my chest, banging on it in an attempt to regulate my breath.

Nothing

The more I try, the more I feel him, next to me. Watching me.

The first time he'd come to my room I'd been barely fourteen. But puberty had hit me earlier, and his eyes had started wandering all too often.

I'd known something wasn't right from the first. He'd watch me in a way that made my skin crawl, his eyes always drifting to my chest and lower…

But he'd been my father's associate, and I couldn't say or do anything. Especially when we'd vacation together in New Port.

He'd always be there with his entourage as he and my father would discuss new business ventures.

It was a known pastime, and Cosima was entirely too excited to be among the high society of NewPort, even though she had to forcefully invite herself to events.

For me?

It had been the start of my hell.

That summer was the first time Clark came to my room. Even now, I can picture the moment perfectly. How I'd woken up to find him at the edge of my bed, his dick out as he'd jerked off while I was sleeping.

He'd noticed I was awake too, but that hadn't deterred him. If anything, it had made him go faster, a sick smile plastered on his face as he kept stroking himself.

I'd been terrified when I had opened my eyes to see him— especially like that. And out of that fear, I'd stayed still. I hadn't moved an inch. Not when he'd come closer to me, and not when he'd come all over my chest.

I stayed still and held my breath until he finally left.

I was so young back then, I barely realized what was happening.

But it persisted. Every day, he would come to my room in the middle of the night and he'd jerk off until he'd come all over my body.

Slowly, though, it escalated until he started using my hand to touch himself.

That's when I first reacted, screaming until he slapped me so hard I saw stars.

The next day I'd feigned serious illness and I'd managed to get home. Still, that didn't mean it all stopped. It just delayed the inevitable.

Tears are running down my cheeks as everything comes crashing in.

Fucking hell, but if I have to marry him…

I don't want to imagine the horrors I'll live through. I don't want to imagine what being near him would be like.

My mind blank of everything *but* that thought, I do the only thing that could save me.

End myself before *he* ends me.

My fingers are nimble as they grasp on to a blade from under the sink. Then, turning the water off so the tub doesn't overflow and alert them to what I'm doing, I simply lay back and bring the sharp edge to my wrist.

One cut on the left one, and one on the right one. Dropping the blade to the floor, I simply lay back, waiting for the blood to flow out of me.

The sting was minimal, the pain dulled by my already fogged up mind.

But as I lay there, my life force slowly leaking out of me, my thoughts slowly turn to *him*—Bass.

Initially someone I hated with every cell in my body, he'd turned out to be my biggest protector.

I wonder… will he feel sad for me?

I've never misjudged anyone as I did him. Certainly, no one's ever proven me wrong before.

But does it even matter now? When I'm not going to see him again?

Maybe in another life we could have met, fallen in love and behaved like normal people.

Not in this one.

Not when I'm anything but normal, and my family is the definition of *abnormal*. Not when my father owns me and can barter me like a piece of cattle, or risk facing the consequences.

At least I had some time with him. Some time to feel what it was like to be touched with affection and care, not in anger or cruelty.

He'd showed me I was more than just my body. More than just my reputation. And more than just a Guerra.

And it was my fault that I believed him and I lost myself in the illusion that maybe, I was more.

Now… my eyelids feel heavy, my breathing labored.

And for one last time, I wish things had been different. I wish I could have been free to be with him, and free to love him.

Love…

The corner of my mouth drags into a languid smile, the image of love burned behind my lids as I let myself imagine the possibilities.

I banish the bad thoughts, instead focusing on the fantasies.

I see us together, his arms wrapped around me, his heat emanating from his body and filling mine up. His smile—that crooked smile that is now the most beautiful sight—as he looks at me. I feel his hands on my body as they show me that love doesn't have to hurt—on the contrary, it heals.

His breath is on my face as he peppers my skin with kisses, moving down my body before stealthily sliding a ring on my finger and asking me to be his wife. His voice as he tells me he loves me like he's never loved anyone in his life.

His promise of eternity.

I feel sleep claim me—slowly. But I'm happy. Trapped in my illusion, I feel content for the first time in my life.

And I let go.

The beeping sounds from the machines wake me up. It takes me a moment to open my eyes and realize I am not—yet—dead.

Or at all.

By the windows, a man is with his back to me—a very familiar back.

"Bass?" I croak, my throat dry, my voice rough.

He turns, his features grave. He doesn't seem pleased.

He doesn't seem pleased at all.

He's slow as he comes towards me, taking a seat on the chair next to the bed and simply staring at me. He doesn't speak. He doesn't even blink.

He just stares at me as if he's seeing a ghost.

That's when I become aware of my surroundings—of the fact that I am in the hospital, hooked to machines, my wrists bandaged.

"Bass?" I ask again, the silence unnerving. My tongue peeks out to wet my lip as I bring my hand up to brush the hair out of my face.

There's some residual pain as I move, and Bass' eyes follow the white of the gauze closely, his gaze fixed on my wrist.

"You're scaring me, Bass..." I whisper.

And he does. Never mind the fact that I'm still alive. But the way he's looking at me, as if he's deeply disappointed in me, breaks me.

"I scare you?" He rasps, frowning as he shakes his head at me. "Me? I scare *you?*" he repeats. "You fucking scared *me*, Gianna. You went and..." he purses his lips, his eyes still on my bandaged wounds.

"How could you think of doing something like that?" His voice is soft as he brings his gaze to mine. "How?"

"I..." I trail off, unable to find the words to explain.

"I thought you were dead, sunshine," he breathes out, and I note the weariness on his features. "I thought you left me," he continues and he looks... desolate.

For me?

"I'm sorry," I say in a small voice, suddenly feeling guilty about worrying him.

The thing is that I've never had someone to care about me before. And in a not-so-great state of mind, I'd simply assumed no one would miss me.

"You're sorry for what? For not dying? Or for putting me through the worst fucking time of my life?"

"Both," I answer without thinking, and my eyes widen at the slip of tongue.

I meet his eyes and I see the same reaction.

"Sunshine, talk to me. What happened?"

"I can't marry him, Bass. I can't," I shake my head, tears already coating my lashes.

"What did he do to you?" He suddenly demands, his tone harsh and unyielding.

"He…" I pause, ashamed to tell him. "He's a bad man. A very bad man. And death is a hundred times more appealing than marrying him."

He frowns at my statement.

"I'll end up dead anyway," I give a bitter laugh, "but this way it will be by *my hand,* not his."

"What do you mean?"

"He's a sadist. He must have killed his last wife. Wouldn't be the first, or the last."

"How do you know that?" He fires back, looking at me intently.

"He…"

"He hurt you." He states point-blank, sparing me the pain of telling him—of reliving that.

I give a jerky nod.

"Fuck," he rises up, his hands on his face as he paces around the room. "You're not marrying him, sunshine. That I can promise you," he tells me confidently.

"Bass, I appreciate the thought but…"

"No. It's not just the thought. I'm going to work something out. That I promise you," he says as he comes to my side, seating himself on the bed next to me, his arm suddenly around me.

He leans down to kiss the top of my head, his hand closing over my shoulder in a tight embrace.

"If I have to get us fake identities and leave the country, I'll do it. I'll figure something out, but you're *never* marrying him. Or anyone else."

I raise my head to meet his gaze, his silvery eyes clear, his features full of determination.

"Bass," I smile at him, his words touching my heart.

Even if it's just platitudes, the fact that he wants to help me warms me on the inside.

"You're mine, Gianna, and I'm not going to let anyone harm you. Ever again," he emphasizes the words. "I knew something was up from the moment you saw him, and I was going to ask you about it but… Fuck, you have no idea what the sight of you in that tub, your blood in the water, your pulse barely there did to me. I…" he stops, closing his eyes on a deep sigh.

"I care about you, sunshine. *Deeply*." I blink repeatedly as I stare at him, shaking my head slightly to clear my ears in case I misheard him. "I can't bear the thought of losing you. The time between your house and the hospital alone took a decade off my life. The uncertainty of whether you were going to make it… I *can't* have that again."

"Bass, you… care for me?" I ask slowly—tentatively.

Yes, I'd known there was an insane chemistry between us from the beginning—regardless how much I tried to deny it. But I'd never expected his feelings to go deeper than attraction. To hear him say he cares for me is something I hadn't dared hope for.

"Of course I do, sunshine," his hand comes down to cup my face. "You're an amazing woman. Maybe it took me a while to see behind the mask you put to the outside world," he chuckles," but once I did there was no going back. There *is* no going back. You're mine."

His thumb moves slowly in circles across my cheek as I lose myself in those stunning eyes of his—finding that my own are getting teary again.

"I care about you too," I reply, a blush staining my cheeks as I quickly look away from him. "A lot," I feel the need to quantify it.

Because he has no idea how hard it is for me to trust another person—with my heart, with my body, with everything. Yet, in spite of all the walls I've put up, he's managed to crush them all, slowly embedding himself in my heart.

Maybe it was the way he shielded me with his body when the car exploded, or the way he'd stood up to me in front of Cosima. Or maybe, it was simply the way he accepted the real me, with my dreams and my aspirations, with my sadness and regrets.

He's the only one who's ever touched me with tenderness, and he's the only one who would have cared enough to see me live.

"Good," an arrogant smile appears on his face. "Then it means we're on the same page."

I nod.

"I'm going to say this only once, Gianna, so listen closely." His voice is low and rough, his tone serious. "You're not marrying Goode. You're not marrying *anyone* but me. I don't care if I have to go against your father, or whatever army of goons he has. I don't care if I have to kill every fucking man standing in my way."

"Ok," I reply softly, for the first time willing to place my trust in someone else.

"I'll never let another man put a finger on you, sunshine. They can look, but they can't touch," he speaks gently as he lowers his lips to my forehead. "You're mine and mine alone, and everyone who thinks to dispute that can fucking go to hell."

"Thank you..." I reply, my voice filled with emotion and every bit of love I have for him.

"Don't thank me. Not yet. Not until we're as far away from this place as possible. However," he playfully narrows his eyes at me, "don't think you're getting away for this stunt of yours. Fuck, you almost killed yourself, Gianna."

"I know," I sigh. "But at that moment, all I could think of was getting away. By any means."

"You have me now. Let me slay your monsters," he says in the softest tone, and my heart melts a little.

"I do," my lips tug up in a smile. "I have you now," I say just as I bring my hands to his face, cupping his cheeks and bringing him closer to me.

Closing my eyes, I let my lips hover over his, enjoying his proximity and bathing in his protective aura.

Because that's what he is.

My protector.

The slayer of my demons.

Leaning forward, I brush my lips against his, a small tremor going down my body at the contact.

Soft. They are so soft. From the beginning I've marveled at how soft they are when the rest of him is so hard.

I continue to tease his lips before I lick the seam with my tongue.

He growls low in his throat before his arms close around me, bringing me flush against his chest and deepening the kiss.

He sucks on my tongue, devouring me whole as I feel the desperation underlying this kiss—the intense emotions he stirs in me, and I in turn awaken in him.

Even as the kiss ends, we do not break apart, breathing in and out like one—his air, my air; my essence, his essence.

"Promise me you'll never try to do this again. Please, promise me," he rasps in a broken voice, and it finally dawns on me how much I hurt him.

And how much he cares.

"I promise," I immediately reply.

"Good. Good," he nods, more to himself. "I'll hold you to that."

Scooting over in bed, I let him join me as he tells me what had happened after he'd found me. How he'd alerted my father and Cosima but neither had seemed to care much as long as I survived.

They'd visited once while I'd been sedated, and after they'd ensured they hadn't lost their future investment, they'd promptly left the hospital, instructing Bass to be extra vigilant so I don't attempt to kill myself again.

Truthfully, I hadn't expected any other reaction from their part. But I can't help the way a part of me is hurt by my father's negligence, and the fact that he doesn't care about me aside from my financial value.

It's funny how I've had eighteen years to realize that he's never going to care about me, but every time he snubs me like this, he kills a small part of my soul that kept hoping…

FRIVOLOUS

I shake myself from my musings, snuggling deeper into Bass' arms and going back to sleep.

Chapter Thirteen

Gianna

The days pass, and I'm forced to remain in the hospital under medical supervision for my suicide attempt. My father, of course, is not happy about this.

He visited me exactly once—the day after I woke up. He only had a few words to say to me, all of which included the shame I've brought to the family and how I'd made him look weak in front of Goode because he can't control his own daughter.

Of course he'd also promptly ordered me to get well soon, because the preparations for the engagement party cannot wait.

I'd still been dazed from the drugs in my system, and before I could reply to him, he'd been gone.

He hasn't visited since.

Bass has been the only one by my side at all times, and his attention has been nothing short of astounding.

For someone who is used to suffering in silence, his treatment amazed me.

He's been a constant presence, always making sure I'm ok and asking if I need anything.

But more than that, his tenderness had shocked me.

FRIVOLOUS

Looking at him, you would only see his hard side—the violence reflected in his scars, the promise of even more violence at every flex of his muscles. Yet for all his imposing appearance, he's been so gentle with me, taking care of me even when I didn't know I needed it.

Cooped up in the hospital room, we've also managed to get to know each other better, playing games, watching shows together, or just joking around, recounting anecdotes from our lives.

He'd been even more forthcoming than usual, even sharing with me how he got the scar on his face.

Although I could see he was still affected by the incident, he'd told me in detail how a number of people had taken him by surprise, ambushing him and holding him down while one person had cut away at his face, the threat of losing an eye always hanging over his head while he'd been powerless to stop it.

I'd been shocked at his story, especially since I find it hard to believe anyone would be able to hold *him* down. But when I'd asked how many people had jumped on him, he'd grimly replied six—seven with the one cutting.

I'd desperately wanted to inquire more, but at seeing how upset he was by everything, I'd refrained from it.

"I brought you your favorite milkshake and cheesecake," his voice interrupts me from my thoughts as he comes inside my salon, closing the door behind him.

"Really?" My eyes widen in excitement as I all but jump out of bed.

"Easy," he chuckles when he sees my expression.

Setting up everything on the table, he invites me to take a seat before spreading everything in front of me.

"God," I whisper in awe, "you went all the way to the Cheesecake Factory?"

Since the incident had happened at home, I'd been rushed to the closest hospital in upstate New York. The closest Cheesecake Factory is all the way in the city, so it must have taken him a few hours for a round trip.

"I had some time while you were sleeping," he gives me a sheepish smile, raising his hand and tucking my hair behind my ear. "Besides, I quite like spoiling you."

A blush creeps up my cheeks and I suddenly avert my gaze.

You'd think I would get used by now with flirtation and men making advances towards me, but with Bass everything is different.

Not only does he have a novel effect on my body, but in his presence I feel like a shy schoolgirl—not at all like the modern woman I pretend to be to the outside world.

"And that blush right there tells me I'm doing a good job," he drawls as he brings his hand down my cheek, his thumb hovering over my mouth.

"You got me all my favorite flavors too," I comment, switching the topic as I realize I'm getting increasingly hot from his touch alone.

"Dig in," he prompts me, leaning back and watching me eat.

We make pleasant conversation while I savor the cherry flavored cheesecake.

It's been so long since I last ate something with this much gusto, without my anxiety threatening to upset my stomach, or influencing my appetite.

And I think everything is because of *him*.

He makes me feel safe.

Smiling at something he says, I'm startled by the sound of the door opening and closing, my father striding in.

Bass immediately gets to his feet, trying to keep a distance away from me so that my father won't get suspicious about the nature of our relationship.

"Leave us, Bailey," he barely even looks at Bass as he orders him.

He grinds his teeth, reluctant to go. I give him a slow nod, knowing that my father won't stay for too long.

"I've spoken with your doctor," my father starts the moment Bass is out of the door. "You'll be able to go back home tomorrow."

"How?" I frown. "When I talked to him he said I needed to be under supervision..."

"I talked him out of that bullshit," he interrupts, waving his hand dismissively. "Bailey will watch out so you behave yourself. Especially since the engagement is less than three weeks away."

"What..." My eyes widen at his shamelessness. "You're crazy," I mutter, unable to believe he'd be this cruel.

"Maybe. But you're marrying Clark as soon as it can be arranged and that's final, Gianna." He shrugs, looking at me with a bored expression on his face.

"I'm not marrying him. I can't," I shake my head. "I won't."

He stares at me for a second before bursting out loud laughing. "Yes, you will," he chuckles.

"We can still find someone else. It doesn't have to be him," I attempt to pacify him. Anyone but Clark would do at this point.

"Someone else?" He raises an eyebrow at me.

Striding to the window, he removes a pack of cigarettes from his pocket, lighting one up and opening the window for the smoke to go outside.

"Someone else," he gives a dry laugh, taking a big drag from the cigarette before turning to me.

Leaning against the windowsill, he looks me up and down in distaste.

"There's no one else, Gianna. Do you really think that *anyone* will have you after everything you've done?"

"Everything *I've* done?" I ask, confused.

"Oh, don't play dumb," he rolls his eyes at me, bringing the cigarette back to his lips.

"Everyone in the Tri-State area probably knows how easy it is to get between your legs," he says derisively.

My mouth drops open in shock, both at the fact that he'd know about it or mention it so carelessly.

"Wow," I exclaim, shaking my head. "You're going to throw *that* in my face? Since when do you care anyway?" I give a bitter laugh. "You've been parading me around for so long, hoping I'd ensnare some rich husband that you turned a blind eye to *everything* going on in my life."

"Of course I did," he replies, almost exasperated. "I must admit that in the beginning I thought you'd find some rich snob, get yourself knocked up and trap him. But it seems to have backfired." He adds pensively.

All the while I can't erase the shock from my features.

He's known... He's known all along what people were saying about me, but he hadn't interfered because he'd thought to use it to his advantage. I almost want to laugh out loud at this.

"Of course," he nods, "no self-respecting fellow would buy the cow after the entire village milked it."

"What?" The words are out of my mouth before I can help myself.

I simply can't believe what he's saying, or the manner in which he's saying it—as if he couldn't care less about it, about me, except that it had hurt his business interests.

Hell, I've always known my father was a mercenary bastard. But I've never realized he could be this cruel.

"Drop the scandalized look, Gianna." He tells me, flinging his cigarette out the window. "I should have realized you're cut from the same cloth as your mother," he shakes his head in disgust as he comes closer to me. "Good for a fuck, but not much else," he all but spits in my face as he backs me towards the wall.

I back away, not wanting him anywhere in my personal space—not after he just said.

I've never held out hope for a good relationship with my father. But this one conversation will serve as the moment I truly cut my ties with him.

"Get out," I whisper, my entire body shaking with anger. "Get out," I say louder, noticing the surprised look that crosses his face.

For a second I think he will, but before I can even blink, he has me against the wall, his fingers around my neck.

"Don't you ever dare to do something like this again and jeopardize my deal with Clark. You will marry him, or else I'll be forced to do something more drastic," a cruel smile tugs at his lips, "like say... have your brother pay for *your* mistakes."

My entire body is quaking, and as I look into his eyes, I *know* he means it. He's never cared about Michele anyway, just like he's never cared about me, either. And all because he loathed our mother and the fact that he was forced to marry her.

"You'll turn those wiles of yours on Clark and make him happy like the little whore you are, and I'll keep your brother out of this."

Terrified by this side of him, I simply nod.

"Words, Gianna, words."

"Yes. I'll marry him," I whisper.

"Good," he gives me a satisfied smirk as he releases me. "I'm glad we understand each other."

And with that he's gone.

My fingers go around my neck as I massage it, feeling the bruising way with which he'd dug his fingers in my flesh.

"Sunshine?" Bass' worried voice registers late, and I raise my head to see him back in the room.

"What did he do?" He demands, coming close to me and taking me in his arms.

I shake my head at him, assuring him I'm fine.

I give him a quick rundown of the conversation and the fact that he'd threatened me with Michele's safety.

"I can't leave him here, Bass. We need to find a way to take him with us."

"I agree. I like your brother, and he shouldn't have to be subjected to Benedicto's scorn just because. He's already dealt with enough as it is." He nods grimly. "It will be harder, but I'll make it happen. I promise you."

He takes me into his arms, bringing me to his chest as he lays a kiss on my forehead.

True to his word, my father convinces the doctor to discharge me the next day. And as I get back to the house, I can't help the doubts that start clouding my mind.

Bass assures me he'll be able to plan our escape in time, but can he really?

He's just an ex-army dude against a billionaire and a mafia boss. Can he really ensure everything will go smoothly?

It's even worse knowing that my brother's wellbeing is at stake too. Whereas Raf has always been in safe hands, coddled by both

Cosima and my father, Michele has been left to fend for himself his entire life.

If it weren't for me, I don't know what would have happened to him, since Cosima can't stand the sight of him.

He would have probably ended up dead. Like my mother.

Because of that, I'm a little reluctant to hope about escaping my fate. If anything, I want to take advantage of the time I have left and make memories for the future.

If all should fail, at least I'll have something to hold on to.

And when night time comes, it's time to put my plan in motion.

I take a quick shower, changing the bandages on my wrists to the best of my ability and donning on a sheer nightgown. Stepping in front of the mirror, I take a moment to inspect my appearance.

I hope he'll like it.

The gown leaves little to the imagination, my naked breasts visible as well as the outline of my panties.

I may not be ready to go all the way with Bass—likely won't ever be—but I want to experience at *least* something.

I want him.

Undoing my hair and letting it fall down my back, I give it a quick brush before I'm ready to go to him.

Fucking hell but my nerves are killing me. I'd made sure to take a pill beforehand so I don't have an attack while we're together, but even so, I feel a tingling low in my belly, my entire being trembling from a mix of fear and anticipation.

Closing my eyes, I take a deep breath and I go knock on his door.

Just like before, he opens the door dressed in nothing but a pair of gray sweatpants, his chest muscles flexing with every move and making my mouth water.

I've never openly admired the male form before. But seeing Bass' sculpted chest and arms, I can't help the sigh that escapes me as my eyes greedily rove all over his delectable planes.

I want to run my tongue all over his flesh.

I don't know where that thought comes from, but as I raise my eyes to his it's to see a dangerous glint in them, as if he knows exactly what's on my mind.

FRIVOLOUS

I don't even get to speak as he pulls me inside, his own eyes looking appreciatively over my body in a way that makes me blush to the roots of my hair.

"Damn, sunshine," he whistles as he peruses my curves.

"You like it," I twirl for him, trying to push down my sudden shyness. "I put it on for you," I wink at him.

He's watching me with glazed eyes, slowly licking his lips as he zeroes in on my breasts.

"Did you?" He intones on a husky voice.

Without another word, he strides to the bed, sitting on the edge and leaning back on his elbows.

"What are you doing?" I ask, almost breathless.

I am way out of my element here, and he's just sitting on the bed, watching. Like a predator leading his prey on a merry chase.

"Strip." He commands, his voice booming in the room and causing my skin to break out in goosebumps.

"What..."

"Strip, sunshine. You said you put it on for me," he smiles. "Now take it off for me."

That smirk of his is back in place as he watches me closely, almost daring me to disobey him.

Over the last few weeks I'd gotten so used to his gentler side that I almost forgot about this *other* side of him. The harsh, demanding one. The arrogant, drop your panties at my command one that *actually* makes me want to drop my panties.

It might have been hard for me to come to terms with my attraction to him, but from the first he'd been a force to be reckoned with, wreaking havoc over my senses and destroying everything I thought I knew about myself.

Moving slowly in front of him, I undulate my body in a sinuous manner, watching his pupils as they expand with desire.

"Strip," he reiterates his command, staring at me like a starved man being served a five-course meal.

Crisscrossing my hands, I bring them to the tiny straps of the gown, teasing him as I drop one inch at a time.

He can't take his eyes off me as he follows every small move I make.

But I don't want to give him the satisfaction of seeing me naked just yet. Not when I feel a power unlike any other as I control what he can see and what he *cannot* see. And as his hungry gaze seems to eat up every bit of flesh I unveil, I become bolder and bolder.

Taking a few steps back, I situate myself in the center of the room, my straps already off my shoulder but my gown is still firmly in place and covering my breasts.

The anticipation must be killing him, especially as he brings his hand to the front of his trousers, adjusting his obvious erection but never once taking his eyes off me.

I start a slow dance.

I've taken enough classes over the years so I know what I'm doing, especially as I bring one hand to my neckline, holding the dress in place while I move my hips like a born seductress.

Slowly—ever so slowly—I start releasing the material of the dress bit by bit, the swell of my breasts the first to peek through, before I uncover my nipples, pebbled and as erect as his cock.

I might be playing this game of arousal with him, wanting to drive him mad with lust, but I'm falling prey too. Because I can't not feel an overwhelming desire when he's simply worshipping me with his gaze.

He might control me with his commands, but I control him with how I affect him.

Turning my back to him, I bend down, curving my spine and thrusting my ass towards him as I lower the rest of the gown over my hips.

It's only when the material is bunched up at my feet that I turn.

He's no longer relaxed and leaning on his elbows. His new position is tense as he looks about to bolt from the bed. His features strained, there's a twitch in his jaw as he seems to hold himself together—but barely.

"Take your panties off," he says low in his throat. "Slowly," he commands, and I comply, my fingers grabbing to the edge of the material as I pull them down my legs.

"Good. Good," he praises. "Now get on your knees like the good girl you are," he purrs, his voice doing strange things to my body.

My clit is already tingling and he hasn't even touched me. And as I palm my panties, I know I drenched them, the wetness unmistakable on the inseam.

Dropping to my knees in front of him, I await his next instruction.

"Bring those panties to me, sunshine. On your knees," he rasps, almost impatient.

I comply, moving sensuously towards him and handing him my panties. I bat my lashes at him as I place my hands on his knees, waiting for his reaction.

"Fuck," he curses as he brings them to his nose, inhaling. "You fucking soaked them. That sweet pussy of yours is ready for me, isn't she?"

I can only nod, my tongue peeking out to wet my lips. I clench my thighs as I seek to appease the ache forming inside of me, but the more he speaks, the more I feel even more wetness gush out of my pussy.

"Fuck, Gianna, you creamed all over your panties," he drawls, his eyes closed, "was it my tongue you imagined in your tight little cunt when you drenched these fucking panties?"

I gasp, an intake of breath that alerts him to my heightened arousal.

I feel my juices pooling between my pussy lips and flowing down my thighs, and I don't think I've ever been so turned on in my entire life.

"Come here and sit on my face, sunshine," he growls before swooping me up, his arms around my waist as he drapes me over his body.

"Ride my face and let me taste that fucking cream," he continues, and his language would have made me blush like hell if I weren't already so turned on.

I don't think about our position, or the fact that he's still semi-clothed while I'm completely naked. Climbing up his body, his hands settle on my ass as he brings my pussy right on top of his mouth.

"Fuck, you're killing me Gianna," he speaks against me, his voice sending vibrations to my clit and making my muscles twitch at the sensation. "You're so fucking wet, sunshine," he groans as he presses me down on his open mouth.

His tongue goes right between my folds as he gives me a long lick, a moan escaping my lips as a spear of pleasure goes right through me.

His lips wrapped around my clit, he sucks it into his mouth, the tip of his tongue playing with the small nub until I'm writhing on top of him.

For a moment I feel like I can't continue this. Not when my entire body is close to convulsing.

His hands on my ass, he keeps me firmly in place as he drags his tongue down my slit, sucking and nibbling and kissing my pussy in what can only be described as torture to the senses.

And as he moves lower, he thrusts his tongue into my opening, using it to massage my walls. There's a ticklish feeling shrouded in the most blinding pleasure I've ever known. And as he keeps teasing my entrance, thrusting in and out of me while making out with my pussy, I find that I'm unable to stop myself from coming all over his face.

"That's a good girl," he speaks as he comes out for air, "you like it when I fuck you with my tongue, don't you?"

I'm so gone I can't even answer. But he's not mollified. No, he demands me to answer, promising me more of the same pleasure if I do.

"Yes," I whimper.

"Say it. I want to hear it from your lips."

"I like it when you fuck me with your tongue," I give him the words, feeling him smile against my pussy when I do.

"Good, because I fucking love it when you come all over my face, sunshine," he says just as he gives me another long lick. "I want your cream coating my tongue. Fuck, I want you to drench me in your cum," he blows softly against my sensitive flesh, "so that everyone knows I belong between your legs," he grunts before diving in again, bringing me to the brink again and again until my body goes numb from too much pleasure.

I feel limp as I barely hold myself upright.

"Bass," I moan when he sucks my clit into his mouth, wringing yet another orgasm out of me.

It's only when I almost crash that he finally puts me out of my misery, dragging me down his body for a heated kiss.

I taste myself on his lips, but I find I don't mind it. It only enhances the eroticism of the moment and the fact that just moments ago his tongue was buried in my pussy as he gave me more pleasure than I've ever known in my entire life.

And to my everlasting shock, he once again doesn't ask for anything in return. If anything, he seems content to just hold me in his arms.

"Bass," I whisper his name, my mouth peppering kisses all over his neck as I go lower.

"You don't have to," he stops my hand when I cup him through his pants.

"I want to," I raise my head to gaze at him.

He still has that glazed look on his face, and I want to give him the same pleasure he's given me.

"I want you to come in my mouth too," I tell him, moving slowly down his body while keeping eye contact.

He doesn't protest again, giving me a jerky nod of approval and it's all I need to proceed further.

I reach the band of his pants, dragging it down. He helps me as he quickly divests himself of both his sweats and boxers, his cock springing out and slapping against the hard plane of his stomach. He's so hard and seems to grow even harder under my perusal.

I tentatively wrap my hand around him, once more reminded of his daunting size.

He hisses at my touch, but I promptly realize it's a good hiss.

"That's it, pretty girl," he hums, eyes half closed as I slowly stroke him—up and down.

His skin is soft and warm under my palm, and as I lay between his spread legs, I lower my mouth to lick the head.

"God," he groans out loud. "Give me that mouth, sunshine. Take me into that pretty mouth of yours," he continues to talk as I open my mouth to take him inside, careful to sheathe my teeth so I don't hurt him like last time.

I'm a little clumsy in the beginning as I find what works and what gets the most reactions out of him.

He continues to praise me for every little thing I do right, holding my hair to the side as I kiss and lick him, giving special attention to a spot right under the head that seems to make him go crazy.

"Yes, suck on that cock like the good girl you are," he says on a strangled moan.

His words of encouragement only make me want to try harder—give him the same pleasure he gave me.

And as I further lean in, attempting to take his entire length into my mouth, I hear him curse, his fingers wrapped in my hair as he groans in pleasure.

"Fucking hell, sunshine," he rasps, "take all of me, let me feel the back of that lovely throat," he says as he pushes me down, the tip of his cock hitting the back of my throat and making me gag.

"Fuuuuck," he exclaims.

And as I look up at him, tears in my eyes from the exertion, I see that he's barely holding himself together. The muscles in his torso are strained and bulging, a vein protruding in his neck and telling me exactly how much I affect him.

"I'm coming," he warns, holding me down until I feel the warm spurts of his cum shoot into my mouth. I swallow every little bit, earning myself a satisfied smile from him.

"You're going to kill me, sunshine," he chuckles as he gathers me in his arms, my pussy resting on his still hard dick.

"I loved this," I confess, "I loved doing this with you," a smile tugs at my lips as I give him a quick kiss.

And it's true. I can't imagine doing this with anyone else.

Anyone but him.

We give in to a passionate kiss that threatens to make me melt, and it soon becomes clear that he's ready for another round.

But no matter how much I try to give myself to his embrace, I realize I'm not ready for the last plunge. I might have gotten comfortable being naked in his arms and sharing intimacies I'd never thought possible, but there is still a small part of me holding back.

I'm not ready.

Will I ever be? The thought that I may never feel ready to give myself fully to him scares me. But somehow I know he won't pressure me. He will let me take the reins and go at my pace. He's already shown more patience than any other man would have.

Just as I contemplate telling him to stop, we're both startled by a loud knock on the door.

"Mr. Bailey?" I quickly look at Bass with wide eyes as I hear Mia's voice. "I tried knocking on Miss Gianna's door, but she's not answering. Considering the circumstances…"

"Shit," I mutter, climbing off him and throwing my robe back on while Bass pulls on his sweats.

"Keep out of sight," he murmurs, kissing the top of my head before going to deal with Mia.

"Yes, Mia," he opens the door slightly, listening to the housekeeper's complaints.

"Maybe she got hungry and she's downstairs?"

"But I just came from there…" she frowns.

"Why don't you check again and I'll go knock on her door. Maybe she's sleeping soundly," he tries to placate her.

Eventually she agrees, after which I quickly sneak back to my room.

And as Mia returns, I open the door, looking sleepy and disheveled and giving her a questioning look.

"I… I'm sorry to bother you, Miss." Mia apologizes and she seems genuine. "Your father asked me to check on you often," she explains, almost embarrassed.

"It's ok, Mia. I understand. Have a good night," I give her a strained smile as I dismiss her, happy at her fortuitous interruption. She'd saved me from having to tell Bass that I wasn't ready to sleep with him yet and from having a painful conversation that is nonetheless unavoidable.

"We need to be more careful," Bass whispers after she leaves. "We can't afford any suspicion while I work on our escape plan."

I nod grimly, reality once more settling in.

Because I have a feeling things are not going to go as smoothly as Bass makes them out to be.

Chapter Fourteen

BASS

Time is running out as I do my best to stay under the radar with my inquiries. Not only do I have to bypass Benedicto's notice but also Cisco's. The latter will prove harder, since we share some of the same contacts, and loyalty is not to be taken lightly in the famiglia.

But covering my tracks with every query makes my job even more time-consuming.

And time is something I no longer have.

Not when there's only one week left until Gianna's engagement party.

From the moment she'd woken in the hospital, I hadn't left her side even for a minute. And though Benedicto had insisted she meet with Clark at least once a week, I'd served as a buffer between the two of them, ensuring that Clark doesn't get close to Gianna at all times.

She might be on to something when it comes to him, though. I've seen the way he looks at her. There's a perversion in his gaze that goes beyond mere lust. There's a need to hurt there that makes even *my* skin crawl.

Fuck, but I'd rather die than let her become a sacrificial lamb for that bastard.

She hasn't gone into the details of what he'd done to her, and I hadn't pushed her for them, but I can see he terrifies her. Hell, it's more than that. At the mere mention of his name she simply closes herself, her features pale, her limbs shaky. That she's managed to last even five minutes in his presence astounds me.

But she's a good actress.

That she is. And she'd definitely seemed entirely unperturbed on the outside, even though *I*'d known she was probably hyperventilating on the inside.

Picking up our new identities from a jail buddy who dabbles into this stuff, now I only have to figure out the travel arrangements out of the country.

Since both families' connections extend throughout Europe, that is out of the question. I'd made a list of a few countries in South America and Asia that we could move to.

The trickiest part will be moving Michele across the border, since he is still a minor. I'd suggested passing him off as my son, and the new IDs I'd gotten identify Gianna and I as a married couple and Michele as my child.

Still, we won't know how hard it's going to be to leave the country securely until we're at the border. The plan is to head straight to the airport before anyone can sound the alarm and have us chased around.

Satisfied that at least half of the plan has been taken care of, I head back home, swinging by a dealer to get a refill of Gianna's pills.

"You're back early," she notes when I find her in the living room, hanging out with her brother.

She's sitting daintily on the couch, a cup of tea in her hands as she slowly brings it to her lips to take a sip.

The model of decorum.

To say I'm impressed with her poker face would be an understatement. She's truly mastered her disguise over the years, and that only gives me hope that she's going to adapt just fine regardless of the country we end up in.

Besides, she's probably going to charm the socks off everyone she comes into contact with—not that I will like that, and it might make me commit one or two murders. I'd promised her, though, that I'd go easy on the killing to not attract any unwanted attraction towards us.

But how could we truly go under the radar when Gianna only has to step in a crowd, and it immediately parts like the Red Sea, everyone's eyes on her—women or men alike.

Her beauty is something out of this world, and I'd be lying if it didn't make me feel self-conscious at times. Especially when I see people staring at me in disgust and at her in adoration.

What a funny couple we make...

As long as I have *her* adoration, I don't care. I *won't* care.

Michele is by her side, a notebook in his hands as he's drawing something.

"Bass," he nods at me as I enter the room, giving me a slight smile.

I hadn't lied to Gianna when I'd told her I liked the kid. He's quiet and he usually minds his own business. Likely because he knows he's not welcomed in anyone else's.

As usual, Cosima and her son are not around, while Benedicto is off getting himself in God knows how many more debts in his attempt to rectify his finances.

That's another thing I'd noticed about Michele and Rafaelo. While their relationship is strained at best, it's not of any fault of their own. Rather, it's Cosima's machinations that create strife between the brothers. And if what she's saying is true, that Benedicto had decided to name Rafaelo his heir, then it would only cause more conflict moving forward.

But it won't.

Not when we're going to be gone from here in less than a few weeks.

Gianna had had a talk with Michele and he understands the importance of leaving as far away for his sister's sake, and he's been nothing but cooperative.

"What are you drawing?" I ask as I take a seat next to them on the couch.

"My sister," a smile pulls at his lips as he turns the drawing slightly towards me.

My eyes widen as I take in the realistic features of the drawing, as well as his unmistakable talent for it.

"Wow," I whistle, meeting Gianna's eyes. "Did you know your brother can do that?"

"Let me see," she scoots closer, leaning forward to look at the drawing.

Her expression mirrors mine as shock is written all over her features.

"Michele," she breathes out in awe, "that... You never told me you could draw like this before. It's spectacular," she praises quietly.

Michele just shrugs.

"I only do it at home. And it's only a hobby, nothing else," he's quick to correct himself.

"No, no," Gianna shakes her head. "You should pursue this. Right, Bass? This isn't just regular art. God, but I have no words," she keeps on staring at the drawing.

Truth to be told, it is exquisite. Even though he's only drawn it in pencil, the details are so vivid it's like seeing Gianna in the flesh. But more than anything, he's captured her beauty in such a way that you can't help but be mesmerized by the sight, a warmth reflected in her features, her eyes full of love, her smile full of optimism.

How Michele sees his sister.

And she notices this too because she dabs the tears from the corner of her eyes before tugging Michele in a hug.

"I'm proud of you. We'll definitely find a way for you to continue to study this."

"No," he frowns, suddenly looking at her confused. "I don't want to. Like I said, it's just a hobby," he disentangles himself from her hold, putting some distance between the two of them.

"But that would be a waste of your talent."

Michele shrugs.

"Why?" I ask, intrigued by his sudden reaction.

His eyebrows shoot up before furrowing in a frown.

"It's not a manly pursuit," he says with conviction.

"And who told you that?"

"Everyone. They said it's for cowards and sissies."

Meeting Gianna's grave expression, she nods at me, getting up and leaving the room.

And I spend the next few hours trying to explain to Michele that drawing and art have nothing to do with cowards, or sissies, or anything.

Pleased when he seems to understand what I'm saying, I can't help but feel that the absence of a father figure has impacted him more than he lets on.

"Thank you," Gianna mentions a while later as I'm watching her put on make-up for the evening. "Michele really looks up to you, you know," she sighs. "He doesn't tell me everything, but I think they're bullying him at school. Otherwise where would he have gotten those ideas?"

"He's a strong lad. He's going to be fine," I assure her.

He may be quiet and often blend in with the background, but there's a quiet strength to him. You don't survive what he has, and at such a young age at that, without having inner strength.

"You can be very sweet when you're not surly," she says cheekily as she finishes adding the last touches to her make-up.

"Well, enjoy my non-surliness for now, because once we're at that party I'll be glowering at every man who comes near you," I retort playfully. Little does she know I'll probably be doing more than that.

This time her attendance at the party had been requested by Benedicto himself, since he is about to close a deal with the hosts.

I keep my distance as Gianna plasters on a fake smile and enters the venue on her father's arm. Benedicto looks smug as he leads both Gianna and his wife inside.

Everyone is already staring at their entrance, especially as they eyes zero in on Gianna in her glamorous golden dress. It complements her blonde hair perfectly and makes her look like a goddess.

And as I see more than one fool salivate after her, I can barely stop myself from dragging them in the middle of the floor to beat them to a pulp in a big display to show that she's off the market.

But I can't. Not yet.

It's becoming increasingly hard to pretend I'm just her bodyguard. To pretend like I have no right to intervene when any of these fools try to fuck her with their eyes.

Fuck, it's becoming increasingly hard not to act according to my nature—kill every single one of these idiots for even being in the same room as her.

Soon, her friends demand her attention and with a sad smile, she follows them to the other end of the room.

I make to follow, but Benedicto stops me.

"Don't think I don't see how you look at my daughter," he scowls.

Ignoring the tick in my jaw for the mere fact that he dares call her his daughter when he's never treated her as such, I force myself to reply.

"How so?"

"Like you want to fuck her," he pauses, "or you've already fucked her." He shrugs, as if he couldn't care less. "I know she has that effect on men, but I won't let anyone jeopardize my deal with Clark. Not you of all people," he sneers at me.

"There's nothing going on between me and your daughter, sir," the words burn on my tongue as I say them, as well as the tone of subservience I'm forced to adopt.

But I grit my teeth and keep myself in check.

"Keep it that way. Otherwise I won't be so kind."

"Is that a threat?"

"It's a promise, boy. You may be a tough guy, but I'll make it so that your body is never found," he smiles arrogantly.

"Right. Understood," I literally have to pinch myself to get the words out of my mouth, my body rebelling at the very action.

Why didn't Cisco ask me to kill Benedicto instead? It would have been so much easier...

"I'm glad we understand each other," he smirks, patting me on the back before joining his wife at the refreshment table.

The act that Benedicto has been putting for the world never fails to surprise me. In public, he shows himself to be a devoted father who would do anything to spoil his daughter. More than that, he shows himself as a man willing to give his daughter any luxury and whatever her heart desires. It had certainly fooled Cisco and the others into thinking Gianna is his weakness when she's nothing but a pawn.

But I've seen the other side of him—the one that's been secretly hoping she'd find herself a rich husband at these parties, forcing her to attend and essentially thrusting her into the role of the perfect society girl. It had certainly helped him find business partners and investors over the years.

I'm starting to realize that Benedicto doesn't care about anyone other than himself—the supposed love of his life included.

As my eyes search for Gianna, I'm surprised to see that she and her friends have disappeared from the main floor, and it takes me a while to meet with her again.

She's giggly and entirely too drunk—just as her other friends—and as I tug her to my side, it's to have her pass out on me.

Not one to despair, I simply inform Benedicto of what had transpired and I take Gianna home, tucking her in bed and waiting by her side in case she gets ill.

Damn, when did she have time to drink so much to get wasted?

I thought all my inquiries had gone under the radar. But when I get a call from Cisco asking me to meet him urgently, I have to ask myself if I slipped.

There's no way...

I'd covered my tracks perfectly, and I'd reached out to people outside of the family's sphere of influence. There's absolutely no way Cisco would have eyes and ears *everywhere*.

For fuck's sake, he's only been at the helm of the famiglia for a few years. For a young don, that's hardly enough time to make lasting connections or get people's respect. Still, there's no denying that Cisco has a certain intelligence and cunning to him that would give him an advantage over most.

And I am to find out just how much when he greets me in his cold manner, his shrewd eyes seemingly seeing everything.

"Uncle," he greets.

I nod, taking a seat across from his office and waiting to see what was so important that he'd call me here in person.

"What was so urgent you couldn't tell me on the phone?" I ask directly.

"Damn, Bass. There's no beating around the bush with you, is it?" he chuckles, his fingers playing with the silver necklace around his neck.

"Cut to the chase."

"If you say so," he shrugs, a lazy smile still on his lips as he regards me. "I wanted to know how your little mission is going," he raises an eyebrow.

"Better than your attempt on Benedicto's life," I throw, watching his lips stretch wider across his face.

"Hmm," he hums, opening the drawer and taking out a pack of cigarettes. Lighting one up, he maintains the silence a moment longer, and I'm forced to admit that Cisco is not the same person I used to know. "Not mine if you want to know."

I frown, tilting my head to the side and waiting for him to continue.

"Dario's got it in his head that he needs my approval," he rolls his eyes. "Do you really think I'd be so stupid to try to kill him with a *bomb*?" He almost looks disgusted at the thought. "Safe to say he's not allowed to handle any type of weapons for the foreseeable future. I swear that boy was born with one neuron and even that one is half dead," he shakes his head.

"Right," I grunt, narrowing my eyes at him. It does make sense that Cisco wouldn't go for something as paltry as a bomb, but I feel there's more to the story than he's letting on.

"Alas, that's not why I called you here. I thought that maybe you need a little more motivation to see this through—and fast. The engagement is in a week, is it not?" he raises an eyebrow. "A perfect occasion for ruination. Why, everyone will be able to witness the ruination. And by all accounts," he pauses, giving me a sharp look, "you've already succeeded with the seduction stage."

I press my lips in a thin line trying not to show my surprise at his words. And not for the first time, I have to wonder how he knows this.

"It's working," I shrug, trying to seem blasé.

It's better if he thinks I'm indifferent towards Gianna. That way, he won't suspect my commitment to the cause.

"But it's working slowly," he sighs. "That's why, I thought I'd show you a little something."

"What?"

A confident smile on his face, he pushes an envelope towards me. Opening it up, I realize I'm looking at the profiles of the men who'd held me down and cut my face. I go through each one of them, noting they had all been freed soon after they'd attacked me.

"Why?" I meet his gaze. "Why are you showing me this?"

"Why?" he chuckles. "I thought you'd want your revenge," he leans back in his seat, continuing to smoke. And as he sees my ground jaw and the tension in my expression, he pushes the pack towards me, urging me to bum one.

"And what does this have to do with Guerra?" I ask the more glaring question.

"Ah, good on you to notice. You see, I did some digging, and all of those men," he points at the sheets in my hand, "are connected to a certain Franco Guerra."

"Benedicto's brother."

"Indeed. So you can see how the dots connect."

"But it doesn't make sense," I frown. "Why would they hire me if they knew who I was?"

"Did they though?" Cisco inquires. "They only needed to know a DeVille was in prison to order an attack. You know how it is," he waves his hand. "Besides, you were rather infamous in that prison. Was there even *one* person who didn't know who you were?"

"No," I grit my teeth. It's true that everyone had known I was the enemy on the inside and they'd certainly behaved as such.

Still, I see what Cisco is trying to do. He's trying to get me to act faster and more viciously. If he thinks I have a personal stake in this, then he assumes I'll go harder on the Guerras.

And though I will, at some point, my personal revenge has to wait until everything else is secure.

"Thanks for the heads up," I nod. "I'll use these wisely," I smirk at him, holding up the papers and getting up to leave.

He must have noticed that I hadn't been too affected by the news, so what he says next does stop me in my tracks.

"Mr. and Mrs. Chadwick," he says, satisfaction dripping from him when I turn around and level him with my stare.

Our fake identities.

"I didn't want it to come to this," he sighs. "I really thought you'd be more sensible, Bass. That's why I sent *you* on this mission. I knew you could never fall for someone like Gianna. She's too much like your mother," he drawls, rising up from his chair and pacing across the room.

"I was so sure you were the perfect choice because only *you* would be indifferent to her charms, all things considered. But you weren't, were you?"

"I don't know what you're talking about."

"Yes. You do. And I'm sorry to say that you've been duped. Really uncle, I thought you'd be more discerning than to believe whatever sob story she told you. Let me guess, she said that people are jealous of her and that's why they spread the rumors, didn't she?" He smirks.

I don't reply, I simply narrow my eyes at him waiting for him to say his piece.

"I see that she did. What else? Oh, that she's afraid of her fiancé? What's his name? Clark Goode?"

"Where are you getting with this, Cisco?" I can barely contain the anger that rolls off me.

"Did she also tell you she fucked him?"

I clench my fists at his words. I don't think I'd make it out alive if I were to kill the head of the family—all things considered too.

"He's a goddamn pervert," I grit my teeth.

"Right," he laughs. "That's what she told you." He makes a tsk sound as he leans against his desk, putting the cigarette out in an ashtray nearby. "Let me enlighten you, uncle. She fucked him. Two years ago. In a public bathroom, nonetheless. You should ask her. Even she can't lie about that when everyone knows. They caught them together, you know."

His brows shoot up in a challenge as he all but shoves his phone in my face, a picture of two people naked on the screen. I do my best not to look, but I feel a pang in my chest as I recognize Gianna's features and her honey blonde hair.

Schooling my features, I try not to show how much this affects me, or how the thought of Gianna with anyone else makes me want to go on a rampage. But when I'd faced my feelings for her I'd decided not to hold her past against her. Especially not in this case, since it's clear who the guilty party is. If anything, I feel even worse for Gianna and the fact that she had to go through that—or that evidence of it was circulating online for everyone to see.

"Two years ago she was sixteen, Cisco. And he's Benedicto's age. That only tells me he fucking took advantage of her." I tell him, my voice firm.

"What about a few days ago?" He raises an eyebrow, a perfidious smile playing at his lips.

"What do you mean?" My breath catches in my throat at his insinuation.

"Damn it, uncle, but I didn't think she'd play you like this," he purses his lips, shaking his head.

Without another word, he turns his computer screen towards me, clicking on a video.

"Watch and tell me you'd risk your *family* for a whore," he sighs in disappointment, moving aside to let me watch whatever clip he has on.

I'm skeptical in the beginning, but it soon becomes clear when the video was taken.

Frozen to the spot, I can only watch the sequences as they roll on video, almost unable to believe this is Gianna.

My Gianna.

The video starts with her and her friends at the party we'd attended with Benedicto a few days ago. The golden dress she's wearing is proof enough of that.

I recognize the layout of the venue where the event had taken place, and I realize this is somewhere on the top levels, where there were actual rooms.

They are all talking and passing around drinks, joking about guys.

Gianna seems to be enjoying herself, and it's like I'm seeing her for the first time—so carefree and happy.

At some point, one of her friends spreads some lines of coke, and all of them do one each.

It's also becoming increasingly clear that the footage had been filmed with a hidden camera somewhere in the room.

I continue to watch them talk shit about everyone, and it's like this is an entirely different version from the Gianna I know—or the one she led me to believe she was.

Suddenly her friends are gone, and Gianna is sitting alone on the bed. The door to the room opens and a man comes inside. He's wearing a tux like all the other guests had, but I don't think I've seen him before—and I know most of her friends.

He looks to be in his twenties, with a handsome face and fit body.

"There you are," he drawls, his eyes roving all over her body, a smirk pulling at his lips.

"You're here," she breathes out, the sound almost muffled. Her hands go to the fastening of her dress as she's impatiently trying to remove it.

"You're so fucking hot," he shakes his head at her, looking her up and down with a satisfied smile. He takes his blazer off, folding it neatly and placing it on the back of a chair.

Slurring, she says something I can't quite make out, but it's definitely something the man approves of, because he's palming himself through his trousers. Though the light in the room is dim at best, I can still see the way she's *also* looking at him, her lip between her teeth as she gives off a *fuck* me vibe.

He grabs her roughly by the throat for a bruising kiss before shifting her around so that she's lying on her belly. Lifting her dress over her ass he all but rips her panties out of the way as he starts fingering her.

I already feel sick to my stomach as I know what's going to happen. But I need to force myself to watch. I *need* to know she took the betrayal to the point of no return.

He quickly undoes his pants, lowering his zipper and taking his dick out. He impales her in one thrust—bare. He's fucking her raw.

Somehow that feels like an even worse punch to the gut, and I barely hold myself still as my knees feel wobbly, my chest constricting in a painful squeeze.

He starts fucking her. Moans fill the room—his and hers.

Fuck, but I don't think I can watch or listen to this. Not when I feel like puking my guts out, a visceral feeling enveloping my entire body and seemingly making my organs stop.

Making *one* organ stop.

And as I continue to watch Gianna, *my* Gianna, get fucked by a random man, I can't help but feel my soul quake with unprecedented anguish.

But she's not my Gianna. She never was.

I can only close myself off, knowing that I'll be driven to madness if I allow the enormity of what I'm seeing take root. I'll truly lose it if I let my feelings take control of me.

And the worst thing? She's enjoying it.

"Harder," she cries out at some point, and I feel my heart squeeze tightly in my chest.

"She looks like a good lay," Cisco comments when Gianna gets to her knees, sucking the man off. "Did you at least fuck her?" He asks flippantly.

I can only shake my head, my eyes fixed on the video still playing, my heart breaking piece by piece.

"I'm sorry, Bass," Cisco adds, patting me on the back. "I told you that the rumors weren't unfounded. And you know I have my sources," he adds and I nod, almost absentmindedly.

Because he had. He'd told me all there was to know about her. But I hadn't listened. Instead, I'd let myself be played by her. By that innocent bat of her lashes, or the few glimpses beneath the mask that I assumed were insights into who she *really* was.

"Damn," he curses. "Well," he pauses, his eyes on the screen as the man continues to fuck Gianna until he comes inside her. "You still have your chance," he says.

I do, don't I?

The video ends with the man leaving the room and Gianna wiping the cum from between her legs, trying to put herself together to rejoin the party.

And to think I'd held her in my arms that night. I'd stayed by her side the entire time she'd been ill from the alcohol.

An ironic laughter bubbles inside of me.

I'd been tending to that man's leftovers. Because that's the truth, isn't it? He's good enough to fuck, but I'm only good enough as her servant.

As all our interactions play in my mind, I can't help my feelings from threatening to burst to the surface—love, lust, anger, loathing—but most of all a gut-wrenching disappointment that obliterates what all that was left of my heart. Everything is mixed together in an awful combination that only makes me more bent on destruction.

Her destruction.

Suddenly it makes sense why she'd always seem hesitant when we're together, or how she'd stop things before they went too far.

I disgust her.

I have since the beginning, only she managed to fool me with her acting. She'd managed to convince me she desired me. I have to wonder how hard it must have been for her to bear my touch when she's clearly repulsed by it.

"Yes, I do, don't I?" I mutter drily, realizing exactly what I have to do.

I don't think I've ever felt worse betrayal than seeing the woman I love—loved—purposefully fucking another guy while keeping me on the sidelines. But of course, I was her little project.

Let's charm the beast...

Gianna and her friends must have had a nice laugh over me. Why, I can already see them daring her to seduce her ugly ass bodyguard and turn him into an adoring pup—joining the other army of fools who fall at her feet.

And I had.

By God, but I had.

I'd literally been ready to worship the ground she walked on. And for what?

A cruel smile pulls at my lips as all sorts of thoughts filter through my mind.

I'd been victim to her fucked up pranks once in the past, so I can only assume she had been trying to win my trust for another one. I can imagine the moment when she would have made me a laughingstock in front of everyone, bragging how she'd fooled her *mutt* bodyguard into thinking she was into him.

Why, she'd probably go even further and laugh at me for imagining we could have had a life together.

"You really think I could stomach looking at that," she'd wave her hand to my face, "for my entire life?" she'd laugh derisively, inviting all her friends to do so too.

Because that's just who she is.

A fucking mean bitch.

And it's no one's fault but my own that I'd bought her lies and that I'd let her wrap me around her little finger.

To think that I'd been about to betray the famiglia for *her*—for a faithless whore.

I shake my head in disgust.

Ah, but it's never too late for revenge.

Fool me once, shame on me. Fool me twice? I go for the fucking kill.

CHAPTER FIFTEEN

BASS

I don't know how I make it out of Cisco's office without killing someone. And as the video replays in my mind without pause, I feel a thirst for blood simmer in my veins, my head pounding with unreleased tension.

I let her make a fool of me.

You'd think my pride would have taken the biggest hit at being played so deftly by a slip of a woman. But no. It's not my pride that's bruised and bleeding.

It's my heart.

Fuck. Fuck. Fuck.

I can't believe that the first time I let myself feel something for a woman—even going against my own self—and it ends up being a complete hoax.

I fell for an illusion.

Because that's the reality. The Gianna I fell in love with didn't exist—has never existed. She was just a projection she used to ensnare me. And maybe partially it's my fault too, since I'd been so infatuated with her, I'd grasped at any morsel of humanity she'd displayed. I'd taken every positive perceived trait of hers and magnified it in my mind until she became incomparable.

Until she became uniquely mine.

Like an idiot, I put her on a pedestal. I excused all her past behaviors by blaming them on her circumstances, because it was better to believe she was abused and misunderstood but deep down a good person than what she really is—a spoiled little bitch that thrives on causing unhappiness.

Just like my mother.

Cisco is right that I should have been the last person to succumb to her charms. Not when she's the epitome of everything I loathe.

And as I close my eyes, the crippling disappointment I feel in my heart mixes with the terror I'd felt at seeing my mother's body fall to the floor, blood seeping from her a wound in her forehead.

The ground seems to shift with me as memories I'd long thought buried start to surface.

"Be a good boy and wait outside the door, ok?" She'd patted me on the shoulder, giving me a wide smile as she instructed me to wait outside her bedroom.

Taking an unknown man by the hand, they'd both headed inside the room, closing the door in my face.

I'd stood still, as I usually did, my attention focused on my surroundings. After all, my mother had told me that she counted on me to tell her when my father got home.

I'd taken my responsibilities very seriously, because when my mother asked for something, I delivered. I was, after all, the man of the house when my father was away. It hadn't been the first time but it always gave me a sense of importance when she delegated such tasks to me.

That time, though, I'd been curious. For the first time, I'd wanted to see what was happening behind the closed door and why my mother was taking strange men to her room.

Knowing I couldn't get caught or I'd risk a scolding, I'd tiptoed around the hallway until I was in front of the door. Sticking my ear to the cold surface, I'd tried to listen to the noises inside.

At first, I couldn't make out much. But as I strained my ears, I heard the first scream. It shocked me. More than anything, I'd been petrified about what was happening to my mother.

When more screams permeated the air, I couldn't wait any longer. Without even thinking, I'd burst the door open, dashing inside and ready to defend my mother.

It hadn't mattered that I'd been all of eight years. Or that the man she'd been with was maybe three times my size. Or that I was just a child playing adult games. No, nothing like that had mattered. It hadn't even registered in my mind.

All I wanted was to rescue my mother. And as I'd burst into the room, I'd found her being suffocated by that man.

He was on top of her, fully naked—just as her. He was doing things to her that couldn't have been good. Not when she was yelping in pain and scratching at his shoulders.

I'd imagined myself some sort of little soldier, ready to defend the honor of the fair maiden. So of course I'd launched myself at her attacker.

"Get off her," I'd yelled at him, trying to kick and punch with all the strength of an eight year old. It had only enraged him as he'd flung me off him, kicking me to the floor.

"Leo, don't," my mother had yelled, but just as I hadn't stopped going for him, he hadn't stopped hitting back.

The back of his hand had caught my face, splitting my lip into two. The blood had tasted bitter as I'd continued to flay my arms, trying to land a hit on him while avoiding getting hit too.

"Leave my mother alone," I'd yelled.

But just as soon as the man had raised his arm to hit me again, he'd dropped to the floor, a deafening sound making me place my hands over my ears.

I'd watched, stupefied, as blood poured out of his body, his eyes open and unfeeling as he'd stared at me.

"Bastiano," my father's voice had rang in the room, and I'd turned my head to look at him. To say I'd been shocked at what had transpired had been an understatement.

I was young enough to not realize what my mother had been doing with that man, but I'd been old enough to know the blood on the floor meant he was dead.

That my father had killed him.

"He was hurting my mother," I'd stood up straight, pointing at the man's body and telling my father everything I'd witnessed.

"Is that so," he'd turned towards my mother. "He was assaulting you naked?"

"Lorenzo, please," her pleading voice had become embedded in my memory as she'd kneeled in front of my father, still naked, her eyes filled with tears.

"It's not what you think, I swear. He... he was raping me," she'd accused. "Bass was helping me, isn't that right, *amore*?"

I'd nodded. It was true. He had been attacking her.

"Does your son even know what a filthy whore you are?" My father had scoffed, all but dragging my mother by her hair out.

"Stop!" I'd gone for his hands, trying to get him to release her.

"Lorenzo, not with Bass here, please," she'd asked, all the while I'd started crying, begging my father to let her go.

"Fucking whore," he'd spit at her, throwing her to the ground.

My mother had scrambled back, a terrified expression on her face.

Her mouth had been open in shock as she'd just looked at my father.

One second.

Two seconds.

Three seconds.

That's all it had taken for my father to cock his pistol and aim at her head. A small hole had formed right between her eyes, blood slowly leaking from it. Her eyes had been wide open, her mouth still agape as she'd stared at me.

I shake myself, my hands going to my eyes to try to erase the image from my mind. Easier said than done when all it takes is to close my eyes and I can see her face—her hauntingly beautiful face—pale and devoid of any life.

That was the first lesson my father had given me.

My mother had been a faithless whore and she'd paid the ultimate price. In my young mind, I'd been split between condemning her for what she'd done and mourning her for the mother I'd lost.

But as my father withered away and died as a result of *her* escapades, I'd started seeing things more clearly.

It wasn't just the fact that she'd slept with half the male population, or that she'd lied and cheated to do so, going as far to use her eight year old son to cover for her affairs. No, the worst had been the deceit behind all those actions. The selfishness as she hadn't cared who she'd hurt as long as she got what she wanted—as long as *she* was happy.

Just like Gianna.

She doesn't care who she hurts or humiliates as long as she can derive some sort of pleasure or amusement from it.

But this time around, it's going to be her on the receiving end.

I don't even realize when the blood spatters all over my face, bathing my clothes in red. I don't even know how I got here in the first place, or how my hands seem to be buried in brain matter as I punch and punch, shattering bone and erasing any semblance of humanity from the man's face.

With the detailed lists Cisco had given me, I'd tracked down at least three of the men, all working for the same underground casino in the area that Guerra manages.

And as I take in my surroundings, I realize that in my rage I'd simply burst in through the back, finding the men and beating them to death.

Well, at least two out of three.

I throw my gaze across the room, spotting another man huddled in a corner as he tries his best to get away from me.

My lips twitch in a cruel smile as I stride towards him.

Not so strong now when they can't hold me down.

And as I look into his cowering face, I realize exactly who he is.

The one who cut my face.

"Well, well," I drawl, crouching down in front of him. "Who do we have here…" I say as I look him up and down.

He's so scrawny and sickly looking, and as I take a closer look at his arms, I realize that he's full of scars.

A junkie.

I purse my lips in annoyance, since where is the fun in killing someone who is already weakened? I've never seen much to brag about winning over someone who is clearly inferior in every aspect.

But alas, I'm here, and I've already killed his friends. It wouldn't be fair to let him live. It wouldn't be fair to me either since I'd probably regret it later.

Grabbing him by his shirt, I drag him to the table in the center of the room, picking up a bloody knife on the way.

And as I pin him to the table, I take a moment to survey him.

Maybe I don't have to kill him.

After all, isn't he already one overdose away from the grave anyway? With how many needle marks he has on his arm, he won't last much longer.

But to satisfy my own morbid craving, I hold tightly on to his neck, positioning the blade to the start of his hairline.

His screams are music to my ears as I drag the knife down, blood pouring out, flesh opening up like a spring flower in bloom, the flaps of flesh letting me know just how deep I've dug it in. And when I reach his eye, I take it one step further. They may have spared my sight, but that doesn't mean *I* will return the service.

After all, in my world, it's not an eye for an eye. It's an eye and you're done for.

The tip of the blade reaches the white of his eye. In spite of his screams, in spite of the way he's trying to move his arms and legs, my hand is uncharacteristically precise. I dig the blade in until the eye comes out with a pop. Cutting all the connective tissue, I fling it to the side, enjoying the way his socket is filled with blood, his throat already hoarse from all the screaming.

But he's not out.

The pain must be a lot too since his entire body is shaking— although it may be from his drug addiction.

Still, I don't stop as I do the same honors to the other eye, taking it off his socket and letting him wail some more.

A smirk of satisfaction is painted on my face as I take a step back, watching my work of art.

There are already people banging on the locked door, probably drawn to his hellish screams of pain. But before I leave, I cannot help myself as I pick up the discarded eyeballs, placing one in his hand, and one in his mouth as it opens on a deafening shrill.

The timing is just right as he clamps down his teeth on the eyeball, the jelly-like consistency exploding in his mouth.

Satisfied with half of my revenge, I leave the room, some of the murderous rage simmering inside of me exercised on those good for nothings.

Still, the prospect of going back to the house and knowing I'm one wall away from Gianna does not help. At all.

How am I going to not fucking kill her?

It's the dead of the night when I get to the house, going straight for my room and pulling at my bloodied clothes.

My knuckles are stained with red, just like the rest of me, and I reek of all the destruction I'd wrecked.

I reek of death.

Flinging the shirt off my back, I make to undo my trousers when I hear the creak of the door.

My head snaps towards the direction of the noise, noting small, dainty feet step inside the room.

She's dressed in her pink nightgown. The same one that always gives me wet dreams, and visions of sinking deep inside of her.

But now, as I see her—the real her—the only thing I want to sink inside of her is my knife.

Maybe after she chokes on my cock.

The treacherous bitch has the gall to look shy as she gazes with trepidation at me, her lower lip trembling as she scans my body, her eyes widening at the sight of blood.

A small gasp escapes her, and it takes everything inside of me not to pay her back for the fool she's made of me right here and now.

Already I can feel my rage returning tenfold, along with my barely buried feelings. But all the love I'd felt for her—and it had been love—has already turned to deep, gnarly, festering hate. Much as I'd like to deny that I'd ever had feelings for her, I can't. Not when she's the only woman who's made me feel like that, the only one I would have considered opening up and sharing all of myself with—my strengths and my weaknesses. And because of that deep love, I'm now dealing with the polar opposite. A loathing so strong my entire body is rebelling at trying to keep myself from harming her.

From fucking her so bad and hard I'd erase all other men from her body. From finally getting the heaven her body promises before ensuring she *never* sees heaven again.

I can already see myself, cock buried to the hilt, my lips on hers as I breathe in her treachery, making hate to her duplicity. All before I bring my knife to her lovely throat, cutting from ear to ear and feeling as life leaves her body, her blood painting me red—the red of her betrayal.

Fuck, but she's driving me crazy even now, when all I want is to watch the life leave her body—punishment for her Judas' kiss.

"Bass?" she asks tentatively, that soft voice of hers doing wonders to my cock even in my murderous state. The bastard would take her anyway—Jezebel or not.

Ah, but who wouldn't?

"What are you doing here?" My tone is flippant, but it's the best I can muster all things considered. That I'm not already pinning her to the wall and fucking her to oblivion shocks me—it fucking astounds me.

"I..." she trails off, wetting her lips. Her eyes are still on my bloodied torso.

"Did you kill someone?" She asks, and I note a small tremor in her voice.

"Why?" I take a step towards her.

She's stuck to the spot, but I can tell her body is rigid as she keeps herself still.

"Do I scare you?" I ask, almost mockingly.

But I do. I definitely scare her as her eyes flicker over my face, slightly widening when she gets a better view of the red that's seeped into the ridges of my scars. I must look like a true Halloween treat.

"I was worried," she adds, once more going for that insecure tone that she knows gets me *every single time.*

"Were you," I drawl, taking another step towards her.

This time, the fear is clear on her features as she backs away from me.

I continue to tease her like this until her back hits the closed door.

"What happened, Bass? Are you hurt?" She feels the tension rolling off me and she's trying to de-escalate.

"No," I answer curtly, my hand going to the top of her gown as I brush past her erect nipples. The reaction is immediate as a shiver envelops her body, goosebumps appearing all over.

She's primed for fucking. One touch. Just one touch and she's begging for cock.

Her eyes are already glazed as she looks at me, biting her lower lip in a come hither way—not unlike the one she used on the other man.

The thought is sobering, and without even thinking, my hand wraps around her neck, my fingers caressing her pulse point.

Ah, but it would be so easy. One squeeze and I'd snuff the life out of her.

But I can't. *Not yet.* Not when the worst is yet to come.

And no matter how much my cock is begging for me to just lift up her dress and fuck her like the common whore she is, I can't.

Not yet.

Because I know that one thrust and I'll crack—I'll show her exactly what she deserves for cheating me.

No, I'll keep that last step for the final humiliation. When I show *everyone* what a fucking devious slut she is.

"Why did you come here, Gianna," I lean down, whispering in her ear. Her breath hitches, her pulse throbbing under my fingertips.

"I missed you," she whimpers as I continue to massage her flesh. "I missed you today," she repeats, turning those big eyes towards me and fuck me if she doesn't look like a goddess fallen from the sky.

"Did you," I tsk at her, my other hand already moving down her body. "How much did you miss me, sunshine?" I rasp, so much violence inside of me threatening to burst through the surface.

"So much," she says on a half moan as I lift her nightgown, my fingers trailing over the surface of her barely covered pussy.

"Who did you wear these for, Gianna? Who did you want to have access to your pussy?" My voice is rough as I palm her mound, pressing the back of my hand over her clit and making her moan in reply.

"You," she breathes out. "Only you."

"Hmm."

The little liar.

Without any preliminaries, I tug her panties to the side, surprised to be met by her dripping lips.

Either she's mastered full control of her body, or she's horny for every fucking dick. The thought doesn't help as I slide two fingers between her folds, searching for her hole.

A sick thought forms inside of me, and I can't help but wonder if I'll find another man's cum inside of her. A deep and ugly jealousy rears its head at the idea, and I all but jam my fingers inside of her.

"Ah," she gasps, almost jumping in my arms as I push inside of her, feeling her velvety walls surround me—strangling my fucking fingers.

She's tight. Fuck but she's tight.

No wonder those fools would give their right arm to have their cocks slide inside this tight, warm heaven.

"Bass," her hands come to rest on my upper arms, her fingers digging in my skin as a strangled moan escapes her. "That... slower," she whispers, but I'm not about to give her slow. Not when this is the only thing keeping me from turning her around and taking her like an animal.

"Shh, sunshine," I coo, my breath fanning on her cheek. "I have you," *you dirty little whore.*

"It's too much," she opens her mouth to say something else but her eyes close, her spine arching as she seems to find her pleasure.

I thrust in and out of her, watching in fascination the ecstasy that appears on her face as she comes, even more juices dripping out of her.

She's limp against the door as I remove my hands from her person. She titters a little before her knees buckle, her breathing still harsh.

"Wow," she exclaims, her voice rough. "That was the most powerful orgasm I've ever had," she shakes her head, a small smile on her lips.

"Why don't you show me how grateful you are then, sunshine?" I say just as I unbuckle my belt.

She peers at me from beneath her lashes, and her innocent act is starting to grate on my nerves.

"Show me how you can be my dirty little slut," I tell her as I fist my cock in front of her.

"Your... dirty little slut?" She repeats, her cheeks flushed, her tone unsure.

"Yes," I smirk at her. "That's what you are, isn't it? My dirty little slut," I bring my other hand to her face, gripping her jaw and tilting her head so she can look at me, "my very own fuck toy," I continue, watching a small frown appear on her face. "Tell me, sunshine, aren't you hungry for my cock like the dirty little slut you are?"

For a second, I don't think she's going to reply. Not as she looks at me with those big eyes of hers that even now reek of contrived innocence. She's looking like she's never seen a dick before, much less sucked one.

"I..." she starts, still unsure.

"Tell me how much you want my cock between those lips," I slip my thumb between her lips, urging her to suck on it. "If you don't tell me, I won't give it to you." I smile at the outrage that crosses her features.

Of course, even deep in her acting she wouldn't miss on being a cock slut.

"I want to suck your cock," she finally says, but her voice isn't firm enough.

"And...?" I tease her, bringing my cock to her mouth and brushing the head against her lips, pulling back when she opens her mouth to take me inside.

She's watching me with confusion in her eyes—but oh, so much desire she could burn down a building with the fire in her gaze.

Licking her lips, she's watching my movements closely as I bring my thumb over the head of my cock, swiping some of the pre-cum and bringing it to her for a small taste.

"The words, sunshine, and this cock is yours."

I don't know why this one act makes me so fucking hard I'm about to burst. But there's something to be said about the way she's on her knees before me, forced to beg for my fucking cock. It's the high of being in control of her arousal and most importantly of myself. Because even with my dick so hard, cum straining in my balls to be released, I'm still not giving in and allowing her to put her mouth on me.

I'm not a slave to her.

It might be a small comfort, but it is one, nonetheless. Especially seeing how I haven't fucked or murdered her tonight. I'd say it's a big fucking achievement.

"I want to suck your cock," she says again, with more determination, "because I'm your dirty little slut," she smiles, almost proud of herself for saying it out loud.

"That's a good girl," I smirk at her, finally bringing my cock to her lips and allowing her to take me inside.

I let her play with me for a moment, her attempts clumsy but driving me crazy at the same time.

She'd never get an award for sucking cock, but her enthusiasm earns her bonus points.

When she's had her fun, I hold her hair in a tight grip, my fingers on her scalp as I thrust my dick all the way inside her mouth, instantly hitting the back of her throat and making her gag.

She's making choking sounds as spit dribbles down my length, her lips wrapped around the base of my cock in quite possibly the most beautiful sight I've ever seen.

I grip even tighter as I realize it's a sight everyone's probably seen.

The jealousy inside of me threatens to spill forward, and in turn I keep on thrusting inside her mouth, fucking my aggression on her, ignoring the way tears are running down her cheeks, her entire face a wet mess.

She keeps gasping for air and I keep feeding her my cock until I feel my balls contract, my shaft trembling with the force of my release. Drawing back slightly, I let her take a deep breath just as my cum hits the back of her throat, coating her entire mouth and tongue.

"Show me," I command her, grabbing her jaw and prying her lips open.

She blinks rapidly, but does as instructed, opening her mouth and thrusting out her tongue towards me.

Cum mixed with saliva drips down her chin as she keeps her tongue out on display.

I can't help the smile that forms on my face as I look at her, somehow wishing I could take a picture to immortalize the moment.

"Swallow," I give her the order, satisfied when she does, audibly gulping down all of my cum.

"You're such a good little slut, sunshine. You love being ordered around, don't you?" I ask as I tentatively caress her cheek.

She gives me a small nod, almost as if she's ashamed of it.

"Then how about this," I lean in to whisper. "I want you to crawl to your room and dream of me fucking every single one of your holes," I pause as I feel her whimper. "Because that's what's next on the menu, sunshine. My cock in *every fucking hole.*"

I don't stick around to see her reaction as I get up and head inside the bathroom.

Ah, my dirty little slut, but this is just the beginning.

FRIVOLOUS

Chapter Sixteen

GIANNA

The engagement party is quickly approaching, and every time Clark comes to the house, I have to force myself to be in the same room as him.

"Oh, look what time it is," I give him a fake smile. "I need to head for a dress fitting," I say as I stand up.

Bass is by the door, his eyes not missing anything as usual.

He's the only reason I'm able to withstand Clark's visits. Him and the fact that our plans will soon materialize.

He's already told me that he's managed to find us new identities and the itinerary for our escape is almost done.

"Not so easy," Clark drawls, and before I know it his hand is on my wrist, pulling me back.

Revulsion fills me as the acid in my stomach churns and churns, threatening to make me ill. Still, I keep my forced smile on, not wanting to show him how much his presence affects me.

"Not even a kiss for your fiancé?" He asks, his voice grating. But not more than the way he looks at me, his eyes dipping to my chest.

I pull at my hand.

"After the wedding," I say stiffly.

From the corner of my eye, I see Bass' stance and I know he's ready to act if things escalate.

Leaning down, Clark whispers in my ear. "You won't have your bodyguard forever, little girl." That appellation is somehow the worst as it reminds me what an old pervert he is, "and I can't wait to fuck you into submission when I have you alone."

My mouth drops open, but before I can act, he releases me, heading out the door.

"Are you ok?" Bass asks when he reaches my side.

I nod.

"He's just a dirty old man," I make a disgusted expression. Bass grunts, not offering a reply.

Raising my head to look at him, I take in his imposing frame and cold countenance. Not for the first time, I feel that there's something seriously wrong with him.

Ever since that night when I'd found him covered in blood, he's changed. His attitude towards me has changed. He's colder, more demanding, preferring to order me around instead of carrying a normal conversation.

And it worries me. Because I want to know what brought this one.

Who did he kill?

And why is he so mean to me?

He'd also been rather insistent that I tell him what happened at the event when I'd gotten drunk. I'd answered him honestly, that one minute I was having a great time, drinking in moderation, and the next I'd blacked out, only remembering snippets of the night—like him taking me home and taking care of me.

Maybe my behavior had worried him? Truthfully, even for me it had been odd, since I'm always careful about how much I drink and I pace myself while doing so. That I'd gotten so drunk had been a little disconcerting.

Regardless, I can't let that cloud my thoughts—not when I'm so close to finally be free.

Since being with Bass I've started seeing a new side of myself coming to the surface. Or maybe it's just an old side that has been suppressed for too long. But for the first time, I find myself daring to do a lot of things that would have sent me into overdrive in the past.

I've even started taking my pills less and less, now taking one only if I feel an incoming attack, but not preventively as I'd done in the past.

With this development comes a new type of freedom as I slowly start to feel more in control of my own body.

For the first time, there's hope.

Hope that I don't have to live in perpetual fear, hope that my body is once more my own.

And there's nothing more liberating than the act of giving myself to the man I love.

The more time we spend together, I become increasingly sure that soon I'll be able to take the last step—give myself completely to him. Every intimacy gives me new confidence.

A while ago I would have never imagined myself in this position. Hell, I could have never imagined myself letting someone touch me. But with Bass... I'm letting him do a lot more.

A whole lot more.

A blush envelops my features as I think of his mouth on my pussy, of his hand around my throat as he thrusts his fingers in and out of me...

With my past, I've never thought I'd enjoy being dominated like this—allowing him to subdue me as I give him full control over my body.

But there is only one reason for this.

Trust.

I trust him more than I've trusted anyone in my life. Lord, but I trust him *with* my life.

For someone who's been let down by everyone since birth, I've never thought I'd ever willingly put my life in someone's hands. Yes, I've had bodyguards over the years, and I'd even had a cordial relationship with Manuello, my previous one. But they had just done their job, while I'd kept my walls up, maintaining a distance between us perhaps even larger than that of an employer and employee.

Bass' arrival in my life, though, changed everything.

He showed me that I don't have to always be alone—lonely. It's ironic that for all my reputation as the queen bee, I've never known true confidence until *he* made me feel confident.

Confident to be myself, confident to be vulnerable, and confident to proudly wear my imperfections just as my imperfections.

"You're sure everything is set for Saturday?" I ask, needing to have the confirmation.

"Yes. I have our IDs and our travel route set. We leave immediately after the party," he nods at me before ignoring me once more.

I feel a little disheartened at his reaction, since it's not the first time he's come across as closed off. I have to wonder if maybe he's regretting his decision to elope with me. After all, he will be forced to leave his life behind as he knows it, and he will likely be unable to contact any friends or family or risk putting them in danger.

There's also the small matter of his feelings towards me. Sure, he's told me he cares about me, but that's not the same as love.

It's a whole lot different from love.

I should know since what I feel for him goes beyond mere *caring*. It's this deep need that gnaws at me, threatening to drive me crazy when he's not near. I feel like an addict binging on her favorite drug and wishing the supply would never stop.

It's an entirely foreign feeling, but one that's overtaken my entire being. There's no me without him anymore, and that's a sobering realization.

"Do you... regret it?" I make the courage to ask.

I pull backwards before flinging myself forward, the swing carrying me in the air with a whoosh. We'd relocated to the garden in an attempt to enjoy some of the nice weather, but Bass has continued to keep aloof, standing by me but somehow doing his best to ignore me.

"Regret what?" He asks, his tone clipped—like it usually is these days.

I stop, my feet propped on the ground as I look at him. Bringing my hand to shield my eyes from the sun, I take in his grave expression as he stares forward—as if he can't bring himself to even glance at me.

"Running away with me," I say, noting the slight clench of his jaw. "Leaving your life behind."

"Of course not," he replies. "After all, I'll have you, won't I?" he turns to me, his expression inscrutable.

I nod, reaching out to take his hand in mine. "You know you have me." I bring his hand to my cheek, closing my eyes and reveling in his nearness.

Just knowing he's by my side makes me want to confront all of my demons—make everyone who's ever hurt me *pay.*

"That's right, sunshine." His entire stance is stiff. "You're mine, aren't you? All mine."

"All yours," I reply, trying to meet his eyes with mine.

"Good. Good," he nods, but why is it that I don't believe him?

I shake myself. I shouldn't question my good fortune when it's been so hard to obtain it.

And because I've gained a new confidence in myself, I know exactly what I need to do.

I need to close that painful chapter from my life—once and for all.

"We need to apply more blush. You're looking a tad too pale, dear," the make-up artist adds as she dusts some of the powder on my face, focusing on my cheekbones and trying to add more definition to my features.

She is right. I am pale.

I'm beyond pale.

Because what I'm about to do will mar me forever. But before I can start a new life, I need to put the old one behind.

"Done. My God, but you look like a doll, Gianna. Your fiancé will not be able to take his eyes off you," she comments sweetly and I force a smile.

That's the goal, after all, for what I have in plan.

The make-up artist soon leaves, and I have some time to dress and get everything ready.

I quickly put on the gown, fastening it in place. Then, making sure the door is locked, I lift my mattress up, looking for a bag with fine white powder—cyanide.

The quantity isn't much, but according to some sources, enough to kill a person.

Knowing time is of essence, I make sure I'm handling it properly as I take the powder from the small bag and place it on a sheet of paper.

Then, opening my jewelry case, I take out the antique ring I'd bought. From the outside, it looks like a regular ring, and wholly inoffensive.

A small mechanism on top of the ring and under the central stone opens an empty compartment. Historically used in assassinations, now it's all but a relic of the past and thus it ensures that people are *never* suspicious of a mere ring.

Propping open the lid of the ring, I fold the sheet of paper into a funnel, pouring the white powder inside and snapping it closed. Satisfied that it won't accidentally open, I quickly slide it on my finger.

A knock on the door startles me, and as I open it, I come face to face with Bass.

His eyes rove over my body, his gaze seemingly eating me up alive.

"Like what you see?" I trail my hand over his chest in a seductive attempt. It's hard to believe that a few more hours and we'll be able to leave everything behind.

"When do I not," he drawls, his hand on my jaw as he slips his thumb inside my mouth. I suck on it, hypnotized by his gaze that promises to do wicked things to me.

"A few more hours," I breathe out, the anticipation clear in my voice.

"Indeed," he purrs, his tone sending shivers down my back.

And as we take the car towards the venue, I can't help both fear and happiness from forming inside of me, like a knot waiting to be unraveled, the outcome of tonight's party and our escape the deciding factor.

"We'll talk later," I tell Bass, briefly kissing his cheek before we step out of the car. He grunts, not adding anything else, but I've already come to expect it from him. He's not exactly the most talkative person.

As we step inside the venue, the ballroom is to the right, taking over the half of the entire ground floor.

We'd visited it a couple of times before to approve everything. An old aristocratic manor, the entire location screams expensive. There are different rooms in the house, all put at the guests' disposal for entertainment and photoshoots.

The guests are already here. I wade through an army of obsequious people, all kissing my cheeks and congratulating me on my engagement.

Not even half an hour into the event and I already feel overwhelmed by the fake pleasantries everyone is offering, or by the strained smiles on their faces.

Everyone realizes what this engagement means, and considering Clark's age, everyone can tell I'm marrying him for money—nothing else.

"Finally, a good use for your daughter, love," Cosima jibes on a fake laugh, holding tightly to my father's arm.

"She's doing what she was raised to do." Throwing his gaze around the crowd, he grunts in satisfaction.

"Is that what you raised me to do, papa?" I throw the question at him, my eyebrow raised in a spontaneous show of rebellion. "Then you shouldn't complain the next time you call me a whore either," I add, watching the scandalized looks on both Cosima's face and my father's. "After all, that's what you raised me to be," I tip my glass towards them in a mock salute, moving away before they decide to reply.

I might not get to give my father his due—or even better, Cosima—but I want him to know I'm *not* what he raised me to be. I won't ever be. And tonight should prove it.

Bass is by the entrance with the other bodyguards, his eyes following my every movement.

I know he won't like what he sees in a moment, but I can't *not* do it.

Turning my back to him, because I don't think I could stand to see the disappointment on his face, I go to where Clark is currently deep in conversation with some men.

Already I feel my stomach knotting in disgust, the mere fact that I'll have to pretend to like his company making me feel even worse.

Still, I've spent my entire life pretending. What's one more moment?

I'd fully prepared myself and I'd taken my pills before the event so I wouldn't have any attacks—knowing fully well that his presence would trigger me.

"Clark," I let my lips dance in an open smile.

"And there she is. Gianna, meet..." I can't even hear the words when I feel his arm snake around my waist, his touch burning like it's the hottest coal. It's killing me inside to stand like this and welcome his attention when all I'd like is to gut him like the sewer rat he is.

Instead, I just keep wearing my smile, nodding my head as he makes the introductions. A small mantra in my head, and I'm back on track. After all, I know very well what this situation entails.

The men are quick to give us a moment alone, and it gets increasingly harder to pretend he doesn't make the hairs on my body stand up—in the worst possible manner. He's like a horror movie playing inside my mind, the jump scare just around the corner as it waits to pounce on me when I least expect it.

And I know that no matter how hard I may try to keep my guard up, his rat-like antics would ensure he gets away with his evil plans—it's already happened once when he'd cornered me in that bathroom, locking me in a stall, alone and at his mercy.

"Where is your goon, Gianna," Clark mocks, "I haven't seen you without him so far."

"Around," I shrug, seeming unconcerned.

"I must say, I'm impressed. You're not afraid of me anymore," he smirks as he comes closer to me, his fingers brushing over my naked arm.

It takes everything in me to keep my expression in check. But as I meet his gaze, my smile is unflinching.

"I'm not afraid. In fact, I've been wanting to talk to you," I start and his eyebrows immediately shoot up in surprise. "Since we're going to get married anyway, we might as well be cordial to each other."

"Cordial," he chuckles, the sound making my skin crawl. "I don't want cordial with you, Gianna," he suddenly says, coming closer to me until his mouth is close to my ear. The proximity is killing me, but I'm staunch in my stance, not betraying my fear or revulsion.

"I'm going to train you as my little pet," he continues, his tone suddenly affectionate. "And you know what pets do?"

I shake my head.

"They listen, obey and *never* talk back. Not even when the skin on their back peels away. They don't make a sound."

He seems rather satisfied with himself, and I bet he wants me to quake in fear at knowing what awaits me.

Instead, I decide to play his game.

"We haven't seen each other in two years, Clark," I turn to him, showing him he doesn't scare me. "You may have heard what they say about me," I say in a seductive tone, my fingers playing with the lapels of his coat. "I might just like it," I whisper as I lean into him.

"Damn," he whistles, his eyes glazed, his arousal already clear. "You've grown, Gigi. We might yet have some fun together," the corner of his mouth pulls up.

"Why don't we drink to that?" I suggest, giving him one of my blinding smiles.

"Why don't we…" he repeats, looking at me as if he'd fuck me on the spot.

The table with refreshments is but a step away, so I turn around, undulating my body for him as I walk towards it. I sway my hips, pushing my ass back so he has something to pay attention to.

And as I grab two glasses of champagne, I slip open the secret compartment, pouring the white powder inside one glass, quickly swirling the liquid with my finger so it mixes well.

Then, as if nothing happened, I turn to him, offering him the glass while I bring my own to my lips.

"To… submission," I breathe out, noticing he's still staring at my body in that lascivious manner of his. He's so enthralled by what he's seeing, he doesn't even glance at the glass, quickly downing it.

"To submission," he agrees, a wide smile stretching across his face before he leans down to press his lips to mine.

Disgust is the last thing I feel as I try my best to keep my mouth shut so no residual cyanide transfers from him to me. And when he finally releases me, I excuse myself to go *fix my lipstick,* all the while wiping at my lips.

I swipe a glass of water on my way out, trying to thoroughly cleanse my mouth.

Damn!

Just as I'm out of the ballroom, though, I see Bass quietly follow behind, his expression grave.

He must have seen the kiss.

Needing to explain to him what I'd done, I turn to him.

"Bass..."

"Not now," he stops me from continuing, taking my hand and dragging me somewhere down the corridor to a different wing of the house. Stopping in front of a door, he pushes it open, tugging me inside.

"It wasn't what it seemed," I immediately start.

"It wasn't?" He raises an eyebrow.

He seems calm, yet there's an anger radiating off him that I can't really pinpoint.

He turns the light on and I note the room is a library of some sort with a study desk in the middle. Everything is a deep mahogany wood, ornate designs carved on every inch of furniture.

"I had to do it."

"What did you have to do?" He slowly takes his coat off, flinging it around before returning his attention to me.

"I had a plan," I take a deep breath. "I wanted to close a painful chapter in my life so we could start a new one."

I move towards him. His neck is tense and I can see a vein protruding and extending to his jaw.

"I love you, Bass. I would never do anything to hurt you," I tell him honestly. "I needed to put on a good show so they wouldn't expect our escape. Besides..." I bite my lip, a little apprehensive to admit I'd planned to kill a man—have almost succeeded. It's just a matter of time before Clark drops dead, and then I'll be forever free of his shadow.

"You love me," he repeats, his voice sounding weird to my ears. "*You* love *me?*" he asks on a chuckle.

"What's so funny. You must know that already," I frown. Have I not shown him so far how much I love him? How much he means to me and how he's fundamentally changed my life?

I used to be a broken toy for people to play with, but since meeting him I finally feel like I've regained some of my agency back.

I'm not broken.

I'm not helpless.

And most of all, I'm not a victim—not anymore.

"Prove it," he raises his chin in a quiet dare.

"What do you mean?" I tilt my head, studying him and trying to see how *this* is the man I love. Something doesn't quite make sense.

"Prove it. Let me fuck you."

My eyes widen at his request.

"What..."

"We've been playing cat and mouse for months already, Gianna. Every time we got closer to doing it, you chickened out."

"But you must know already," I whisper, blindsided by his demand. "I wasn't ready."

"Will you ever be?" He throws the question casually. "Or will you just dump me when I'm no longer useful to you."

My mouth parts in shock.

"Is that... Is that what you think of me? That I'd abandon you after I got what I wanted?"

"Isn't that what you've led me to believe?"

I pause a second, trying to think about it rationally. Have I been too selfish with him? All this time, have I been so wrapped up in my own trauma that I didn't realize he felt like this?

The answer is... maybe. Ok, maybe yes.

I hadn't stopped to wonder how long he'd be fine with me putting off sex and asking him to *always* stop before doing it. But looking through his perspective, I can see that it may have seemed as if I was purposefully withholding it to control him.

"But you know it's not true. You're the only man I love—I've ever loved. That has to count for something," I attempt a smile.

"So prove it. Prove it you're not playing with me." He throws the challenge again and I can see it in his eyes that he means it.

But... Can I do it?

I raise my gaze to meet his, and my decision is solidified.

This is Bass. The man I love. The man I trust with my entire heart. And if he needs this to feel confident in our relationship, then so be it.

"Ok," I nod. "I'll do as you want."

"Good." He grunts, his eyes studying me in my cocktail dress.

"Go to the desk and put your ass in the air."

Chapter Seventeen

Gianna

"Go to the desk and put your ass in the air."

I blink at him, thinking I didn't hear him right.

"You want me to… now?" I ask, incredulous.

In two steps, he's in front of me, his thumb tipping my jaw up as he looks down at me.

"Show me you're mine, sunshine. Show me you're *only* mine," he says, an odd cadence to his voice.

And as I look into his eyes—those steely eyes that have become my safe haven—I find myself nodding.

"Alright," I whisper, raising myself on the tips of my toes to give him a kiss.

Even in my six inch heels, I still have trouble reaching for him. But as my lips meet his, everything fades away.

There's no more fear. No more dread. There's just the safety of his arms as he wraps them around me, holding me tight as the warmth of his body seeps into mine.

For as long as I live, I don't think I'm going to forget the happiness that blossoms in my chest at knowing he is mine, and I am his.

He moves, maneuvering us until I feel the hard edge of the desk hit my back, a gasp escaping me at the contact.

"Bass..." I break the kiss, raising my gaze to his.

There's lust there, but there's something else. Something that both scares and excites me at the same time.

"I love you," I tell him, my arms twined around his neck as I keep brushing my lips across his, slowly making my way all over his face as I try to put into action what I feel deep in my heart.

It's inexplicable, and words fail me as I try to convey everything he makes me feel—everything he awakens inside of me.

Suddenly, he leans back, watching me with hooded eyes, an inscrutable expression on his face. Before I can ask him if something's wrong, he twirls me around.

My hands come to rest on the edge of the study as I steady myself.

He's behind me, his presence burning a hole through my back. And though the stance is oddly reminiscent of that night, I don't let panic overtake me. I thrust it out of my mind as I give myself to the moment—to the man I love more than anything.

His rough hands are trailing up my legs, bringing my dress up and settling it over my ass.

Pushing my chest down on the surface of the table, he uses his foot to separate my legs. I'm quick to note what he wants, so I accommodate him by widening my stance.

The air feels cold as it caresses my private parts, my panties the only thing still standing between us.

"Bass?" I utter his name, a sliver of uncertainty going through me. "Can we maybe..." I trail off, biting my lip as his hands are back on my legs, and he slowly brushes the tips of his fingers up and down my thighs. "Can we do this facing each other?" I ask, a little unsure of myself.

Although I'm making a conscious effort not to think about that night, my body still remembers it, and I can barely stop myself from shivering.

"Tell me, sunshine," his breath caresses my ear, his front almost flush to my back, "tell me you're only mine. Tell me that I'm the only man for you. The only one you welcome in your tight pussy," he rasps, and suddenly, his fingers are there—in that place that aches for his touch.

My panties become scraps on the floor as he searches for better access to my pussy, his fingers probing deep and finding me wet for him—when am I not?

"You are," I answer on half a moan, already forgetting about my previous concerns as he starts stroking me, expertly flicking my clit and making me squirm under him. "You're the only man for me," I say on a gasp when he pushes two fingers inside of me, working them in and out in a slow and sensuous torture.

"Really?" he drawls, his breath on my nape as he licks my skin. "Does that mean your pussy belongs to me and *only* me?"

"Yes," I cry out as he increases his speed, my orgasm within reach.

And as he opens his mouth over my flesh, biting into my neck, his teeth a sweet pain dulled by the soothing of his tongue as he licks and sucks on that tender spot, I come.

Hard.

So hard I start screaming with the force of my release, my walls contracting around his fingers. He pumps them a few more times in and out of me, but I'm already gone as I slump on the desk.

That burst of pleasure still dancing in front of my eyes, I'm almost unaware of his movements behind me.

It's with a blissful delay that I realize he's undone his pants, his cock at my entrance as he swipes the head over my pussy in a soft caress.

Even more pleasure erupts through me as he teases my sensitive flesh. But the pleasure is deceiving as he pushes inside of me with one thrust, burying himself to the hilt.

My back arches, my eyes widening in pain as my mouth parts on a silent moan.

The pain is almost blinding as I feel him deep inside of me, surging forth and retreating. Every time he thrusts into me though, there's a deep sting at my entrance that makes my sight blurry with tears.

I clutch at the edge of the table, holding tight as he keeps on thrusting into me, not even noticing that he's literally tearing me apart.

"Bass," I say his name on a strangled moan.

"Fuck, Gianna," he rasps. "You're so fucking tight you're strangling my cock," he continues to speak, moving his hand to my neck and holding tight, bringing my back flush to his front.

"Ah, sunshine," he groans, his hips pistoning in and out of me as he holds me tightly by my neck, his fingers massaging my pulse point.

The pain, though, is slowly dissipating as he trails his other hand to my front to touch my clit. A whimper escapes me as I feel the sensations shift inside of me. From insufferable pain to a sweet numbness accompanied by bursts of pleasure, I can barely control myself as I let out moan after moan.

And through the massive sea of sensations, there's only one thing that matters—the way I feel about him.

Because as I feel his cock so deep inside me, touching me in a way I'd never thought possible, I can't help but tear up, my emotions spilling forth. There are no words to describe the way he completes me as he finally makes me his, this joining physically solidifying the way our souls are already joined.

"That's my dirty little slut," he nibbles at my ear lobe, his hand still on my neck as it slowly starts tightening and restricting my airflow, my euphoria climbing as I become lightheaded.

"Yes," I quickly say, "I'm your dirty little slut," I give him the words, because I am—only for him.

"Tell me how much you love my cock destroying your pussy, Gianna. How I'm fucking wrecking you for any other man. Fuck," he shouts. "Tell me you're a slut *only* for my cock, sunshine. Tell me!"

His movements are becoming increasingly more aggressive, his cock still leaving a burning trail behind as it moves in and out of me.

"I am," I cry out. "I'm a slut only for your cock. Please..." I don't know what I'm asking, but as I feel something build deep inside of me, I can't help the way I keep on pushing my hips towards him, wanting to take him deeper, wanting to hurt more so the pleasure can be so much sweeter.

As his hand is massaging my neck, he moves it slowly to my hair, his fingers gripping tightly as he pulls my head back, placing open mouthed kisses all over my cheek before biting it.

"Who's fucking you, Gianna?" *Thrust.* "Whose cum is gonna fill up this pussy?" *Thrust.* "Who's fucking owning you, my dirty little slut?" *Hard thrust.* "The words, Gianna. I need the words," he speaks in my ear, his voice chilling and almost emotionless.

But I'm too far gone to wonder about that. Not as he pulls on my hair so hard I'm both hurting and tingling from the pain, my pussy contracting around his length in an attempt to keep him inside— merging us as one.

"You," I moan out loud. "I'm yours, Bass. My pussy is yours. *Everything...*"

Everything I am is yours.

"I own every hole in your body, don't I, sunshine?" There's a slight chuckle as he taunts me with the words.

"Every hole," I answer.

"Every fucking hole, sunshine," his voice is low, the bass reverberating through every cell in my body. "You'll take all of me as I fucking breed you. Pump you so full of my cum you overflow with it. I want to see it spilling from every fucking orifice. Your mouth," he yanks me closer to him as he bites my lip, "your pussy," he grunts as he slips out of me completely before slamming back at full force, my body reeling from the impact, "and your ass. Isn't that right, my dirty little slut?" He coos low in my ear.

"Yes," I breathe out, my vision swimming from the combination of pain and pleasure he's wrecking on my body. "My body is yours," I strain to speak, my mouth seemingly unable to cooperate. "You can do anything to me."

"That's right, sunshine. You're fucking mine," he growls in my ear.

Suddenly, he pushes my face down on the table, my cheek against the cold surface as he keeps me pinned in place.

He thrusts into me as if he'd like to imprint himself on my very soul.

"Fuck," he curses out, suddenly stilling as his release claims him.

I'm breathing hard, sweat clinging to my body from the exertion. He's not any less affected than me, barely getting himself together to move.

His cock slips out of me, leaving a burning trail that culminates in an aching emptiness.

As soon as I'm out of his hold, I turn around, trying to regain my equilibrium.

There's a deafening silence as Bass stares at me, his eyes wide with horror.

"What?" I frown, following his gaze down my body. "What..."

There's blood on my dress and between my thighs, red splattered all over. And as I look back at him, I realize I got some on him too, the condom splattered with red just like the base of his cock.

"I'm so sorry," the words tumble out of my mouth immediately.

"Shit," he curses, suddenly looking worried. "Are you ok? Did you just get your period?"

He quickly gets rid of the condom, zipping himself back up and I feel slightly put on the spot. I bring my teeth over my lower lip as I bite it in uncertainty, giving him a small shake of my head.

"Then... why..." his brows are knit together in consternation as he keeps on perusing my bloody thighs.

I pull down on the dress to cover myself, self-conscious about his examination and a little embarrassed about what had happened.

Maybe I should have told him beforehand, but I don't think he would have believed me—I don't think anyone would have believed me.

"Gianna," he calls my name, his eyes still fixed on the spot between my legs. "Please tell me it's not what I think it is," he whispers, his voice almost anguished.

Raising his gaze to meet mine, he asks again. "Tell me. Just tell me it's not..."

"I'm sorry," I reply with the only thing that comes to mind. Because I *should* have told him.

"What... how..." he shakes his head. "I don't understand," his voice seems broken as he keeps on shaking his head, a lost look in his eyes that tugs at my heartstrings.

"It's not your fault," I'm quick to assure him. "It happens sometimes during…"

"During the first time," he completes my sentence.

I nod.

He takes a tentative step towards me. And another. Until he's standing in front of me. There's so much torment etched in his features, and I feel guilty for having caused it.

"I'm fine, I promise," I raise my hand to his cheek, slowly caressing his unmarred flesh.

"How?" he croaks. "How…" he shakes his head. "Clark, he…"

"He didn't. Not like that," I answer, feeling a pang in my heart at hearing his name mentioned. I'd never told anyone what had happened that night for two reasons. For the longest time it had been hard to even think about it, much less recount it to someone else. And there was also the issue with people already thinking the worst of me. No one would have ever believed me.

But because he's Bass. Because he's *my* Bass, I find myself confiding in him.

"He's had an obsession with me since I was fourteen," I start, telling him about the incidents where he'd visit my room at night. "He would always try to corner me alone and touch me. I was usually pretty good at avoiding him. Until I wasn't," I whisper.

"I was sixteen," I tell him about *that* night.

How Clark had cornered me in the bathroom, pushing me inside a stall and all but ripping my clothes off me. How he'd restrained me, a knife on my cheek as he'd threatened to disfigure me if I didn't let him have *a taste*. How he'd touched me all over, my tears and screams all in vain. And then how he'd unbuckled his belt, and I'd felt his erection touch me. I'd threatened to tell everyone that he'd raped me, but he'd just laughed at me, telling me there would be no proof. Because he could still fuck me and I'd remain a virgin. And no one would be able to tell.

"Sunshine…" Bass stops me, and I note a lone tear in his eye. I bring my thumb up, wiping it away.

"He tried. God, Bass, it was so painful. He kept trying to push it in my ass, and I kept on screaming, my throat raw from pain. I don't know how I managed to get my bearings together. But at that moment,

I knew that I'd rather have my face ruined than let him ruin *me*. I fought back. His knife cut me on my back and on my arms, but I fought back until I managed to run away."

"Gianna, baby," his arms come around me in a tight hug. I feel his chest contract and I realize he's crying—for me.

"You want to know what was equally as bad?" I lean into him, everything I'd kept buried suddenly finding its way to the surface. "My best friend walked in on us. In the bathroom. She stayed long enough to take a picture under the stall, and then she told everyone I was a slut who likes to take it up her ass. That's how the rumors started," my voice feels painful as I relive that betrayal. "That's how everything started."

I lean back, trying to gauge his reactions, a little disconcerted when I see him white as a sheet of paper.

"Bass? What's wrong?"

"I didn't know… Honest to God, sunshine… I didn't know," he keeps saying, his eyes on me, his gaze filled with so much anguish I feel his pain as my own.

"Bass, you couldn't have," I tell him tenderly. "I swear it wasn't as bad as the blood makes it seem. It didn't hurt that bad," I blush as I tell him. "But I'm glad it was you. I'm glad he didn't take that from me. You're the only one for me. Always," I give him a tentative smile.

Without notice, he takes a step back. And another. And suddenly, he falls to his knees in front of me.

"I'm so sorry, sunshine. I didn't know. I swear I didn't know." He continues to speak and my confusion mounts as I see him repeatedly say he's sorry for something that isn't even his fault. It's mine because I didn't tell him.

"Bass…"

"Please forgive me. Fuck, they lied to me, sunshine. They lied… And like an idiot I bought it. I fucking believed all the shit they told me," he continues to say, his features ravaged with agony.

Just as I'm about to ask what he means, the doors to the library open, my father striding in. He makes a straight line for me, the back of his hand connecting with my cheek as I'm sent flying to the floor.

Bass makes to help me, but he's quickly restrained by my father's guards.

"Papa, don't," I yell as I see them drag Bass out the door.

But the worst? He's not even fighting it. There are only two people handling him, and I know his strength. I *know* he could out-power them. But he doesn't. He doesn't even try.

Instead, there's a resigned look on his face as he gives me one last nod, his eyes sending me another apology. For what, I don't know.

"Let him go, please. Nothing happened," I turn to my father, quick to jump at Bass' defense.

"You're fucking stupid, Gianna, that's what happened. Fucking whore sullying the family name," he mutters under his breath. "And you know what's worse?" He gives a maniacal laugh as he stares at me. "You went and fucked our enemy of all people."

I frown at his words. "What do you mean?"

"There's no Sebastian Bailey. But there is a Bastiano DeVille," he almost spits the name, and I cower back, thinking he's going to strike me.

"I... I don't believe it." I say rather confidently. I know Bass—I know *my* Bass. He wouldn't do something like that. It must be a misunderstanding.

"You don't believe it," my father chuckles bitterly. Roughly grabbing my arm, he all but drags me out of the library and into the ballroom, where everyone seems to be focused on a projection on the wall.

I don't see it at first. But I hear it. And what I hear is like a spear through my heart.

"Gianna Guerra, or should I say the DeVille whore?" the voice says, laughing. And I recognize that voice. I *love* that voice.

No! Bass couldn't do that. He wouldn't do that.

But as I extricate myself from my father's grasp, I realize people are starting to stare at me.

One step. Two steps. Three steps.

And I see it.

My arms fall by my body as I feel my entire body go numb—my heart shattering in a million pieces never to be put back together again.

I own every hole in your body, don't I sunshine?
Every hole.

Every fucking hole, sunshine. You'll take all of me as I fucking breed you. Pump you so full of my cum you overflow with it. I want to see it spilling from every fucking orifice. Your mouth, your pussy, and your ass. Isn't that right, my dirty little slut?

Yes. You can do anything to me.

The words echo in the room, the sound of flesh slapping against flesh resounding even louder. My moans, his moans.

Everything.

I'm stuck to the spot as I see Bass fucking me on the desk, the video filmed from a vantage point in the study. You can't see much of me except his hips pumping in and out of me.

But the damage is done.

The damage is more than done.

I keep shaking my head, hoping this is all a bad dream. That I haven't just been betrayed in the worst possible way by the man I love. That a video of me isn't playing for over two hundred people, all already with their phones out to record what they can. That I haven't just lost *everything*.

He used me.

He used me for revenge.

The realization is startling, and my breath catches in my throat, my lungs constricting and making me gasp for air.

It feels like I'm suffocating.

And as people continue to stare at me with their condemning gazes, the words *slut, whore, tramp* sounding in my ears, I can barely hold myself upright.

How could you, Bass? How could you...

My sight is hazy as my eyes fill with tears. Still, I continue to watch that one scene on repeat. The video had been customized by someone to have the message and a short snippet of Bass fucking me, ensuring people knew I was now a DeVille whore.

The pain in my chest continues to expand until a hollowness overtakes me.

The man I'd fallen in love with. The man I'd given my trust to. The man I'd given *myself* to.

He was an illusion.

He'd never said he loved me back.

He'd never said anything except his need to own me—to actually turn me into the whore everyone condemns me to be.

God, but how could he?

I bring my fist to my chest, banging on it in an effort to alleviate some of the pain I feel in my heart.

All our moments dance before my eyes, and I try to identify signs of his deceit.

He played me so well. I can't help but be astounded by the way he'd toyed with me, using all my weaknesses to promptly catch me at my lowest. And when he'd managed that, he'd turned himself into my protector, making me trust him with my very life.

And I had. That's the bitter truth, and why this betrayal cuts so deep.

I'd trusted him so unconditionally, giving him all the love I had to offer, and he'd simply stomped on it.

Now I'm here… a shell of myself, an emptiness that echoes back at me and lets me know I've truly lost myself.

But this time… I don't think there's a way back.

I'm slow to get out of my shocked state, but the first thing I see when I become more aware of my surroundings is my brother.

Michele is standing right in front of the video projection, watching his sister get fucked by her bodyguard in the most vulgar way.

Without even realizing, my feet take me to him, my hands covering his eyes as I beg him to stop looking.

"Don't," I whisper, my heart breaking even more that my baby brother had to witness it.

"Gianna!" someone yells my name.

By this point, the crowd had parted, seemingly no one wanting to be close to the *whore.*

The whispers are bad enough, all of them calling me slurs unbefitting the ears of an adult—much less a child. But I can't shield my brother from everything.

And as I see Clark saunter towards me, his face a mix of embarrassment and mottled anger, my entire body starts trembling, my knees almost buckling.

But as he makes to reach us, he suddenly clutches at his heart with his hand, foam appearing at his mouth as he drops to the ground.

Dead.

He's dead.

I can't even gloat.

Because soon, I'll be dead too.

Chapter Eighteen

BASS

I try to open my eyes, but there's not much I can see. My eyes are swollen shut, and I've already lost count of the amount of punches I'd taken to the face. If I'd been scarred before, I expect now I'll be downright disfigured.

Nothing less than what I deserve.

Fuck, but I deserve so much more.

Leave it to Benedicto to draw out my death, though. By the end of my miserable life, I'll have endured enough pain to atone for at least *some* of my sins. Because there are some things that not pain, nor death, nor any other fucking thing can erase from my mind.

It's been a day now, or maybe two? I think I've lost track of time as I'd been in and out of it for most of the time.

His guards had taken me to a dark room—a basement I assume, since there are no windows—and since the beginning, they'd tied me to a big, wooden X on the wall. Securing my arms and legs with barbed wire, they'd ensured that I'd have perpetual wounds— bleeding and festering and bringing me closer to my death.

And it won't be too long until I'll be dead. I know it deep in my gut, just as I know that after the second or third beating I started to become numb to the pain, my body taking it in stride.

But while my body has become inured to fists and wounds, my heart has been hemorrhaging in my chest, the pain so intense it's like I feel every drop of blood as it spills from that vital organ.

I don't think I've ever experienced more self-loathing than the moment I'd been faced with the consequences of my actions. With the fact that I'd been fucking manipulated into killing my own heart.

And there's nothing worse than knowing it's no one's fault but my own for falling for Cisco's lies.

From the beginning, I'd been primed with skepticism, and because of my own issues with my mother's death, I'd been easy to fool into believing Gianna was just like her.

Fuck... Gianna.

I don't even dare say her name in my thoughts, the act seeming like the highest offence after what I did to her.

I can still picture the way she'd looked at me, so much love in her eyes as she'd been willing to do *anything* for me.

Fucking hell, but she shouldn't have had to prove me anything in the first place. I should have been the one to question everything I'd been told and just... trust her.

Her smile is ingrained in my mind as she'd whispered words of love, the trust she'd placed on me so undeserving. And that's the one sight I want to take to my grave.

As I replay every single interaction with her in my mind, I can now see the signs perfectly.

From the very beginning she's been a vulnerable woman doing her best to protect herself while hiding her weaknesses. The mask she'd shown to the world was the only thing helping distract from what was really going on with her—she was fucking terrified.

Everything is starting to make sense—the pills, the way she'd react if men touched her unwarranted, as well as her bitchiness. They were all coping mechanisms and ways to keep people away from her. She'd come across as heartless and mean when she was only a traumatized woman thrown to the wolves to devour her.

What had she said? To assimilate, she'd started behaving like one too. She'd assumed the mean girl persona to keep people at arms' length.

And knowing what I do now about what Clark did to her, and about her best friend's betrayal?

It doesn't fucking surprise me.

If anything, I'm in awe of her strength. All this time, she's had absolutely no one. Everyone had condemned and maligned her, branding her the vilest of whores when in fact she was anything but.

Until I turned her into one.

Fuck…

I can't help the way my eyes tear up, even busted up like this.

Because my darling girl had been living with that stigma for so long, the rumors never far from her hearing, and I'd just turned them into reality.

I'd made her into the whore everyone thought her to be.

To my dying breath, it's going to be the one thing I will never be able to forgive myself for.

And as things start to shift into perspective, I realize that I'm no better than Clark.

I'd taken advantage of that innocence that had somehow remained untouched even under layers of sophistication and worldliness. In spite of all the depravity and malice surrounding her, she'd maintained her naivete, until I ruthlessly stripped her of it.

The first time I'd forced her on her knees comes to mind, and how I'd mocked her for her lack of skill when it had in fact been just inexperience.

The signs had been there. Fuck, but the signs had been there. But I'd been so deep into my warped perception of her that I could not see past them.

Every single intimate interaction we'd had had been filled with apprehension on her part, her tentative touches a result of her trauma, not as I'd arrogantly thought—a way to wrap me around her little finger.

It's too late. It's too late to realize that she'd been the only innocent one in this whole debacle.

And now? I'll die knowing I caused the woman I love extreme anguish. That I destroyed her entire life.

Cisco is probably patting himself on the back now, knowing he's reached his goal and he'd made an utter fool out of me.

And if I have a dying regret, it's that I can't kill the motherfucker from the grave. That, and knowing my girl will hate me forever.

I'm once more in and out of consciousness. I'm vaguely aware of Benedicto paying me a visit and promising me he's going to send my head to Cisco as a present after he's done with me. Of course, as if Cisco would care.

He'd gone through so much trouble to make sure his plan worked, and *it had.* He must be gloating at the success.

Defile. Debase. Destroy.

Why, I'd fulfilled each of his orders. But I hadn't done that only to Gianna, I'd done that to myself too. Because there's nothing worse than knowing I forced a girl to blow me, or that I broadcast a video of me fucking her to the entire world. Her destruction had been my destruction.

I'd known the moment I'd seen the blood on her thighs, the implications slowly entering my mind and making me realize what I'd done—that I'd ruined the only good thing in my life with my own two hands. I'd known right then and there that there was no other fate for me than death. So I hadn't resisted when they'd come for me. Hell, I'd wished they would have just pummeled away, hoping physical pain would alleviate the spiritual one.

But it hadn't.

Nothing could.

I'd let my jealousy fester into something so ugly, I'd ended up destroying *everything.*

Because that's the only reason I'd been willing to do Cisco's bidding.

Even now, knowing the video must be fake, the memory of it is enough to get a rise out of me—shackled as I am.

The sight of her fucking another man when she should have been mine had been my undoing. And I'd let myself go. I'd let myself fucking sink.

And there's no excuse.

I jump up, startled, the barbed wire cutting deep in my wrists and ankles. Water splatters all over my face, washing away some of the blood already caked around my many wounds.

But as I open my eyes, it's to come face to face with a vision—or at least it seems so. Because why would Gianna Guerra be standing in front of me right now, if she's not a figment of my imagination?

"You're awake," she nods thoughtfully, turning her back to me to pick up another glass of water, dumping it all over my face again.

The liquid also helps with my sight and I'm able to see her better as she plops herself in front of me, her features exquisite as always, but emotionless.

"What..." I croak, my throat dry, my voice hoarse from unuse. "What are you doing here?" I ask again, this time managing to get the words out.

She looks me up and down, and she doesn't seem particularly impressed by the state I'm in. If anything, she looks bored.

And it's breaking my heart.

Maybe she's here to kill me. Put me out of my misery herself. It would be her right to do so, and for all that's saint and pure, the thought of being dispatched by her would actually warm my already dead heart. Because then I'd have paid at least a fraction of my dues to her.

"I see they took care of you," she purses her lips.

There's nothing in her expression to suggest she's happy, or sad at the state I'm in. If anything, her apathy is even more disconcerting because I fear I may have broken her—for good this time.

"What are you doing here?" I repeat, and she raises her eyes to look at me.

"I know they're going to kill you," she says blatantly. "I didn't come here to gloat, if that's what you're thinking. Although," she pauses, her gaze studying my wounds, "I'm happy to see you suffering as you deserve." She shrugs, as if she didn't just confess her love to me a few days ago, and now she's looking at me as if I were a mere stranger—a stranger she would rather see dead.

"Then why?"

"You don't have much longer," she continues. "Not with the state you're in. A day? Maybe two if you're lucky. Though those must hurt like a bitch," a smile plays at her lips, the first sign of anything other than apathy on her face.

"Why are you here, Gianna?" My tone is rather brusque, the total opposite of what I'm feeling for seeing her one last time.

I must have done something right in a past life seeing that I'm blessed with seeing the woman I love once more before dying. Although the joy is immense at seeing her again, I can't help but hurt all over as I take in her features.

She's pale, her skin sallow. She's wearing a pink dress that's entirely too big for her, the wide fit masking her figure.

She doesn't look good. She looks anything but good. And that makes me die a little at that very moment.

Because I did that to her.

"I want to know why." She straightens her back, pushing her chin up as she gazes at me unflinchingly. "Why me? Why..." She pauses, shaking her head. "Why did you have to do *that?* Was anything real?" The questions pour out of her, and I note the confusion in her eyes.

For as much as she'd like to look unbothered, she's not.

"I..." I don't even know what to tell her. I could excuse myself all day long, but the truth is that I *am* guilty.

"It was all supposed to be a revenge plan," I start, telling her about my bargain with Cisco. "He'd just gotten me out of jail, and this was my payback."

"Jail?" Her brows shoot up in surprise.

I nod, or at least try to. My neck is too stiff for that type of movement.

"I got caught killing someone," I add jokingly, cracking a smile. But she doesn't laugh. If anything, she frowns more.

"Go on."

"The mission was to ensure you wouldn't be able to marry anyone," I proceed to recount Cisco's plan and how he'd wanted to keep Benedicto bankrupt for as long as he could.

"I see. So that's why you approached me," she nods thoughtfully.

"But things changed." I state grimly. I don't want to throw myself a pity party, but I don't want her to believe that what we shared—or at least part—was fake.

Her eyes widen as she tilts her head to look at me, waiting for me to continue.

"I started seeing you in a different light." I swallow deeply. "I fell in love with you," I admit, and if the circumstances had been different, I would have loved the expression on her face—shock and pleasure mixed in one.

"How can I believe you?" She whispers the question, and it hurts that I put us in this position, where even the truth is seen as a lie.

"Everything was real. I even got us fake identities," I give a dry laugh.

"Then why? Why would you do something like that to me? Why, Bass?"

"I'm not going to excuse my actions in any way, sunshine." She flinches when she hears the pet name, and the taste of bile inundates my mouth at her reaction.

"Someone lied to me." I take a deep breath. "I was ready to leave my family behind—betray them. I was ready to leave everything behind for you."

"What could they have told you that..." She shakes her head. "What you did to me, Bass... I don't think you realize that you didn't just humiliate me. You *destroyed* me," she says and a lone tear falls down her cheek.

"I'm sorry," I give her a quiet apology, even though as I see her face scrunch in disgust, I know no amount of sorry is going to cut it. I blew everything.

"Go on," she invites me to continue, seemingly getting herself under control.

"It was a video. I realize now it must have been doctored somehow... But when I saw it, I went mad with jealousy."

"A video?" She frowns.

"Of you fucking someone the night you got drunk at that event," I explain and I tell her everything I'd seen in the video.

"I don't remember everything from that night, but I would have never done that, Bass. I would have never done that to *you*." She shakes her head. "How could you think so little of me that I would cheat on you?"

Even I am disgusted at myself for buying Cisco's lies.

"The video was flawless, Gianna. But even if it wasn't... I was so angry, so fucking angry..."

"That didn't give you the right to do that, Bass. That didn't give you the right to ruin me."

"I know, sunshine. I know. And I'll gladly take my punishment. I just..." I sigh. Now faced with her like this, I can't even find the words to let her know how much I regret how everything turned out.

"I'm sorry. I know you will likely never forgive me, but I want you to know that I do regret what I did to you."

She looks away, her chest rising and falling with every breath.

"Did you... love me?" Her voice is barely above a whisper as she asks me, her gaze not meeting mine.

"I did." I answer honestly. "I do."

She nods, her hands clenched into fists by her side.

"Thank you. For telling me." She says right before she turns. With her back to me, she stills for a moment.

"I loved you too, Bass. Or I thought I did. Because how can you love someone you don't know?" Her profile swathed in darkness, her words cut me deeper than any blade. "You didn't love me either. Yes, you might think you did, but you only loved an idealized version as me, just as you hated the perceived one." She takes a deep breath. "You know, they say we have three great loves in our lifetimes—the fairytale love, the hard love, and the forever type of love. Maybe I'm lucky and I had the first two with you. Because you were my fairytale, Bass. You were the hero I thought was going to save me from my tower. But then you weren't." She pauses. "You turned into the villain who set fire to the tower, gladly watching me burn."

"And I did burn," she gives a dry laugh. "Maybe I'm still burning a little. But just as you gave me happiness in the beginning, you also gave me the most important lesson."

Spinning on her heel, she turns, coming even closer to me, those gorgeous eyes of her clear and full of strength as she stares into my pain-filled ones.

"No one can save me but myself. I don't need a fairytale. And I don't need a hero. I only need myself. So thank you for that." A sad smile pulls at her lips.

"Sunshine..." I croak, unable to cope with the pain in my heart.

"And maybe in the future I'll be ready for the forever love too. Because I won't let what you did to me define me. I know that now. I'm not a whore. I never was," she raises her hand to my face, her fingers brushing against my bruised flesh. "I gave myself to you in love, or at least what I thought was love. And there's nothing to be ashamed about that. But you..." she stops, her fingers coming up coated in blood. "You should be ashamed for turning my love into something dirty."

"It wasn't dirty. Fuck, sunshine. I know that now. It was the purest thing in the world and I..."

She doesn't let me continue as she places her finger over my lips.

"What's done is done."

And with that she's gone.

I'm dying. I know I am. I feel myself getting weaker and weaker and I can barely feel my limbs anymore. My mouth is dry, my lips chapped, my entire mind foggy as I struggle between a state of being and not being.

Benedicto's men visit me once more, beating what's left of me, before leaving, convinced I won't make it through the night.

I'm convinced too.

That is until her voice makes me struggle to open my eyes.

She's here.

Again.

"I have a deal for you," she says, and I can barely focus on her figure.

"I'll let you go, and you give me the IDs you got for us," she continues.

When she sees I'm not replying, she brings a bottle of water to my lips, wetting them and letting me drink.

"More," I croak.

She feeds me all the water before stepping back, assessing me with narrowed eyes.

"Do we have a deal?" She asks, and my mind can't make sense of why she'd do something like this.

"Why?"

She grimaces.

"Clark isn't dead. They got to him before the poison did its job," she says, telling me about her plan to kill him and how she'd almost succeeded. "He wants to marry me tomorrow, and I can't have that. No, I won't have that," she states determinedly.

There's something different about her, but in my wretched state, I don't trust my perception anymore.

"Where... where will you go?"

She shrugs.

"That's for me to figure out. But we need to hurry before anyone notices I'm down here."

I want to argue. Tell her I'm not worth saving—that I'm not worth anything. But maybe helping her this time might lessen my own sins, since I'd never want her anywhere near Clark—or Benedicto for that matter.

"What about Michele?" I ask, knowing she'd wanted to leave with her brother.

She looks as if someone struck her when I say his name, and she slowly shakes her head.

"He won't be coming."

"I'll help you," I agree, knowing I'd do more than that. I'd fucking do anything for her.

But that's neither here nor there. She needs my help and I'll give it to her. Besides, I don't know if there's anything left of me that's salvageable—both physically and mentally.

She cuts my binds, quickly helping me clean up before ushering me towards the house and to my room where I'd carefully stashed all the paperwork.

I hand her everything she needs before we both head downstairs to the garage.

She's carrying a small bag that barely fits her necessities, but as I ask if that's all she's taking, I can see she's completely determined to leave everything of her old life behind.

Hotwiring a car, I quickly drive out of the estate, surprised to see that no one's giving chase.

"I put some sleeping pills in the guards' dinner," she says flippantly, before ignoring me for the rest of the journey.

I'm hanging by a thread as I drive into the city, surprised I'm able to fully focus on the road. Knowing what's at stake, though, helps me push through one last time, dropping her off at the train station as she'd instructed me.

Stopping the car, there's a moment of silence as we both stay still.

"This is goodbye, Bass," she speaks first, not looking at me.

I try to blink some clarity into my eyes but my sight is already leaving me. Still, as I slip out of consciousness, I think I hear her something more.

I even think I feel her kiss my cheek.

But she wouldn't.

Not anymore.

It's all just an illusion.

"Look who's rejoined the living," I hear a voice speak.

Opening my eyes, I bring my hand up to shield my eyes from the light, noting the bandages secured around my wrist and up my arm.

"Where am I?" I ask, disoriented.

"Uncle," I turn to see Dario roll his eyes at me. "Is that my thanks for taking care of you when you were at death's door?"

"What do you mean? How did I get here? Last I remember..."

I watched Gianna leave. For good.

"I have no clue. Someone called me and told me there was a package waiting for me at Penn station. I couldn't help my curiosity so I went. Imagine my surprise when I find *you*," he laughs. "Looking like a corpse too. Really, Bass..." he shakes his head.

"You must have heard what happened," I grunt.

Everyone should have heard what happened at Gianna's engagement party.

My eyes swipe across the room and I recognize the furniture. *Cisco's home.*

"Of course. You're famous now. Or should I say notorious," he chuckles. "Everyone thinks you're a hero. Why, several of Cisco's men want to name their newborns after you for the set down you gave Guerra. One of the best," he brings his fingers to his mouth, imitating a chef's kiss.

"Where's Cisco?" I ask, my voice strained. Because if this is his home, then it must mean the bastard's close by.

If I am still alive, I'll just count my blessings and do the one thing I wanted to before—fucking end Cisco. I'll probably die afterwards anyway, but at least I'll know that fucker won't be able to hurt Gianna—ever.

"He should be coming by later," Dario shrugs. "I knew you'd be surly so I brought you some magazines," he adds, dropping a few in my lap.

"Seriously?" I roll my eyes at him, brushing the porn magazines off the bed.

"Where's your sense of humor, uncle?" He groans.

But I don't let him say anything more as I shoo him from the room, taking some time to ground myself.

My body feels fine—all things considered. There's still some pain in my extremities, where the barbed wire had cut into my flesh, but as I go to the bathroom to inspect my face, I realize the damage had been minimal.

The swelling must have gone down while I'd been out of it, and though I forgot to ask Dario how long that was, I can only assume it's been at least a couple of days.

Looking around the room, I find a new phone and some toiletries laid out for me. Meanwhile, a doctor also comes by, checking in on me and congratulating me on my speedy recovery.

Feeling stronger than I have in days, I finally go after my fucking nephew.

"Damn, uncle, you don't look that much worse for the wear," he chuckles when I open the door to his study to find him smoking out the window—a common occurrence with Cisco.

"Is that how you greet the *hero?*" I ask mockingly, closing the door behind me and advancing towards him.

"Right," he shakes his head, "where are my manners?" He quickly disposes of his cigarette out the window, opening his arms to give me a hug.

I don't even think as my hand shoots out, my fingers wrapping around his neck as I lay him down on his desk, sweeping all his things to the floor.

"Damn, a little violent, aren't we?" He keeps joking, giving me a lazy look.

Cisco isn't a fighter. He's never been one. He's always been a ruler—the one who orders others to do his bidding.

And though our frames are of similar sizes, I know he's no match to me, even in my half dead state.

"You knew," is all I say as I grit my teeth, my fingers squeezing at his neck. "You fucking knew."

"What are we talking about?" He asks, feigning ignorance.

"You knew the truth about Gianna. You knew the rumors weren't true."

"Ah," he scoffs. "But of course," his wide smile resumes. "That's why I sent you there, didn't I? To make the rumors true."

"Cut the crap out, Cisco."

"Tsk, tsk, uncle. You're ruining my favorite suit, you know?" he says jokingly as he straightens his coat.

"Why?"

"Why not?"

"Damn it!" I curse, banging his head on the table. "Have the decency to tell me why. Why did you doctor that video? Why do you hate Guerra so much? Why do you fucking hate *me?*"

"I don't hate you," his expression immediately changes from playful to serious. "You were just the perfect scapegoat," his shoulders angle up in a lazy shrug. "The video..." he trails off, "they call them deepfakes. You can't trust anything these days, uncle."

"You knew how I'd react. You fucking knew..."

"Yes. I was banking on it. And you acted brilliantly. The video from the engagement party was amazing too. I told you she'd be a good lay." He has the gall to smirk at me.

"Because of you I..." I can't believe how stupid I'd been to fall into his trap.

"No, uncle. Because of *you*. You were the one who never once questioned whether the video was real or not and that's on *you*. You can sit there and blame me all you want, but I merely gave you the push you needed. The destruction... That was all you."

I raise my fist, bringing it against his cheek and feeling the burn as bone meets bone.

Still, Cisco's sporting the same amused expression on his face, even as I keep on pummeling him.

"Why? WHY? Fucking tell me why!" I yell as I continue to punch him, blood already pouring from his lip and nose.

"Because it's fun," he drawls, a maniac laughter escaping him. "Because it's infinitely more fun watching people flounder than watching them be happy."

"You're sick," I snarl at him. "Fucking sick," I continue to punch, even as my wrist hurts like hell, the skin off my knuckles peeling away, I keep on punching.

"Yes! I'm fucking sick. So bring it on, uncle. Show me what you've got," he laughs, his white teeth stained with red as he keeps on baiting me with his words.

"I'll fucking kill you," I say as I fling him to the floor, my foot connecting with his stomach.

He starts coughing blood, but the laughter doesn't stop. If anything, it's stronger.

"Come on, you can't say you didn't enjoy fucking her. Was her pussy as good as they say? Come on, old man, share the details."

Something doesn't fit as I realize I'm just beating him to death and he's not even defending himself. If anything, he's baiting me to hit him harder.

He's on the floor, gasping for air as he spits more blood, but that sick smile is still on his face as he looks at me with a twisted grin.

One more kick and I have my foot on his chest, keeping him down.

"Do it," he taunts. "Fucking do it!" He yells at me, and in that moment, all I see is Gianna's face as she'd walked out on me—for good. The ending of a life I never even had.

And for that, he doesn't deserve to live either.

"Come on!" He yells at me. "Fucking do it! Who do you think hired those people to cut you? Who do you fucking think orchestrated the entire thing? Because I knew you'd fall for every *single* one of my traps, uncle," he laughs.

I still, my eyes wide in shock.

"You..." I trail off, my voice filled with horror. "You hired them to cut my face?" I ask incredulously. "Why... What the fuck?"

I shake my head, unable to believe I'm staring at someone I'd watched grow up—that I'm staring at my fucking family.

"Because you fit my plans," he shrugs. "And because I could," he winks at me, his entire face bloody and looking like a fucking freak show.

"What's wrong with you..." I shake my head at him.

"Guerra took everything from me," his lips curl in contempt. "It's only fitting I took everything away from them too," he chuckles. "After all, Benedicto only ever cared about his social standing. Now he has *nothing*," he continues to laugh like a madman, going on and on about his perfect plan for Guerra and how I'd been the perfect pawn.

"But there's one last step," he grins like a fool. "So do it! Fucking kill me and get *your* revenge," he laughs manically, and I realize what he means by the last step.

He *wants* me to kill him.

I don't know what Guerra took from him, but this isn't the Cisco I know. This is a deranged version of him, possibly on the brink of a mental breakdown.

But as he continues to hurl insults at me, taunting me with Gianna, I don't care whether he's got a death wish or not.

"I promised my men they could take a turn too," he chuckles. "That video certainly whet their appetite. And she'd be willing wouldn't she? She already spread her legs for a DeVille once, what's a few more times?"

My fists connect with his jaw again—and again.

There's just so much a man can take before reaching his boiling point. And Cisco just sent me to mine. Betrayal after betrayal, he fucking ruined *everything*.

And I'll ruin him—literally.

Lifting my foot up, I draw it back to gain momentum before going for the region right under his chin, knowing that if I hit hard enough it's going to kill him immediately.

But just as I'm about to go for the kill, I feel a knife plunge deep into my skin.

"What..." I mutter, bringing my hand back and feeling for the wound. It had definitely come from the direction of the window. I remove the knife from my shoulder, surprised to see it's tiny—and likely hadn't done much damage.

I barely have time to register what's happening when Cisco's expression changes completely.

He's looking at something behind me with a mix of awe and shock, his eyes wide, his mouth parted open.

Finally turning, I note the presence of a newcomer—a woman.

Dark hair, and dark eyes, her features are emotionless—dead—as they gaze upon Cisco.

"You don't kill him," she states, not even looking at me. "I kill him," she proclaims in a foreign accent.

Cisco still hasn't reacted, looking at her as if he'd seen a ghost.

"He needs to die," I grind my teeth, ready to fight her for that right.

"Why?" She finally turns to look at me. "He wronged you?" She raises an eyebrow, and I nod, a little surprised at her question. "He wronged me too." She tilts her head as she meets Cisco's gaze.

Of Asian descent, she's around five foot four, but there's a nimbleness to her movements that is quite impressive. Especially as she managed to take me by surprise enough to stab me in the back.

"You can kill him after I kill him," I add drily, turning back to Cisco.

He seems to have forgotten I even exist as he all but gawks at the woman.

"No." She says again, this time more forcefully. "I don't think you understand me. *I* kill him. Because he wronged me first."

"Right. Debatable, but let's just kill him together and be done with it," I suggest, a headache mounting both from the sudden exertion and from arguing about fucking killing a man and *not* killing him yet.

"No." She says again, and I get the impression she likes to speak in short sentences. "He's mine. And if you try to steal my kill," she slowly turns towards me, "then I'll kill you too."

"Wait, wait, wait," I roll my eyes. "First of all, I don't hurt women. No offence," I point towards her outfit, which is clearly designed for fighting. "But I don't see why we couldn't cooperate and kill him together."

"Stay out of what doesn't concern you, stranger. He wronged me first. He's mine to kill."

"Fine, let's do it another way. What did he do to you? Because I'm pretty sure he didn't orchestrate an elaborate scheme to get you to destroy the woman you love, all in the name of some fucking gratuitous revenge."

"He dishonored me," she says through gritted teeth, throwing Cisco a glance full of disdain.

"He… dishonored you?" I ask tentatively, because my mind is sending me to one place and one place only, and that might be the worst offence.

"Yes. He betrayed me and married a bitch," she rasps, her eyes wild as she seems barely in control of herself. "And now that bitch will be a widow," she says with a sick smile on her face.

She's holding a blade in each hand—butterfly swords. She slowly brings one to her lips, her tongue dancing over the sharp edge as her eyes are focused on Cisco.

Looking between the two of them I debate whether I should push the issue or not. But since she seems quite possibly more determined than me to end his life, then who am I to stand in a lady's way?

"He's yours," I nod, taking my foot off him.

"I'm done, Cisco. I'm done with you, I'm done with the famiglia, I'm done with *everything*."

It feels like a weight's been lifted off my chest as I renounce my affiliation with the famiglia once and for all. Because I may have been their lackey my entire life, but no more.

Everything was over the moment they destroyed my heart.

I make to leave, only pausing one moment to ask.

"What's your name?"

She frowns, as if she can't understand why I'm asking, but after a prolonged pause, she does answer.

"Daiyu. My name is Daiyu."

"Good, Daiyu, make sure he dies a slow death. The bastard deserves it."

A smile pulls at her lips.

"Oh, by the time I'm done with him, he'll wish *you'd* have killed him," she gives a sinister laugh as she approaches Cisco.

I shrug, closing the door behind me. But as I leave the house that used to be my *home* at some point, I can't help but feel like I'm closing an important chapter in my life—at last.

Passing by what used to be my mother's door, the memories aren't as painful today as they used to be. Instead, they've dulled to a slight buzz, the images blurry.

It's perhaps the first time that I haven't felt a deep revulsion towards the events of that day, and how I'd played a role in both my mother's and my father's demise.

But as I leave—for good—I know a new chapter awaits me.

I'm still alive.

She's still alive.

And that means I'm chasing after my sun, even if my wings might melt along the way.

CHAPTER NINETEEN

GIANNA

ONE MONTH LATER,

The entire floor is bathed in darkness. Using the flash from my phone, I light the path to my apartment, quickly fumbling to get my keys out and unlock the door.

Once I'm inside, I firmly lock it, releasing a deep breath.

I don't think I'm going to get used to coming home after dark anytime soon. Yet it's my new reality.

I'll survive. I always do.

For a studio, the place is pretty spacious, even though the kitchen and the bedroom are in the same room. I'd had to make some tough decisions after I'd put as much space between me and my family as I could. And that had included seriously downsizing my previous life.

I'd chosen this place for the low rent, and for the relatively safe neighborhood.

Or as safe as it can be.

That has been the hardest.

Before, I'd had my guards with me everywhere, and no one dared to say a word to me. Now? The amount of times I'd gotten hit on and cat called in the last month is astounding.

It's particularly worse at night, when my shift at the restaurant ends. I always walk back in fear, clutching my bag and making sure I don't draw any unwanted attention to myself.

Taking my blazer off, I quickly put some food in the microwave before showering. When the food is done, I take it with me to the bed, quickly eating while reading from my textbook.

The decision to run away had been a spontaneous one.

When I'd heard that Clark had in fact survived the cyanide poisoning, I'd known things could not possibly turn out well for me. While he hadn't directly accused me of attempting to murder him, he'd declared he was going to marry me as soon as he was out of the hospital.

Since that had been out of the question, I'd known that I couldn't stay there any longer.

So what if Bass had betrayed me? I was still my own person, and for the first time I'd decided to take my fate into my own hands.

The most unforeseen thing, though, had been Michele's reaction.

He'd been the first person I'd gone to, knowing I could never leave without him.

"No," he'd said in that quiet voice of his, raising his gaze to mine and looking nothing like my baby brother.

"But Michele, you can't stay here…"

"No," he'd interrupted me, his eyes cold. "I'm fine on my own. I've always been. But you…" his lip had curled in disgust. "You've shamed us, Gianna."

The moment he'd referred to me as Gianna instead of Gigi, I'd known that something was wrong—something was terribly wrong. Because Michele had *never* called me by my full name.

"Michele…"

"You know that they make fun of me at school. That I had a whore of a mother and a whore of a sister. I always defended you. But I shouldn't have, should I? Because it was true. Everything was true."

"Michele, I know what you saw there…" I'd tried to explain to him, but he wouldn't have it.

"I know," he'd stated point blankly. "I'm not a child, Gianna. And like everyone else present that night, I had to see you—my sister—getting fucked from behind like a common whore."

I'd gasped in disbelief. Michele had never talked to me like that before. *Never.*

But no matter how much I'd tried to get through to him, I couldn't.

"You've done enough damage to this family. You need to leave and never come back. I don't have a sister, much less a loose one like you," he'd told me right before shutting his door in my face.

I'd barely made it to my room before tears had racked my body. But even then, I knew I couldn't waste any time.

In a way, wasn't it better that he renounced me as his sister? That way he'd never miss me again. But even that platitude sounded fake to my ears when my heart was breaking that my own baby brother—the one I'd basically raised—had shunned me.

Getting myself together, I'd started planning my escape, knowing I'd have to depend on Bass to make it out.

But was it really only that?

The grim truth is that it hadn't been *only* that.

Even knowing he'd stabbed me so deeply my wounds would not stop bleeding, I still could not let him die.

How could I when I loved him even if I hated him?

There was this part of me that still hurt for him. Especially after I'd seen him so beat up in that cellar. I'd known he had one foot in the grave, so I'd gone against myself—against that part of me that hated him more than anything—and I freed him.

I'm even more mortified to admit that I'd been worried sick in the days following our escape. He'd looked awful as he'd dropped me off at the train station, and I'd known from his slurred speech that he was almost out.

And so I'd once more done something that went against everything I *should* have done.

I'd called his family.

Why, I can't say.

I should have prayed for his death. I should have rejoiced at his pain. I should have fucking killed him myself.

Yet, I couldn't do any of that. Not when all I wanted was for him to live.

That worry hadn't helped with my new adjustment to the real world.

According to plan, I'd pawned off some expensive jewelry and I'd managed to get enough to pay the deposit for the studio apartment. But knowing the money I had wouldn't last, especially since I'd taken with me only a couple diamond necklaces to not tip off anyone, I'd had to get a job.

The only option for someone who had zero experience had been waitressing. I'd been lucky enough to find a position within a week of moving to a new city, and for a while now I've been working there.

The pay isn't great, and the job isn't easy either, but at least the tips are good and will help me put some money aside to start my studies in the future.

To escape notice and take advantage of my new identity, I'd also had to change my looks. I'd gone for dark hair, and I'd put on blue contacts. I'd also gotten a fake tan to make my skin slightly darker. Why, I almost look like a different person. Now, I only need to lay low and make sure I don't get on anyone's radar.

The first few weeks I'd survived on my stubborn will alone, spending ten plus hours at the restaurant and the rest crying at home.

It hadn't helped that I'd felt more alone than ever coming home to find it empty, the silence almost deafening. I'd missed my brothers, I'd missed home, and more than anything, I'd missed *him*—the bastard who threw me to the wolves and laughed as they chewed me up.

Soon, though, the crying stopped, and while my heart was still broken, I had a goal. After all, I finally had the freedom I'd always dreamed of, so why wouldn't I take full advantage of it.

Why let anyone stop me when I could do whatever I wanted if I worked hard enough?

Slowly, I started befriending the staff at the restaurant, even getting friendly with some of the regular clients. And while the emptiness in my heart was still present, step by step, I was learning how to live again.

After a couple hours of studying, I tuck my textbook in a drawer, and make my bed.

If I'm disciplined enough with my schedule, I might be able to take the GED and apply to some of the local colleges.

Early the following day, as I head to the restaurant, I can't help the nagging feeling that I'm being followed. Yet every time I turn to look behind me, there's absolutely nobody.

It's not the first time this has happened, and for a while now I'd felt like someone was watching me. Still, not having any evidence, I can only assume it's my paranoid mind. After all, I'd tried to find out some news about my family in the first week since leaving home—I couldn't help my curiosity. But the only online articles about Guerra had been dedicated to my engagement party and the video of me and Bass. Following the party, the video had been uploaded and re-uploaded *everywhere*.

Throwing that out of my mind, I increase my pace, making it just in time to put on my uniform and clock in.

Since it's Friday night, the shift is getting increasingly busy. My feet hurt like hell and I barely get a reprieve to rest them a little.

"Lara, table five needs you," my coworker signals me, and it takes me a moment to realize he's addressing me.

That's right. I'm Lara now.

Gianna is all but gone.

I head to table five, ready to take the order.

Once again, all the hairs stand on my arms as I feel someone's stare boring into me. Shaking my head, I take a deep breath and paint a big smile on my face.

"Hello. What can I help you with?" I ask in a pleasant tone.

The secret to hospitality is to always wear a smile on your face, even when you want to kill the customer. Besides, the nicer I am, the more tips I get, so it is to my advantage.

"Hmm, what would you recommend," the man asks.

He looks to be in his early twenties, with curly brown hair and dark eyes.

"We have a steak special," I point to the menu, going through my rehearsed lines of praising the food.

"I didn't ask what the special menu was. I asked what *you* would recommend," he turns his eyes towards me, and the perusal in his gaze makes me slightly uncomfortable.

"I like the steak," I strain a smile.

"Then I'll have the steak," he answers smoothly. And when I take the menu from him, he brushes his hand intentionally across mine.

Almost as if burned, I pull my hand away, still maintaining a pleasant smile.

"Right away," I say as I scurry away.

It's not as if it's the first time that a customer's hit on me. But no matter how many times it happens, I can't help but feel put on the spot, a sliver of panic threatening to overtake me.

Since I no longer have money to buy Xanax without a prescription, and I have no health insurance, I'd had to resort to some cheap alternatives—usually combinations of magnesium and valerian. While not as effective, they help me stay afloat. But there are moments when I feel like passing out, my mind closing up to the outside world and going into overdrive.

It will be a long time until I get used to being on my own and vulnerable—the perfect combination to get me primed for a panic attack.

But I'm tackling it one day at a time. I'm not going to let my issues define me or enslave me to a life of what ifs. Because I've seen how it goes—how living but not really living hurts worse than any panic attack. You're just watching your life pass by you, standing on the sidelines and seemingly unable to interfere.

It's *my* life. And I need to take the reins.

The shift continues and the man from table five keeps on trying to engage me into conversation.

I do my best to deflect the more personal questions, happy when he finally pays the bill and leaves.

"He was quite taken with you," Marie, one of my coworkers, comments.

"I'm sure he was just being nice."

"Nice? He left you a hundred dollar tip, girl. I want that kind of nice," she laughs.

"I tried to tell him it was too much, but he wouldn't have it." I explain.

"Lara, girl, are you for real? You get a hundred bucks, you don't ask questions. Go get yourself something nice," she winks at me and I give her a smile.

I'd felt a little uncomfortable taking that much money because I didn't want to give him the impression I was beholden to him in any way.

Getting my bag, I exit the restaurant through the back, pulling my hoodie over my head and trying to look as low-key as possible.

I have a small knife in my bag for emergencies, but I hope I won't have to use it. One attempted murder is enough on my conscience—though I wish it had been actual murder.

As I walk towards my apartment block, I can't help but feel that I'm being followed, the shadows playing with me and making me think there's someone behind me.

Turning around, I see a dark figure a few feet away from me and panic takes hold of me. Without even thinking, I start sprinting, running towards my apartment at full speed.

It's in vain, though, as the other person gives chase too.

But just as I think he's going to catch up with me, he stops.

Breathing harshly, I look back, noting there's no one behind me at all.

"Am I going crazy?" I mutter to myself, shaking my head.

I don't linger, though, running the remaining distance and closing myself in my studio, happy to have made it home in one piece. *Damn, but I need to be more careful.*

"Isn't this the guy from the other night?" Marie asks me as I put on my uniform. I lean forward to look at the newspaper in her hands, noting that there is a picture of that man.

"Yes. I think so,' I nod.

My eyes widen when I see the headline. His body had been found in a nearby park and he'd been stabbed to death, his hand cut off from his body.

"Good God," I mutter, horrified by what had happened to him. He might have come across as a little creepy, but that is too cruel a death for anyone.

"Poor guy. The police doesn't have any suspects yet either," she shakes her head, pursing her lips.

"I hope they catch whoever did it," I add sympathetically.

That night, when I go back home, I instinctively know something is wrong. I don't even have to turn on the light to realize that someone is inside.

My first thought is that my father's men have found me, and I quickly grab my small knife, ready to fight to the death for my freedom if need be.

But as I click on the light switch, it's to find the one person I didn't expect.

"What are you doing here?" The words tumble out of my mouth, my fingers tightening on the hilt of my knife.

"What does it look like I'm doing, sunshine?"

He turns slightly towards me, and I get a good look at him. There are a few new marks on his face and his nose seems a little crooked to the right. Other than that, though, he looks exactly the same.

"Get out," I tell him when I've managed to recover from my shock.

"No," he replies, standing up to his full height, and I'm once more taken aback by the discrepancies in our sizes.

He could crush me.

A sad smile forms on my lips. He *did* crush me.

"What are you doing here, Bass? Need to add something more to your revenge? What is it this time?" I raise an eyebrow. "Want another video? A close up porno?" I snicker at him, infuriated by his audacity.

"No," he repeats, coming closer to me.

"Stand back," I wave the knife in front of him. "Or I'll stab you."

"I don't care," he says, continuing to advance towards me.

Those steely eyes of his are watching me with a crazed intensity, and for a second, I can't help the fear that passes through me—but not because he might hurt me. No, the fear is because I might soften towards him. And after everything he did to me, he deserves to rot in hell.

To show him I'm not playing around, I hold on to my stance, watching him approach before I stick the blade in his shoulder.

He doesn't even wince. In fact, there's no expression in his face save for a savageness that seems to be barely contained.

My mouth parts, my eyes wide with shock.

"Stay… stay back," I whisper when I see it didn't affect him as I'd wanted to.

"No."

I step away from him until my back connects with the door and I realize I have no way out. I feel his breath on my skin as he's almost flush against me. Keeping eye contact, he brings his hand up to remove the knife, throwing it to the floor with a thud.

"What did I tell you, sunshine," he tsks at me, his deep voice caressing my senses.

I turn my head away, not wanting to lose myself in his hypnotizing gaze.

"You're mine. You were mine from the beginning. And I. Don't. Share." He enunciates each word, taking a strand of my hair and bringing it to his nose, inhaling.

He looks almost feral as he studies me, his nostrils flaring, his breath coming in short spurts.

I feel entranced as I look at him, and for a second I feel rooted to the spot as I lose myself in his gaze. It's invitation enough for him to bring his mouth to mine.

His hand on my nape, he holds me captive as he seeks to ravage my mouth, his teeth nibbling at my lips and urging them to open up for him.

I push my hands against his shoulders, trying to get him to release me. But he's unyielding in his attempt to get me to submit.

My body is flush against his, and I feel him hard and ready against my stomach. It should make me sick. It should make me turn away and run. But if anything, it reminds me of the ephemeral happiness I found in his arms.

And just as that melancholy seeps into my body, my mouth softening against his, I'm also reminded of his perfidy and the way he'd sold me out, causing me such immense pain I'm still reeling from that hurt.

So my struggle begins anew as I bite and claw at him, trying to get him to release me. Clamping my teeth down on his lip, I'm happy to feel his blood hit my tongue—evidence I'd bit hard enough. Still, he doesn't let go. No, he only leans back, watching me with hooded eyes.

"That's it, sunshine, hate me!" he rasps, his tongue peeking out to lick the blood from his lip. "Hate me, and take out on me all that anger you have inside," he takes my hand and brings it to his cheek, making me slap him.

Wide eyed, I watch as he folds my fingers in a punch, telling me to hit him.

"What... I'm not going to hit you," I mumble, shocked he'd resort to something like this.

"Do it! Make me hurt as much as you did. Because I know you did, sunshine. I know I bruised that beautiful heart in your chest and I'd do anything to soothe it," he looks so lost, his eyes two empty circles as he keeps hitting himself with my hand.

"Stop it, Bass. This won't solve anything," I say softly.

"Yes, it will. Fucking hit me, Gianna. Hate me, hurt me, fucking *destroy* me," he breathes harshly, "do whatever you want to me but understand you're mine. And I'll never let you go."

"You're insane," I shake my head at him.

"No. I'm desperate," he simply states.

His hand comes to rest against my neck, his thumb propped against my jaw as he tips it up so I'm looking straight into his eyes—witnessing the pure madness that seems to have made its home there.

"You might hate me. You might despise me. But I'm never letting go. And know this," he takes a deep breath, "you let any man touch you and they're fucking dead," he threatens.

"So that's it? You're just going to stalk me forever and kill anyone I come into contact with?" I ask, my voice unflinching.

"Damn right," he all but growls. "You're not getting rid of me. Ever."

"Really?" I roll my eyes at him. "See, that's your problem right here," I jab my finger into his chest, focusing on the area I'd injured earlier. "You were all too willing to believe I was a slut slumming it with just about everyone. But the moment you find you were the first to plow the field you turn all caveman on me. It doesn't work like that, Bass."

"Plow the field?" He repeats, amused.

"Sure, laugh about it. It doesn't erase the fact that you're a fucking hypocrite. I'm yours now, but what about before?"

"You were mine from the very beginning sunshine. Don't even think otherwise. I admit I messed up because I was too fucking jealous to see straight…"

"No," I interrupt him, my tone brisk. "You had your chance, Bass," I tell him, my expression serious. "And you blew it." I shrug. "You have absolutely *no* claim on me. Not after what you did."

"That's where you're wrong, Gianna. Did I fuck it up? Yes. I fucked *everything* up, and believe me that I know exactly what I lost. But I'm not giving you up. Not while I'm alive."

His fingers move up my jaw, slowly caressing it. His touch brings back memories—of tenderness, of love, but also of humiliation and deep betrayal.

"Stop touching me," I hiss.

"I told you, sunshine," he leans in, his lips hovering over mine. And as I quickly turn, I feel him smirk against me. "I'm the only one who's *ever* going to touch you."

"We said our goodbyes, Bass. Please just leave me alone," I take a deep breath as I say it, trying to maintain my calm. Because while I still feel something for him—my heart beating wildly in my chest at his proximity being proof—I can't trust him.

That's the crux of the issue.

He hurt me worse than anyone's ever hurt me. Because with others I'd expected betrayal at every corner. But with him? He'd been the only one I'd let my guard down with and he'd fucked me over.

"Why? So you can find that forever love with some polished little shit? That's what you want, don't you?" He grits the words, his fingers back on my chin as he forces me to look at him.

"So what if I want that? I think I deserve it after everything I've been through. I deserve someone who will *never* hurt me. Someone who will love me unconditionally. Yes. I want the forever type of love, and I will find it."

"Look no further, sunshine," he smirks and I roll my eyes at him.

But before I can reply, he's suddenly serious again.

"If you think to let another man as much as brush his hand against yours, I'll fucking chop it off. And next time I'll bring it to you in a box, just so you see I'm not playing around."

"Next time?" I frown, but he just lets his lips curl up in a satisfied smile.

"One already down," he whispers against my ear.

Then I remember the article. The man from the restaurant had had his hand chopped off.

"You…" I trail off, unable to understand him. "Why? Why are you doing this to me?" I ask softly, tired of heartache and tired of pain. "Why can't you just leave me be?" Tears coat my lashes as I look into his eyes.

"I just want to *not* hurt anymore," I continue. "Why can't you give me at least that?"

"Because I can't," he rasps against me, burying his face in the crook of my neck. I feel his breath on my skin, his lips almost touching my collarbone.

Goosebumps erupt all over my skin as I hold myself still. But the proximity is too much. My body is starved for him just like my heart is starved for love—so much so it's still looking in the wrong place for it.

"I can't let you go, Gianna. I can never let you go." He pauses, the heat of his frame engulfing me and cocooning me in a protective layer. "I love you, sunshine. I'm so fucking in love with you I can't function if I'm away from you. I'm fucking gone for you…"

"Bass…"

"No, listen to me." He shushes me. "I know I fucked up massively. I know I broke your trust *and* your heart, and sunshine, it's been killing me inside. That day, I was ready to let your father's men kill me. I thought I could maybe pay for what I did to you with my life. But I didn't die," a sad smile spreads across his lips. "*You* didn't let me die. I don't care that you used me. I don't care that you had an ulterior motive. But you didn't let me die. And because of that, you're stuck with me."

"Really?" I raise an eyebrow at him. "What about your family? What do they think of this sudden change of heart you had?"

His family would *never* let him be with a Guerra. And from what I'd learned about Bass' real identity, he's nothing but loyal to his family.

"I don't care," he shrugs. "I stopped caring about them the moment they deliberately manipulated me into destroying myself."

Seeing my frown, he clarifies. "I renounced them."

"But you can't... It doesn't work like that." I add, a little flabbergasted at his claim.

"It did this time," he assures me. "I cut ties with them completely," he adds vaguely, without explaining how.

"Why?" I whisper.

Because I know men like him. I grew up with them. Their loyalty to the don is their entire identity. They would *never* willingly betray or leave the famiglia. And especially not someone like Bass. It's in his blood. He's a true DeVille and that means he was born and reared to do this.

"You don't know?" He asks, his eyes fixed on mine.

I shake my head.

"Because I can only choose one. You or the famiglia." He pauses and I can feel the intensity rolling off him. "And I chose you."

I'm simply stunned. That's the only way I could describe what I'm feeling when he utters those words.

"Bass," I close my eyes, taking a deep breath. "You *hurt* me. You *betrayed* me. And you think you can just force your way into my life? I don't think I can ever trust you again."

"I know." He nods, surprising me again with his easy acquiesce. "And I'll work for it. I'll show you that you can trust me

again, and I'll show you just how much I love you, sunshine. Just…
give me the chance to prove to you that it was a stupid mistake.
Please," he rasps, looking as if he's in physical pain.

I shake my head, my own mind filled with jumbled thoughts.

"I'll be good," he continues. "I'll be fucking good to you
sunshine. This time it's only us. Just you and I. No more family
rivalries. No more stupid revenge. No more lies."

His hand comes to cup my cheek, his thumb brushing over my
lips.

"Just us," he repeats.

"I…" I trail off as I look into his eyes, recognizing the sincerity
in them. Still, my heart is too wary, too raw from the last betrayal.
"How will I know it's not another elaborate scheme? That you won't
hand me to your family just to twist the knife further into the wound?"

He scowls at my words.

"I would never do that," he grits. "I'd never do anything to hurt
you, sunshine. Not again."

Silence descends as we just stare at each other, our breaths
coming in short spurts, the beats of our hearts seemingly in unison as
thump after thump resounds in the air.

"Give me time. Space. I can't forgive you, Bass. I don't know if
I ever will," I breathe out, surprised at my own words.

"I'll give you all the time you need, sunshine. Just… I need to
be close to you. I need to know you're fine. I… fuck," he curses, and
for a moment I get a glimpse into a hidden vulnerability. "I can't be
without you. I just can't. This past month's been pure hell. I've been
near, but not near enough and it's been fucking with my head. I feel
like I'm on the brink of collapse…" he shakes his head. "Just let me
protect you."

My brows shoot up at his request.

"Protect me?"

"Not from the shadows like before," he says and it dawns on
me that he's been the one following me around all this time. My
intuition had been on point. "I need to be by your side."

I blink away the wetness in my lashes, not wanting to give
away how much his words affect me.

"You need to leave, Bass," I tell him firmly, pushing against him and heading towards the kitchen counter. The space seems to help clear my head a little, even though my heart is still beating wildly in my chest, the desire to nestle into his arms too overwhelming.

"This isn't giving me space," I motion to him coming into my personal space and messing with my head. "You may try to prove to me that you're sincere, but *not* by stifling me, or by being an overbearing boor."

His expression falls, his hands balled into fists by his side.

"I'm finally free, Bass. I'm finally living on my *own* terms. And I'm not about to let anyone take that away from me."

"I understand," he nods, looking at me like a freaking lost puppy.

Does he really think that will help his case?

"Good," I cross my arms over my chest. "Goodnight then," I motion to the door.

He moves his gaze between me and the door, looking uncertain for a second. Eventually, his shoulders slump in defeat as he leaves the apartment.

I hurry to lock the door after him, sighing deeply as I slide down to the floor.

My entire world's been turned upside down—again. And I don't think I would survive another betrayal, not when I'm still nursing old wounds.

Still, his presence here had been like a balm to my battered heart and for a moment I'd faltered.

He says he's chosen me over his family, but how can I trust that when I know loyalty to the famiglia is the most important thing for a made man?

The dilemma is killing me, and that night my sleep is fitful.

Because what if he's lying?

But what if he's not?

FRIVOLOUS

Chapter Twenty

BASS

Bringing the glass to my lips, I tip my head lower so that no one can get a glimpse of my face. I wouldn't want any children to start screaming.

Still, my eyes are fixed on her.

Dressed in a pair of black jeans and a white shirt with the restaurant logo on it, Gianna prances from table to table, taking orders and somehow ignoring the way all the men are staring at her body like *she's* on the menu.

I grit my teeth as I watch their eyes follow her around, the need to prove to everyone that she's *not* available eating at me.

But I can't do that. No, I can't do that when I'm supposed to be on my best behavior.

It's been two weeks since I've been to her apartment, and every single day without fail I occupy a table at the restaurant and I watch her.

I'd told her it was for her protection because men are unpredictable, and the *real* world as she likes to call it is a dangerous one.

In the beginning she'd protested my presence, but slowly she'd started getting used to it.

After all, I have one schedule *every fucking day*.

In the morning, I show up at her door to take her to work. I wait around at her work place until she's done, and then I walk her back home.

I'd been very lucky that her landlord had seen the urgency in my fists when he'd declared the unit next to her had suddenly been freed up.

And so I don't need to worry about anything happening to her at all times, since I'll always be close.

But it's not enough.

It will never be enough.

Not when she can barely look at me, much less talk to me.

Even when we walk home at night, she's quietly pretending I'm not there.

And I don't fucking like it.

In the beginning, I'd thought that she'd come around eventually if she recognizes that I am serious. But now...

"Do you need a refill of that?" Someone asks, and I spare the waitress a quick glance, grunting.

"You don't have a chance with her, you know," she continues. "You should quit before it becomes creepy. Just a friendly advice," she says before she disappears.

I narrow my eyes in the direction she left.

Of course people would think I'm a fucking creep if I'm here almost twenty-four seven. But she's not wrong. At some point, people are going to become suspicious and some might even call the cops on me.

And that's the last thing I need.

Although, seeing that our fake identities share a last name, and an equally fake but nonetheless real marriage certificate, there might be something extra I could do.

A smile pulls at my lips at that thought.

And when the waitress stops by my table to refill my coffee, I casually add that tidbit of information.

"That woman," I point towards Gianna. "Is my wife."

Her eyes widen in shock, and she towards Gianna and back at me, likely unable to believe someone of her beauty would marry someone like me.

"I'm just looking out for her," I shrug. "There are a lot of *creeps* around."

"Right," replies, looking unconvinced.

A while later I see her speak with Gianna in hushed tones, and I know she's recounting what I said. Especially as Gianna comes strutting towards me, her features drawn in anger.

There's my sunshine.

"What do you think you're doing," she hisses. "How could you tell her we're married?"

"But we are, aren't we?" I smirk, reminding her of the fake identities.

"God," she groans, raising a hand to massage her temples. "I've had enough of your antics, Bass. You need to stop this."

"Why?" I raise my eyebrows at her. "Ah, wait. Because you want to find your forever love and you can't if we're married."

"We're not married," she snaps.

"This says we are," I answer smugly as I take out my own ID from my wallet, pointing at the last name.

"You know it's not true," she rolls her eyes at me.

"But they don't, *Lara.*"

"You're taking this too far, Bass."

"I'm not. I'm simply ensuring people know you're off limits." I shrug, leaning back in my seat.

"You said you were going to leave me alone."

"I didn't. You assumed. I told you I was going to give you time, but get used to it because I'll be in your life whether you want it or not."

The outrage is slow to enter her features, but the way her small hands are clenched into fists, her lips pressed together in a thin line, and I know I've hit a nerve.

"Damn you, Bass," she turns on her heel, going back to her job.

After I drop her off at her door, I go to my own apartment, all the while ruminating about what I could do to change her mind.

The thing is that even I am so fucking disgusted with what I did to her that I wouldn't forgive myself either. But that doesn't mean I'll stop. Not when she's my only reason for living.

I start doing a few pushups, thinking some exercise could clear my head and give me some new ideas.

Since proximity does not seem to help very much, I'll have to change tactics. But I know Gianna, and I also know I hurt her a lot. No amount of apologies will help until *she* is ready to forgive me—if ever.

She's right that she finally has a chance at living on her own terms, and I won't do anything to jeopardize that.

I'm halfway through my set when I hear some noises from the other side of the wall. I frown.

Thud. Thud. Thud.

It sounds like someone is remodeling the apartment. And knowing Gianna and her lack of experience with those things, I highly doubt it.

Fear pools in my stomach and I don't even think as I dash over, knocking loudly on her door.

"Gianna! Open up!"

Thoughts of someone having broken into her apartment, or her being attacked plague my mind, and I'm one step away from kicking the door open.

"What is it?" She finally opens the door, slurring her words. Her entire face is tear streaked and there is a gash on the inside of her arm.

"Sunshine," I stride inside, locking the door behind me.

She's clutching a bottle of alcohol, blood running down her hand and over the bottle.

She's also looking at me with a mixture of happiness and sadness, more tears forming at the corners of her eyes.

"I hate you," she slurs, taking a wobbly step forward and pointing her finger at me. "I fucking hate you! Why couldn't you leave me alone?"

"Sunshine…"

"Don't *sunshine* me! You son of a bitch!" she says right before she attacks me. Dropping the bottle to the floor, she starts banging her small fists into my chest, and my heart breaks at her meager attempt.

Her eyes are so full of hurt and I feel like the worst motherfucker for knowing I put that there.

"Gianna," I whisper, letting her pour out all the hurt on me.

Her little punches feel like nothing, but when she does hit some of my unhealed wounds, it takes everything in me to keep still and let her express her anger.

Soon, sobs start racking her body, and she fists her hands in the material of my shirt, burrowing her head into my chest.

"Shh," I slowly pat her hair.

"Why?" she croaks. "Why couldn't you leave me alone," she sniffles, blowing her nose in my shirt. Well, if that's to be part of my punishment, I'll take it.

When I see she's calmed down a little, I swoop her in my arms, taking her to the bed. That's also when I realize that her wardrobe had collapsed on the floor—probably the source of the noise.

Laying her gently on the bed, I take her arm to inspect her wound.

"That's a pretty nasty wound, sunshine. You need to get it dressed," I add softly, raising my gaze to find her watching me closely. Her eyes are swollen and puffy, her lashes still damp with tears.

She gives a jerky nod, and I quickly go back to my apartment to get my first aid kit.

"What made you so angry that you destroyed that poor closet?" I ask as I clean the wound, trying to distract her from the pain.

"You," she pouts. "You always make me angry."

"Do I?" I chuckle. Angry is good, because that means she's not indifferent to me.

I can take all her hate, anger, and tantrums. The more the better because it shows me I still affect her.

"You're a brute," she continues. "Why do you have to hurt me so much? Why do I have to care about you?" she jabs her finger into my chest.

"I like that you care about me," I tell her as I catch her finger, lifting it to my mouth for a kiss.

"I don't," she sighs.

I try to bandage her wound properly, but she keeps on moving and interrupting me.

"Gianna, how much did you have to drink?" I ask as I lean a little closer, a strong whiff of alcohol greeting me.

She shrugs, pushing me slightly before climbing off the bed to get her bottle.

Raising it up, she squints as she tries to make out how much she'd drank. But going by the half empty bottle, I'd say *a lot.*

"Not enough," she says before bringing it to her lips and chugging.

"Shit," I curse, grabbing her and the bottle and separating the two, making her sputter in the process.

"More than enough," I correct her.

I'm holding on to her with one hand, while keeping the bottle away with the other. She keeps on struggling to get close to the bottle, her face so fucking cute as she pouts at me. The puffiness on her face makes her even more adorable as she keeps on flailing her arms in her attempt to get the bottle.

"No more vodka for you," I tsk at her.

"Please," she puckers her lips in an attempt to charm me, but I'm already up and heading to the sink, emptying the contents of the bottle.

"You..." she stares in horror as the liquid goes down the drain. "Do you know how expensive that was?" She dashes to the sink, looking even more forlorn as she takes in the empty bottle.

"You're not going to solve anything by drinking your sorrows away."

"Yes. I am," she crosses her arms over her chest. "I'm going to have one moment of peace where you don't intrude in my thoughts." She says confidently, not seeming to realize she's just admitted she thinks about me.

"And how often do I intrude in your thoughts?" I inquire, moving closer to her.

"Too often," she promptly answers before her eyes widen, her hand going over her mouth. "I didn't say that," she makes a feeble attempt at backtracking.

"You did," I smile, caging her in. "Don't worry. I think about you often too. Too often," I lean in, watching the way her pupils dilate at my proximity. Her nipples, too, are pebbled beneath her flimsy shirt, and I can't help the rush that goes through me knowing she's not indifferent to me.

"You should go," she whispers, never taking her eyes from mine.

"Mhmmm, why should I?" I ask, bringing my hand to her cheek.

"You need to go," she reiterates, "before I do something stupid."

"Something stupid you say? Like what?" I drawl, watching a blush climb her cheeks.

She doesn't move as I continue to caress her face, moving my hand down her neck and towards her cleavage. Her breath hitches, her lips slowly parting.

"What are you going to do?" I dare her, because I know what she has in mind—I have the exact same thought.

"You're a bad, bad man," she tells me, "and you need to go. Now."

"Why? Tell me why and I'll go."

"Because if you don't..." those beautiful eyes of hers are looking at me as if I had all the answers in the universe, and I feel my chest constrict with an unfamiliar feeling. "You make me feel hot, and I don't like it. No, I don't like you," she's back to jabbing her finger in my chest, looking entirely too contrite about how I make her feel.

"Sunshine," I close my eyes, her allure too strong. Still, she's drunk, and I'm not going to take advantage of her like that. Not even knowing that if I closed the distance between us and pressed my mouth to hers, taking her lips in a scorching kiss, she wouldn't deny me. If anything, she'd probably beg me for more.

And then she'd hate me in the morning.

"You're going to bed," I rasp, none too nicely. Swooping her up, I lay her on the bed, draping a sheet over her body so I'm not tempted anymore by the sight of the luscious wonder hiding underneath.

She stretches lazily in bed, seemingly forgetting our exchange as she makes herself comfortable, releasing a sigh and closing her eyes.

"Sweet dreams, sunshine," I whisper, slowly caressing her hair and embedding her image of her like this in my mind.

Precious. She's so fucking precious, and I can't believe I let Cisco cloud my mind when I should have known she would never do something like that.

I keep my distance in the morning, still trailing behind her and ensuring she's safe, but without bothering her anymore. It seems that the more I try to ingratiate myself in her life, the more I hurt her—and that was never my intention.

Maybe I should change strategies and stop forcing my presence on her. And so I attempt to do just that.

For the first half of her shift, I manage to lie to myself that I'm fine not being there and watching out for her. In fact, I actually convince myself I can stay away—for an hour.

And as I take a seat at my regular table at the restaurant, I have to admit that I *can't* stay away.

I can barely go a few minutes without having her in my line of sight.

She sees me too as I order my usual, pursing her lips and looking at me with an inscrutable expression.

I turn my attention to a newspaper, reading the news section when I feel someone slide into the seat next to mine.

"What are you doing here?" I frown when I see her place a plate of food on the table.

"It's my break," she shrugs.

"Yeah, but what are you doing *here?*"

She doesn't reply. Instead, she digs into her food, her eyes skittering between me and the plate every now and then.

"Why did you leave last night?" She finally asks, making the courage to look me in the eye.

I tilt my head, studying her and trying to understand what exactly she's asking.

"You fell asleep."

"Oh," she nods, a sudden shyness to her demeanor.

"Did you think I wouldn't leave?"

Her eyes widen at my question.

"Or," I pause, narrowing my eyes at her. "Did you think I'd take advantage of you?"

She shrugs.

"Why didn't you?"

I'm surprised by her blasé attitude about it.

"You could have, you know," she continues, playing with the food on her plate.

"I know." I grunt.

"Then why didn't you?"

"Because you would have hated me. And you would have hated yourself. I don't want half of you, Gianna. And I certainly don't want you to allow my touch just because you're drunk. I want *you*." I tell her seriously.

She nods thoughtfully, her gaze back to the food.

Silence descends, and I just watch her as she tries to look unbothered, slowly bringing the fork to her lips for a bite of steak.

Fuck, but she's beautiful.

Even with her new look, she still looks like a goddess.

"You said your nephew showed you a video of me—or at least someone who looked like me," she suddenly speaks. "What was it like?"

"Why do you want to know?"

"I want to understand, Bass. I want to know what could have made you think I'd betray you like that," she says softly.

So I do. I tell her in great detail everything that had happened in the video, watching her expression morph from one of curiosity to one of horror.

"And she looked like me?" She asks, stupefied.

"They doctored the video. But it looked so real," I shake my head, ashamed that I need to continue to justify my mistake.

Yes, it looked real, but I should have trusted her more.

"I don't remember what happened that night. I know I went upstairs with the girls and they kept feeding me drinks. I was having fun. For the first time in forever, I was having fun. Especially knowing you were nearby and nothing would happen to me. I must have passed out at some point," she says pensively.

"And they took your dress to film the video," I add.

"That's a horrible thing to do to someone, Bass. Why..." She shakes her head, sadness enveloping her features.

"My nephew, Cisco... I don't think he's right here," I add as I bring my finger to my temple. "He did this too," I point to my scars.

She blinks repeatedly, shocked.

"He did *that?*"

"I was in prison," I grimly admit, telling her most of my sordid past and how Cisco had decided to give me a reason to hate the Guerras as much as he did by setting it up as if Franco Guerra had been behind my attack.

"That's horrible, Bass. I have no words. Why... why would he do that to his own family?"

I purse my lips.

"After leaving the famiglia, I did some digging. Apparently, Cisco sent his right-hand man to spy on your father a year or so ago. He disappeared."

She frowns, looking unconvinced.

"All this for his right-hand man?"

"There are rumors that they were more than friends," I grimace, since look where rumors had gotten me.

Still, only if he'd loved that man would he have reacted so viciously, disregarding even his own family in the process. It would also make sense with what I know about him. While all his cousins had been whoring around and doing everything under the sun, I'd never heard a thing about Cisco getting involved with *anyone*. Maybe he *was* in love with his right hand man. But since loving another man is unacceptable in the *famiglia*, most of all for the heir, he could have never acted on it.

What had he said? That Guerra had taken everything from him.

Who knows just how many others he's hurt because of that? Daiyu's claim that he had dishonored her comes to mind. Just how far would he have gone for his revenge?

"That's why you were so intense that day," she adds with a blush. "It all makes sense now."

"Sunshine," I reach across the table and I take her hand in mine. "I won't sit here and place all the fault on Cisco when I know I did the damage with my own hands. He was damned smart, that's for sure. He knew I had my own issues due to my mother's death, and the rumors about you only exacerbated the image I already had of you," I say as I explain that I had never realized just how much my mother's reputation and her death had affected me.

"Bass, I'm sorry," she whispers, but I stop her.

"Don't. I was nothing but a prejudiced bastard. That's why it was so easy for Cisco to poison my mind. Because he knew exactly where to strike. He knew I hated women like my mother so he painted you like one."

She gives me a tight smile.

"That's why I didn't tell you I was a virgin either. With my reputation, who would have believed me?" she gives a dry laugh. "You'd have probably thought I was trying to manipulate you."

"I'm sorry," I tighten my fingers over hers. "And that is my fault too. I should have made it easier for you to trust me. To trust that *I*'d trust you."

Her lips press in a thin line as she lowers her head, almost in shame.

"My panic attacks started after the incident with Clark," she confesses. "I couldn't let *any* man touch me or I'd have a breakdown."

"Shit, sunshine! I should have known. I should have fucking known, because it was right there in front of me. But I was so set in my ways I couldn't see past that. All I saw was your beauty and how every fucking man was obsessed with you and it was enough to believe you were everything they said you were."

Her eyes widen at my outburst, but I just continue.

"Because I hated it. I fucking hated the thought of *anyone* touching you. I hated to think you with another man and fuck... sometimes I'd have sleepless nights imagining you with others..." I breathe harshly, the admission pouring out of me.

"Your inexperience was right there for me to see, but I was too blind. I was so wrapped up in you that I didn't even stop to think about that, and *that* is on me."

"Bass," she wets her lips, taking my hand between both of hers, her touch tentative and soothing. "I can sit here for an eternity and claim you should have trusted me, that I would have never betrayed you like you saw in that video. But the truth is, if roles were reversed, I don't know if I'd have reacted any differently. There was just so much we hid from each other..." She shakes her head. "We didn't know each other. That's the reality, and the reason it was so easy for others to poison us against one another."

"And where does that leave us? Now." I ask, almost afraid of her answer.

"Lara, your break's done, girl. Kayla needs your help in the back," someone yells at Gianna.

"I'll be right there," she says right as she gathers her plate and what's left of her food and gets up.

"Walk me home tonight?" Gianna turns to me, giving me a small smile.

I find my own lips twitching as they stretch across my face.

"I'll wait for you," I nod at her.

CHAPTER TWENTY-ONE

GIANNA

It's late at night when my shift finishes. My entire body aches from the exertion since it had gotten quite busy late in the afternoon.

Changing out of my uniform, I go out, a little too excited at the prospect of seeing Bass again.

Hearing more about what had happened and what had prompted Bass to act as he did had helped me understand him better—understand us better. It has helped me put things in perspective in order to make a decision for my future—for our future.

It may not be the easiest thing, but if possible, I do want to get to know him as *him*. No more secrets and no more lies. I want to see if there's a chance for more. Because if he's truly sincere about everything…

I don't dare hope. My heart is already doing somersaults in my chest, my palms sweaty, my entire being restless as I think about seeing him.

But as I go out, I realize that he's not here.

He'd left soon after we'd talked, but he'd promised he would be back.

My smile falters as I look around, and a deep disappointment settles in my gut.

This is what I get for getting my hopes up.

With a forlorn sigh, I clutch my bag next to my body and I start walking home. I barely get to the side of the road, though, when a car pulls up.

"Hop in," Bass swings the door open, inviting me inside.

I blink at him, wondering where he would have gotten the car from.

"Bass?" I ask tentatively as I slide into the passenger seat.

"Sorry I'm a little late. I had to take care of something."

I frown.

"Of what?"

"There's a present for you in the back."

"For me?" My eyebrows shoot up in surprise, and I'm quick to turn to look in the back.

"Not yet," he chuckles. "You'll see when we get home. But first," he switches hands so he can maneuver the car easier, taking a tablet from a compartment and passing it to me.

"Search your name on the internet."

"What, why?"

"Do it. Please," he gives me half a smile, so I indulge him.

I type up my name and hit search.

My mouth hangs open in shock as I look through page after page, checking each article in part.

"The video," I whisper. "It's gone."

He nods.

"I had someone delete it from the internet. He thinks he caught most of them, but if anything related pops up, he'll make sure it's deleted."

"Wow, thank you," I tell him sincerely, but he just grimaces.

"Don't thank me for something I caused in the first place, Gianna. You have no idea how sorry I am about what I did to you."

"Still, this means a lot. Thank you."

We drive in silence the rest of the way, and as he parks the car, he goes to the back to remove a big box.

"I'm guessing that's my present?" I crack a smile when he doesn't let me touch it.

"It is. And you'll see what it is when we get to your house," he adds a little sheepishly, which only serves to make me more curious.

"Just promise me you won't scream."

"Damn, Bass, but you're really keeping me guessing."

"It's... personal," he chuckles.

I walk briskly as I fumble with my keys to open the door, inviting him inside.

He places the box on the kitchen counter, turning to me rather sharply.

"Oh no, something is leaking," I point to a wet corner on the package, the white of the box turning a muddy red. My eyes widen as they swing to him. "Bass... tell me that's not what I think it is."

"I don't know what you think it is, or who..." he trails off as he turns to unbox it.

I take a hesitant step forward, gasping when I see what's inside.

"You didn't," is the first thing that's out of my mouth. "You... How? When? Bass... I don't know what to say."

And I don't.

Because I'm staring at Clark's decapitated head laid in a box, his eyes wide open, his mouth parted. There's blood leaking from the place where it had been severed, and it's soon going to stain my kitchen counter.

Turning to Bass, I jump on him, wrapping my arms around his neck as I give him a loud kiss on the cheek.

"Thank you! This means a lot," I tell him, tears glistening in my eyes.

"I know you tried to kill him and it failed. You'll never have to worry about him again, sunshine. For good now."

"God," I whimper, burying my face in the crook of his neck. "I can't believe you did this for me... Bass... Thank you," I continue to speak until my words turn into sobs, a freedom unlike any other claiming my body at knowing that he can't hurt me anymore.

I am free.

I am finally free.

"But please get rid of it now," I whisper. "I appreciate the gift. I've seen it, and I'm now convinced he is dead, but please get rid of it before it stains my counter, or worse, before it starts smelling."

"Your wish is my command," he says, giving me a kiss on the forehead before wrapping things up and taking the head with him.

"I'll be right back," he says before he leaves.

Meanwhile, I start cleaning my room a little, suddenly self-conscious about the sorry state of my accommodation.

"I should at least make my bed," I mutter to myself, debating what requires more effort. "But maybe we'll make it messy again..." I blush at the sudden idea, and instead of focusing on the room itself, I decide to pay more attention to *myself.* I take a shower and I make sure my skin is moisturized before I put on some of the nicer underwear I own. It's not much, but since I don't have that many clothes anyway, it will have to do.

Taking out my contacts, I put on a little make up and finish everything with a dab of perfume.

And when the knock comes at the door, I take a deep breath and I answer the door.

"Damn," he whistles as he sees me.

"What did you do with the head?" I ask, worried it might lead back to him. With his record, it wouldn't be a good idea.

"It's gone," he winks. "No one will find it."

"Thank you. I mean it. You have no idea how at peace I feel now."

"Oh, sunshine." His arms come around me, bringing me against his body, and for the first time I let myself breathe, relieved.

He scoops me up, depositing me in the middle of the bed before joining me, his arm around my shoulders as he settles me on his chest.

"Can we..." he trails off, clearing his throat. "Can we try again? This time as ourselves—our true selves. I want you, sunshine, and I want to make you happy. I want to be what you need, when you need me."

Tipping my chin up, I see the sincerity in his eyes as he gazes at me. Bringing my hand to his cheek, I trace the hard planes of his face, the harshness of his scars but also the sharpness of his features.

His eyes are fixed on me, intently watching my every move.

Making courage, I raise myself up his body, straddling him as I prop my hands on his big shoulders.

"What are you doing, sunshine?" He asks in a rough voice.

His hands are twitching by his side, yet he's not touching me. He's letting me go at my own pace, and that makes me even more daring.

Settling my body against his, I feel his unmistakable hardness under me, and for the first time, there's no fear, no dread—just anticipation.

I cup his cheeks in both my hands, leaning forward to brush my lips against his.

Closing my eyes, I simply inhale his essence. Our lips are barely touching, yet I feel this one kiss in my very soul.

Drawing back, I realize tears are pouring down my cheeks, yet they aren't sad tears. They're tears of relief.

"Oh, sunshine," he finally brings his hands up as he swipes the tears from my cheeks, his face full of worry. "We don't have to do anything," he assures me, and I give him a tight smile.

"I'm just... " I swallow, "I can't believe it's over. It's so hard to think that the bad times are in the past. I keep thinking that something else is going to happen and..."

"I know," he pulls me close, resting his chin on top of my head. "I know. And I promise that I'll never let anyone harm you again. It's the vow I make to you, Gianna."

I pull back, inspecting his features and finding myself nodding in return.

"If you hurt me again," I shake my head. "I don't think I could bear that, Bass."

"I won't. I'd rather die than see you cry because of me again."

"I do love you, Bass," I confess and his features light up. "I love you more than anything, and because of that love I am willing to try again. But there won't be a third chance. There won't be two and a half either. You hurt me, and against everything telling me not to, against my common sense, I am willing to try again."

"Sunshine," he groans, his eyes glossy with tears. "I promise you won't have to give me two point one either," he fires back and I feel a smile pull at my lips.

"Do you know why I call you sunshine?" He suddenly asks, serious.

I shake my head, raising my eyebrows in question.

"Because the first time I saw you, you were like the sun. The brightest fucking star, and I felt myself blinded by your light. You shine brighter than anyone I've ever seen, Gianna, and I can only say I'm the luckiest motherfucker that you choose to share your light with me."

"Bass," I smile, his words touching me. "You can be very sweet sometimes."

"I love you, Gianna. I may not have told you before, but I've loved you for so long it feels like forever. That you're giving me another chance..." he shakes his head in disbelief. "I'll cherish it, and I'll cherish you, my very own ray of sun."

"Flatterer," I poke at him.

"I miss your blonde hair, you know," he notes as he brings a strand of my hair to his nose, closing his eyes and inhaling my scent.

"I'll grow it back. For you," I add cheekily, and he regales me with a smile.

"What a good girl you are," he drawls, and the atmosphere suddenly shifts. There's a heavy current that moves between us, and before I know it he has me flush against his body, his mouth open on top of mine as he ravages my lips in a kiss that has my toes curl in anticipation.

Because God, this feels like heaven on earth.

There's absolutely no panic, no anxiety as I find myself cocooned deep into his arms, his mouth plundering mine as he kisses me so deep I don't ever want to reach the surface again.

My body, too, rejoices at the reunion, feeling at home for the first time in forever. He's everywhere, surrounding me with his heat and that raw energy he emanates when he's taking over me.

"Fuck," he curses as he breaks the kiss, his eyes glazed with desire as he stares into mine. "You're driving me crazy, sunshine, and I want to take this slow. Make up for the last time. Fuuuck," he closes his eyes, reaching between us to adjust his erection.

"I don't want slow, Bass. I just want us."

I reach out to caress his face, my lips pulling up in a smile meant to convey everything I'm feeling.

"I don't know what I've ever done to deserve you, Gianna. But I promise you I'll spend the rest of my life showing you how much you mean to me." He pulls my hand to his lips.

"Ok," I breathe in, biting my lip. "Why don't you start now," I move my hand down his chest, feeling the hard muscles under his shirt. Reaching for the hem, I pull the shirt over his head, unveiling his sculpted torso.

Just like the first time I'd seen him naked, I can't help my fascination with his form. I bring my fingers over his pecs in a light caress, noting the twitch of his muscles under my touch.

Not everything is flawless, though. There are countless scars that run all over his chest, some more recent and angry looking, while others are old and faded.

Keeping eye contact, I move closer, placing my lips on the wound I caused when I'd stabbed him with my knife. Opening my mouth, I let my tongue skirt around the wound.

He's breathing harshly, and I know my small ministrations are driving him crazy, even though he's trying his best to hold himself still.

And as I move my hand lower, brushing against the band of his pants, he finally stops me.

"My turn now," he rasps, and I don't even get to reply as he has me on my back, his big body looming over me as he simply watches me.

His eyes move over my body, and I'm happy I put some effort into my appearance. Because if the glint in his eyes is any indication, he likes what he sees.

"This needs to go," he says as he all but rips the shirt off me, quickly unsnapping my bra too until my breasts bounce free under his hungry gaze. And it is hungry as he lowers his mouth to my neck, trailing his lips in a ghost of a touch.

My thighs clench together, goosebumps covering my entire body as the anticipation grows and grows.

He stops right above the swell of one breast, opening his mouth and licking a trail down to my nipple before wrapping his lips around it, sucking it into his mouth.

I release a moan, my hands going to his shoulders as I hold him to my chest, urging him to keep doing what he's doing. The flick of his tongue against my nipple is making me writhe under him. My panties are already soaking wet, and I can't wait until he'll get *there*.

He moves from one nipple to the other, giving each the attention they crave, biting, licking, sucking until I'm thrashing so bad he has no choice but to move even lower—to that place that demands his attention *the most*.

"Your greedy little pussy missed me, isn't that right, sunshine?" I feel his breath on my stomach, his fingers grabbing on the band of my panties and slowly pulling them down my legs.

"Yes," I whimper. "Please," I whisper, my eyes fluttering rapidly as my arousal mounts.

"Did you touch yourself?" he suddenly asks.

My pussy is already bared to him, and I can feel the warm air fanning over my wet lips, the sensation only driving me crazier.

"Yes, yes," I answer promptly. Everything so he would just touch me and put me out of my misery.

"Show me," he demands, taking my hand and bringing it between my legs. "Show me how you pet your pussy when I'm not there, sunshine!"

There's a harshness to his tone that speaks of urgency and need, not the slow torture he thinks to wreak on me as he denies me his touch.

My fingers meet my wetness as I dip them low between my legs.

He's watching intently, almost in awe.

"Tell me you were thinking of me," he grunts. "Tell me!"

"Yes," I breathe out on a moan as my finger brushes against my clit. "I was thinking of your rough hands. Of your big fingers sliding inside me, stretching me."

"Fuck," he curses, his pupils engulfing his irises and showing his desire for me.

Closing his eyes, he brings his face closer as he inhales my scent, licking his lips before taking hold of my wrist.

"You're my fucking temptation," he says as he sucks on each one of my fingers, tasting my arousal. "Do you know how many times I jerked off to the memory of your taste?"

I shake my head, heat climbing to my cheeks at the image.

"Too many times. Too many fucking times, sunshine."

There's an intensity to him as he tries to keep himself in check, going at my own pace. It would be sweet if my need wasn't as great as his.

Giving me one of his lopsided smiles, he grabs my ass in his big hands, spreading my legs further.

"Give me that sweetness, sunshine," he murmurs as he lowers his mouth to my pussy, his tongue giving me a long swipe before settling against my entrance, thrusting slowly into me. My walls contract as I feel his tongue caress me on the inside, his touch feather-like and making me squirm in pleasure.

Of their own accord, my hands find their way in his hair, holding him there as he fucks me with his tongue. And as he wraps his lips around my clit, sucking on it, I know I'm losing it.

"Bass," my scream echoes in the apartment as I fall apart, tremors racking my body as my orgasm ripples through me. I can't stop shaking, especially as he continues to lick me, tease me so much until another one is imminent.

"That's it, pretty girl. Come for me. Let me feel that cream on my tongue, Gianna," he rasps. "Been too long without it," *lick*, "without you," *lick*, "without my fucking heart." He bites down on my clit, and pain and pleasure mingle in that tight bundle of nerve endings, making me open my mouth in wonder, no sound coming out as the entire world seems to dance before my eyes.

Words—even sounds—fail me as he makes me come for the third time.

"Bass, please," I whimper, pulling at him, knowing I can't take anymore.

"Making it up for the last time," he grumbles. "I know you didn't come last time, Gianna, and it's been fucking with my head. I want you sated, pretty girl. Sated and fucked. In that order, you get me? Your pleasure comes first. Always."

Languidly, I give him a nod that earns me a smile from him.

"But I want to get fucked now." I pout at him. "Pretty please?" I bat my lashes at him.

He chuckles, that deep voice of his touching every fiber of my being and making me even more turned on—if that's possible.

I watch, almost hypnotized, as he leans back, quickly taking off his pants and boxers. His cock immediately juts out, straining against his stomach as he moves towards me.

There's mild trepidation as he parts my legs, settling his hips against mine.

"Give me that mouth, Gianna," he orders, his hand on my nape as he brings my lips to his in a rough kiss.

Rubbing the head of his cock against my clit, he doesn't push in.

"Slow, sunshine. We're going slow," he says, almost to himself, his tender concern for me moving me to tears.

And as I open my eyes to gaze at him, I see *it*—I see everything.

There's love, acceptance, protection. Everything I've ever wanted before. There's him.

This hulking beast that I'd tried to fight and push away, but that had ended up worming his way into my heart. This man that broke my heart yet came back to put it together.

"I love you, Bass," I tell him, taking advantage of this moment when our souls seem to be in alignment.

"I love you too, Gianna. So fucking much." His lips pull up in a smile, and I bring my hand to cup his cheek.

"Not afraid of STDs now?" I joke, since he didn't bother with a condom.

"No," he answers immediately. "I trust you," he simply states.

His words warm my heart as I note the sincerity in his eyes.

"There's only ever been you, Bass," I move my thumb in a circle over his scar. "There will only ever be you."

"Ah, Gianna," he groans, closing his eyes. "You've been *it* for me since the first time I saw you, sunshine. I may have hated it, but any other woman ceased to exist from the moment I laid my eyes on you. You're my fucking everything,"

"Then make me yours," I urge, pressing myself against him. "I want to belong to you, feel you so deep inside of me…" I trail off as I feel the head of his cock at my entrance, stretching me.

There's still a slight burning sensation as he slowly pushes inside of me, but the pain from before is gone. And when he's seated fully within me, I release a breath I didn't realize I was holding.

"Don't hold back. Please, Bass. I want everything you can give me," I tell him, wrapping my legs around his waist and tilting my pelvis to fit him deeper.

A whimper escapes me at the sensation.

"Fuck, sunshine. You're going to kill me," he groans in my ear, slowly starting to move.

"Your pussy's fucking heaven. So fucking tight, and milking my cock… Sweet Jesus, but I don't know how I'm going to last," he rasps as he thrusts, his movements starting to gain speed.

I feel a tightening inside of me every time he pushes to the hilt, the head of his cock hitting something deep within me.

His thrusts become increasingly more aggressive as my nails dig into his back. He grunts his approval as he urges me to claw at him harder. His mouth on my neck, he sucks on my skin as he pummels into my pussy at a speed that makes me see stars, the combined effect of his cock stroking my walls and his mouth caressing my pulse perpetually having me on the edge but not quite ready to fall.

"Bass," I moan out his name, the pleasure so fucking intense it's messing with my brain.

Everything is foggy as pleasure seems to emanate from all parts of my body, my nails on his back already drawing blood.

"You're mine, Gianna," his teeth scrape at the sensitive skin right under my jaw. "All fucking mine, baby," he continues to lick the skin.

"Yes, all yours, Bass," I say as he brings his mouth to mine, swallowing my cries. His hands holding my hips in place, he thrusts into me like a madman, pulling all the way out before slamming back in.

Without warning, he switches position, his back hitting the mattress as I bounce on top of him, his cock buried so deep inside me, I can't help the moan that escapes me.

"That's it, sunshine. Ride me. Ride my cock, pretty girl. I want to see how you take all of me in that juicy cunt of yours," he says as he brings his hands up my waist, reaching my boobs as he palms both mounds in his hands.

My body is already flushed from the exertion, but his words only serve to make me hotter, my walls clenching around him.

"Ah, fuck, you're strangling the life out of me, Gianna. You're about to come, aren't you? My pretty girl's about to come," he smirks, trailing his fingers down my front.

I can only nod, arching my back and riding him harder, pleasure building inside of me and waiting to be released.

"Then come. Come for me, pretty girl and drench my fucking dick in your cream," my breath hitches at his tone. "Now, sunshine," his command washes through me just as my orgasm hits.

My hands on his pecs, I grip him firmly to support myself as my mouth opens on a scream. My walls close around him, holding him so tightly his own shout of release follows mine as warm jets of his cum flood my insides.

I'm back on my back as he slips from my body, an emptiness already forming from his absence.

"Fuck. Me," he whistles, one finger trailing down my pussy. "Your pussy's greedy for my cum, sunshine, eating it up like honey."

I feel his cum slowly ooze out of me, but his finger stops it, pushing it back inside and smearing my walls with it.

"You're going to look so pretty swollen with our child," he drawls.

"Hmm, and how many do you want?" I ask lazily, opening my arms for him to nestle inside.

"However many you'll give me," he lays a kiss on my forehead before turning me so he's spooning me from behind. "Although I'm pretty sure I just put a baby in you," he whispers in my ear sheepishly.

I pinch him playfully, laughing at his words.

Little did I know that nine months later his words would come true.

Epilogue

BASS

EIGHT YEARS LATER,

"Shh, you have to be quiet, lovelies," I put my finger to my lips as I attempt to keep Arianna, my seven-year-old calm, while settling her four year old sister, Ariel, on my hip. "It's starting," I point to the screen.

The ceremony is in full swing as all the graduates are on one side of the arena, the camera focused on them.

I spot my ray of sunshine immediately, her honey blonde hair long and contrasting against the blue of her robe.

She looks nervous as she clutches her hands in front of her, waiting for her name to be called.

"It's *mamma*," Ariel lifts her arm to point at the screen.

"Yes, it's your *mamma*," I nod.

Both girls are in awe as they watch their mother walk on the podium to receive her diploma.

FRIVOLOUS

Gianna herself is looking flushed as she shakes hands with the dean.

In the meantime, I'm trying to juggle a child in one hand, and a camera in the other so I can immortalize this moment forever.

Since I'd had quite a bit of money stashed away, Gianna didn't have to work anymore. Instead, she'd spent her time studying. She'd breezed through college, earning the respect of her professors for her intelligence and work ethic, and she'd quickly received an invitation to apply for their doctoral program in cognitive psychology.

After she'd been accepted, it had been a hard couple of years as she'd started her own research, filled with sleepless nights and copious amounts of coffee. It hadn't helped that Arianna had been a toddler by then and she'd soon fallen pregnant with Ariel.

I'd taken over most of the chores around the house, staying home with the girls while she'd continued her research.

Though it had been a rocky road, she successfully managed to complete her PhD program almost two years earlier, graduating with an offer to continue her postdoctoral work with her senior professors.

In the years that had passed, I'd watched Gianna bloom from a young woman who'd been afraid of her own shadow into a smart and confident woman who knew what she wanted—and of course, always got it.

There's nothing I wouldn't do for her and seeing the smile on her face as she waves her diploma in the air for us to see on screen, I know I did the right thing when I decided not to return to work and take care of our little girls instead—giving her the time to pursue her dreams.

With the ceremony done, she hurries towards us. The girls immediately jump from their seats as they dash towards their mother, both hugging her and giving her the flowers we'd bought her.

"Congratulations, *mamma*," Arianna and Ariel tell her, kissing both her cheeks.

"Thank you, sweeties," Gianna gives them a hug before turning her gaze towards me.

"Looking hot enough to eat, Doctor," I wink at her, opening my arms for her to fly into them.

"Hmm," she purrs against my chest. "You can eat me later all you want," she whispers right before our girls call our attention again.

"You said we're going to the restaurant to celebrate," Arianna reminds us.

"Yes! Restaurant! I want pizza," Ariel chimes in.

Holding my hand for Gianna, she gives my cheek a quick kiss as she takes it, signaling for the girls to follow suit. They jump up and down as they talk about some new fashion, the stifled energy from before fully unleashed.

"I'm so happy, Bass," Gianna says as she places her head on my shoulder. "I'd never dreamed I would get here. And yet... Here I am. Sometimes it feels like a dream."

"Me neither. Maybe we didn't have the best start, but this..." a smile pulls at my lips as I nod towards our little girls. "This is the best gift I've ever been given."

"Do you ever miss it? That life?" She asks suddenly.

"Why are you asking this?" I frown, wondering where it had come from.

"You gave up your work, your family..."

"Gianna, you and the girls are my family. That's it," I interrupt her. "And there's nothing more important than you three." She looks up at me with those gorgeous eyes of her that even now never fail to mesmerize me. "What brought this on?"

She shrugs, pursing her lips.

"My colleagues were talking the other day, and some were saying that it's weird you'd choose to be a stay at home dad while I pursued my studies."

"Sunshine," I groan. "You know I never cared about that. Seeing you happy while pursuing your dreams has been my one priority, and you know how proud I am of you."

"I know," she sighs, nestling closer to me.

"Besides," I lean in to whisper, "how many made men do you know whose wives have a PhD?"

"None," she answers cheekily.

"See? I hit the jackpot," I wink at her.

Because it is true. I'd never give up the life I made with her and with our girls. And that's why my grudge towards Cisco had faded with time too—especially considering the bastard is still alive and well. Without him sending me on that mission, I would have never met Gianna. I would have never known what I was missing in my life.

I would have never known happiness. Plain and simple.

"Yes, we're going for pizza," Gianna chuckles as she takes Ariel in her arms, Arianna quickly coming next to her to grab her mother's hand.

Looking at the three of them together, I can't help the way my heart swells in my chest.

Yes, I made the right choice.

Because there had never even been another choice.

GIANNA

TWO MORE YEARS LATER,

"Bass, love," I call out to my husband.

The kids are already asleep as I make my way towards our bedroom. He's already in bed, a book in his hands as he looks up at me.

"What is it, sunshine?" He places his book on the nightstand next to him, lifting the blanket for me to snuggle inside.

"Someone knocked at the door, and when I opened it, I found this."

I show him a white envelope. It's entirely blank—no sender, or receiver.

"That's odd," he frowns, taking it from me to inspect it.

"Right. Who could have sent it?"

"Well, let's open it up and see," he says, making quick work of tearing a corner and opening the entire thing up.

Inside, there's only a folded piece of paper.

"What…" I mumble as I take it out, reading the few short lines.

Father is dead. Cosima is dead. Rafaelo is gone.
You can come home, sister.
No one will harm you while I'm in charge.
-M

"That's…"

"Michele. It has to be Michele. But what does he mean that they are dead? And what about Raf?" I shake my head, unable to comprehend what's happening. "Do you think it's safe to return?" I ask Bass, a sliver of hope blooming inside of me.

I haven't seen my brother in ten years. Not since he'd renounced me as his sister, telling me to never come back.

I must admit I'd thought about him often over the years, since our type of bond isn't one to be severed so easily. But that doesn't erase the hurt in my heart for what he'd said to me.

That also doesn't erase the fact that I'd failed him as his sister.

"I don't know. I'll make a few inquiries," Bass grunts, not looking too pleased about the possibility of returning. "Do you want to, though?" He eventually asks.

"I... I don't know. I miss Michele. I'd love to see him. But," I purse my lips. "I'd never willingly bring Arianna and Ariel into that life. You know how they treat women," I shake my head, the thought of putting my children through that absolutely appalling.

"My thoughts exactly. We can arrange for you to meet with your brother, but I don't think it's wise to resume our affiliation—with any family."

"You're right," I sigh.

His arms come around me as he takes me in his embrace, making me forget about all my worries in the way only Bass knows how to.

But as the days pass, I can't take my mind off the letter, the thought of seeing my brother again becoming close to an obsession.

He'd be twenty-four this year. A young man. I wonder if I'll even recognize him.

And as I find myself thinking about him more and more, I finally relent and ask Bass to set up a meeting.

"Wow, you're quick," I exclaim when he tells me it's all done. Michele had agreed to meet me in Central Park so that it's neutral territory, agreeing to all Bass' terms.

"I'll be waiting at the entrance," Bass tells me. "And if anything," he says grimly, "press your alarm button and I'll come get you."

I nod. "I'm sure I'll be fine," I give him a tight smile.

I'm the first to arrive at the designated location. Sitting down on a bench, I wait.

A young man catches my eye as he strides towards me. He's dressed all in leather, his dark hair long and curling around his shoulders. He has a pair of sunglasses on his face, and as he stops in front of me, lowering them down his nose, I come face to face with a pair of startling amber eyes.

"Michele?" I croak, a feeling of familiarity suddenly enveloping me.

"Sister," his mouth pulls in a crooked smile.

His voice is deep and smooth, and I note that puberty's really done a number on him. There's a cockiness to him that's not unwarranted, his pale skin making him look like a young Lestat waiting to take the country by storm in a rock revolution.

"It's been… forever," I say the first thing that comes to mind, because really, it feels like talking with a stranger.

"Indeed, it has," he takes a seat next to me, leaning back and placing his leg over his knee.

Pulling a cigarette out of his jacket, he extends one to me too.

"I don't smoke," I tell him.

"Not anymore?" His brows pull up.

"No," I reply, a little thrown off that he'd know that small detail from ten years ago.

"You look the same, Gianna. Just as beautiful," he drawls, looking me up and down.

There's something about him that doesn't sit well with me though. There's a coldness to him that chills me to my bones, and it takes everything in me to act normal.

"Thank you for reaching out," I start, "but I won't be able to come back. I have my own family now."

"With the bodyguard," he nods.

"Yes. With him."

"I've been keeping tabs on you over the years. I'm proud of you," he says, releasing a cloud of smoke. Why is it that his words sound fake to my ears?

"Thank you."

"It's a pity you've decided against coming back. Especially now that the entire *famiglia* is mine," he smirks.

"How did they die?" I can't deny I'd been curious about that.

He shrugs.

"How people in this life die," he answers cryptically, "when their time comes," he winks at me.

His eyes are an eerie light shade, almost as if there was no melanin in them. And as he sets them upon me, looking at me over his glasses, I can't shake the feeling that there's something very wrong with him.

"I'm glad I could see you. And I'm glad you're doing fine," I add, trying to find a way to end the conversation and get the hell out of here.

"Am I... doing fine?" he chuckles, shrugging. "I am. Power sure tastes nice."

He says it in a way that it's unmistakable that he's had something to do with Benedicto and Cosima's deaths—not that I'm ever going to mourn either of them.

"What about Raf?" I ask before I can help myself.

His features darken immediately, and a sinister smile appears on his face.

"Raf," he grinds his teeth as he repeats the name. "Raf..." he laughs. "Don't worry about Raf, Gianna. He's finally where he was meant to be," he pauses, tilting his head back, "at the bottom."

His lips are ever so slightly curled upwards, the satisfaction rolling off him unmistakable.

God, Michele... What happened to you?

"I should go," I stand up, trying my best to paint a smile on my face. "We're taking the children to the zoo today."

"Children," he nods, an odd expression on his face. "Take care of them, will you?" He throws the words at me before he's gone. No goodbye, nothing.

He's just... gone.

"So? How did it go?" Bass asks me when I get back to the car.

"Good. Or at least as good as can be. I think some things should just be left in the past."

"That bad, huh?" he chuckles.

"He's not my baby brother anymore. In fact, I don't even know who he is."

"It's better to keep interactions to a minimum then," Bass adds and I agree.

The rest of the day, I try to take my mind off our short meeting, but I can't help the disappointment that envelops me.

I'd taken care of him since young. I'd basically raised him. And the man I saw today... I couldn't recognize him. I couldn't find even the smallest trace of the Michele I knew inside of him. And that breaks my heart.

"Stop worrying, sunshine," Bass' arms come around me in a hug. "He's not your concern anymore."

"You're right," I sigh, raising myself on my tiptoes to lay a kiss on his lips.

I have my own family to think about now, and their safety comes first.

I'd never willingly pull us back into a world that demeans women and regards them as inferior. I'd *never* do that to my girls.

"I love you, sunshine," Bass whispers in my hair.

"Love you too, big guy."

And sometimes I can't believe how lucky I'd been to escape that life and build my own with Bass and the girls.

This is love.

This is happiness.

And I'll protect it to my dying breath.

THE END

AFTERWORD

Thank you so much for reading!
If you enjoyed this story, please consider leaving a **rating** or **review**
on any retail platform.
For more news, subscribe to my newsletter:
Veronicalancet.com/subscribe

Check out the other books in the Morally Questionable Series:

MY NAME IS PINK

MORALLY CORRUPT

MORALLY BLASPHEMOUS

MORALLY DECADENT

MORALLY AMBIGUOUS

CPSIA information can be obtained
at www.ICGtesting.com
Printed in the USA
LVHW091635221121
704107LV00008B/57